FATES' FURY

FURY

LIZ BUTCHER

Copyright © 2019 Liz Butcher
Cover Design by Andrew Butcher
Background vector created by freepik: www.freepik.com
Editing by Kathrin Hutson at KLH CreateWorks:
Klhcreateworks.com

ISBN: 978-0-646-80830-7

To Jonah, one of the brightest souls I've met.

Keep shining, wherever you are...

ACKNOWLEDGMENTS

A huge thank you to my mother Catherine, my husband Andrew, and our daughter Lola. Your unconditional love and support keeps me going.

Kat, the most epic editor/mentor there is, thank you for helping me turn this story into something I'm so proud of.

CHAPTER ONE

THE YOUNG MAN'S gait was a little unsteady. As if he were sleepwalking, he was only vaguely aware of the fact that his body was no longer in his control. He had no idea where he was going or how long he'd walked, but he did know it had been many hours, judging by how far the sun had traversed across the sky. The rough, and rocky ground cut into the already raw soles of his feet with every step, coating them in blood and dust. Each breath grated along the sandpaper of his throat. In his fugue state, he longed for water.

Even then, he couldn't stop whispering to himself, willing his body to stop, to let him rest. But his feet just continued, stepping one in front of the other. As he longed for unconsciousness to take a firmer hold, for the relief of the darkness, of death, his body stopped. Before he could pin down his gratitude and relief, he was forced to his knees. His yowl of pain sounded raw and primal to his own ears, but the rock cutting into his knees was the least of his concerns. His hands moved on their own, sweeping away the sand and dirt in front of him. Then his fingers dug beneath the surface of the hard terrain, clawing at the rock and the packed earth, and he was completely powerless. The sharp stones cut his hands, his fingernails snapped and ripped from their beds, and his silent screams echoed only within his own mind.

JONAH SANDS STEPPED out of the bustling Brisbane airport. He turned his face towards the fierce Australian sun and smiled, relieved to be home. As he joined the taxi queue, he glanced at his watch and realised he hadn't changed the time after leaving Greece. He moved to the next available taxi and greeted the driver politely, helping to load his bags into the trunk.

"Are you visiting or returning home?" the driver asked.

"Returning," Jonah replied, running his hand through his shaggy blond hair. He wiped his sunglasses on his shirt before putting them on.

"Where are you returning from?" They both got into the car.

"I was over in Greece for a few weeks for work."

"What do you do?"

Jonah pulled his phone from his satchel and turned it on. "I'm a photojournalist."

"Nice. Plenty to photograph over there, I'm sure. So, where are we headed?"

Jonah gave the driver his address, then his phone rang—his best friend Tristan calling. "Excuse me. I need to get this," Jonah said.

The driver nodded, navigating his way through the traffic.

"Happy birthday, mate! Glad you finally decided to join me in the thirties."

Jonah chuckled. "It's my birthday today? I was hoping I'd skipped it somehow with the time difference. Are we still on for dinner at your folks' tonight?"

"You know it. No one can escape the family birthday dinner. Not even you. Hey, what was with the cryptic emails while you were away?" Tristan asked.

Jonah sighed. "I don't know how to explain it without sounding paranoid. It just felt like someone was watching me from the minute I got there."

"What's the saying?" Tristan asked. "Just because you're paranoid doesn't mean no one's after you?"

"Thanks, mate. That's helpful." Jonah stared out the window.

"Well, did you see anyone who looked suspicious? Or any sign someone was watching or following you?" Tristan asked.

"No, I didn't," Jonah admitted. "It was more like a feeling I couldn't shake. It didn't stop until I left the country."

"That's weird, dude. Are you sure you didn't unlock some kind of mummy's curse while you were there?"

Jonah laughed. "Not likely, considering I was in Greece and not Egypt."

"You know what I mean," Tristan countered. "What if you triggered a curse or something? You *were* on an expedition."

"I know, but I don't believe in curses. And I only take the photographs. It's not like I touched anything."

"If you say so. At least you're back now. Anyways, I have to get back to work, so happy birthday. I'll pick you up at six."

Jonah ended the call and smiled.

"Couldn't help but overhear it's your birthday," the driver said, meeting Jonah's gaze in the rear-view mirror.

"Yeah, mate. The big three-oh."

"Ah… well, it's been a while since I was that age, so enjoy it."

"Thanks. Will do," Jonah replied and finally settled into his seat. The fatigue from his journey swept over him, and he wound the window down halfway to keep himself awake.

The driver chuckled.

"What's so funny?" Jonah leaned forward.

"There's a birthday song for you on the radio, though you may be too young to know it," the driver declared as he turned up the volume. Jonah couldn't help but laugh as Blue Oyster Cult's "Don't Fear the Reaper" filled the car. The driver turned around. "Happy birthday."

Jonah's attention moved in horror from the driver to the windscreen. A woman stood facing them in the middle of the road, and they were headed right for her. "Look out!" he yelled.

The driver's head swivelled around in surprise.

Jonah braced himself as the driver swerved sharply to avoid hitting the woman, then swerved again to dodge the oncoming traffic before losing control and ploughing into a parked car. Jonah felt his belt snap. He gripped the seat in front of him, his breath catching in his throat as the car flipped in the air.

JONAH MOANED WHEN the pain pulled him back to consciousness. He opened his eyes and looked around. It took him a moment to realise he was lying on the side of the road and could see the crumpled, smoking taxi up ahead. The buckled door was forced open, and a bloodied, injured driver eased himself out. Jonah tried to call out to him, horrified to find himself mute. He wanted to raise his arm but couldn't move. Panic seized him when he wondered if he'd been paralysed in the accident.

The driver's face contorted in pain, blood dripping from a gash in his forehead as he slumped to the ground beside his car. Despite the fact that they'd been driving in heavy traffic only moments ago, now there was only the flipped taxi on the other side of the road. Jonah tried to move his head, to look for anyone who could help.

What the hell is going on?

Beyond the driver, he caught movement at the edge of his vision. With slow yet purposeful steps, the woman who'd caused the accident approached him. Jonah tried again to call out, but still, his body would not respond. Any fear he'd held for his own well-being disappeared beneath the sudden dread he felt now for the taxi driver.

Something about the woman made him wish he could run and hide.

Why is she moving so goddamn slow? It infuriated and terrified him all at once. The taxi driver managed to prop himself up to a seated position against the car. When he noticed the woman approaching, he called out to her for help, his voice cracked and gasping. The woman continued toward him in silence, without reaction or emotion, and the man stared at her in helpless confusion.

She stopped in front of him and stared down at his bloody face. Flaming red hair starkly contrasted her ivory skin, illuminated against the flowing black dress she wore. She slowly raised her arm, clutching in her hand a strange, glowing cord, which seemed to resonate with its own internal life force.

The driver's confusion bloomed into panic the longer the woman stared at him, unblinking. Without diverting her intense gaze, she raised a gleaming pair of silver scissors in her other hand. In one sweeping motion, she severed the cord between the scissor blades, and Jonah swallowed hard when the driver's head fell back against the car, his dead, blank stare aimed upward into nothingness.

The woman then turned her gaze to Jonah. With slow, languid steps, she made her way toward him, as though she knew full well he could not flee. Immobilised, he heard his own heart pounding in fierce protest.

She stopped, tilted her head, and stared straight into his eyes. He held his breath. Her mouth twisted upwards in a sneer before she turned and walked away, red hair billowing behind her by a wind Jonah could not feel.

Then she was gone.

He could barely move to look around, wondering where the hell she'd gone and how she'd disappeared. Whatever paralysis had gripped him abruptly ceased, engulfing him in even more pain, and all thoughts of the woman vanished. He finally called out for help as the world blurred before him.

Right before he lost consciousness, he heard the radio in the taxi still playing in the now-silent street.

"Come on, baby. Don't fear the Reaper…"

CHAPTER TWO

LAUGHTER ERUPTED, SHATTERING the silence of the hospital ward. Jonah had just finished telling Tristan about the redheaded woman. "How is any of this funny?" Jonah asked.

Tristan stood and tried to look serious. "Look, man. I'm sorry I laughed. I am. It's just… you tell me you're fine except for your broken arm and some bruised ribs. Then you tell me about a freaky hot chick wielding a pair of big-arse scissors."

"I never said she was hot."

"It was implied." Tristan raised a hand to silence Jonah's protests. "A woman you believe caused the car accident before killing the driver with a piece of string."

"Not with the string. She cut the string."

"Right. Well, mate, you must have a concussion, because you're talking shit."

Jonah stared at his best mate. Tristan had an almost identical mop of hair, only jet-black instead of Jonah's fair blond. He also shared the prominent shadow of unshaven facial hair, and he actually managed to make it look good. On Jonah, it only gave him a dishevelled appearance.

As Tristan marched about the room with his casual air, Jonah couldn't help but smile at what he referred to as Tristan's uniform—jeans, scuffed where they dragged on the floor around one of his numerous pairs of Chucks, paired with a t-shirt depicting whichever band or musician Tristan favoured most that day.

Jonah tried to get comfortable on the hospital bed but grimaced at the pain pulsing through his bruised and battered body.

Tristan saw that grimace and approached the bed. "Jonah, you know I'm your best mate, but you understand how it sounds, right? Can you at least consider the possibility that what you saw was just a result of the accident? I mean, you came to on the side of the road. You have no idea how hard you hit your head. Mate, you're lucky to be *alive*."

Jonah gazed out the window as he thought about those words. "Wait…" He sat upright with the sudden realisation. More pain took his breath away, and he waited for it to dull. "It couldn't have been my imagination. I saw the woman before the accident, remember? She was standing in the middle of the road."

Tristan said nothing. He paced beside the bed, trying to come up with an alternative explanation. "Okay, so maybe you saw the real woman standing in the middle of the road. But what if the second time you saw her was a hallucination? Your way of coming to terms with witnessing someone die?"

"Shit, Tristan, you sound like your sister."

"Speaking of which, I'd better call her. Ava's going to have my neck for not calling her sooner."

"No, don't! You pretending to be a shrink is bad enough. I can do without a real one here." Tristan didn't look convinced. "There's no point in worrying her, mate. I just need to get my head straight first, okay?"

Tristan shrugged. "Okay, but only if you admit what I said is plausible."

"Okay, I admit, it's plausible. But if that's what happened—and I'm not saying it is—where did she go?"

"Beats me." Tristan flopped into the chair beside the bed and propped his feet on the edge of the thin mattress beside Jonah's legs. "Maybe she just bolted when she saw the damage she caused. People can be arseholes like that."

"It seemed real to me."

"Look, mate, I know this is the last place on earth you want to spend your thirtieth birthday. If I could change things for you, I would. But I think you need to follow the doctor's orders on this one. We can celebrate all you want when they give you the all-clear, okay? My shout."

"You? Shout me drinks?"

"What? It wouldn't be the first time."

"You never shout."

"Well, I'm shouting, all right? No arguing."

"Must have hit my head harder than I thought," Jonah said and grinned.

TRISTAN MADE HIS way to the ferry dock. It had been a long day, made longer by the fact that his car had refused to start in the hospital car park. He resigned himself to leaving the car overnight and tackling that issue in the morning, too worried about Jonah to think about much else.

He glanced down at his Batman wristwatch, which he always said served as a reminder not to take life too seriously. It failed to ease his worries today, but he was relieved to see he still had plenty of time.

It surprised him to find the ferry already docked. Despite being early, it was already boarding passengers, and Tristan broke into a jog, amazed by his turn of good fortune. He greeted the captain, moved down the aisle, and took up a window seat. Gazing out at the city lit up along the waterfront was his favourite part of travelling on the ferry at night. As it pulled out onto the dark, murky river, the water's surface looked to Tristan like a black mirror, reflecting the sparkling lights of Brisbane back at him. Mesmerised, he let his thoughts drift back to Jonah.

He felt like he'd somehow let his mate down by not taking him at his word. As much as Tristan wanted to believe him, there was no way Jonah's account of what he'd seen before and after his accident could be true. The more he thought about it, the more he convinced himself that the woman was a hallucination. Things like that just didn't happen. It occurred to him that Jonah was likely to come to this same realisation once the concussion wore off.

He leaned back in his chair, relieved by and confident in the fact that he hadn't broken any vital code of mateship. Just as he was finally relaxing, the ferry gave a long, loud groan just before the engine cut out. The lights flickered, then left the cabin in darkness, the only light coming from the buildings lining the riverbank. Tristan looked around in confusion while the other passengers voiced their concerns in increasing volume.

Someone shouted from the front of the ferry. "Attention, passengers!" Tristan struggled to make out the captain standing illuminated by the lights outside. "I am sorry for the inconvenience, but we seem to be having some technical difficulties."

"What kind of technical difficulties?" a passenger in the front asked.

There was a pause. "Please rest assured, we will have one of the other ferries join us soon. We'll transfer you all over if we haven't fixed the problem by then."

Protests rose all around, and Tristan sighed in disgust. He leaned his head against the cool glass of the window, closing his eyes and trying to ignore the racket of disgruntled passengers. When he opened his eyes again, he saw another ferry approaching them across the water. The mood around him shifted from annoyance to relief, but Tristan found himself fighting off fierce stabs of dread at the sight.

"All right, everyone. If I could just have your attention, please. I'm going to head up and speak to the driver, and then we can start moving you across."

Tristan's apprehension only intensified when he stared back at his own concerned expression in the window. He had never been superstitious and didn't believe in the paranormal, but if there was such a thing as a sixth sense, his own was going crazy. The whole situation creeped him out, and he couldn't figure out why. He watched the two ferry captains bring their boats together so the passengers could easily step from one to the other. As the men stood talking, it seemed to Tristan that their rescuers had appeared all too quickly. Not to mention the fact that this new ferry was empty.

In the middle of peak hour.

He gave himself a mental slap. *Stop it! It's just a bloody boat, for crying out loud.* Jonah's story must have unnerved him more than he thought.

The driver of the second boat stepped inside the stranded ferry, and Tristan took an instant dislike to the man when a tingling up his spine told him to stay away. The new driver made his skin crawl, and he scrunched down into his seat.

"Good evening, ladies and gentlemen. If you can please make your way forward in single file, we'll have you back on land in no time." The man's cordial tone sounded forced and fake, only cementing Tristan's desire to steer clear of him. He stayed in his seat and watched the other passengers move out, then ducked his head into the aisle for a better look. The man stood at the entrance and greeted each passenger with a friendly pat on the shoulder as they exited. For all intents and purposes, the new captain seemed pleasant enough, and Tristan could find no reason for the unexplained warning telling him not to follow the others. He only knew that he wanted to get off the boat, and he wanted to avoid contact with the captain.

Most of the passengers formed a line down the aisle closest to the exit. Tristan walked down the outer aisle and moved around to the front of the cabin. He squeezed past as the captain greeted a passenger, forcing himself between the passenger and the wall. He ignored the shouts of protest and flying insults as he stepped out into the fresh night air and climbed onto the next boat before he allowed himself to turn around.

He immediately wished he hadn't.

The driver stood at the entrance of the ferry, his head turned toward Tristan with a cold glare that sent a chill down his spine.

Yep. My Spidey senses are tingling.

He turned and kept walking, choosing not to sit in the cabin but to stay outside on the deck. He'd hoped the feeling of dread would ease once he was on the next ferry. It only intensified.

Finally, all the passengers had boarded, and Tristan found himself the only one sitting outside. A nervous flutter filled his stomach as the ferry pulled away and headed across the river. He fished his phone out of his pocket in the hopes that some music would distract him. Chris de Burgh playing "Don't Pay the Ferryman" blasted into his ears, and he ripped out his headphones in disgust. Then he shoved the phone back into his pocket, leaned against the rail, and cupped his face in his hands, wondering what the hell was wrong with him. He reassured himself that in under an hour, he'd be in the comfort of his own home, enjoying a beer and laughing at what a sook he'd been. But for now, fear sat like a lead weight in his stomach, and his mouth was as dry as dust. Tristan forced himself to take three deep breaths to calm down.

He opened his eyes and exhaled, his heart skipping quickly at what he saw. The city lights faded away along the riverfront, hidden by the thick, ominous fog creeping towards them across the river.

Ice crystallised in his veins as the boat transformed before his eyes. He stepped back from the rails when they slid out from under him. The deck narrowed on either side while stretching out in length. The exterior of the boat morphed from fiberglass and chrome to an aged and brittle-looking wood. Tristan forced himself to turn around. A moan escaped him when he saw the rest of the boat changing too. He gripped his forehead, watching the cabin disappear completely. The passengers, still in their seats, moved and merged until they sat two abreast.

It stupefied him that no one else acknowledged what was happening. A woman knitted where she sat, silently counting stitches; a businessman clattered away on his laptop, brow furrowed in concentration; a teenager scribbled hearts and initials in a notebook as she silently sang along to her phone. In disbelief, he stared as one by one a handprint illuminated across each passenger's right shoulder blade.

I'm losing my bloody mind!

The ferry had now completely transformed into a gig-like boat minus the oars. Tristan peered down the vessel's great length, trying to locate the captain.

Then he found the man standing at the bow.

The ferryman's uniform faded away, starting at his feet and moving upwards and replaced by a black cloak. Tristan almost lost sight of him as the cloak rose up over the captain's head to form a hood. In his hands, the man now suddenly held a single wooden staff. When he used it to pierce the water's dark surface, the staff illuminated like a lantern to guide them forward.

Tristan lurched backwards in fear, only to trip and clatter against the stern.

The hooded figure turned his head to look back at him, but Tristan could see nothing but darkness under that hood. Silver eyes flashed, and in a deafening voice, the ferryman commanded, "Get... off... my... boat."

With a vibrating *boom*, Tristan was flung off the back of the boat, flying high into the air before landing a hundred metres away. He sank into the cold, dark river, the silver eyes still on him even as he lost consciousness.

CHAPTER THREE

FTER TWELVE HOURS in this bed, Jonah was bored. He'd tried calling Tristan several times, but his calls went straight to voicemail.

He heard the rattle of wheels outside his room and waited in anticipation for his meal to be brought in; he hoped the hospital food had improved since his childhood.

"How are you this evening?" the nurse asked as she rearranged his table and poured him a glass of water.

"Bored but okay, thanks." He eyed the tray of food before him, his hopes dashed when he saw that jelly was still on the menu. He nudged it with his finger, impressed that it didn't move at all.

"How's your pain?"

"Well, I can't feel much of anything so long as I don't make any sudden movements."

The nurse smiled and made notations on his chart.

Jonah's gaze shifted to the muted television suspended from the ceiling. A news headline flashed along the bottom of the screen, and he sat forward in a rush, the pain masked by his shock.

"Can you turn that up, please?"

The nurse complied, startled by the urgency in his voice. She said something, but Jonah didn't hear. Then she turned, headed toward the door, and stopped. He felt her gaze on him but ignored her.

The only thing he could see now was the television screen and mind-numbing update on the news. Jonah only saw in tunnel vision as he stared at the screen in front of him.

"Strange reports have flooded in today of a number of bizarre and unexplained deaths. A currently unidentified woman has been described as the alleged cause of the deaths, despite their occurrences all across the country. For more on this story, we now cross to Anna Port, live from the City Police Station."

"Good evening. Now, what's interesting about this is that witness reports of the woman are almost identical across the board, despite the fact that the accidents themselves are varied and have occurred in different areas across the country. The first incident was a car accident on the outskirts of the CBD around 7a.m. this morning, in which a cab driver lost his life and his passenger was found unconscious on the road. Police had previously believed the passenger's account to be a result of head trauma but were forced to reconsider after similar accounts and descriptions of the woman were repeated over the course of the day.

"The most recent incident occurred in Perth less than half an hour ago, involving two window-washers working

downtown. Witnesses holding a meeting within the building were all able to describe the events with the same details."

"Anna, are we any closer to learning the identity of the woman, what role she plays in these incidents, and how she might be connected to the victims?"

"Well, at this stage, authorities have yet to identify her but have given the following description. A Caucasian woman with fair skin, approximately six feet tall, with a slim build, long red hair, green eyes, and wearing a long black dress. As for her connection to the witnesses, victims, and the accidents themselves, we have received no news. The fact that the same woman appears to be responsible for every strange occurrence is definitely unnerving. The police have stated they will not be releasing any further details on the disturbing events until they finish interviewing witnesses. They're also asking for anyone who may have come across the woman or know anything about her to please contact the Crime Reporting Hotline as soon as possible."

"Thank you, Anna. We'll cross back to you later as the story develops. Now for a short break, and we'll be right back."

The newsreader stared at the camera, all shiny white teeth, and the ad break began.

Jonah eased himself back onto the pillows.

He was no longer hungry.

TRISTAN'S HEAD HIT the stone wall lining the riverbank, and he came to with a start. After flailing around for a moment, he realised he was still in the water. Recalling how he got there, he was overcome with a panicked need to get onto land. He launched himself upwards, grabbing onto the shallow wall, and hoisted himself out of the water.

Once flat on his back on the grass, he wondered what the hell had happened. He looked at his watch only to find that it had stopped working. Then he wriggled his phone from his back pocket, but it didn't take long to see the water had also gotten the best of it. Exhausted and confused, he would still rather walk home, even if it took all night, than go near any more public transport.

The fact that he'd never called his sister hit him like a blow to the head. Her mobile number was one of only a few he actually knew by heart. Now he just had to find a payphone—not an easy feat these days. After walking a couple blocks, he stumbled across one just off the street and thanked his semi-lucky stars that he still had his wallet in his pocket. He fished out some change and dropped it into the phone before punching in her number.

She answered on the third ring. "Hello?"

"It's Tristan…" He was more relieved to hear her voice than he expected to be.

"Are you okay? You sound funny. What's up?"

"Um, I need you to come pick me up." He gave her his location and asked her to hurry. Then he waited, trying to think of anything other than the night's events.

After what felt like an eternity, his sister arrived and jumped out of the car, looking at her brother with bewilderment and concern. He could only imagine how he looked, especially since he stood on the side of the road, illuminated only by the flickering light of the phone booth.

"Tristan, what the hell?" she asked, arms in the air.

He let out a huge sigh. "It's a long story, Sis, and I promise I'll tell you everything. But first, I'm in dire need of a beer."

Ava rolled her eyes. They decided it was unlikely that any local pub would permit him inside, given how soaked he was. It didn't help that he was only wearing one shoe, which he'd been oblivious to until Ava pointed it out. He convinced his sister to pick up some beers to take back to her house; he didn't feel like being alone. Or sober.

He climbed into the front seat and was distracted by a hat sitting on the dashboard. He picked it up—an old-school *X-Files* hat with the words 'The Truth Is Out There' across the front. He grinned, recognising it as Jonah's, and pulled it on. He was more than aware of his sister's frequent sideways glances, and he leaned forward to turn on the radio, hoping the noise would prevent Ava's questions for the duration of the trip.

"WHAT HAPPENED? SHE asked when she got back into the car after a brief stop at the liquor store. "You seem pretty shaken. Do you want to just crash at my place tonight?"

Tristan didn't need to be asked twice and cracked open a beer.

"Could you not wait five minutes until we get home?" His sister glared at him between glances at the road.

"Nope." He skulled half the bottle in one long drink. Ava let out a long sigh but said nothing.

When they got to her place, Tristan juggled the beers in his arms and followed her inside. He put the cans down on the coffee table before he took off the hat and ran his hands through his almost-dry hair.

Ava gave out an almighty shriek.

"Damn it, Ava! I'm sure I look like crap, but was that really called for?"

"Tristan! Your hair!" She pointed at his head.

He gave her a puzzled look before walking toward the bathroom to see for himself. "Holy *shit*!" Tristan took a moment to compose himself, then looked up at the mirror again, sifting his fingers through his hair and peering at it from every angle. A thick stripe of white hair ran along the right side of his head from his hairline to the nape of his neck. He shook his head in disbelief, then walked back into the lounge room, where Ava handed him a fresh beer.

"I think you'd better start at the beginning," she said, worry written all over her face.

Tristan nodded, sat down beside his sister, and took a deep breath. He started off by telling her about Jonah's accident.

"Oh, my God, Tristan! Why didn't you call me? Is he okay?" She punctuated each word with a whack to his arm.

"I know. I'm sorry! I was going to call, but Jonah asked me not to. He wanted to get his head sorted first before telling anyone else. Especially since my reaction was hardly helpful." *If only I knew then what I know now,* he thought.

"What do you mean?"

Tristan took a long drink from his beer, then repeated Jonah's account of the accident. When he finished, Ava sat completely still, gazing at the opposite wall. She opened her mouth to speak, but Tristan stopped her with a raised hand. "There's more." Her eyes grew wide. Then he told her about his own experience that evening on the ferry. He resented the cold shiver spreading through him when he recalled the intensity of the ferryman's eyes.

"Tristan… I…"

He could tell just by looking at her that she didn't believe him. "Look, I know how this sounds. Believe me. I felt the same way when Jonah told me what had happened to him. I can see that brain of yours ticking over, trying to come up with some psychological explanation for it. Come on, Ava, you know me. You know Jonah. I don't believe in any of this weird shit. It's always been more Jonah's thing, but there's nothing like almost drowning at the hands of someone straight out of a horror movie to convert you. I'm telling you now… it happened."

Ava still said nothing, doubt and confusion flashing simultaneously across her face.

"For crying out loud, Ava! Some of my hair turned white. White! Now tell me, how terrified does someone have to be for that to happen?" He paced around the lounge room in frustration.

"I don't doubt that something terrified you, Tristan. It's not that I don't want to believe you. It's just that I can't comprehend what you're telling me. I believe that you believe what happened to you."

"That sounds like a load of crap you would say to placate your patients."

Ava sighed. "I don't know what you want me to say. Even if I could believe what you just told me, what does that mean?"

Tristan leaned back against the wall, letting his head fall back to look up at the ceiling.

I have no idea.

JONAH JOLTED AWAKE. His room was dark save for the low light coming from the corridor and the flickering glow of the television. He realised he must have dozed off while watching for further updates on the mysterious woman.

Damn painkillers. He sat up, feeling groggy, then groaned as his bladder indicated a visit to the bathroom was in order. He slid himself out of the bed, feeling stiff, and found that things were trickier when doing them one-handed and injured. He grabbed his IV pole and used to it make his way across the room to the bathroom. After some rather skilled fumbling, he achieved his goal and hobbled back towards the bed. He was all too aware of just how many muscles there were in the human body; every single one of his screamed at him.

Halfway across the room, he jumped when a dark shadow blocked out the light, just for a moment. Jonah stood motionless, his heart pounding, gripping the IV pole as if it were his life support. He was particularly grateful that he had already been to the bathroom. When nothing else happened, he moved back towards the doorway.

He hated being so jumpy and chastised himself for not managing to move any faster. At the door, he poked his head out and glanced both ways down the corridor, but it was empty and dim. The only light came from the nurse's station to the left—currently empty He was about to turn back into his room, then glimpsed movement again off to the right and immediately tried to find the source. He saw the tail end of a black dress flowing through the doorway about six rooms down. Jonah's heart thumped hard against his chest as he struggled to control his breathing.

What the hell?

He half hoped that he'd imagined it, but there was no way he could go back to bed until he knew for sure one way or another. Closing his eyes, Jonah tried to swallow the fear, then glanced towards the nurse's station to ensure the coast was clear. When he saw no one, he shuffled towards the room, hugging the wall, trying to make himself as small as possible—a difficult task while attached to a pole. He cursed the squeak of the IV wheels magnifying in the quiet hall. Then he stopped again at the entrance and made a silent plea to whomever would listen for the room to be devoid of everything but patients.

Slowly, feeling just a little foolish, he turned his head into the entry and gave a small sigh of relief. There were only sleeping patients along the right side of the room. He stepped sideways to stand directly in the doorway and almost fell back in terror.

There she stood at the foot of the last bed. The moonlight streaming through the semi-closed blinds illuminated her skin.

It was the red-haired woman.

Jonah watched, frozen, as she enacted the same ritual he'd witnessed earlier that day. He squinted, trying to make out the string-like object she held. He could have sworn it was much longer than the one he'd seen her holding in front of the cab driver. Then he turned his attention to the woman lying in bed, who was now awake and pleading.

"Please. I don't want to go." Her watery blue eyes focused on the stranger in front of her. She was an elderly woman, quite thin and with snowy-white hair. But there was a vibrancy about her still. "Why won't you answer me? Who are you?" The anger and annoyance rose quickly in the elderly woman's voice. The red-haired woman stood motionless, unblinking and silent. The only thing moving was the silvery, glowing string.

The elderly woman forced herself to sit up in defiance. "Fine! Do whatever it is you're here to do. Get it over with."

Jonah turned his head away when he heard the metallic snap of the scissors. In his heart, he'd known what was coming and couldn't bear to see it a second time. Startled by the sudden glare of beeping machines, he backed away from the door but lost his balance and tripped backwards over the IV pole. He landed hard on the floor, yowling in pain as his already battered body protested.

The woman in the black dress turned, unimpressed to see him again. She walked towards him, her intense gaze locked on his, her eyebrow raised in question. Jonah scurried backwards until he felt the wall behind him.

"Hey! What are you doing?" A gruff-looking nurse stomped in his direction as more staff flocked out of nowhere to attend to the already deceased woman. Jonah didn't even attempt to answer her and struggled to ease himself upright. The nurse helped him up and told him to get back to his room before she turned and followed the mechanical beeping. Jonah tried to look past her to where the red-haired woman had stood, but she'd vanished. All who remained were the deceased and the startled patients awoken by the commotion.

He couldn't help but feel like a chastised child as he hobbled back down the corridor. When he reached his room, he paused; he now felt quite scared of the dark.

Damn it, you idiot. You're acting like a bloody child.

He forced himself into the room, trying to ignore the quickening of his pulse, and focused his attention on the lamp by his bed. A few minutes later, he was still trying to get comfortable when the gruff nurse walked into his room.

"Now, Mr Sands, just what did you think you were doing walking around in the middle of the night?" she asked, checking his chart then fussing over his IV.

Jonah ignored the question. "What happened to the old woman?" He tried to sound nonchalant.

"She passed away, I'm afraid." The nurse matched Jonah's forced apathy completely.

"Was she very ill?"

Confusion flashed across her face before her brows furrowed. "She was going home in the morning. But that's no concern of yours." Realising she had said more than she should have, she took up her coarse attitude once more and shoved a little paper cup of pills towards him. Jonah downed the pills with the glass of water provided and lay down.

The nurse rambled about nothing important, and Jonah yawned. He felt tired—physically, emotionally, and mentally. As if on cue, his body decided he'd had enough for one day, and he drifted off into blissful oblivion.

CHAPTER FOUR

AVA STARED DOWN at her brother, astounded that he could sleep after everything he'd told her. She could only assume it was out of sheer exhaustion. Either that, or the beers had caught up with him in the end.

She was as far from sleep herself as she could get. Her mind still reeled after Tristan's story, wondering what to make of it. So she decided, despite the hour, that she would head back to work; gods knew she always had paperwork to do. She grabbed her things and left without her brother ever stirring.

AT WORK, AVA headed straight for the staff lounge for a cup of coffee.

"Oh, good evening, Bob. How are you?"

One of the night staff sat in the lounge on his break. "Hey, Dr Carter. What are you doing back here? Shouldn't you be at home fast asleep?"

"In a perfect world, yes, Bob." Ava laughed. "But since I can't sleep, I thought I might as well catch up on some work." She poured herself some coffee from the hot urn.

"How is everything tonight? Nothing out of the ordinary?"

"All good, Doctor. Though I am a little concerned about Caitlyn."

"How so?" Ava asked, surprised. Caitlyn had been progressing well.

"Well, it's probably nothing, but a few times today, I found her whispering to herself."

Ava looked up from her cup, trying not to show how concerning she found the news. "Did you approach her at all?"

"Yeah, I did the first couple times. She just looked at me as if she didn't know what I was talking about and walked away. I documented the details in her file and included the time of each instance," Bob answered.

Ava said nothing as she ran through the new development. Finally, she gave a little nod. "Great, Bob. Thank you. If it happens again, I don't want you to approach her. Just leave her be and get me, okay? I would like to observe her myself."

"No worries, Doctor." Bob waved as she left the lounge.

Once in her office, she sat back in her chair and reflected on Caitlyn while she waited for her computer to boot up. Ava had first met the girl three months ago. Caitlin had been admitted after a suicide attempt in response to losing both her parents in a house fire after she had fallen asleep with a lit candle. In the past few weeks, however, Ava had noted a significant improvement in the girl's behaviour and outlook on her own life, and this setback troubled her.

Taking a few steps back during treatment is normal. But this... She sighed and rubbed her eyes. *Great, now I'm tired.*

But she was already here, so decided to push past it and get some work done. After a big gulp of coffee, she pulled Caitlyn's file from the cabinet and had to read the same notes three times; her mind remained on her brother, Jonah, and the day's events. Ava wanted to speak to Jonah but knew it was far too late—or too early. She would have to wait until later in the morning. Part of her hoped that Jonah and her brother would laugh it off and tell her that the whole thing was a practical joke. Their sense of humour could be questionable at best. This was the one time Ava would be more than happy to bear the brunt of their warped sense of humour. But then she reminded herself of Jonah's injuries and Tristan's latest hairstyle, and it gave her little hope.

She got up in a huff, annoyed by her inability to focus, then went to check on Caitlyn for herself. As she turned the corner, she ran straight into Bob again.

"I'm so sorry, Dr Carter," Bob said, catching his breath.

"It's okay. I'm just heading down to check on Caitlyn. Are you all right?"

"That's what I was on my way to see you about, Doctor. She's talking to herself again."

Ava tried to conceal her surprise. Bob was usually an unshakable man, but as he stood in front of her now, his face was ashen, and Ava thought it looked like fear. "Thank you, Bob. I'll take it from here." She moved at a quick pace until she reached the girl's room.

As she peered through the window in the door, she saw Caitlyn sitting on the floor at the foot of the bed. "Caitlyn? It's Dr Carter. I heard you were awake and thought I would say hello."

She took her time in entering the room, not wanting to startle the girl.

Caitlyn didn't respond but only stared at the wall, whispering quietly to herself. Ava sat down in the desk chair to observe. Folding her arms across her chest, she tilted her head and watched in concentration. After a few moments, she opened Caitlyn's file to search for even the smallest clue as to why this new behaviour had appeared so suddenly.

There were no amendments to her medical chart, no reports of aggression. The day's documentation stated that Caitlyn woke late despite attempts from nursing staff to get her up sooner. She had appeared groggy and complained of being tired, then refused breakfast but drank several glasses of water. The girl took her medication without fuss but didn't eat lunch, opting for more water. She failed to interact with other patients during the day and in group therapy. She spent most of the day by herself, staring off into the distance and talking to herself. She didn't eat dinner but drank water. Medication was taken before bed with an additional three glasses of water.

With still no acknowledgement now from the girl, Ava decided to go check the visitor's log; perhaps a visitor had been the trigger today. "I'll be right back, Caitlyn," Ava said softly, giving the girl one last look before walking out of the room.

As she stepped into the hall, the evening RN Mary approached her. "Hi, Mary."

"Good evening, Dr Carter. What are you doing here on your day off?"

"I decided to come in and catch up on some paperwork. Just as well, too. I take it you're aware of Caitlyn Johnson's behavioural changes today?"

"Yes. I didn't think it severe enough to call you about, though."

"That's fine, Mary. I'm not checking up on you." Ava glanced toward the door. "Caitlyn is displaying that same behaviour again now, and I'd like you to sit with her while I look into a few things."

"Of course."

Mary headed towards the girl's room, and Ava went down the hall for the guest registry. She scrolled down the day's visitor list, as well the previous days', and saw nothing out of the ordinary. She sighed.

What's going on with you, Caitlyn?

The silence was shattered by a piercing scream ringing out through the ward. Ava stiffened for a moment, then realised the scream had come from Caitlyn's room. The folder fell from her hands, and she raced down the hall. Bob ran toward her from the opposite direction, also at high speed. They met at the door, exchanging bewildered looks before entering.

Ava first saw Mary, who was partially obscured by the desk as she huddled in the left corner. The evening nurse stared wide-eyed across the room, terror distorting her features. Ava stepped farther inside to get a better look.

Against the wall, almost touching the ceiling, was Caitlyn. The girl was pinned there as if by an invisible force, her body contorting in impossible angles.

"Oh, my God!" Ava's hands flew to her mouth in horror. She stepped backwards into Bob, who followed her gaze and swore. He fell hard against the wall in his hurry to get away.

Ava forced herself to take another look.

Caitlyn's clothes hung from her body, half torn off, and sweat beaded across her exposed skin. Despite the unnatural positioning of her body, the girl's face appeared serene. Her eyes were closed, lips parted, and a light frown drifted across her brow. Ava removed her hands from her mouth and took a tentative step forward. "Caitlyn?" she said softly. "Caitlyn, can you hear me?" There was no response or any sign that the girl was aware they were even in the room.

Ava turned back towards her staff. Mary still huddled in the corner, now with her head in her hands, and Bob was trying to regain his composure as he picked himself up off the floor. For the first time in her professional career, Ava was completely at a loss for what to do. She felt her own panic rising, threatening to overcome her, and she forced herself to take a deep breath in response.

Approaching Caitlyn with slow steps, she had no idea what to expect. When she was close enough, she reached up and gently touched the girl's ankle. As though that released her, Caitlyn fell to the floor in a heap. "Caitlyn?" There was no response, and Ava checked the girl's vitals. Caitlyn's pulse raced, her breathing laboured. Ava forced herself to take another deep breath and focus. "Bob, call an ambulance."

Bob launched himself into the hall, and Ava couldn't tell if it was in eagerness to help or to get as far away from the situation as possible. She felt the girl's forehead. As impossible as it seemed, Caitlyn's temperature rose by the second. When Ava pulled her hand away, the girl went into a violent seizure. Ava quickly rolled her onto her back and grabbed a pillow from the bed to place beneath her head.

She glanced at her watch, timing the episode, and had to force herself to focus on the task at hand and not on the cacophony of thoughts flooding her head. A seizure, at least, she understood. A seizure she could manage.

When it passed, she looked down at the girl's face with trepidation. A soft sigh emanated from Caitlyn's lips, and her whole body relaxed into the floor. Ava leaned forward to check her vitals again, but this time found no pulse. She sprang into action, removed the pillow from beneath the girl's head, and tilted Caitlin's head back in preparation for CPR. But before she could begin compressions, she was abruptly thrown back against the wall. Stunned, she watched in mute horror as Caitlyn's body lifted once more into the air.

As the girl rose higher, her body rotated forward until she suspended vertically, her feet hovering a metre from the ground. The girl's arms lay limp by her sides, and her chin rested on her chest, rolling slightly to the right. Her face was mostly obscured by her hair, which had fallen across it.

Ava rubbed the back of her throbbing head, picked herself up off the ground, and reached up to touch Caitlyn's idle hand. Instantly, the girl's head snapped upright, and her hair blew away from her face in a breeze that did not exist in the room, floating around her head as though it had a life of its own. Her eyes opened, and Ava gasped. Gone were the beautiful hazel eyes she was used to seeing, replaced now by white, opaque orbs.

"Caitlyn!"

The girl spoke in a delicate whisper, and Ava found herself leaning forward to hear the words. "The Dawn of Metamorphosis is upon us. The Age of Man hangs in the balance, for they come. So too the three rise. Seek the wisdom of Hephalion."

Ava stared up in confusion, and Caitlyn slowly rotated backwards until she lay perfectly straight again in mid-air. Then her body slowly lowered itself onto the bed. Ava had to take a few seconds before approaching the bed with cautious steps. She gripped Caitlyn's wrist and was amazed to find a pulse again—a strong and steady one at that. The girl's breathing had stabilized, too, and Ava could only stand there watching her. It was like the girl had been there, asleep, all along.

The sudden quiet was interrupted by a whimper, and Ava turned to see a forgotten Mary still huddled in the corner. She went to her and coaxed the woman upright.

"I'm losing my mind," Mary said, her eyes bulging from their sockets.

"I promise you, Mary, you're not. But you have had quite a shock. We all have." Ava glanced back at the peacefully resting Caitlyn. She decided the girl would be okay for the moment while she escorted Mary to the staff lounge. They found Bob waiting for them.

"The ambulance is on its way," he reported.

"Thank you, Bob. Now I just have to work out what the hell to tell them," Ava said with a tired sigh.

"What do you mean? Just show them that poor girl's body."

"That's the thing, Bob. She's now breathing steadily, her pulse is regular and strong, and she's sleeping." Ava massaged her temples.

"Oh, well done! I knew you could revive her, Doctor." Bob patted her on the back. Ava went to correct his misconception but instead realised he had given her a way out of telling him— and the paramedics—the truth.

"Thanks, Bob. Would you mind going to the foyer and keeping an eye out for the paramedics? They'll still need to check her out. And Bob, for now, don't mention what happened. Just tell them she suffered a seizure resulting in cardiac arrest."

Bob's face darkened, her statement forcing him to recall what had preceded the seizure. "Don't worry. I told them as much on the phone."

Ava turned her attention to Mary, who now looked slightly more composed—only slightly. "How are you holding up?" she asked and sat down beside the nurse.

Mary took a deep breath before turning to face Ava with a look of determined resolve. "As far as I'm concerned, Caitlyn had a seizure which resulted in her heart stopping, and you revived her. That's it. Nothing else happened."

"Mary…"

"No, Doctor. With all due respect, I know what you're going to say, but right now, if I try to think beyond that simplified medical scenario, I'm afraid I might start screaming. I'm even more afraid that I won't be able to stop."

Ava acknowledged the pleading look on Mary's face and gave the woman a small nod. "Okay, Mary. On one condition. If you need to talk, or you need anything at all, you call me straight away. Do you understand?"

"Thank you." It took Ava completely by surprise when the nurse leaned over and hugged her briefly before leaving.

Ava still had the paramedics to contend with before she could go home. Not that it mattered; she knew she wouldn't be sleeping. Instead, she decided to stay a while longer and keep an eye on Caitlyn until the morning staff arrived.

AVA STOOD IN the doorway of Caitlyn's room, watching her sleep. The girl now rested on her side, curled up under her blanket as though nothing had happened. Try as she might, Ava could find no logical or scientific explanation for what she had witnessed.

"Thought you might need this."

She turned to see Bob standing there, a hot cup of coffee in his hands. "Oh, Bob, you're my hero." She gratefully took the steaming mug from him, trying to hide the shake in her hands. "What time is it?"

"About three-thirty," he replied and took a sip from his own cup. "Crazy night."

"That's for sure."

"What do we do now?"

Ava thought for a moment. "I think we should keep it between the three of us for now. I'll document the medical aspects of tonight's events, as well as the report from the paramedics. All staff should be aware of that much, at least. But I think we should keep quiet on the rest until we know how much Caitlyn remembers."

Bob nodded slowly. "What do you think really happened in there?"

Ava sighed. "I honestly don't know. But whatever it was, I have a feeling this is just the beginning…"

CHAPTER
FIVE

I T TOOK ALL the strength and concentration Ava could muster to turn the key in the lock. When she stepped through her front door, she was surprised to see Tristan awake and looking relaxed on the couch.

"Hey, Sis. I thought you were still in bed. You look like crap. Where have you been?"

Ava shook her head. "I need a nice long shower before I say anything." She ignored the concern on her brother's face and walked past him.

"I'll put the coffee on," he stated, then walked off to the kitchen.

A HOT SHOWER made all the difference. Ava sat on the couch, towel-drying her long dark hair, gratefully accepting the fresh cup of coffee her brother placed on the table in front of her. He sat in the armchair across from her, and she smiled, watching him fidget; it was something they both did when unsure of what to say. She marvelled at the near-mirror image that was her brother. They were quite often asked if they were twins, with their raven hair and bright blue eyes. She sighed, aware that she was procrastinating but grateful for the moment's silence. While she knew her brother thoroughly enjoyed teasing her ninety-five percent of the time, he always knew when she needed timeout. She took a sip of coffee before she let out another sigh and relaxed into the couch. Tristan stared at her; the worry on his face made her feel mean for making him wait.

"I'm feeling a sense of deja-vu, only in reverse," she stated with a hint of a smile.

"And with no beer," Tristan pointed out.

"And no beer." Ava paused. "So, for starters, I should say I believe your story from last night."

"Are you serious? I'm not even sure I believe it."

"Well, they'll have to lock us both up, because once you hear what I saw, you'll wonder which one of us is crazier."

"Really?"

Ava took a deep breath, and Tristan leaned forward to listen to her tale, which she recounted from beginning to end in just a few minutes. When she finished, Tristan hadn't moved an inch, only now his mouth hung wide open.

"Oh, come on!" she demanded crossly. "How is that any more unbelievable than what happened to you?"

Tristan shook himself out of it. "No, it's not. I guess because it happened to you and not me, you know? I mean, holy crap. That sounds like it should be a scene directly from *The Exorcist* or something. If only her head had done a three-sixty and she'd vomited pea soup—"

"Tristan, this isn't a joking matter."

He scoffed. "Who's joking?" Tristan took a sip of his now-cold coffee. Ava stared at him with raised brows. "What?"

"We need to go see Jonah."

THE SLEEPING PILLS had left Jonah feeling groggy, and he poked, disoriented, at his breakfast. Recollections of the red-haired woman flooded his consciousness the moment he awoke. It left him feeling alone, confused, and scared. He didn't understand what had happened. Or why.

His pensive mood was interrupted by the sound of arguing voices wafting down the corridor and quickly growing louder. The familiar sound made him smile, and he looked up as Tristan and Ava entered.

"Morning, slacko. Can't believe you're still in bed." Tristan lightly punched Jonah on his unbroken arm.

"You're a comedian," Jonah said with a smile.

Ava leaned forward and gave him a kiss on the forehead. "Happy birthday for yesterday. We got you a couple presents to tide you over until you get well and can celebrate properly." She placed flowers, balloons, and a couple of wrapped presents on his nightstand.

"Thanks, guys. You didn't have to do this. But Ava, now that I think about it, you're just in time for my sponge bath." Jonah tried to muster an innocent expression.

Ava only rolled her eyes. "Now who's the comedian? You'd be lucky if I didn't drown you in it after you told Tristan not to call me yesterday."

"I know," Jonah said. "I just didn't want you to worry. That, and assuming Tristan has filled you in on the more curious aspects of my accident, I didn't want you to lock me up with the loonies." His smile disappeared when Ava glared at him. "I'm sorry. I meant the mentally ill." Then he flashed another grin. Ava ignored him and sat down on the opposite side of the bed.

"As it turns out, mate, they'd have to lock all three of us up," Tristan declared.

Jonah looked from Tristan to Ava, who had developed a fascination with her hands. Then he glanced back at Tristan, who was apparently trying to play it cool but seemed eager to elaborate. "Okay… so spill," he said with trepidation.

"You better make sure you're comfortable first." Tristan stood and stretched, making sure Jonah had a full view of his shirt.

Jonah groaned. "Dude, tell me that isn't a Blue Oyster Cult shirt."

Tristan did his best to look innocent while Ava started humming "Don't Fear the Reaper".

"Oh! Well, look at that! I suppose it is. What a coincidence that I should be wearing this," Tristan announced in mock surprise.

Jonah shook his head, unable to stop the smile forming at his friend's obvious amusement. "Bull, mate. I've never known anyone who chooses their t-shirts each day with more purpose than you do."

Tristan laughed as he sat back down. "I couldn't help myself. You have to see the funny side." Jonah stared at him, expressionless. Tristan averted his gaze towards his sister. "Too soon?" he asked. She just laughed.

"And that's my *X-Files* hat you're wearing," Jonah added. He really only wanted to change the subject.

"Mate, not my fault you leave your crap all over the place. Besides, I think it's an appropriate time for me to get my Mulder on."

"No way. It's my hat. I'm Mulder. You can be Scully," Jonah said.

"Whatever, mate. I'm the one wearing the hat. End of story."

Jonah opened his mouth to argue the point, but Ava interrupted them. "Don't you boys think we have more pressing issues to discuss?"

Jonah felt a little foolish, but he was grateful for the familiar banter. He also knew Ava was right. "Sorry. So, Tristan, fill me in."

"I think you should be the one to tell him," Tristan told his sister. "It'll sound more credible coming out of your mouth." He leaned forward and stole a bite of Jonah's breakfast, then pulled a face and leaned over to spit it out into the rubbish bin beside the bed. Then he turned to his sister and with a gallant wave of his hand said, "You may speak, ma'am."

Jonah grinned, and Ava shook her head. "You sure don't do yourself any favours in the credibility department." She took a deep breath. "I don't know where to start, to be honest. I mean, when I picked Tristan up last night looking like a drowned rat, I didn't know what to think."

Jonah turned to Tristan for an explanation, only to find his friend was the one now engrossed in studying *his* hands, too.

"Then he told me the circumstances of your accident. First, I attributed the account to a hallucination brought on by survivor's guilt—"

"See? I told you," Tristan interjected, and Jonah's laugh made him grimace in pain.

Ava ignored the pair. "But then I saw his hair and heard what happened, and I had no idea what to think."

"Hang on a minute," Jonah said. "What happened to you? What about your hair?" He glanced back and forth between his friends before Tristan sighed and removed the hat.

"What the hell is that?" Jonah almost couldn't move.

"It's not that bad, is it, Ava?"

She looked like she was going to try reassuring her brother, but instead, she only shrugged.

"Okay," Jonah said. "I think it's safe to say I'm confused. You better tell me what happened after you left here yesterday."

Tristan sighed and told his mate of everything the night before that had led to his not-so-flattering hairstyle.

"Shit, mate. That's intense. I don't know what else to say."

"Oh, dude, it gets better. Over to you, Ava."

Jonah turned to Ava, amazed that there could be any more. "Don't tell me something happened to you, too?" He tried to ignore the stab of concern he felt at the thought of her in harm's way.

"Well, not exactly to me," she said before launching into her version of the night's events.

When she finished, Jonah cleared his throat and said, "Okay, my turn again."

"Huh?" Ava and Tristan asked in bewildered unison.

Jonah nodded. He told them about seeing the woman again and the death of the elderly patient. When he finished, they sat in silence, trying to get their heads around all of it.

Then the doctor and a nurse bustled into the room, disrupting the sudden lull. "Mr Sands. How are we feeling this morning after last night's midnight stroll?" the doctor asked with a jovial smile.

"I have no idea what you're referring to," Jonah replied, smiling back.

The doctor chuckled and approached the bed for a closer inspection. "I see you got yourself some birthday presents of the non-painful kind." He checked Jonah's pulse.

"Sure did, but I'm still waiting for yours."

"Mine?"

"Yeah. When can I get out of here?"

"Well, your tests have come back clear. You're lucky to be alive, let alone avoiding serious injury." The doctor shook his head. "Do you live alone?"

"Yeah. Is that going to be a problem?" Jonah tried to contain his pending disappointment. After what had happened, the last thing he wanted to do was spend another night in the hospital.

"Well, yes, to be honest. You still have some recovering to do. It's painful for you to move around and will continue to be that way for the next few days. Plus, that cast on your arm is going to hinder you too. After last night's fall, I would feel better if I knew there was someone with you to keep an eye on you and help out." He scribbled notes onto Jonah's chart.

"He can stay with me," Tristan volunteered. "I have plenty of room, and I can work from home for the most part if I need to."

Jonah looked hopefully at the doctor, who appeared to take his time in considering it. "Okay," he said finally, "but I have a few conditions. First, you come straight back if you experience any increased pain or your condition changes. Second, you make an appointment to see me early next week. And last but not least, you take it easy over the next couple weeks. I mean it. Not that you're going to feel like running any marathons. Are we clear on this?"

"Crystal," Jonah replied with a relieved smile.

"All right, then. Well, Brooke is going to change some of those bandages for you, then she'll help you get dressed. I'll go organise your discharge." He gave Jonah a courteous nod, then left the room.

"Tristan and I will start taking your presents and things down to the car," Ava offered.

"Oh, will we just?" Tristan replied, eyebrows raised at his sister.

"Well, unless you want to watch Jonah get stripped down to his birthday suit, you will." Ava smirked and gathered up Jonah's things.

"Righto!" Tristan jumped out of his chair as though he'd been bitten.

Jonah tried not to laugh while his friends left the room. He felt much better knowing he was leaving with them.

THE CAR RIDE to Tristan's was a silent one. When they got there, Ava helped Jonah get settled on the couch. "Do you want your feet up? I can get the footstool. How about a pillow? Do you want a blanket? Are you thirsty?"

Jonah reached up and gently grabbed her by the arm. "Ava, I'm fine. Really." He stared into her eyes, trying to convey reassurance. She stared back at him for a moment before pulling away, her eyes filled with tears.

"I have to go. I'll see you later," she mumbled and walked back out the door.

Ava braced herself against the car in the driveway. She couldn't catch her breath, and the more she tried to stop the hot tears running down her cheeks, the more steadfastly they came.

"Hey! Ava, are you okay? What's the matter?" Tristan sounded surprisingly alarmed when he grabbed her shoulder and spun her around.

She buried her head into her brother's chest and sobbed, feeling like she was eight years old again. Tristan said nothing and let her cry. After a short while, she pulled back and sniffed. "I'm sorry. I don't know what's wrong with me." She wiped the tears from her face with the backs of her hands, angry at herself for crying like this.

"Don't apologise. It's been an insane twenty-four hours. If I wasn't such a big, strong man, I'd be breaking down into tears too."

Ava rolled her eyes but couldn't help a smile. "I guess I'm just overtired. A little delirious. It feels like weeks since I've slept, not just twenty-four hours. With everything that happened at work last night, and trying to process it all…"

"And I bet Jonah's accident and seeing him banged up like that didn't help much either, huh?" Tristan probed gently.

She could only briefly meet her brother's eyes before she had to look away again. "Well, yeah, I guess that too."

Tristan grinned. "Come back inside, and I'll make you a coffee."

Ava shook her head. "No. Thanks, but no. I have to pop back into work and check on Caitlyn, and then I think I should go home and try to get some sleep. Otherwise, you'll just have me crying all over your house. But we do need to sit down and talk about all this, the three of us, and figure out what the hell's going on."

Tristan nodded. "Well, since Jonah's here and probably shouldn't go anywhere, why don't you come over for dinner? I'll cook."

"You? Cook?"

"By cook, I mean barbecue. How does that sound?"

Ava laughed. "Any excuse for a barbecue."

TRISTAN WAS PARTICULARLY pleased with himself for managing to put a smile on her face before she left. In his opinion, he was seriously the best older brother ever. Hands shoved in his pockets, he turned and headed back inside, excited about planning that evening's barbecue despite the reason behind it.

CHAPTER SIX

AVA SAT ANXIOUSLY in the staff carpark, checking her watch; she'd been there ten minutes. She felt childish and incredibly worn out, both mentally and physically. The idea of facing another 'incident' in her ward made her wonder whether or not she even had the strength to go back inside. Still, she knew she couldn't go home and sleep if she didn't check on Caitlyn first. Finally, she took a deep breath, collected herself, and stepped out of the car.

Inside the hospital, she bypassed her office and walked straight to Caitlyn's room. The poor girl was fast asleep, and Ava grabbed her file to see if anything had happened since she'd left. All notes reflected that Caitlyn had slept right through the night. A staff member had noted that she'd gotten up for a shower but declined anything to eat, complained of a headache, and went back to sleep.

Ava walked toward the girl's bed and leaned forward to check Caitlyn's temperature. It was raised slightly, and she made a note in the file for her staff to monitor it. She didn't know whether to feel relieved or concerned that there was no evidence of Caitlyn remembering what had happened.

As she stepped into her office and turned on her computer, she weighed the pros and cons of raising the issue with her patient. And then she forgot everything else when she found an email from Dr John Aljoy in her inbox. John had been a friend of Ava's all through university, though it had been a while since they were last in touch. She was only too glad to have a positive distraction and eagerly opened the email.

Her eagerness shifted rapidly into despair as she read then reread his message.

Dear Ava,

I know it's been a while, but I need your help. Last night, we had an incident with one of our patients. A teenage girl suffering from depression underwent what I can only describe as a severe relapse. I'm not even sure I can explain it. Suffice it to say, I have never seen anything like it—nor do I wish to again.

I'd rather not say anything more via email, so please call me as soon as you get this. It's imperative.

Yours Sincerely,

John

Ava tried to stay calm, but she couldn't ignore the horrible feeling building in the pit of her stomach. As much as she didn't want to, she decided to get the phone call out of the way.

John must have been sitting by the phone and waiting for her, as he answered it halfway through the first ring. "Hello. Dr Aljoy speaking."

"Hi, John. It's Ava. I got your email." She heard him sigh with relief.

"Ava. Thank you so much for calling. I was worried you might not."

"Of course. So, tell me more about this patient of yours." She tried to hide the trepidation in her voice.

John relayed almost exactly the same chain of events Ava herself had witnessed. The only difference was that John's patient neither undergone cardiac arrest nor had a seizure.

"Did she say anything during the episode?" Ava asked, bracing herself for the answer she knew was coming.

"Well, that's the strangest part, Ava. She spoke your name."

There was a brief silence. "I'm sorry, John. Could you repeat that?"

"She spoke of you specifically and said your name." The sound of shuffling paper came over the line. "She said, 'From the darkness they call her name. Ava Carter. But on deaf ears their cries do fall, and into Hades we will perish."

The words echoed forever in her head, and for a moment, she'd forgotten she was on the phone.

"Ava? Are you still there?"

She cleared her throat. "Yes. Sorry, John. I'm just a little shocked, to say the least." She frantically scribbled down the words on her notepad.

"I know, and I'm sorry. In fact, I'm surprised you believe me at all."

"To be honest, a day ago, I probably wouldn't have."

AS JONAH TENTATIVELY made his way out of the bathroom, he called out to Tristan, "What's a bloke got to do to get a decent feed around here?" He heard his mate rattling around in the kitchen.

"Dude, I'm on it. I'm making us the Tristan Carter Deluxe Brunch. It annihilates that so-called hospital food."

"Well, it's not like that would be hard." Jonah sniggered.

"While that may be true, prepare yourself to be blown away nonetheless."

Jonah made his way slowly but surely to the table, his ribs still giving him grief. He sat and watched with amusement as his best mate flung himself around the kitchen. Then his mind wandered to Ava and her abrupt departure. He was worried about her, but he somehow felt unable to talk to her about it. The only reasonable thing he could think to do was to discreetly ask Tristan about it. No time like the present. He could always blame the painkillers if it backfired.

"So what was wrong with Ava? She ran off in a hurry." He tried to appear as nonchalant as possible, though he didn't miss the smile Tristan tried to suppress.

"I think she was just overtired and overwhelmed. I'm sure she'll feel much better once she gets some sleep."

Jonah took a deep breath and frowned at the table before giving himself a mental shake. He was well aware of the unwritten code stipulating no man could feasibly date his best mate's sister. Not to mention the fact that Ava and Tristan's parents were like his own. He shook his head and changed the subject. "Where's this awesome food you were talking about?"

"Hold your horses." Tristan set Jonah's plate in front of him on the table.

"Oh, man, this looks amazing."

"I told you," Tristan said and joined him with his own plate.

Jonah gazed down at the steaming breakfast in front of him stacked with bacon, sausages, thick, buttery toast, poached eggs, hash browns, grilled mushrooms, tomato, and wilted spinach. He realised he was ravenous.

Tristan laughed when Jonah tried to shovel in a ridiculous-sized mouthful. Then the doorbell rang. He looked hopefully at Jonah, who gestured with his hands that his mouth was full and his ribs were sore. He also pulled the most forlorn look he could muster.

"Poor form, mate," Tristan said, putting his fork back on his plate. Jonah grinned at him and prepared his next mouthful.

When Tristan walked to the door and opened it, Jonah couldn't help but lean back to see who it was, despite his body's painful protest. "Mr Jonah Sands?" asked the policeman standing on the doorstep.

"Um, no. I'm Tristan. Jonah's staying with me at the moment. Is there a problem?"

"Ah, right. Sorry. I'm Senior Constable McMillan. The hospital informed me that Mr Sands had been discharged to this address. I just need to speak with him about his involvement in the recent car accident."

"Oh, right. Come on in, officer." Tristan stepped back to let him in. "He's just eating, but he won't mind."

Jonah looked up, fork poised halfway to his mouth.

"Sorry to interrupt, Mr Sands, but I have a few questions for you. Do you mind if I sit down?"

Jonah nodded at the chair beside him and lowered his fork.

"Don't mind me. I'll just keep eating this delicious, hot breakfast while you two talk." Tristan grinned and sat at the table. Jonah shot him a look.

The officer ignored them both. "Now, Mr Sands—"

"Jonah. Please."

The officer nodded. "Okay, Jonah. I'm sure you heard me at the door, but I'm here to talk to you about your recent car accident. I'd like you to tell me whatever you can remember." He pulled out a small notebook, pen at the ready.

Jonah recounted everything as vividly as he could, right up until the moment he lost consciousness. The officer didn't flinch when he described what he'd witnessed between the red-haired woman and the taxi driver.

"Can you remember what you had to eat or drink in the twelve- to twenty-four-hour period prior to the accident?" the officer asked, staring straight at Jonah.

"What I had to eat or drink?" he repeated in confusion. "How is that relevant?"

"Well, Jonah, due to the number, timings, and locations of these sightings, we think they were most likely the result of hallucinations caused by unclean, undercooked, or rotting foods."

Jonah glanced at Tristan, an eyebrow raised in doubt. His mate looked back, then glanced at the police officer before shaking his head and returning to his meal. Jonah recalled as much as he could about his diet during that time, and the policeman dutifully jotted everything down. "Hallucinations. How do a number of people from across the country all share the same hallucination?" Jonah asked, folding his arms. "One that also coincides with so many deaths?"

"Look, we have a number of experts working on these cases, and they claim, with a lot of proof to support their claim, that some types of bacteria or mould can cause mass hallucinations. Now, they and the TGA are trying to find out what food or ingredient is the same across the board and go from there. Most likely, they'll extend a mass recall and get whatever product it is away from consumers."

"And what if they don't find the link?"

The officer stared back at him.

Tristan cleared his throat. "So, how many sightings have there been of her so far across the country?"

The policeman flipped back to an earlier page in his note-book. "The last updated figure was three hundred thirty-four," he answered impassively. Tristan's mouth opened wide in sur-prise, and Jonah whistled. "But between you and me," the of-ficer continued, "that's just here."

"What do you mean?" Jonah leaned forward.

"The sightings are global. All forty-six thousand, seven hundred and thirty-five of them."

Tristan swore under his breath. Jonah was silent, the number bouncing around in his head. "I take it that's not public knowledge yet," he offered.

The policeman shook his head. "The authorities don't want to cause a social panic."

"Why are you telling us, then?" Tristan asked.

The policeman took a deep breath. "Well, your friend here is a first-hand victim of one of these incidents. He is the only individual to have come into direct contact with the red-haired woman and live through it. All the other incidents were fatali-ties and reported by witnesses only."

There was a momentary silence. "What are you saying?" Jonah asked, his head suddenly empty of cohesive thought.

"I'm saying you may just be the luckiest person on the planet right now, because as far as I can tell, you're the only one who's survived the encounter. Whether or not it *is* a hallu-cination or a woman." He looked directly at Jonah, letting the enormity of what he said sink in. "Well, thank you for your time, Jonah. It might pay for you to keep a low profile for a while. I'll see myself out." He stood to make his way toward the door, then turned briefly back toward them. "And please, keep that information between us, yeah?"

Jonah and Tristan nodded in unison, and Senior Constable McMillan left the house. They sat for a few moments, staring at the front door.

Finally, Tristan asked, "Do you think they're right? That it's all just hallucinations?"

Jonah shook his head slowly. "No. I think they're grasping at straws. They have no more idea than we do."

Tristan sighed. "Yeah, that's what I think's going on, too." He got up to clear his plate as Jonah absently finished his meal.

WHILE TRISTAN SEEMED to find it difficult to focus on tidying up, Jonah tried to get comfortable on the couch. He'd decided not to take his pain medication after breakfast, wanting his head to be as clear as possible if he were to have any chance of figuring out what was actually happening in the world. He flicked on the television and switched straight to the sports channel, looking for a distraction.

He really tried to enjoy the basketball game, but then the channel flicked over to a news update. Jonah looked down, thinking perhaps he was sitting on the remote, but it was lay right there the couch beside him. Confused, he reached for it and changed the channel back to the game. After a few seconds, the TV flickered, and the news came back on. "Tristan, stop messing with the bloody TV!" Jonah shouted, repeatedly punching the number on the remote for the sports channel.

Tristan stepped into the lounge room. "What are you yelling about?"

"You're messing with the TV." Jonah waved the remote at his mate.

Tristan shook his head. "Not me, mate. I don't know what you're talking about." The TV switched back over to the news again. Jonah groaned, and Tristan approached the television set. "Maybe there's something wrong with the box. Might just need to be reset or something." He knelt down to investigate.

Jonah was forced to look at the news report in the meantime, so he turned up the volume.

"... what appears to be a mass suicide. Little is known at this stage about..."

"Wait!" Jonah yelped, startling his mate. He tried to peer around Tristan's body to get a glimpse at the TV. Unsure what the fuss was about, Tristan sat beside him on the couch to watch.

"We are coming to you live this morning from Wacol prison to report what can only be described at this stage as a mass suicide. Authorities have yet to release specifics on what happened here, but we can confirm that last night, around midnight, two hundred and seventy inmates died simultaneously. So far, all officials can tell us is that it appears to be a diversification of suicides. Police are frantically trying to contact the families before further details are released. If you have a family member currently an inmate at Wacol prison, please call the hotline on..."

Jonah felt the hairs on the back of his neck stand on end. This had to be connected to the sightings of the red-haired woman.

"How the hell does a group of people simultaneously commit suicide diversely?" Tristan asked. Jonah responded with a slow shake of his head. "We're going to see more of this, aren't we, like with all the sightings of your lady friend?"

"Yeah, I think we will." Jonah sighed. "But I can't see what we can do about it."

At that moment, the computer in the corner flicked on.

"What?" Tristan exclaimed and went to the computer desk. "There's seriously something dodgy with the power in this place." He was about half a meter in front of the computer before he halted and peered down at the screen.

"What?" Jonah asked, struggling to get up from the couch.

"It… I think… it looks like it's doing a Google search."

"The computer? For what?" Jonah asked in astonishment.

Tristan shook his head. "It's a name. I've never seen it before."

Finally on his feet, Jonah went to stand next to his friend, not knowing whether to touch the computer or completely leave it alone. Once the search completed, a link opened all on its own, and a photo popped up.

"Holy shit!" Tristan said.

"You know who that is?"

"Yeah. That's Grommo. We play basketball together." Tristan stared at his teammate on the screen. "I didn't recognise his name, because I've only ever known him as Grommo. Nikolas Grommonosvki, hey? Wouldn't have picked that," he mused. Jonah nudged him to focus. "I don't know why we're staring at a photo of him, though."

The pair studied the screen for a few moments, then Jonah swore under his breath.

"What?" Tristan asked.

"Look at what he's wearing." Jonah poked his finger towards the screen.

"Well, I'll be damned. It's a prison guard uniform. What do you think the chances are of this being a coincidence?"

"Buckley's," Jonah replied and shook his head. "I think maybe you should give your mate Grommo a call and see if he wants to come over for a beer."

Tristan picked up his phone.

CHAPTER SEVEN

AVA DROVE HOME on autopilot. Her exhausted body ached, and she longed for the comfort of her bed. After fumbling with her keys, she walked through the door and into the house, dropping her bag, shoes, and jacket along the way. She shut the curtains to block out the light and set her alarm before collapsing into bed in a blissful sleep

SHE JOLTED AWAKE, sat up, and looked around her room, feeling disorientated.

She had the distinct sensation that something had woken her. Her heart thundered and sweat beaded on her skin. She reached for her phone before remembering she'd turned it off.

Ava pondered her chances of going back to sleep when she heard the noise—a strange whirring sound. She strained to hear, trying to place the cause of that sound, then decided she wouldn't be able to get back to sleep until she'd revealed the source. She rose, pulling her hair back from her face in irritation. Stepping into the hallway, she paused and listened for the sound.

It came again from the front of her house. As she walked down the hall, the sound grew louder. Whatever the cause, it was in the lounge. She mentally pictured the room but couldn't imagine any responsible object.

When she stepped into the lounge, her eyes fell upon a stranger, and she let out a startled scream. She backed up against the doorframe, her hand over her mouth to smother the sound, then blinked in the hopes that she was dreaming. To her dismay, there was still a stranger in her home. In the middle of the room, with her back to Ava, sat a woman.

Ava lowered her hand from her mouth in confusion. Despite her rather loud entry, the woman hadn't budged. The whirring sound came from in front of her, but from where Ava stood, she couldn't get a clear view of the cause. She took a hesitant step closer, her heart pounding in fear's vicelike grip.

The familiarity of the modern room began to change from the bottom up, morphing into walls of dark stone. Ava looked up as the ceiling and floors altered to match, until the room became a cave. Torches now hung on the rough and uneven walls, the firelight bouncing off the stone, causing flickering shadows.

Still, the woman didn't move.

At first, Ava thought she was completely motionless, but the longer she watched, the easier she noticed movement from the woman's hands and foot. The scientist in Ava overrode her fear, and she wondered if this was the same woman Jonah had told them about. She wore a long black dress over ivory skin, and long, gleaming red hair cascaded down her back.

When nothing more happened, Ava approached the woman, circling her in a wide berth until she faced the woman's profile. Finally, she saw what made the whirring noise.

It was a spinning wheel.

Confusion numbed her fear of the woman and heightened her curiosity. It looked like the woman was spinning yarn, but that yarn had a strange luminosity and movement to it, independent of the woman's hands. The spinning stopped, and the sudden silence snapped Ava out of her fascination. She realised at once that the woman now stared at her, and she backed away, berating herself for entering the room instead of calling for help.

Holding Ava's gaze, the woman reverently lowered the thread in her hands before rising. The woman's height surprised Ava, and her vibrant green eyes entrapped her, rendering her powerless and immobilized. She tried to move but found it impossible. The woman approached her, taunting her fear with each slow and purposeful step.

Then the woman halted, tilted her head, and stared into Ava's eyes, giving her the sensation of somehow already having answered a question without knowing what was asked. The intensity of the woman's gaze unnerved her, and her heart pounded harder against her ribcage.

Without warning, the woman reached out and yanked a strand of hair from Ava's head. Ava yelped in pain, shocked to find that no sound actually escaped. Terrified, she watched the woman almost float back to her spinning wheel, sit, then turn back toward her with a knowing smirk before returning her attention to the wheel. Ava looked on, powerless and confused, while the woman attached the strand of hair to the glowing thread.

The woman recommenced her spinning, only this time in reverse.

The muscles of Ava's body suddenly ached, and her skin tingled. As mobility returned to her, she lowered her trembling hands before gasping again in horror. Her skin changed before her eyes.

What the hell is happening? Ava thought as she struggled to hold back the panic spreading through her.

In answer to her unspoken question, the woman nodded past Ava's shoulder and continued to spin. Ava turned to find a gilded mirror now hanging on the wall of the cave around her. What she saw in the mirror made her fear her heart would stop altogether. Her skin was not only changing but aging visibly even as she stared at her reflection. Tears ran down her face, and her hair dulled in colour before turning grey, then white. Heavy, deep-set wrinkles appeared, lining her face and neck. Her hands shrunk and curled in on themselves, and the veins beneath her thinning skin stood out as if she could touch them. Ava tried to scream, but to no avail. Her reflection morphed into something hauntingly inhuman.

The woman laughed—a deep, throaty sound.

Ava continued her silent scream, helpless as her now brittle hair fell out completely. She felt herself growing thinner and thinner, shrinking into her own body until she looked like a skeleton wrapped in skin and could no longer even attempt to scream.

SHE AWOKE WITH a start, heart pounding and tears still wet on her cheeks. Her throat was sore, as though she'd been straining to scream. Ava leaped off the bed and jumped in front of the mirror. She sobbed in both relief and terror when she saw that she looked fine—normal. It had only been a horrible nightmare, yet she felt deep down that it had been more than that. She felt threatened. A nightmare had never left her feeling so deeply shaken.

As she drove to her brother's house, she fought the urge to check her reflection. This was far from her first nightmare, but it was the most vivid and the most terrifying. She debated whether to share the dream with Tristan and Jonah, unsure which reaction would be worse—that they laughed it off or took it seriously.

She walked up to the house and knocked on the front door, trying to make up her mind.

"Well, look who finally decided to show up," Tristan stated with mock surprise when he whipped open the door.

She managed a half smile. "Sorry I'm late. I overslept."

"Are you sure about that?" Tristan asked, stepping back to let her through. "You still look exhausted."

"I'll just have an early night tonight." Ava took off her coat.

"Well, I have just the thing for you. How about a nice big glass of wine?"

"That would be fantastic. Just not *too* big. I still have to drive home later."

"Don't. I think we could all use a drink or two," Tristan said. "You can just crash here."

Ava really didn't have to think about it for very long. She was definitely in no hurry to go home while the nightmare still burned fresh in her mind. Perhaps a couple glasses of wine and a sleepover at her brother's was just what she needed to catch up on some sleep. And some sanity.

"Okay. You have yourself a deal." She followed her brother into the lounge room, where Jonah sat flicking through notes he'd scribbled on paper. "What have you got there?" she asked him. Tristan continued past her towards the kitchen, and Jonah looked up, startled.

"Oh, hey! I didn't hear you come in," he said, shoving the papers into a folder before he cast it aside. His attempt to be covert didn't escape her attention, but she decided to let it slide. "Take a seat." Jonah gently moved over to make room for her, but Ava opted to sit beside the couch in the one-seater.

"How are you feeling?" she asked.

"Not too bad," Jonah said, quickly glancing down at his body and rolling his eyes. "The cast is a pain, and I'm finding the ribs a bit of a struggle. I can't seem to do anything without them screaming at me."

"Well, stop trying to do anything." It was a relief that she could actually still manage a smile, no matter how small it felt.

Jonah gave her a wry smile of his own. "Whatever you say, Doc."

She felt ridiculous when she told them that she'd forgotten to bring a salad, but Tristan assured her it was fine. He'd gone and gotten it anyway. He brought their drinks out from the kitchen, and she was more relieved than she thought she'd be to feel the alcohol take effect on her nerves. Her brother left her and Jonah alone in the lounge while he started up the barbeque outside, and she tried to ignore the unfamiliar sensation in her stomach when Jonah smiled back at her.

AS TRISTAN PLACED his tray of barbequed goods on the table, Ava realised she was ravenous. Now that she thought of it, she couldn't recall the last time she'd eaten something.

"Dig in," Tristan declared.

"So, what did you two hooligans get up to today?" Ava asked them, finally feeling more relaxed.

"Who are you calling a hooligan?" Tristan said. They all laughed.

"I guess it depends on whether you mean 'what did we get up to?' or 'what happened?'" Jonah replied, then swallowed a gulp of beer.

Ava glanced quickly back and forth between them. "Why? What happened?"

Tristan nodded for Jonah to continue. "Well, we've witnessed an interesting chain of events," Jonah stated.

Ava sighed, almost gulping from the glass of wine herself. Just when she'd almost been able to pretend that everything was normal, these two had to bring up something else. "Dare I ask what?" She found herself playing with her food, her appetite suddenly gone.

"Well, we had a visit from the cops, wanting a statement."

Ava listened to them recount the story, trying to process the information. Her anxiety grew with new incredulity at the sheer number of sightings reported.

"Wow. This paints a much bigger picture than we first thought," she stated.

"There's more."

"Of course there is." She sighed. Jonah informed her of the news broadcast and the Google search.

"Grommo's coming over tomorrow for a beer," Jonah finished. "We'll see what he knows about it then."

"But given what's happened so far, there's no way his photo just coincidentally showed up," Tristan said.

"Yeah, I think you're right there," Ava agreed.

"So," Jonah started, meeting her gaze head-on. "Did anything else happen to *you* today?"

It took her a moment to decide it would be better not to tell them about the dream for now. The horror she'd felt was far too raw, and she didn't think she could recount the imagery without breaking down. Instead, she told them about the conversation she'd had with her colleague and the patient of his who'd spoken her name. There was a long silence after she finished, and she fidgeted under the bewildered stares of her brother and his mate.

It was a relief when Tristan broke the silence. "Out of all the weird crap that's been happening, that would have to be the creepiest."

Ava rolled her eyes. "Thanks for that insight. I feel a lot better about it now—"

Before she could say anything else, Jonah came to her brother's defence. "What he means is, this is the first instance that confirms we're being targeted. It's one thing for the computer to perform a random Google search, or for someone to survive an accident. But for a complete stranger to say your name while in a trance? Well, that makes me think there's a lot more going on here than we realise."

Ava took a moment to let the notion sink in.

"So what do we think is going on?" Tristan asked.

"All I can tell you is that I don't buy into the 'hallucination from food' theory," Jonah stated.

"Nah, me neither, mate."

"No," Ava said. "It's plausible, though. Mould and mushrooms can have hallucinogenic properties. Some believe it was a factor in the thousands of so-called witches being burned at the stake."

Tristan's dumbfounded expression amused her. "Where do you come up with this stuff?" he asked.

"I read an actual book from time to time."

Tristan nodded. "Yeah, that's a fair call." Then he shovelled more food into his mouth.

Jonah frowned, staring into his plate. "There's something about this that feels kind of familiar, but I can't place it." He glanced up at Ava, confused.

"How so?" She didn't think any of this could possibly feel familiar.

"I don't know," Jonah said. "Something about this is niggling at me. I just can't work out what. But I do think I know who can help."

"Who?" Tristan and Ava asked in unison.

"Your folks."

"No. No way!" Tristan said. "We are not telling Mum and Dad about this. They'll think I've finally snapped!"

"And what, that all three of us lost it together?" Jonah pointed out.

Tristan ran his hands through his hair and seemed to become as disinterested in his food as the others were.

"Look," Ava said, "we're having dinner there tomorrow night for Jonah's birthday. Maybe we can suss a few things out and see where it takes us."

"Like what?" Jonah asked. Tristan groaned in protest.

Ava chewed her lip. "Well, maybe we could start with the name Caitlyn spoke? Hephalion? We don't have to say how we came across the name, but if it rings any bells with them, it might be worth a try."

Jonah nodded, and his eyes lit up a little. "If we do tell them anything else, I don't think it will come as a massive shock.

I'm sure they've heard the news at least once in the past couple days."

"True," Ava said. "The whole world's been following this weird story." She sat back in her chair and felt a small smile. Her appetite didn't seem so completely lost anymore, especially when talking to her parents made more and more sense.

"Sorry to be a downer, but I'm not convinced," Tristan announced. "I mean, we can't manage to wrap *our* heads around it. How do we explain it to someone else and be taken seriously?"

"Tristan, they're our parents. They aren't going to accuse us of making it up," Ava said.

"Really? Are you sure about that?" Tristan sat back in his chair and folded his arms with exaggerated force. "Because I seem to remember your disbelief when I told you what I went through. Not to mention the fact that I laughed at Jonah when he told *me*. What makes you think Mum and Dad will be any different?" There was silence for a few moments, and Tristan just glared at them over the table.

"Look, mate," Jonah said, "what other choice do we have? Things are escalating, and we still don't know why. All we know is that whatever's going on, it's huge. And for some reason, we seem to be at the centre of it. I think if there's any chance that your parents can shine light on what's happening, we need to tell them."

Tristan leaned back in his chair, finally put his hands behind his head, and let out a long sigh. "Okay, fine. But on one condition. We forget about everything for the rest of the night and just enjoy hanging out."

"Agreed."

MANY DRINKS LATER, Ava staved off Jonah's chivalrous offer to sleep on the couch so she could have the bed in the spare room. As she'd predicted, he overdid it in his zeal to feel better.

Tristan muttered something about getting her a blanket, but Ava shushed them down the hall to sleep. She got herself a doona and spare pillow and set herself up on the couch. She was happy to sleep on it; it was a large, L-shaped couch, as comfortable as any bed.

She tripped trying to get her shoes off and realised that perhaps she'd had a little too much wine. She lay back against the pillow and pulled the doona up under her chin, trying to ignore the fear of a repeat nightmare. The memory of it still lingered, despite the great meal and the wine. Finally, she fell into a blissful, dreamless sleep.

The loud cry of a baby pierced the silence, and Ava sat upright. She fumbled for her mobile on the floor to find it was 3:05 am. She pulled a face; she'd only been asleep for a couple hours.

A baby cried out again. The memories of her nightmare came flooding back. An illogical fear kept her from getting up to investigate the noise herself, and when she thought about calling out to her brother, she felt completely desperate. Tristan would probably have ignored her, anyway.

She took a deep breath and swallowed her fear, then got up. Using her phone as a torch, she fumbled for the switch on the lamp beside the couch and turned it on. Relief swept over her as light radiated across the wall.

Until she turned around.

She found herself standing in the corner of a large hospital nursery. Row upon row of sleeping newborns spread out before her. "Okay, Ava, you must be dreaming again," she told herself. "Just breathe and try to wake up." That barely managed to stop the panic from rising in her chest.

Looking around, she was surprised to find that most of the babies appeared to be sleeping. It was really rather quiet. She didn't know why she'd expected a nursery to be noisy, especially in the middle of the night. Another sharp cry startled her, and she glanced around for the source. She thought it had come from the far end of the room, but it was still enshrouded in darkness, and she couldn't see.

But she could sense movement in the dark, and the fear came flooding back. "It's just a dream, it's just a dream," she chanted, standing still and trying to find what was in the darkness. There was another brief cry, then silence.

Ava turned slowly, searching, and her petrified gaze fell on a baby half hidden in the shadows. She jumped in shock when a pale hand reached out of the darkness, a pointed finger hovering over the infant's head. One luminescent spark shot from the bodiless fingertip into the infant's forehead, the baby cried out, and the hand moved across the baby's face from right to left, like waving in a magic trick. There was silence again, and Ava strained to see what had happened to the baby. She gasped and stepped back against the wall, clamping a hand over her mouth, as the figure to which the hand belonged stepped out of the shadows.

The red-haired woman moved to the next baby in the nursery, repeating the process. Ava tried to shrink back further against the wall, her heart threatening to explode and expose her. The woman appeared oblivious to Ava's presence, but she wasn't going to take any chances, dream or no dream.

Watching the red-haired lady, she swore it was a different woman than the one in her last dream. Yes, it was the same long dress, the same pale skin and long, flaming-red hair. Ava couldn't see her eyes but would have put money on them being the same fierce green. It was the shape of the face that was different. Ava forgot herself in her curiosity and tried to move left to get a better view.

The movement caught the woman's attention, and she looked up. Confusion flitted across the red-haired woman's features, followed by a frown of annoyance. She drew her hand away from the head of the next infant and glided down the aisle, her hair billowing around her by some non-existent wind.

Ava's last dream flashed in her mind, and the thought of another such encounter brought panic with it. She turned and dashed to the glass door, banging against it when it wouldn't open for her. She swore under her breath and turned to see that the woman was now at the end of the aisle. The red-haired lady hadn't looked at anything in particular when she moved, but now she paused, turning her head to lock her gaze on Ava; that gaze was fiercely malicious. A sly smirk spread across the woman's face, and Ava realised she was trapped.

"Focus, Ava. Concentrate. There must be a way out," she chastised herself. "I'm dreaming! I should be able to wake myself." She swallowed hard and tried to focus, despite the woman's impending approach that made her feel like hunted prey. "Wake up, Ava! Wake up!"

Nothing happened. Ava tried pinching herself, but if it was a dream, she could not take herself out of it. "Wakeupwakeupwakeupwakeupwakeup!" she yelled, pounding on the door behind her.

The red-haired woman's laugh rumbled as she took the last step to close the distance between them.

"Hey!"

Ava sat up with a start and fell off the other side of the couch in her desperation to get away from the woman. She landed on her hip and yanked the doona from her face to see her brother standing over her.

"Must have been some dream," he said, reaching out to help her up.

Jonah stood in the doorway, his face riddled with concern. Ava tried to smooth down her hair, groaning inwardly at the thought of how terribly crazy she must look. "I'm okay. Just a bad dream. Too much red wine," she joked.

"Do you want to talk about it?" Tristan asked.

"No, thanks. Maybe in the morning. Well, later in the morning, when the sun's up." She forced a smile.

"Good idea, Sis." Tristan gave her a quick rub on the back. "In that case, I'm going back to bed. Can I get you anything?"

Ava shook her head. "I think I might just sit and watch TV for a bit."

Tristan looked at her for a moment, then gave a tired smile. "I'm just down the hall if you need me, okay?" Then he kissed her on the head and turned toward the hallway. "It's all good, Jonah. She was attacked by the vicious doona, but I was able to stave it off."

Jonah chuckled. "Well, I'm wide awake now. Might watch a bit of tele too, if that's okay with you, Ava?"

"Yeah, whatever." Her back was turned to him as she tried to straighten her makeshift bed.

Tristan disappeared down the hall, and Jonah hobbled over to the couch. The stiffness of deep sleep hadn't quite worn off, it was plain to see, and Ava wondered just how much better he actually felt. He groaned as he lowered himself into the chair.

"Are you okay?" she asked, turning in concern.

Jonah smiled through his grimace. "Yeah, I'm fine. Just stiff and sore. I'll be right once I get settled again."

Ava nodded but didn't believe him. Somehow, she felt he was only out here for her sake. "Look, why don't you go back to bed? You'll be more comfortable," she suggested, even though she wanted him to stay. More than anything, the thought of having another dream about the red-haired woman terrified her. Or were there really more than one red-haired women?

"Nah. To be honest, without the pain medication, I'm not comfortable anywhere. And I'm wide awake. If having the TV on is going to bother you, I can just go do something in another room."

"No, no. That's fine." Ava crawled back under her doona and rearranged the pillows so she could see the television screen.

Jonah turned the television on and flicked through the channels while Ava lay still, feeling her muscles tighten and her insides flutter. Despite the fact that Jonah sat a good meter or so from her, she couldn't help but notice that they were alone together, that her hands were clammy underneath the doona, and she couldn't focus on the TV. She kept wondering whether the tingling at the back of her neck meant she could feel Jonah looking at her, or if she was just imagining that.

Stop being such an idiot, she thought. *It's Jonah, for crying out loud! You've only been friends with the guy for nearly twenty years.* Ava made herself close her eyes and think about something else other than her brother's best friend—or the nightmares. She thought about Caitlyn and the undeniable changes she was undergoing. Then she wondered if she was devoting enough time to her patient or if she'd allowed herself to get side-tracked. When Jonah finally decided on a channel, she was fast asleep within seconds.

CHAPTER
EIGHT

J ONAH RUBBED HIS eyes and yawned. He looked out
the window to watch the first rays of dawn spread across
the horizon. He hadn't intended to stay up; he had just
wanted to make sure Ava was able to fall back to sleep. Needless to say, he should have known better than to turn on the TV.
News updates on the red-haired woman had taken a back seat.
The new headline came from reports of inmates from prisons
all over the world committing suicide en masse. The tips of his
fingers felt icy and numb as fear spread through him—the kind
of fear that came when a person knew they had no control over
what was happening. All he knew was that this news terrified
him and that he wanted answers.

Jonah grabbed the folder he'd tucked under the coffee table
the night before and opened it. He had already begun to write
down the facts, as few and far between as they were. He didn't
know if it would help him work things out, but he always felt
better when he had something tangible to work with. The folder

held his recollection of his encounters with the red-haired woman and the stats he'd obtained from the police officer. He now added the extra prison incidences highlighted on the news. All his instincts told him they were connected. Deciding to investigate a bit further with his laptop, he tried to get up and let out a groan. His bruised ribs punished him for sitting in one position for so long.

Ava stirred a little, then opened her eyes. "Are you okay?" she asked with sleepy concern.

He couldn't help but notice how cute she looked first thing in the morning. "Yeah. It's my own fault. I shouldn't have sat so long in the one spot," he explained, trying to hide the fact that he was actually in a lot of pain.

Ava jumped up and came to his aid. "Here, let me help you up."

Jonah groaned again while she first supported his back in bending forward, then his shoulders in standing from the couch. She looked up at him, and he knew what she was thinking without her even having to open her mouth. "I know, I know. I overdid it," he said.

"I didn't say anything!" Ava looked up at him in wide-eyed offence.

He chuckled, then winced and put a hand to his ribs. "You don't have to." The familiar smile tugging at the side of her mouth was a welcome distraction. He cleared his throat. "I'm going to jump in the shower. Maybe the hot water will help."

Ava nodded and took a step back. "I should go. I need to get to work."

"No worries. See you tonight at your parents." He smiled at her, nodded, then put a hand on the doorframe to steady himself as he hobbled down the hall toward the bathroom.

THE FIRST THING Ava did when she returned home was jump straight into the shower. The hot water calmed her, washing the residual emotions from the nightmare down the drain. Thankfully, she'd also had the foresight to turn the coffee machine on when she got home and was now happy to wrap her hands around a steaming mug.

Ava sat at the table and forced herself to confront the two dreams. The more she thought about it, the more certain she was that there had, in fact, been two different women. But the specifics were already blurring. In a moment of inspiration, she remembered the voice recorder buried away somewhere, and with coffee in hand, she went into the study to rummage through boxes of old Uni stuff. Twenty minutes of dusty searching found what she was looking for, and after testing the buttons, she was surprised to see the batteries still worked.

As she dressed for the day, she spoke into the recorder and detailed both dreams to the best of her ability. She felt it was important to record them in as much detail as possible, should she start to forget. These were no ordinary nightmares.

She uttered the last word when she finished brushing her hair and clicked the stop button on the recorder. Then her mobile sounded from the kitchen. She dashed down the hall and grabbed her mobile from the kitchen table with barely enough time to see the call came from the hospital.

"Hello?"

"Doctor Carter? I'm sorry to bother you at home. There was a memo that we were to notify you about any changes in Caitlyn's behaviour."

Ava rubbed her forehead in frustration and listened to the update. "All right. Thank you. Just continue to monitor her until I get there. I'm on my way."

SHE REACHED WORK in record time, striding quickly through the halls and ignoring greetings in her hurry to get to Caitlyn's room. Mary leaned against the doorframe of the girl's room, her arms folded tightly against her chest as she peered through the small square window. When she caught sight of Ava, she straightened and gave the doctor a grim-faced nod.

"What's going on, Mary?" Ava asked.

The nurse's pale face said more than any words. "This just started," Mary said, stepping back to let Ava toward the door. Her voice was almost a whisper, as if she thought speaking any louder would make things worse.

Ava turned the handle and walked into the room. Caitlyn stood in the far-left corner beside her desk, and the doctor thought she heard the girl talking to herself. She took a step forward, and Caitlyn turned slowly toward her. Ava felt the warmth draining from her face, felt that she must look as pale as Mary, but she could only stare at the girl. The tips of Caitlyn's toes only just scraped the carpet beneath them, dangling as if the girl were held up by some invisible puppet strings. Her head hung low against her chest, obscured by the falling curtain of her hair.

"Caitlyn?" Ava whispered. The girl's head snapped upright, and her hair billowed outward, moved again by an unfelt wind. There was no colour in the eyes staring out at Ava, only cloudy white orbs. Ava swallowed, her mouth gone dry, and had absolutely no idea what to do next.

Then the invisible strings holding Caitlyn in mid-air moved her forward, and she floated across the ground like a wraith. The girl's mouth moved again before Ava heard the whispers. She took a step back, and the chanting Caitlyn only glided toward her still. The doctor found herself walking backwards out into the hall, searching the girl's face for any hint of awareness. Mary had pressed herself against the opposite wall, her hands braced against her eyes.

Then Ava found her wits, annoyed by how much the whole thing had caught her so off guard. She stopped her retreat, straining to decipher Caitlyn's whispers, but the words were inaudible. The girl didn't stop when she reached the hallway, and Ava realised she had to do something. She grabbed the girl by the arms, gave her a firm shake, and yelled, "Caitlyn! Snap out of it, right now!"

At once, the white fog cleared from the girl's eyes, and it took a moment for her to focus on Ava. "Help me," she pleaded, then whatever had held her mere inches off the ground let her go, and Caitlyn collapsed on the floor in hysterical sobs.

Ava knelt beside her, pulled the girl into her arms, and let her cry. From the corner of her eye, she saw Mary turn and head off towards the staff lounge. The nurse hadn't said a word through the episode, but judging from her reaction last time, Ava knew the woman would need someone to talk to again. She would have to follow up with Mary later.

It took a few minutes for Caitlyn to stop crying, then Ava helped her back into the room, where she sat Caitlyn on the bed with her back against the wall. The girl pulled her knees up to her chest and tucked a blanket up under her chin. In that moment, Ava remembered how young Caitlyn really was and that she was just as confused and scared as Ava felt herself. Probably even more so.

Ava pulled the desk chair beside the bed and sat down. "Do you want to talk about it?" Caitlyn turned her gaze from the wall towards her doctor. She took a deep, shaky breath as the tears welled up again. "It's okay," Ava said and tried to give a reassuring smile. "We can talk about it later. You can just rest for now, if you like."

Caitlyn shook her head. "No, it's okay. I need to talk about it. I need you to help me make it stop." Her wide eyes begged the doctor for any possible help she could offer.

Ava nodded. "Okay, then. So let's start at the beginning." When Caitlyn looked back at the wall for a moment, Ava worried she had lost her again.

"It started about a week ago. I had a vivid dream." The girl paused, fidgeting with her fingernails.

"Go on," Ava prodded.

Caitlyn finally met her gaze again. "I don't want you to think I'm... well, you know."

"I promise I won't, Caitlyn. You have nothing to worry about. Please tell me about the dream you had."

Caitlyn exhaled a deep breath before continuing. "I was standing in the centre of an old stone building on a hill. Fog was swirling around my ankles. It was really eerie. Then I heard a man's voice talking to me, but I couldn't hear him clearly at first. Then the fog swirled faster and moved up. I could see it moving around a human shape... like he was invisible or something. I walked toward him, but not too close. Just close enough so I could hear what he was saying. He told me I was special and not to be afraid. He knew what had happened to me, and he said everything would be okay. It was all part of the plan. He explained that I had to be prepared to stand at the edge of the crevice, so my mind would be pure for the task at hand. I asked him what he meant. He turned and moved aside a little, then I saw the mouth of a cave behind him. 'You don't expect me to go in there, do you?' I asked him. He told me the choice was mine. He would not try to 'sway' me, as he put it. He said again that I was special and that he knew I'd always thought I wasn't as good as other people. He said I was wrong. That this was my chance to prove it.

"So I asked him what I had to do in the cave. He said I had to release myself to the greater good and just breathe. It didn't sound too hard, so I walked past him. The fog collapsed, like he vanished or something. I walked into the darkness of the cave but stayed by the edge, in case I wanted to get out. I stood there, closed my eyes, and took a deep breath. There was a strange smell. I don't know what it was. And I started to feel faint. I opened my eyes, but the darkness made me dizzy, and I fell. I hit my head on something, and I swear I heard women laughing. Then I woke up, here in my bed, and my head was pounding like I'd hit it on something for real. And I still... I still smelled whatever was in the cave from my dream." The girl's nose wrinkled in distaste.

"Can you describe it?" Ava asked.

Caitlyn grimaced. "Like when someone leaves the gas on."

"Do you remember anything else?"

Caitlyn pulled the doona farther under her chin, as if it made her feel safer. "Well, I didn't think anything of it at first. I just put it down to a weird dream. But then...things started happening that I couldn't explain. I thought I was losing my mind. At least I'm in the right place if that happens, hey, Doctor?" she said with a sad smile.

Ava leaned forward and gave the girl's hand a squeeze. "We can continue this later, if you prefer," she suggested, not wanting to wear the poor girl out any further. She was proud of her for getting this far into the story already.

Caitlyn stared at Ava's pants and swallowed. "No. I think I want to tell you about it now, while I feel... like myself."

Ava nodded and leaned back in her chair again, glad to give the girl whatever time she needed to continue.

"In the very beginning, I was just seeing things. Little glimpses. I'd be doing something, or looking at something, then all of a sudden, I'd see something else that wasn't there. Just for a few seconds."

Ava tilted her head, wondering if the girl was referring to her own hallucinations. She'd never mentioned anything like this before.

"I don't know how to explain it," the girl continued. "It's like, for a brief moment, even while I'm still standing in the same spot, I'm looking through someone else's eyes. It's like... seeing into a different time and place."

The doctor took a moment to formulate her next question. "How do you feel when you experience these glimpses? Do you recognise anything?"

"No. Half the time, I can't even make sense of them. I just feel that it's someone else, in a different place, even in a different time, maybe? Then the headaches started. Pounding headaches, and I couldn't even think straight." Caitlyn put a hand to her head, frowning, and blinked rapidly with the memory.

Ava turned and looked out the window as she thought about the best way to proceed. She'd known about Caitlyn's frequent headaches and had attributed them to more medical causes. It was best not to rule anything out, though, and the girl's story seemed to have vague answers for some aspects of her condition.

"Tell me about the whispering," she suggested.

"Whispering?" Caitlyn glanced up at her with wide eyes and shook her head. Here, they were equally confused.

"Caitlyn, how much do you remember about the past few days?"

"Not a whole lot, to be honest. Ever since that dream, things have been kind of hazy."

"Describe what you mean by 'hazy'," Ava prodded. She took note of how much the girl seemed to calm down the more she voiced her experiences, even though the whispering appeared to be an altogether new concept for her. She wondered just how much of these episodes the girl remembered and what portion of Caitlyn's memories actually made up these strange occurrences.

"Well, I couldn't tell you what I did most of yesterday, for example. When I'm awake, I actually feel like I'm sleepwalking. Like I'm here…but not here. I don't feel like myself anymore, just… disconnected and powerless. Like I'm a puppet and someone else is controlling me or something. Does that make sense?"

Ava nodded, trying to encourage Caitlyn to continue.

"This is the most awake and in control I've felt since that dream. I have no idea how I got out in the corridor." Caitlyn paused with a frown. "So I've said that, and now I realised I wasn't even surprised to wake up there."

"So why do you think you feel more alert now?" Ava asked, interested to know if Caitlyn had any of her own theories.

The girl thought about it for a few moments longer. "I don't know. For the past few days, I felt like someone, or something, has been controlling me. When I manage to regain some kind of control, I feel so drained that all I want to do is sleep." Then she let out an enormous yawn, as if to punctuate her point.

Ava nodded, hoping that perhaps a few seconds more of silence would encourage Caitlyn to share something else. Sometimes, all a patient needed was an open ear, just someone to listen without comment or judgement. If the girl could share more with her, maybe Ava wouldn't have to make the diagnosis that kept creeping back into her mind. Maybe there was more they could do for her.

The girl opened her mouth as if to say something, then shook her head and sighed.

"What is it?" Ava asked. Caitlyn glanced very quickly at her Doctor, then returned to staring holes into the blanket covering her lap. "It's okay," Ava added. "You can tell me."

Caitlyn took a deep breath and closed her eyes. "I know I'm not the only one," she whispered.

Ava had to blink back her momentary surprise. She really didn't want to say the wrong thing here. "How so, Caitlyn?"

"He told me. The man in my dream. He said there were many of us, that we're special, and that's why I shouldn't be afraid. But I am." She very slowly repositioned herself to lay on her side, never having let the blanket fall below her chin. "Now, you can fill in the blanks for me," she stated, her wide, trusting eyes leaving no room for error on Ava's part.

Ava glanced out the window and watched the magpies flying just a few feet from the glass. The sun was bright, casting light on a very dark situation. She had to form her words carefully, had to give Caitlin the correct information without terrifying the poor girl even further. She took a deep breath and opened her mouth, but when she glanced down at her patient, the girl had already fallen asleep.

CHAPTER NINE

JONAH SAT AT the dining table, trying to ignore his discomfort. He was adamant about staying away from the painkillers. He wanted to keep his mind sharp and focused with everything going on. Intrigued to hear what Grommo would have to say, he hoped their friend could shine some light on what had happened in the prison. He spread out his ever-growing collection of notes, but try as he might, he couldn't see any connection or link.

"What's that you're working on?" Tristan asked as he walked into the room, fresh from the shower.

"Not much, mate. Just going over all this stuff we've collected, hoping to make sense of it."

"Let me guess. Makes no sense at all?" Tristan asked as he sat down.

"If it does, I can't see it," Jonah replied, rubbing the bridge of his nose.

Before Tristan could say anything, there was a knock at the door. He looked at Jonah and let out a deep breath as he got up to let Grommo inside. Jonah gathered all his notes back into his folder and put it in his lap. On the table, he had a blank notepad and pen ready in the hopes that Grommo would give him something worth writing down.

Tristan opened the door and greeted his mate with a basketball-bonding, three-part handshake before walking him into the dining room. He introduced him to Jonah, who felt his standard-non-athletic-marginally-masculine handshake was inadequate by comparison.

"Beer?" Tristan suggested as Grommo sat at the table. Both Grommo and Jonah nodded. Tristan went off to gather the beverages, and Jonah felt he needed to dispel the silence with small talk.

"So, you work at the prison?" he asked, not knowing what else to say.

Grommo nodded before letting out a deep sigh. "I don't know for how much longer." He stared down at the table.

"Because of what happened?"

"Well, that would be the main reason. But I can't see them needing a full staff in a prison that has no prisoners left." It was a logical response.

"True," Jonah said. He couldn't believe he hadn't considered that reason as well. Grommo seemed still shaken up by his experience, which only compelled Jonah further to find out all he could.

"Here we are, boys," Tristan said, passing around the beers. All three took long, silent sips. "So…" Tristan glanced back and forth from Jonah to Grommo.

"Look, I know why you asked me over, but you guys are going to think I've lost the plot," he said, shaking his head.

"Trust me, that's the last thing we'll think. We've seen some surreal things ourselves recently," Jonah replied.

"So little has been released in the media," Tristan added. "We just thought you might be able to shine some light on it for us."

Grommo absently picked at the label on his beer. "In all honesty, I've been trying not to think about it. It still freaks me out. But at the same time too, for my own sanity, I need to tell someone else—even though we've been told to keep silent." He paused, reached into his satchel, and pulled out a DVD. He turned it over and over in his hands. "I do have one thing on my side. Proof."

"Of what?" Jonah asked.

"Surveillance footage. From the internal prison cameras."

"How did you manage to score that, mate?" Tristan's eyes had grown wide with excitement.

"Maybe I should start at the beginning." Grommo took a swig of beer in preparation. Jonah and Tristan followed suit. "I work security at the prison, right? I was on the night shift, rostered in the monitor room, observing the screens." He looked up, and Jonah and Tristan nodded in unison, urging him to continue. "It was late, and most of the inmates were asleep. So I almost fell off my chair when I saw a woman on one of the screens. At first, she was just standing there at the entrance to the cell block. I called down to the guard for that section and told him to get her the hell out of there. Only when he buzzed back through, he said he couldn't see anyone. I figured he must have been too lazy to get up and have a look, since I couldn't see him in the frame. So I asked him to step into the cell block. On my screen, I saw him. He was so close to the woman, he could have touched her. Instead, he just looked around, shaking his head. He told me he thought I should take a break from the monitors and go stretch my legs or something. I didn't even reply, I was too confused. I just watched the screen and thought I was losing my mind."

Tristan opened his mouth, about to roll out a smart quip, but Jonah silenced him with a look. Tristan rolled his eyes and took a swig of beer instead.

"I freaked out when she started moving. She walked down the corridor, and it looked like she was talking to the inmates. But she never looked at them. She just stared straight ahead and walked right past. I worked out she was taking about five to six seconds to pass each cell, so she wasn't walking fast by any means. I had to go down and investigate myself. But when I got to the wing, the corridor was empty. No sign of her. Gate was still locked. I went to the guard's station and told the guy to be alert. I think he thought I'd completely lost the plot, but he didn't say anything. I never saw her again when I got back to the monitor room, and that was fine with me. I didn't care if I was losing my mind. I was just relieved that I couldn't see her anymore." He paused to take a long pull on his beer.

"And then there she was again on a different screen. In a different wing. I felt like I was going to vomit, I was so freaked out. She walked toward the camera this time, same kinda slow and talking to herself." He took a deep breath, and Jonah noticed the man's hands were shaking. "I waited for her to walk right out of the camera frame, but then she just stopped. Looked up at the camera and straight… into me. I don't know how else to say it. I actually heard it when she laughed. The monitors don't even have sound, but I heard it, like she was in the room with me. I'm not kidding you, it made me want to crawl under that bloody desk and hide. Then all the screens went dead. Just like that. The lights flickered, so I called through to other guards to alert them of a possible intruder. I didn't tell them they wouldn't be able to see her. Then I called the warden at home. It took me about twenty minutes to get the cameras back up and running, but by that time…"

Grommo's eyes were alarmingly glazed over by the memory. "Well, by that time, all the inmates were dead. I found the footage of the woman on the automatic backups. Just the first camera, not the second closer one. I told the warden what I had, but he wasn't interested in taking a look. I guess he had a far bigger mess on his hands. He told me, if anyone asked, to just say the backup was wiped when the system crashed. And you guys know the *official* story is that all deaths were either natural or suicides." The man's last sentence burst out of him, as if he were relieved to have it out.

"What do you think happened?" Jonah asked.

"I think the warden was half right. I mean, all the inmates did actually show signs of either self-harm or a natural death. But I don't think that's the whole truth. I think she made it happen. I think whatever she said to those men down there either killed them or drove them to kill themselves. How or why, I have no idea. In all honesty, I just don't want to think about it."

"Were any of the guards or other members of staff harmed? Or was it only the prisoners?" Tristan asked.

"Only the prisoners."

"And you were the only one who saw her?" Jonah asked. Grommo nodded, and Jonah leaned back in his chair to let it all sink in. "I think it's time to have a look at that footage."

"Sweet. Let's roll," Tristan agreed, grabbing the disk off his mate as he walked into the lounge room.

AS THE FOOTAGE came to an end, the house was hauntingly quiet. Tristan had his eyebrows raised. Jonah rubbed his stubbly chin and stared at the screen, while Grommo sat with his head in his hands, staring at the carpet.

Finally, Jonah leaned forward and grabbed the remote from the coffee table. He skipped the footage back to where the woman walked along the first few cells of the corridor. He paused it, then stood and approached the TV to have a closer look. He gingerly stooped over, peering at the scene.

"What is it?" Tristan asked.

Jonah shook his head as he half turned to his mate. "This isn't the same woman I saw." He turned back to the screen.

The angle of the camera viewed the woman in an almost perfect profile. Despite her features, the most obvious difference between her and the woman he'd seen was the colour of her hair. This woman's hair was raven-black, but had the same billowy, wind-blown effect to it as that of the red-haired woman. In the paused frame, she appeared to be looking straight down the corridor. She wasn't looking into the cells, yet Jonah noted her left hand trailed along the bars as she walked.

When watching the footage straight through, they had in fact seen her talking, as Grommo had claimed. But none of them had the lip-reading skills to decipher what she said, and the majority of the footage only captured her profile. Her expression and body language gave the impression of enjoyment; it looked like she was taunting them—teasing like a playground bully. The woman took her time, too. She strolled down one side of the corridor before turning and strolling back down the other side, leaving no cell untouched. Jonah leaned closer toward the television, staring at the paused image of her.

"Who are you?" Jonah pondered, and leaned down even closer, bracing himself against the television. Then, as he stared at the paused frame, the woman turned and looked right at him, with an eyebrow raised and a smirk on her face.

"Holy shit!" Jonah yelped, and launched himself away from the TV. In his panic to get away from her, he tripped and fell backwards over the coffee table, landing half on the couch and half on the floor. He swore and groaned as he grabbed his screaming ribs.

Tristan and Grommo, who had jumped off the couch to get out of his way, now stood looking down at him in utter bewilderment.

"What the hell happened?" Tristan asked, glancing back and forth from the still paused TV to his mate.

"The woman... she turned and looked straight at me," Jonah huffed out. He held his ribs and willed the pain to subside.

Tristan looked back towards the TV, where it was still paused on the exact same frame. The woman faced the corridor, away from them. "Are you sure that's what you saw? It looks the same to me as when you paused it." He helped Jonah up.

Jonah turned to see for himself, then frowned at his friend. "I know what I saw."

Tristan stared back at him for a moment before nodding. "Okay, then." He grabbed the remote and turned off the TV.

"Has anyone else seen this tape?" Jonah asked Grommo.

The man nodded. "My boss. Once he realised what had happened, the first thing he did was to check what the surveillance cameras caught. When he saw it for himself, though, he told me to hide it. He said if anyone asked, I was to say that there was no footage, that the cameras had failed when the system went down. But I'm glad he gave it to me. This is the one thing keeping me from checking myself in to the nearest psychiatric ward. In saying that though, I think you guys might want to hold onto it for me."

"Why do you say that?" Jonah asked.

"Well, the first time you see the footage, your attention is on the woman. You need to watch it again. Even though the lighting is bad, you can still see most of it." Grommo sighed.

"Most of what?" Tristan asked, frowning.

Grommo looked at them in surprise. "The prisoners. You can see them dying." He grabbed his satchel and with a nod headed for the front door.

Tristan and Jonah stared after him long after he left the house.

"KNOCK, *KNOCK*," AVA called out, and let herself into Tristan's house.

"In here," Jonah said from the lounge room. He sat at the table again, studying the papers he had spread out in front of him. He looked up with a smile as she walked into the room. "So, your brother is running late, just for something different," he said wryly.

Ava rolled her eyes. "Of course he is." Her brother's bizarre t-shirt ritual had kept them waiting on more than one occasion. She was glad to see Jonah didn't scramble to hide his papers as she approached. "So, what's that you've been working on?" she asked, attempting a blasé approach. That was more difficult than she'd expected.

"I've been trying to apply some kind of order to the chaos. I was hoping that by compiling lists of all the facts we currently have, I'd be able to see some kind of pattern."

"Have you?" Ava asked, sitting down beside him at the table.

Jonah looked down at his papers for a moment. "No, I don't think so. It just looks random, but my gut says it's exactly the opposite." He sighed.

"Well, go with your gut," Ava said. Jonah looked up at her and smiled, and Ava felt her heart skip a beat, suddenly all too aware of their close proximity.

The moment halted as Tristan barrelled into the room. "Oh, hey, Sis! Sorry, running late as usual."

Jonah and Ava both checked to see what shirt he had finally chosen. "Really? You took that long to come up with that band?" Ava scoffed.

Tristan grinned, oblivious to his sister's disdain. "Yeah, one of their songs reminds me of the woman we saw in the footage."

"Hold up, what woman? What footage?"

"You would not believe what Grommo showed us," Tristan answered, shaking his head.

Ava turned to Jonah for clarification.

"Well, he described a woman he saw at the prison. She seems somehow responsible for the deaths of the prisoners."

"Hang on," Ava interrupted. "I thought they all died of either natural causes or suicide."

Jonah nodded. "Exactly. Even better, he brought us surveillance footage."

Ava flashed them both wide eyes. "Seriously? Do you still have it? Is it the same woman you've seen, Jonah?"

"He left the footage with us, at least for the moment. His bosses are pretending it doesn't exist, so I guess it's ours until that changes. I can say, though, with one-hundred-percent certainty, that it isn't the same woman I saw. I think we should wait to show it to you until after dinner. We're supposed to be putting our game faces on, remember?" Jonah smiled.

Ava nodded. She was happy to delay viewing anything else that would keep her up at night.

"How did it go today with your patient?" Jonah asked. "Is there anything we need an update on?"

Ava gave them the shortened version of her day with Caitlyn. She wasn't up to answering their questions and deflected them by declaring they were going to be late if they didn't get a move on.

"You're such a stickler for punctuality," Tristan teased.

"Well one of us needs to be." She turned to Jonah. "Are you sure you're up to going out? You don't want to overdo it."

Jonah patted her on the shoulder. "I'm fine, really. Don't worry about me. All I have to do is get in and out of the car. No drama. And I need to get out of the house. I'm starting to get a little cabin fever."

Ava looked him up and down for a few seconds, then smiled and gathered her bag to head out the door. "Come on," she shouted one last time.

Jonah and Tristan looked at each other over the table and laughed.

CHAPTER TEN

AS THEY DROVE, Jonah had to tune out Tristan and Ava's sibling banter spilling over from the front seats. Instead, he gazed out the window and smiled at the thought of seeing his friends' parents, Alex and Mallory Carter.

JONAH WAS THIRTEEN when he moved in with his aunt after his parents died in a car accident. While she was nice to him, Jonah never felt at home with her. She was a busy, career-driven woman who travelled all over the world for the better part of the year. While he was left to his own devices most of the time, he actually preferred it and took great solace in grieving for his parents.

One Saturday afternoon, about a week after his arrival, there was a knock on the door. Jonah answered it to find a dishevelled-looking boy with a football tucked under his arm.

"Hey! I'm Tristan. I live a couple houses down. I saw you when you got here, but Mum said I had to let you get settled before I harassed you. But it's been a whole week, so I think that's okay. Just wanted to see if you want to come outside and kick the footy with me?" He flashed Jonah a toothy grin. The boy then flipped his head to the side, attempting to toss the hair from his eyes, and in doing so dropped the ball. When he bent down to pick it up, he hit his head on the corner of the entryway's brick wall.

"Ouch!" he cried and stood, sans ball, grasping his forehead with both hands.

It surprised Jonah that he wanted to laugh, and with a smile, he nodded. "Awesome. You can pick the ball up, though," Tristan stated, then ran to the top of the cul-de-sac.

Jonah found it therapeutic just to kick the ball back and forth. Though he didn't feel like talking, Tristan seemed happy to do enough of it for the two of them. Once the day cooled off and the sun dimmed, Tristan finally asked him a direct question.

"So, my Mum said you can have dinner at our place tonight. Do you want to? She's making roast chicken. It's awesome."

Jonah glanced back at his aunt's dark, empty house. He knew the takeaway leftovers in the fridge couldn't compare to a home-cooked roast chicken. He hadn't had a homecooked meal since his parent's death. So he nodded and said he would go leave a note for his aunt first, should she come home and notice his absence.

"I'll come with you. I always wanted to see inside that house. It looks pretty big. Mum will be glad you're coming to dinner, 'cause she likes feeding people. I'll even let you have one of the chicken legs if you want. No one else in my family likes them, so I usually get both, but we can share." Tristan rambled some more as they walked into Jonah's house. Jonah smiled, then wrote his aunt the note and headed back up the street.

As they approached Tristan's front door, anxious butterflies of being a guest in a stranger's house fluttered in Jonah's stomach. Tristan walked inside, dropping the football as he called out to his mum. Jonah hovered at the threshold, unsure of whether he should enter.

"Hey, Mum! We're home. Jonah's going to stay for dinner. How awesome is that!" Jonah listened to his new friend's voice drift away to his right.

"That's great, sweetheart. Go wash up before dinner." Jonah considered turning around and heading home until Mallory Carter stepped into the hall. "Oh, goodness! Has that boy of mine just left you standing there?" she exclaimed, shaking her head. "Please come in, Jonah, and make yourself at home. I'm Mallory Carter, Tristan's mum," she said.

Jonah held out his hand for her to shake. "Nice to meet you, Mrs. Carter."

"Hey, Mum, are you making your special gravy too?" Tristan asked as he came down the hall behind her.

"Yes, I am. Now what's this? You leaving your guest standing in the doorway?" she teased.

Tristan shrugged. "I just figured he was following me," he replied with a grin.

Mrs. Carter rolled her eyes. "Go show Jonah the bathroom please, so he can wash up too. Then you can set the table." She smiled at Jonah again before heading off in yet another direction.

"It's this way," Tristan announced and headed back the way he'd come.

Jonah followed, and he couldn't help but marvel at all the pictures on the walls. He recognized some of them as shots of Ancient Egypt, Greece, and Rome from his lessons at school. Ancient history was shaping up to be his favourite subject.

They washed their hands, and Jonah helped his new friend set the table, listening to Tristan talk. He jumped when a girl came hurtling into the room.

"Mum! Mum! You'll never guess what happened," she squealed in excitement.

"What's that, Ava?" Mrs. Carter stepped around the bench to meet the girl, wiping her hands on her apron.

"I was picked to perform a ballet solo at the end-of-year concert. I'm the only one from my class!" she screeched, jumping up and down and clapping her hands together.

"Oh, sweetheart, that's fantastic. Congratulations." Mrs Carter bent down to give her daughter a hug.

"Yeah, I thought there'd been a murder with all the high-pitched screaming in the studio." Mr. Carter chuckled as he followed his daughter into the room.

"You're so silly, Dad." Ava rolled her eyes at him.

"Yes, I am. Now go have a quick shower before dinner," he replied, then leaned over his daughter to give his wife a kiss.

"Who's that?" Ava asked, finally noticing the extra person in the room.

"Don't be rude, Ava. This is Jonah. He's the boy I was telling you about who moved into the court," Mrs. Carter said.

"Oh. Hi." Ava stared at him with a little scowl.

"Hi," Jonah replied, noticing how fierce her eyes were.

"Don't tell me you have an actual friend now, Tristan." She turned to her brother.

Before he had a chance to retort, Mr. Carter gave her a mock smack on the backside. "Shower. Now."

Ava pulled a face at Tristan before she left the room with graceful skips. Jonah couldn't help but stare after her.

Mr. Carter held a hand out in greeting. "Nice to meet you, Jonah. Tristan has been itching to visit you since you moved in. Needless to say, I'm not always here when my son wants to kick the football around."

Jonah gave a slow smile as he shook the man's hand.

Sitting at their kitchen table brought a pang of loss to Jonah's heart as he listened to the family banter and thought about how much he missed his own parents. His eyes stung, and he fought back the tears by concentrating fiercely on his food. He felt eyes on him and looked up to see Mrs. Carter, her face filled with concern. She gave him a small smile and a nod.

Jonah took a deep breath and smiled back. "So, Mrs. Carter, Tristan was right. This is the best roast chicken I've ever tasted," he stated.

"Why, thank you, Jonah," she said kindly.

"See, I told you. Especially with the gravy, hey? See, I knew we would end up being best mates." Tristan took another huge mouthful. He grinned, gravy smeared around his mouth, and patted Jonah on the back with his spare hand. Jonah laughed at his first ever best friend.

"WHAT ARE YOU looking all goofy about?" Tristan asked as he glanced at Jonah through the rear-view mirror.

Jonah smiled. "I was just thinking about the first time I ever had dinner at your place."

Ava and Tristan both laughed. "You were so shy and quiet," Ava stated.

"And *you* were such a brat," Tristan added.

"I was not!"

"Jonah? Back me up here," Tristan said.

"Sorry, Ava. You were a bit of a brat."

"Whatever." Ava crossed her arms and glanced at her brother from the corner of her eye before they all burst into laughter.

Jonah smiled when they pulled into the driveway. He had such fond memories of the Carter house, which had pretty much been his home and the Carters his surrogate family. He glanced at the house where his aunt used to live, though she'd been living in London for many years now.

Tristan came around to the back to help his mate out of the car.

"I think I've got it," Jonah said, manoeuvring himself with care. Using the arm of the door, he pulled himself up as Tristan stood back and waited should his mate need a hand.

"Nice work, mate. I reckon you've been faking these injuries, if those smooth moves are anything to go by."

Jonah chuckled.

"Do you two always have to be so slow?" Ava asked and gave an impatient sigh. She walked backwards toward the front door and motioned for them to hurry it up.

"Um, bruised and battered body, here?" Jonah replied.

"Yeah, and I'm his nurse," Tristan added.

"And I must say, you make an excellent nurse," Jonah complimented in a mock-posh voice.

"Why, thank you." Tristan gave a low bow. Ava groaned and rolled her eyes as she turned and proceeded without them. "You know what, mate, I reckon I scored all the humour genes." Tristan matched the pace of his hobbling charge.

"She has a sense of humour. It's just buried most of the time," Jonah replied.

"Buried is a bloody understatement," Tristan huffed, and they stepped up to the door.

"Jonah! Happy Birthday!" Mallory Carter exclaimed, beaming in excitement as she waited for them at the front door. She approached him and gave him a gentle hug and a kiss on the cheek.

"Here's the birthday boy," boomed Alex Carter. He reached forward to shake Jonah's good hand with both of his.

"Thanks, guys," Jonah said, feeling his face flush. He had never felt comfortable with a lot of attention, even from people he considered family.

"Yeah, hello? Your actual son, here?" Tristan joked from behind.

"Son? What son?" Alex said.

"Did we have a son?" Mallory added.

"Oh, right. There's the famous Carter wit again." Tristan's parents laughed and greeted him.

Jonah noticed Alex's curious frown when the man's gaze went to his son's hair. He looked like he wanted to ask about it, but his wife's hand on his arm prevented him. Jonah watched their silent exchange. He'd always found their ability to communicate without words fascinating.

"Let's go sit at the table," Mallory suggested. "Dinner isn't ready yet, but I figured Jonah would find it easier not to have to move from the lounge room to the dining room."

"Let's make it all about Jonah, shall we?" Tristan joked.

"Yeah, it's not like it's his birthday or anything." Ava appeared in the doorway to the dining room, glass of wine in hand.

"Jeeze, you don't waste any time, sis." Tristan laughed.

Ava gave a nonchalant shrug and turned back into the room.

"Now, sit down wherever you like—except for Jonah," Alex said, pulling the chair out for him. Birthdays were a big deal in the Carter household, and one tradition held that whoever had the birthday got to sit at the head of the table.

"That roast chicken smells amazing." Jonah tried to make himself comfortable.

"So, how are you feeling?" Alex asked. He took the seat to Jonah's right.

"Yeah, I'm getting there. Pretty much the only thing that still hurts are my ribs. This cast on my arm, though, doesn't make it any easier." Jonah waved his arm in the air.

"Nothing worse than doing your ribs," Alex said. "I don't understand how you're even walking around, to be honest. You should be resting up."

"Good luck with that," Ava muttered. She sipped her wine with a tiny smile, quickly looking away when Jonah met her gaze.

"Pipe down, Nurse Crankypants," Tristan said.

Mallory ignored her children. "Jonah, have you been resting like the Doctor said?"

"Well, sort of," he replied and looked down at his hands.

"What exactly is 'sort of'?"

"I've been resting to the point of boredom, except for a little tumble I took. Other than that, I'm behaving…"

"A tumble?" Mallory prodded. Her smile didn't quite hide her alarm.

"Yeah, what tumble?" Ava echoed.

"Ladies, Jonah is all grown up, now. He's capable of looking after himself," Alex jumped in, raising his hands at their protests.

Jonah looked up to see Tristan shaking his head. "What?" he asked.

"Dude, after all our years of friendship, have you learned nothing from me? You still insist on volunteering information that only gets you in trouble." Tristan's comment elicited laughter and head-shaking all round.

"So, what's news in the lives of the three stooges?" Alex asked with a smile. Mr. and Mrs. Carter had referred to them by the affectionate nickname ever since Jonah had met the family, though the dynamics of their friendship had changed somewhat. When they were in school, it was always 'Tristan and Jonah', Ava tagging along. Now, if anyone took the lead, it seemed to be Ava. For the most part, though, they were on equal footing with one another.

Tristan cleared his throat and made a face. "Well, I've been working from home so I can look after *this* bum—"

"You can imagine just how much work has been getting done," Ava interrupted.

Tristan turned to his sister beside him and gave her a pointed look. "But other than that, it's been a normal week."

"And I've just been resting. Nothing to see here, people," Jonah added.

"All I seem to do is work and check in on these two to make sure they keep their beer-soaked stomachs lined," Ava said.

"Jonah, you're not drinking on the painkillers…" Mallory started with concern.

"Mallory…" Alex warned.

"It's okay. I haven't been taking the pain meds," Jonah replied.

"Why ever not?" Mallory asked.

Alex groaned as he leaned back into his chair and took a swig of beer. Jonah saw both Tristan and Ava's alarmed expressions, warning him not to give too much away. Not yet. Unfortunately, Mallory had also caught their shared glances.

"Uh… I just didn't want to take them anymore. I don't like feeling dopey all the time," he explained. Tristan opened his mouth with a smart retort, but Ava jabbed him in the ribs.

"Hmm… Well, it's your body," Mallory said. "I just don't want you to be in any unnecessary pain."

"That's what beer is for, Mum," Tristan declared before ducking a swipe from his sister.

"You *are* aware of the irony in that, aren't you?" Mallory asked with a smirk.

Tristan nodded. "He's aware. It's the lesser of two evils, Mum."

Mallory shook her head at her son's excuses and Jonah grinned.

He looked around the table at his surrogate family as they continued their banter, and he still felt the familiar grief of wishing his own parents were there to celebrate with him, too. He tried to imagine what they would look like today but couldn't, and the realisation saddened him. But he didn't want to be morbid during his birthday dinner and ruin the Carter-family fun. He focused instead on how lucky he felt that they had welcomed him into their family all those years ago. Jonah was certain his parents would have gotten along like a house on fire with the Carters, and this comforted him. He watched them; Alex laughed, and Mallory rolled her eyes at something Tristan had said.

Mallory was an anthropologist and Alex was an archaeologist. As a boy, Jonah had envisioned the pair of them living an exciting existence—like a real-life Mr. and Mrs. Indiana Jones. Needless to say, that wasn't the case, but they still fuelled his fascination for the subjects.   Jonah had no idea why he'd always felt drawn to ancient civilisations. He and Ava had bonded over those shared interests when they were in high school; once she'd gotten over her snooty stage, they got along pretty well.

Jonah turned to her to find her looking back. She deferred her gaze and raised her wineglass for a nonchalant sip. Jonah frowned; the recent changes in her not gone unnoticed. He couldn't shake the feeling that he'd done something wrong, that maybe he'd offended her in some way. Ever since his accident, she'd been stand-offish and avoidant. With everything else that had happened, he just hadn't found the time to have a serious talk with her. The few times he'd managed to strike up a conversation, she'd put an end to it at the first available opportunity. She'd kept him at arm's length all week, and it made him uneasy. He just wanted to find out what he had screwed up so things could return to normal.

When she laughed at her brother, Jonah couldn't help but notice the laughter didn't reach her eyes. She must have felt his stare, because she turned to face him. The smile vanished, and she turned away. Jonah sighed and looked at Tristan, who was still busy enthralling his parents with another comical tale.

Jonah had struck gold in having Tristan as a best mate. Sure, the man was a clown and didn't take a thing seriously unless he had to—he could come across as a bit flaky—but when it came to the crunch, he was the most dependable person Jonah knew. Tristan was loyal to a fault and would drop everything if Jonah needed him. Tristan and Ava were the only two people who really knew Jonah, and he realised he preferred it that way.

The kitchen timer went off, and Mallory excused herself to dish up dinner. Ava got up to help her.

"I'll top up everyone's drinks," Alex suggested, and he, too, stood from the table.

Tristan turned to Jonah. "How you holding up?" he asked.

Jonah smiled. "You know I love it here."

Tristan rolled his eyes. "I know. You're as big a nerd as the rest of my family."

Jonah laughed. "Well, I must have some redeeming features, considering I've been your best mate for how long, now?"

Tristan pulled a face, making out like he had a hard time coming up with any answer. "Hmm... yeah. I guess you must... I just can't put my finger on any of those redeeming features at the moment."

"You know, I could just pull out the 'it's my birthday' card and tell your mum I want both chicken legs," Jonah teased.

"You wouldn't." Tristan's horrified gasp seemed less of a joke than anything else he'd said.

"I'm pretty hungry... and it's not like I have any redeeming qualities." Jonah pretended to consider the position.

"Dude... there's a line." Tristan shook his head. "You just crossed it."

Jonah laughed at his mate and reassured him his chicken leg would be safe. This didn't stop Tristan from placing a protective arm around his plate while he ate.

The friendly banter continued, and for a little while, the three stooges forgot about their worries. Once the cake was cut and eaten and coffees were served, however, Alex cleared his throat. Everyone looked up at him in surprise.

"So, before we conclude the festivities for the evening, I thought you might like to tell us what's really been going on with you three this week?" The Carters' dinner guests sat in silence, not knowing where to look or what to say.

"Look, it doesn't take a genius to know you're keeping something from us," Mallory added. "I mean, Ava, sweetheart, you look exhausted—more so than usual. Jonah, you look stressed and more pensive than normal. Tristan, no amount of joking in the world can hide the fact that you now have a great big white stripe in your hair."

Tristan ran his hands through his hair, having all but forgotten about the white patch until now. "It's not that bad," he muttered.

Alex and Mallory sighed in marital unison, their faces mirroring one another's concern. "I would recommend one of you start talking now. Keep in mind, this is not the first time we've lined the three of you up at this table for questioning. So, I'm sure you realise it's easiest just to spill it," Alex said with his soft but firm fatherly tone.

Tristan put his head in his hands and groaned. Ava went to speak before Jonah cut in, not wanting her to shoulder the responsibility. He took a deep breath and let out a long sigh. Ava and Tristan nodded for him to continue.

"Well, I guess it started the day of my accident. As you know, I'd been in Greece working on a photo shoot of the restoration of the Acropolis. As planned, I finished the job in time to fly home for my birthday, and as you also know, I got in a car accident on the way home."

Alex and Mallory watched him. Tristan stared up at the ceiling, and Ava alternated her worried gaze between Jonah and her parents like she was watching a tennis match. Jonah continued with his tale but stopped when he came to Tristan's encounter. He turned to his friend to let him pick up his side of things.

Tristan shook his head. "No thanks, mate. You're on a roll." He switched his gaze from the ceiling to the table and ran a hand through his white stripe.

Jonah glanced at Ava, who gave him a small smile of encouragement, so he continued. He explained Tristan's encounter with the man on the boat, then his second encounter with the red-haired woman, Ava's patient Caitlyn, and the revelations of what had happened at the prison. Jonah watched the Carters' expressions through his tale morph from bewilderment to confusion to what he could only describe as oddly misplaced excitement.

When Jonah finished, Alex turned to his wife. "Do we have a pen and some paper floating around here somewhere?"

Mallory nodded. "I'll get something from the study." Then she left the room.

"Excuse me if I seem confused by your reaction," Tristan exclaimed.

Alex stared at his son's head for a few seconds, barely concealing a smirk. "Well, I guess at least we now know what happened to your hair."

"That's all you have to say? Do you have any idea how terrified I had to have been for this to happen in the first place?" Tristan demanded.

"Maybe you're just a big wuss, mate," Jonah suggested. It seemed counterintuitive, but more often than not, the only way to calm Tristan down was to dish him the same kind of joking criticism he gave everyone else.

Tristan scoffed. "At least I'm not the one who passed out when things got weird."

"I had a head injury," Jonah shouted.

"Still piss weak, mate."

"Well, if you ask me, apparently women are still the stronger sex. I didn't pass out *or* change my hair colour," Ava added with a triumphant smile.

"We didn't ask you," the boys said at the same time.

"I think the white streak gives me an air of refinement," Tristan stated, which only made everyone snigger. It was one of the things Jonah had always loved about the Carters; no circumstance was so dire that there wasn't room for humour.

"In all seriousness, I really am intrigued by what you've told us," Alex stated. Mallory walked back in and placed a pad and pen in front of him.

"Intrigued as in you have some idea what's going on? Or intrigued as in you're going to have us committed?" Tristan asked.

Alex chuckled. "Well, I do have a theory, but first I have a few questions." He paused to pick up the pen and prepared for note-taking. "First of all, the red-haired woman. Jonah, you only saw her with scissors. Is that correct?" he asked.

"That's right. Twice."

"And none of you have seen any other red-haired women?" he asked.

"You mean there's more than one crazy lady?" Tristan asked.

"No, it's only been those two sightings of the same woman," Jonah replied, and confusion flashed across Alex's face.

"Um, that's not entirely correct..." Ava interjected.

"You've been holding out on us, Sis?" Tristan asked, miffed.

She turned her gaze from her brother to Jonah, looking extraordinarily guilty. "Well, um... yes and no. I mean, I know I should have told you, but I didn't know how it would sound," she finally said.

"You're kidding, aren't you?" demanded Tristan.

"Well, it's different than what you and Jonah experienced," Ava declared in her defence.

"How so?" Tristan asked.

"Well, for starters, I've had dreams about women." All eyes were on her now and Ava flushed. "What I mean is, I wasn't awake when I saw the women, though they were vivid enough the dreams *felt* real."

"Women? As in more than one?" Jonah asked. He didn't want to show the fact that Ava's secrecy hurt him, but he realised he was frowning at her now.

Ava nodded. "Two separate dreams, two separate women. At first, I thought they were one and the same. They did *look* similar, but their faces were a little different. Maybe this will help." Ava reached into her handbag and pulled out the dictaphone. She placed it on the table in front of her, and with all eyes on her in anticipation, she reached out and pressed play.

When the recollection of her dreams had finished playing out, the only sound in the room was a long, low whistle from Tristan. Alex scribbled furiously on his notepad while Mallory reached out for the old tape recorder.

"I can't believe this thing still works," she declared. "I haven't seen it since your uni days." Ava nodded. In her anxiousness, Mallory lost her hold on the device and it clattered to the floor. A few pieces broke off from the plastic body and scattered about the room. "Damn. I'm sorry."

"Don't worry about it, Mum. It's not the first time that thing has been dropped." Ava joined her Mum on her hands and knees to fish out the pieces from underneath the table.

"Do you have any idea how hard it was for me not to kick?" Tristan asked once his sister and mother had returned to their seats at the table. Alex and Jonah chuckled while Ava ignored her brother, instead holding out her hand for the last piece from her mum. She flipped the dictaphone over and froze.

"What's the matter?" Mallory asked.

Ava turned the device around and held it up so they could all see. There were no batteries.

"The batteries probably fell out when the back flew off," Tristan stated matter-of-factly.

Ava ducked back under the table, joined by her brother in hot pursuit of the batteries.

Alex ignored everyone as he continued to scribble frantically. Ava and Tristan, unable to locate the batteries, sat back at the table in confusion. The whole family gazed at the dictaphone with a mixture of curiosity and trepidation, except for Alex, who stared at it with a grin on his face and a feint flush of excitement crawling up his neck.

"Ava, did you check to see if there were batteries in it before you attempted to record?" he asked his daughter, and she shook her head.

"No, I just tested the play and record, and they worked fine. I just assumed the batteries were in there. How else would it have worked?"

Alex nodded as he jotted down more notes. Mallory looked over her husband's shoulder to read his scribbles. She raised her eyebrows as though impressed with what she saw and nodded.

"Okay. Look, Dad, you know something we don't," Tristan pleaded in frustration. "So can you please share already?"

"Before I propose my theory, is there anything else I should know about?" Alex asked. All eyes turned to Ava. She blushed again. Without looking up she took a deep breath and told them about the conversation with her colleague and about the other girls like Caitlyn.

"I can't believe you hadn't told us any of this before," Tristan said and shook his head.

"I'm sorry. There's just so much info to process already," she said.

"Mate, please tell me you're just as pissed off about this as I am," Tristan said to Jonah, who only looked at his friend's sister with pity. Ava kept her gaze on her hands. Jonah glanced back at Tristan again, who scowled then glared at the tabletop.

Mallory broke the tense silence. "I think I might go fetch a bottle of wine." She stood from the table.

"Make that a beer for me, thanks, Mum," Tristan added.

Alex got up also. "I just need to go double-check a couple things." He left the room in a hurry.

The three of them sat in an awkward silence while they waited. Mallory reappeared, wine and beer in hand.

"Well," Alex began when he re-entered the room, "I think it's fairly safe to confirm my suspicions." He sat down beside his wife, still staring down at the notepad. He didn't seem to notice the four pairs of eyes on him. "I guess the best place to start would be with the red-haired women. So, Jonah, the woman you saw was severing a thread with a pair of scissors. That resulted in someone's death. Is that correct?" Jonah nodded.

"And Ava, the first woman you saw was spinning the thread, which rapidly aged you. The second woman in your dreams appeared to be 'zapping' the newborns, as you put it?" Ava nodded and paled a bit. Alex sighed. "It seems to me the only logical explanation is that you have encountered the Fates."

"Logical? You're kidding, right?" Tristan asked. "Who the hell are these Fates?"

"They are primarily known in Ancient Greek mythology, although you can find stories of them in most cultures," Mallory explained. "The Fates are three sisters, also known as the

Moirae. Some believe them to predate the Gods themselves. They embody the raw forces of nature—forces we can only attempt to understand. Some mythology describes them existing long before anything else, and that they will continue to exist long after there is nothing left. And no matter the myth or the culture, they yield immeasurable power." Alex nodded at the end of his wife's description.

"I can't believe I didn't realise this myself," Jonah said, frowning in frustration. He'd studied these topics for years through his hobbies but never thought he'd be experiencing them first-hand himself.

"So, they're immortal?" Ava asked.

"In a way, yes. But more importantly, the rules of immortality and mortality don't apply to them. They exist above and beyond everything else." Alex paused as he stretched back in his chair and flashed a smile.

Ava's eyes widened at her father. "How can you tell us something like that and still look so relaxed and cheerful?"

Alex tried to contain his smile, but it still wavered at the corners of his mouth. "Ava, honey, you have to understand. You've stumbled upon the Fates! Do you have any idea how huge and exciting this is?" Ava just looked at him without expression. "Help me out, here." Alex turned to his wife, then the boys, for support.

"I can't say I would have chosen the word 'exciting,'" Jonah answered.

"It's official. You've lost the plot, haven't you, Dad? Flown over any cuckoo's nests lately?" Tristan retorted.

"I understand why you're so enthused by all of this, Alex." Mallory said. "I am too. But please try to remember their encounters with these beings have been quite traumatic. Don't be offended if they don't share your enthusiasm." She leaned over and kissed her husband on the cheek. He patted his wife's hand and nodded.

"So, what you're saying is we're screwed?" Tristan added.

Alex tapped his pen against his notepad as he tried to come up with a diplomatic answer. "Well, I guess we won't know until we can determine what it is they're doing here."

"So, what *are* they doing? I mean literally—with the scissors and the spinning and the thread?" Tristan asked.

"For starters, the thread Jonah saw is the Thread of Life itself, hence the luminous glow. That has been a constant in all mythology. Severing it severs the life of the victim. Now, Ava, the woman you saw in your dream at the nursery was Lachesis. She is the Measurer of Life, responsible for allocating a person's lot. Their fate."

"Is that what she was doing to all those babies? Locking in their life plan?" Ava asked. She scowled, and her paleness almost seemed to turn green with repulsion.

Alex nodded. "Yes. Sealing their fate, so to speak. The other sister you saw in your first dream was Clotho. She's the Spinner of the Thread of Life. Her role is to determine how long the thread will be, therefore dictating the length of someone's life."

"So, when Clotho spun the wheel backwards with Ava's hair in it, that's what prematurely aged her?" Jonah asked, finally having found his voice in the conversation.

Alex offered a proud smile, and Ava shuddered. "We'll come back to that in a minute. The third sister is the one you encountered in person, Jonah. Atropos. As you witnessed, once she severs that thread, the victim's life ends. Atropos has always been the most feared of the sisters. Legend claims she cannot be swayed. No amount of begging, pleading, or even bribery can stop her once she decides to cut the Thread of Life. Not even the gods themselves could change her mind. Like

Mallory said, the three sisters are older and more powerful than any other being in existence." Alex's smile faded then beneath a small frown.

"What does all this mean?" Ava asked. Tristan and Jonah echoed her sentiments, and Alex held up his hands to quiet them.

"There's still more to explain. Maybe it's better for me to touch every subject before we get to questions," he stated.

Jonah thought the man would have made an excellent professor. Mallory tried to cover her smile as she proudly put her arm around her husband's shoulders. He was clearly in his element.

"Oh, man..." Tristan muttered. His surprise didn't dull his ability to dodge another jab in the ribs from his sister.

"Next, Tristan, we'll revisit your encounter on the river," Alex started.

"You mean you know who that weird boat guy was?" Tristan asked, his eyes wide again after just having looked heavy with the burden of new information.

His father nodded. "I have a theory, at least, though I don't know if your term 'guy' is accurate. I think you encountered an entity by the name of Charon, the Ferryman. His role is to escort souls into the Underworld." Tristan swallowed hard, and Jonah let out a low whistle. "The fact that he escorted a whole boatload of the living is disconcerting, to say the least. Given everything else that's happened, I'd be surprised if that was an isolated incident. Then we have Caitlyn, Ava's patient, and the other girls like her. Given the description of her dream, Ava, I can only theorise, but I think she may have become an Oracle. As have all the other girls like her."

"You mean like the Oracle of Delphi?" Jonah asked.

Alex nodded again, clearly impressed. "Exactly. But I will explain that further in a moment. Finally, we have the incident at the prison. I believe that to be the work of the Erinnyes, or at least one of them. You may have heard of them referred to as the Furies, and with good reason. Again, we have three sisters; Tisphone, Megaera, and Alecto. They exist solely to punish those who have wronged. Now, what makes them such a ferocious force is the fact that they don't just kill their victims outright..." Alex paused for effect, ensuring his audience hung on his every word. "They torment them. They get inside their victims' heads, and they don't stop until that person is dead. More often than not, the victim will commit suicide just to end it."

"Oh, my God. How awful!" Ava put a hand to her mouth.

"Hmm, well, yes. Keep in mind, the Erinnyes only pursue those who have done evil things," Alex said, and Jonah thought it was meant as a justification.

Mallory got up with a blank, distracted look, then collected the glasses on her way back to the kitchen for the coffee. No one said a thing until she returned. "You said you thought it was Charon Tristan encountered, yet all the people on the boat were still alive. I thought he could only transport the deceased," she said.

"That's an excellent point, dear. Truth be told, I don't know the answer to that." Alex sighed in frustration.

"Well, what about the Erinnyes?" Ava asked. "I mean, such a mass attack like that has never happened before, or else we would know about it. Right?" Her father tapped his notepad with his pen.

"And how come I've been conscious for my run-ins with Atropos, and Ava has only seen the sisters in her dreams?" Jonah added.

"Look, before you ask any more questions, keep in mind, my theories are based on ancient mythology," Alex advised. "I don't think any archaeologist or historian worth his salt has ever put much credence into the actual existence of these creatures. I know I certainly hadn't... before now. But you've described these entities with such specific detail, I can't find any other explanation as to who they are. Aside from what I've already told you, there really isn't much more known about them. At least, nothing more that would explain all of this."

"I will say one thing," Mallory added. "The fact that they're appearing now, after all this time and in such brazen fashion, cannot be a good omen."

"Agreed," Alex said.

"I don't understand." Ava frowned at the table. "I mean, why now? Why are we involved?"

"I'm sorry, sweetheart, but your guess is as good as mine," her father replied.

"I think it's safe to say this isn't a coincidence," Mallory concluded. "Something huge is happening here. As unbelievable as it all seems, we have to try to determine what's actually at the root of these occurrences. And why." She glanced pointedly at each of them in turn.

"Dad said you can't stop either the Fates or the Erinnyes, so what good is investigating any further?" Tristan asked.

"Let me put it this way, son. Would you rather sit and worry about what you can't control, or would you rather get off your butt and work with the few small things you *can* control?" Mallory said bluntly.

"Will you still love me if I say I would rather sit on my butt?" Tristan's half smile seemed to lighten the mood, but Jonah knew his mate was only half joking. Everyone else seemed to pick up on that fact as well.

"In all honesty, though, there's no realistic way to attribute your involvement in all of this as coincidence," Alex replied. "I believe everything you've seen has been intentionally shown to each of you." He paused to let this sink in. "Which means the three of you are somehow supposed to be a part of all this. You have roles to play, whether you like it or not."

Ava took a deep breath followed by a long sigh. "So we should anticipate things will get worse before they get better?" she asked.

Alex glanced up at the ceiling and chewed his bottom lip. "I think, for whatever reason, they want your attention. I think things will get worse until you can determine what's going on, what they want, and why. Maybe then you can start to take some kind of action."

"In the meantime," Mallory interjected, "I would stay vigilant in search of any clues or signs."

"Clues or signs?" Jonah asked, brows furrowed in confusion. He couldn't possibly imagine what other signs any of them could catch before it was too late. They'd already experienced some pretty big *signs*.

Mallory nodded. "Yes. Anything strange that appears to be a coincidence, write it down. Or anything that grabs your attention for no apparent reason. These could all be of use to you."

"Are there any incidents like this you can think of?" Alex asked, his pen poised once more.

"You mean, like my computer turning itself on and running its own Google search?" Tristan joked.

"Or with my recorder?" Ava added.

"Exactly. Though for the most part, I would imagine they wouldn't be quite so obvious."

Jonah watched his friends sifting through recollections of the past few days, and he joined them.

"A few weird things did happen with my phone," Tristan said.

"Such as?" Mallory prompted.

"Well, it sounds silly, but when I was on that boat, I tried to chill out a little with some music. But the song that came on was "Don't Pay the Ferryman". Then when Ava picked me up, the song on the stereo was another song, kind of about this Charon."

"Yeah, and when I was in the accident, just before I saw Atropos the first time, the song on the radio was "Don't Fear the Reaper"," Jonah added. He felt the pieces fitting together in his head but couldn't make out just what they meant yet.

"Well, I guess in hindsight, they were both very relevant," Mallory stated.

"Or they could have just been coincidences, Mum," Ava said with her usual scepticism.

"No, no. I think your mother is right on this one," Alex said. "I think it would pay to be alert at the moment and take note of everything."

"Well, it can't hurt, can it?" Jonah asked. He glanced at Tristan, who shrugged, and was only met with a yawn from Ava.

"Excuse me," she said. "Sorry. I guess I haven't been sleeping very well. I think I just hit the wall."

"Don't apologise," Mallory said. "I think that might be enough to process for one evening. Jonah, I'm sorry your birthday dinner took on such a sombre tone."

"Are you kidding me? It's been great. Enlightening, in a dark way, but great. Besides, anything is worth that roast chicken." Jonah moved to reposition himself in the chair and grimaced in pain.

"Are you okay?" Mallory asked, her expression of concern mirrored by the others'.

Jonah couldn't help but laugh, albeit in pain. "I'm fine. I just forget I shouldn't sit for so long. I'll be right as soon as I start moving around." He tried to force himself to ignore the blaring aches in his ribs and hunched over, trying to hide his discomfort by setting his elbow on the table and placing his chin in his hand.

"Never fear! Nurse Tristan is here!" Tristan stood to assist his mate out of the chair and moving again. Jonah glanced at Ava and saw her face darkened by concern. But when she met his gaze, she quickly looked away and stood from the table.

"Ava," Mallory added, "I think your focus should be on finding out all you can on the other girls like Caitlyn. If they have in fact become Oracles, I imagine they would have some very useful knowledge to impart." Ava nodded and stifled another yawn as they all walked out to the driveway.

"Damn, it's gotten humid out here," Tristan said, pulling a face and plucking his tee shirt away from his body.

Jonah made his own face. "Too early in the year for it, if you ask me."

AS THEY DROVE, Jonah and Tristan discussed the evening's events, and Ava spent her turn in the back seat in silence. Tristan pulled the car into the driveway, and Ava leaned forward to kiss both men on the cheek before getting out. "Are you okay, sis?" Tristan asked.

She nodded. "Just really looking forward to some sleep."

Both men watched her shuffle into her house and close the door behind her. They even waited for a few seconds longer, but she didn't turn on a single light.

"She hit the wall pretty hard," Tristan muttered.

"Not really that surprising," Jonah said. "She hasn't had a lot of sleep lately. All this new information didn't exactly give me *more* energy, either."

Tristan sighed. "Yeah, I know. But I'm worried about her, man. Aside from the nightmares and not sleeping, she just seems a lot more affected by everything going on. Ava's always been—"

"The strong one?" Jonah finished for him.

Tristan sighed and glanced at his friend. Jonah was certain the concern behind Tristan's eyes matched what he felt.

CHAPTER ELEVEN

AVA OPENED HER eyes, completely disoriented. She found herself lying clothed and sprawled diagonally across her bed, then looked up at the alarm clock on her bedside table and groaned. It was only three in the morning. Her muscles were stiff from heavy slumber, and she rolled onto her back to stretch out. With a gasp, she shot upright and pushed herself back against the headboard. Clamping her hand against her mouth, she stifled a panicked scream.

Someone sat in the window seat only a meter away from the foot of the bed. Ava sat completely still, trying to make out who it was, but a breeze coming through the open window billowed through the curtains and kept the person's features from view.

The figure, apparently aware she was now awake, moved. Ava struggled to contain the scream she felt rising up within her. The curtains parted on their own as the dark figure took slow, purposeful steps toward the bed. A car drove past the house, illuminating the intruder through the window. Ava's fear was suddenly replaced by confusion.

"Caitlyn?" she whispered.

"Hey, Doc," the girl replied in a quiet voice and finally approached the foot of the bed.

"How did you get in here? Is everything okay?" Ava's brain scrambled into overdrive. Caitlyn glanced back towards the window as if she'd find her answers there. "Caitlyn?" Ava prompted and scooted forward on the bed to be closer to the girl.

"Don't be afraid, Doc," the girl said.

"Afraid? Afraid of what? Caitlyn, how did you get here?" She got no response, and fear threatened to overtake her again. "*Answer* me."

Caitlyn tilted her head, fixing Ava with an only vaguely lucid stare, as though she struggled to decide what to tell her. "He sent me here," she finally whispered.

"Who sent you here?"

Caitlyn sighed. "I don't have time to explain right now. Don't be afraid. You'll see soon enough. He's coming. Soon."

"What? Caitlin, who's coming?" Ava turned to her nightstand and fumbled with the switch of the lamp. In an instant, she felt better as the light engulfed the shadows. Then she turned back toward the girl, expecting an answer, only to find Caitlyn gone. "Caitlyn?" She looked around the room before dashing to the glance out the window.

There was no sign of the girl.

It had been so real; she could have sworn she was actually awake. Yet there was no way Caitlyn could just vanish like that. It had to be another nightmare. Ava let out a frustrated scream before collapsing onto her bed with exhausted sobs.

JONAH LAY AWAKE, staring at the ceiling. He tentatively lifted his arms to fold them underneath his head and felt the pain in his ribs and the pull in his muscles. He let out a long sigh and waited for the pain to subside. The room grew lighter with the beginnings of a new day, and he ran through his recollections of the past few days. It was time to go home; he needed his own space to try to get some clarity. He realised then that he hadn't had any time to go over the pictures from his trip, and he had a sudden yearning for his computer. With the realisation that he could lose himself in his work, he took advantage of the time he had to pack his things while Tristan slept.

AVA SAT OUTSIDE on her balcony, nursing a cup of coffee that had long since gone cold. She had lost track of how much time elapsed while she sat staring into space, trying hard to rationalise what had happened. Yet as dawn broke, she felt too dazed to do anything other than continue staring. Giving herself a mental shake, she forced herself to get up. Nothing could be done until she'd spoken to Caitlyn.

TRISTAN WANDERED OUT into the living room, groggy and still half asleep. He wasn't surprised to see Jonah at the table, reviewing his notes. What did surprise him was the sight of Jonah's packed bags on the floor. He rubbed a hand through his hair and stared at his mate.

"So, I take it this means you want a divorce."

Jonah laughed. "More like a trial separation. I just feel I need to get home and get organised. Clear my head a little, you know?"

Tristan nodded. "All good, man. I was starting to get sick of having to look at your ugly mug all the time, anyway." He smiled and poured himself a cup of coffee.

"Don't hate the face. It's hard work being this handsome." Jonah grinned.

"You might be handsome, my friend, but I'm a Greek god," Tristan declared.

"You're an idiot is what you are."

"It's a widely known fact." Tristan winked. "How about I drink my coffee, jump in the shower, and then drop you home on my way to work?"

Jonah nodded. "Sure. No hurry, mate."

Tristan glanced at Jonah's belongings stacked up against the lounge. "No hurry?" Jonah shrugged and turned back to his notes.

AS AVA WALKED into her office, she realised she had no idea what time it was. Feeling all too acutely the effects of no sleep, she grabbed the clock next to her computer to find it was 7:30 a.m. Caitlyn should be awake and dressed by now. Without a second thought, she walked down the hall to the girl's room.

It was empty.

The familiar sinking feeling fell in the pit of her stomach, and she stuck her head out the door to see Bob approaching in the hallway. "Bob," she called. He smiled at her. "Have you seen Caitlyn this morning?"

"Yep. She's in the dining room having breakfast with everyone else. Is everything okay?" His smile faded when he took a closer look his boss.

Ava shook off his concern. "Yes, everything's fine. Can you please go ask her to return to her room immediately? I need to speak to her."

"Sure. Okay…" Bob nodded and took a few slow steps backwards before turning around and heading back down the hall. He turned back once. Ava stood there, arms folded across her chest, frowning as she stared straight through him.

JONAH STEPPED THROUGH the door into his townhouse and couldn't help but smile. It felt good to be back in his own home.

"Hurry up, will you?" he called to Tristan, who struggled with Jonah's belongings in the driveway. Tristan only grunted at him. Jonah chuckled and walked into the living room. Cautious of his injuries, he opened the curtains and windows, then walked toward his unpacked luggage from the Greece trip still sitting on the coffee table. Ava had dropped it off for him while he was in the hospital.

Leaving the suitcases untouched, he proudly pulled out his camera case and walked into the study. While the computer booted up, he removed the memory card and listened to Tristan come banging through the house.

"I'll just dump this stuff in your room," his friend shouted.

"No worries," he shouted back. Once he got focused on his photography, there was really nothing else that mattered. The photos loaded on the computer, and Tristan appeared in the doorway.

"So, I was thinking I wouldn't mind heading down to the pool to do some laps after work. I'll swing by after?" Tristan suggested.

"Can I come watch?" Jonah asked.

"Won't that just piss you off? You can't get in yourself."

Jonah nodded. "Sure. But no more than having to spend another day inside. I'll just bring a book, or my camera, or something."

"Yeah, bring the camera. You can shoot me. All the chicks will think I'm a super swimming legend or something." Tristan pumped a bicep.

Jonah laughed. "Has anyone ever told you you're a tool?"

"Not today, mate," Tristan said with a wink.

Once Tristan left, Jonah made himself a coffee before hobbling back to his computer. He clicked on the first photo to enlarge it for a better view and broke into a smile with the focused image; there was nothing he loved more than standing amongst some ancient ruins, camera in hand.

He believed himself beyond lucky to have a job that combined his passions—photography, ancient history, and archaeology. He had never been able to put his finger on it, but something about ancient civilisations had always called to him. Even places to which he'd never been gave him a sense of familiarity, like an old memory that couldn't quite surface. The sensation was always strongest in Greece, and for some reason, it had been magnified during his last trip. Perhaps he'd just been more sensitive to it; he *had* felt particularly paranoid under the constant sense of being watched.

Jonah's original assignment had been to photograph the restoration of the Acropolis. While he was there, a previously unknown tomb was discovered. The site was in a remote farming area of Greece and not thought to be a region of particular archaeological significance, and Jonah had been thrilled when he received the reassignment. The details of the tomb's discovery were restricted on a 'need-to-know' basis, to which he hadn't been privy. Still, he *had* been able to deduce on his own merit that the circumstances surrounding this new tomb were unusual at best. But what was a new discovery without a little mystery?

The tomb was not quite like anything seen before, and it had the archaeologists and historians baffled. Despite the assignment being a prestigious career opportunity, Jonah also had a great deal of personal interest in it.

Now, he inspected the images on the screen. After briskly scanning through the first few, he had to stop. There was something on the left of the photo that he couldn't quite make out. After closer inspection, he attributed it to a reflection or light anomaly. Moving on to the next frame, he found the same anomaly, though a little more prominent. He flicked through the following frames, his annoyance growing as this reflection grew and grew within his photos. Jonah rubbed his forehead in frustration; he had checked the stills on site, and they had been perfect. He let out a groan and leaned forward again to take a closer look. He clicked for the next photo to slide across.

"What the hell?" he muttered and enlarged the photo. In this frame, the anomaly almost appeared to hold form. Jonah flicked through the next few frames as his heart pounded in his chest. What he'd first thought a trick of the light now appeared to be the apparition of a woman.

She'd moved closer and closer to him in every shot. He couldn't make out her features, so he scanned through the next few frames until the form came into focus. The photo was taken at the tomb's entrance—a close-up shot to capture the details of the inscriptions.

It was here the apparition now stood, her hand placed against the doorway of the tomb as though about to step inside. Now that she fully faced the camera, her features were finally clear enough to reveal a cunning smile.

"Shit!" Jonah exclaimed in horror.

It was the red-haired woman from his car accident.

CHAPTER TWELVE

AVA PACED THE paced the length of Caitlyn's room as she waited for the girl to arrive. So engrossed in her own thoughts, she jumped when the girl appeared, more startled than she should have been.

"You wanted to see me?" Caitlyn asked, hovering in the doorway.

Ava gave a quick nod. "Take a seat."

Caitlyn complied in silence and sat on the edge of her bed. Ava pulled the chair out from under the desk and sat down before jumping back up to continue her pacing. Feeling Caitlyn's eyes on her, she finally said, "Caitlyn, I need you to tell me what happened last night."

Caitlyn just stared at her with wide eyes. "What do you mean?"

"What do I mean? Don't play dumb with me, Caitlyn. I want to know how you managed to leave here in the middle of the night and then break into my house."

"What? I didn't leave my room at all. I slept through the whole night," Caitlyn said, visibly upset by the accusation.

"Don't lie to me, Caitlyn. I saw you with my own eyes. I spoke to you, for God's sake. Just tell me what you were talking about!" Ava yelled, unable to contain her frustration any longer.

"Dr Carter!" came a stern, angry voice from the doorway. Ava turned to see her boss Dr Fraser standing there, Bob hovering in the hall behind him. "Please go wait for me in my office."

Ava glanced sideways at the teary Caitlyn before storming out, refusing to meet Bob's gaze.

Once she was in the director's office, she forced herself to sit. As soon as she did, she felt an overwhelming remorse come over her. Ava rested her elbows on the desk and placed her tired head in her hands. "What did I just do?" she whispered.

Dr Fraser himself appeared somewhat calmer as he entered the office and closed the door behind him. He sat behind his desk and waited for Ava to look up at him.

"I am so sorry," she started, ashamed of her unprofessional conduct. "I don't know what came over me."

Dr Fraser took a moment before saying anything. "I know that I've been away for the past couple days, but I still can't help but notice there's an awful lot of tension in this place. Most of which seems to stem around you, Bob, and Caitlyn. Not to mention the fact that Mary Sullivan has submitted her resignation, effective immediately. She cited undue stress on which she refuses to elaborate. But you're still here, Ava. So start talking." Ava stared at the director, feeling like a deer caught in the headlights as she tried to think of a way out. "And don't even think about telling me anything less than the whole story," he stated firmly.

Ava sighed and rubbed her tired eyes. Taking a deep breath, she launched into her account of what had happened, attempting to downplay some of the more extreme occurrences as much as possible. When she finished, she watched Dr Fraser for the disbelief she knew was coming.

The director didn't look at her. Instead, he sat back with his chair turned sideways behind the desk. With his left hand, he toyed with a pen, twirling it atop his blotter.

Ava sat for what felt like an eternity of silence, wanting to break it but too afraid to speak. She tried to steal glances at him, maybe find out what he was thinking, but his face was a blank canvas. Just when she felt she couldn't take it anymore, Dr Fraser cleared his throat.

"I'm sure you had every intention of reporting this to me upon my official return," he stated, eyes still fixed on the pen.

"Of course. Had I known you were back already, I would have come to see you first thing this morning," she lied.

The director stared out the window as he drummed his fingers on his desk. "I am also quite sure that you're more than aware your earlier conduct with Caitlyn is unacceptable."

Ava said nothing but gave a small nod.

"What you are not aware of is the number of emails that awaited me this morning. They reported similar incidences from other facilities. All of them involved girls around Caitlyn's age, and they all displayed the same... anomalies... in behaviour."

Ava's mouth fell open. She was half tempted to mention the email she herself had received but thought better of it.

"I want you to take some time off. A few days, at the least."

"What?" Ava exclaimed. "There's no way."

Dr Fraser finally met her gaze with a demanding authority. "That was not a request, Dr Carter."

Ava sighed. "I can't believe this," she mumbled.

"Based on both what you've told me and the things of which I've been notified, the situation at the moment is worrisome, to say the least. Aside from that, you look like hell. I assume you haven't been sleeping, and what I witnessed in Caitlyn's room makes me think you need to take a step back. So, I don't want to see you back in here for the rest of the week. Understood?"

"What about Caitlyn?"

"I will see to her."

Ava nodded and stood to leave. She opened the door but briefly turned back towards the director. "Please tell Caitlyn I'm sorry for the way I treated her this morning." Dr Fraser nodded curtly, then Ava took a deep breath and stepped out of the room.

TRISTAN TAPPED THE steering wheel as he made his way home. He couldn't help but let his mind wander over the past few days. As he pulled up at the next traffic light, he leaned forward to turn on the music; it would be a welcome distraction. The melody filled his car, and without thinking, Tristan found himself singing along. Halfway through the song, he realised he was actually singing about danger and warnings. Agitated, he turned the music off, swore, and thumped the steering wheel in anger. He couldn't shake the feeling that the one thing he loved more than anything in the world was somehow being used against him.

AVA STA IN in the window seat of her bedroom, contemplating the morning's events even through her exhaustion. She felt awful for the way she'd treated Caitlyn and was angry with herself for having momentarily lost control.

After a shower, she felt calmer, and her wet hair was a soothing relief against the back of her neck. The unseasonal rise in humidity made the shower that much more of a refreshing reprieve. More than anything, Ava wanted to sleep, but she was too afraid. She knew she had to get back her equilibrium, had to take the steps to regain some control within the surrealism of everything happening around her. Then a strange tingle ran down her spine, striking her with a sudden inspiration.

During Caitlyn's original episode, the girl had whispered the name *Hephalion*. Hearing that name at the time had confused her, because it had sounded so incredibly familiar despite the fact that she knew she'd never heard it before. Finding out who this Hephalion was would be an excellent first step.

Feeling renewed with energy, she got up and went into the lounge room where she'd left her laptop. Ava curled up in her favourite chair and ensured she was comfortable before switching it on. She typed the name into the search engine, relieved to see a number of hits show up. After closer inspection, she was a little disconcerted when the first page of hits all seemed to be in reference to a character in a computer game. She patiently clicked for the next page of hits, and the next, but the only deviation from the game character was when the results changed languages.

Ava set the laptop in her lap and gazed around the room, thinking. She considered searching the name *Hephalion* with the word *oracle* or *prophecy* to see if anything more relevant came up. But when she looked back down at the laptop, the device appeared to be doing its own research on her behalf. Ava watched in astonished silence. Windows popped open and minimized on their own. As pages of text scrolled by, highlighted passages flashed out at her.

Ava lifted the laptop and held it out in front of her with her fingertips, fearful that if she moved suddenly, the activity would stop. Rising gingerly from her chair, she placed the laptop on the coffee table before dashing off to find a notepad and pen. She was a little old-fashioned, just like her father, and preferred to write notes herself. The act in itself seemed to help her process the information more effectively.

By the time she returned, the search was complete. Not wanting to miss anything, Ava decided to begin with the first of the open windows and work backwards from there. With her pen poised in anticipation, she took a deep breath and read the first section.

JONAH GAZED OUT his study window, watching the leaves on the trees moving with the breeze—a breeze that provided no relief from the rising and extreme humidity, even for Brisbane. Feeling calmer, he let his mind wander back to the photographs and the woman. He realised now why she seemed to recognise him after the accident. But why had she left him unharmed? Even more perplexing was the question of why he had been unable to see her in Greece. She'd obviously been right there with him, yet he'd not seen her either with the naked eye or through the lens of his camera.

He sighed. The list of questions seemed to grow exponentially, and for the most part, the answers remained elusive. As far as he could tell, it all started with the excavation site. He didn't want to believe that his presence had any significance other than being in the wrong place at the wrong time. But the fact of the matter was a clear connection existed, and Jonah was determined to find out what that was.

As he swivelled his chair back around to face the computer again, he was stunned to find a new message waiting for him in his email, blank and ready to be written and sent. The email address had already been entered into the 'To' field to complete the process. Jonah recognised the name as the archaeologist in charge of the excavation. They had only met briefly when Jonah had first arrived at the dig site. Dr Sydney had been courteous enough at their first meeting, though distracted. Jonah shook his head, not wanting to put too much thought into how this not-so-subtle nudge had occurred. Instead, he took a deep breath and began to type. The archaeologist was as good a place to start as any, and Jonah hoped to continue his rapport with Dr Sydney by mentioning his review of the photos—without mentioning the red-haired woman—and asking if the man and his team had discovered anything interesting within the tomb site.

As he sent the email, his phone vibrated beside the keyboard. He glanced down to see a message from Ava. He instantly refocused his attention and opened up the whole message.

Ava said she'd been spending her involuntary time off work wisely by doing some extra research and wanted to swing by her parents' house again later in the day. When Jonah told her that he and Tristan were going to the pool first, she quickly asked if they'd pick her up to go with them. Jonah replied with, 'Okay,' knowing they all could probably use a good reprieve from the humidity, before texting Tristan the change of plans.

Just as he finished, his computer pinged to notify him of a new email. Jonah had thought his email to Dr Sydney was just a stab in the dark, and it surprised him now to receive such a prompt response.

'Dear Mr. Sands,

The timing of your email is eerie, to say the least, given the subject matter of your questions. There have been a number of... incidents... since the discovery of the tomb. All but one occurred after your photo assignment. Many of those who are involved with the dig liken these incidents to the aftermath of Howard Carter's discovery of Tutankhamen's tomb in 1922. I myself have never put much stead in superstitions. Yet even I have to admit that certain events I find difficult to rationalise, most of which I would prefer not to explain in any great detail via email. Perhaps we can make a time to have a meeting on Skype? In the meantime, I can answer two of your questions for you.

As you know, we were part of the team working on the preservation of the Acropolis. During the project, one of my post-grad archaeology students went missing. Two days later, he was found in the middle of nowhere in the Greek countryside, with no recollection of getting there. He was barely conscious, his bare feet cut and bloodied, and his hands were extraordinarily dirty and missing a few fingernails.

When he was rehydrated and able to speak, he told us he'd awakened from a deep sleep and felt compelled to walk. According to my student, he had been driven by a sense of urgency but didn't consciously know where he was going. He stated it had felt like something forced him to walk, as if he had no physical control over his body. When he reached his destination after hours of walking barefoot, he was then overcome by the compulsion to dig at the exact spot in the ground upon which he stood. Not having any tools on hand, he dug through half a meter of hard, rocky earth, using only his hands. At some stage, he collapsed from exhaustion. This was how we discovered the tomb. He refused to allow the paramedics to take him to the hospital until we had promised him we would continue digging. It was difficult to maintain secrecy from the press and University about this strange method for initiating a new dig site, but I feel it was managed well for the time being. Still, I felt compelled to see my promise to the lad fulfilled, in addition to finding a strange urgency in continuing the dig once we had his story. I admit, I was both professionally and personally intrigued. Obviously, my intuition had been correct, and we found something, indeed.

Once properly unearthed, the tomb entrance was closed. We had yet to work out a way to open it without causing any structural damage. Then one morning, we arrived on site to find it open—only none of us were able to enter. It was as if some invisible force prevented us from doing so.

I am sure this is enough information for you to process until our Skype meeting...'

Jonah sat back and processed what he'd just read. Something wasn't quite right, but he couldn't put his finger on it. He tried to think back to his photography session at the tomb, closing his eyes and frowning in concentration.

"Shit!" The realisation hit him; he had himself been inside the tomb. Not the all the way in, of course, but he'd never experienced the same sensation of restriction Sydney and his team had encountered. Jonah got up and rummaged through his camera case until he found the right memory card. As he waited for the photos to upload, he tried his best to recall anything unusual.

He had stood in the entryway of the dark tomb, yet something had managed to catch his attention. The sunlight shone through the entrance at such an angle that it appeared to bounce off a dull reflection farther inside the tomb. This had led him to take a closer look; he'd stopped inside, waiting for his eyes to adjust to the minimal light. A couple metres inside the door stood a small wall, only about as wide as the entryway and as high as Jonah's waist. It seemed to be made of the same stone as the tomb itself, but set in this small wall was a metal inlay, like a large plaque. Jonah had assumed it was made of gold and this was what had caught the light. He'd leaned down to have a closer look. Despite the dust, the hieroglyphics were set deeply enough into the metal that he could still make them out. They were unlike any markings Jonah had seen before, but they were visible. He'd taken photos of the plaque but had wanted to run them by Sydney prior to including them in his final assignment.

He decided then that it would be best to hold off telling Sydney about having been in the tomb and taken the photos until he was able to talk to the man via Skype. Instead, he sent a brief reply with a thank you for the information and times for the call. After sending it, Jonah sat back and lost himself in scrolling through the photos again. Once more, he felt as though he had answered one question only to discover another ten

CHAPTER THIRTEEN

WITH A YAWN, Jonah felt a wave of exhaustion sweep over him. Tristan was due to pick him up, and if it wasn't for his inability to find reprieve from the humidity, Jonah would have decided to stay home. Despite the hot and heavy cast on his arm, the prospect of the pool sounded better than feeling sorry for himself at home, alone. Not content with sitting on the edge with his legs in the water, he hunted through the kitchen for something with which to cover his cast. When Tristan came strutting through the front door, Jonah was struggling to disentangle himself from a plastic garbage bag and a long piece of masking tape.

"Dude, you're hopeless!" Tristan exclaimed in amusement.

"Well, it turns out my idea wasn't as easy to execute as it appeared in my head," Jonah replied dryly, realising he was only tangling himself further.

"Nothing ever is, mate." Tristan went to help him out, shaking his head. "Let's get some fresh tape and a new bag and get out of here. You know how Ava gets when we're late."

Jonah smiled at the image. He had always thought Ava's annoyed frown was pretty cute.

AS ANTICIPATED, THEY pulled up to find Ava standing in front of her house, strumming her fingers on the mailbox. Jonah was grateful his dark-lensed sunglasses, which enabled him to appreciate the bikini underneath Ava's sheer kaftan. As she climbed into the car, fanning herself with her hand, Jonah averted his gaze.

"Can it get any more humid? This is insane. I don't know how the hell you can wear those jeans, Tristan," she exclaimed.

"You know I refuse to wear shorts. Besides, people wouldn't recognize me if I didn't wear jeans. Hell, I would even do laps in these babies if I didn't think they would slow me down," Tristan admitted. "Just because you're a chick and have the luxury of walking around half-naked doesn't mean that *we* can. Isn't that right, Jonah?"

"Uh… yeah…" Jonah muttered, trying hard to not think about the fact that Ava was indeed, half-naked.

Ava just scoffed. "Whatever, you pair of twits. Are we there yet?"

Jonah grinned at her cue. "Yeah, Tristan… are we there yet?" he asked with feigned innocence.

Ava leaned forward towards the front seat, preparing for a Jonah-and-Ava tag- team.

"Are we there yet?"

"Are we there yet?"

"Are we there yet?"

"Don't make me pull this car over," Tristan stated when he could no longer stand it.

Ava patted her brother's shoulder, and they all laughed.

JONAH HAD ANTICIPATED the pool would be packed given the weather, so he was surprised to find it almost empty.

"Awesome, no sharing the lap lane." Tristan fist-pumped the air as he hurried toward the water. As Tristan warmed up, Jonah gingerly took his shirt off and slipped his plastered arm into the plastic bag.

"Here, let me help you with that. You have to make sure no water can get in. Don't want to make this any worse on yourself," Ava stated, smiling up at him as she took charge.

"No, I think the bloody humidity's managed that," Jonah replied. He struggled to ignore the proximity of their semi-naked bodies and turned his thoughts to the red-haired sisters.

Yep, he thought, *that'll do it*.

He cleared his throat and forced his gaze towards Ava's handiwork. When she'd finished, he felt both disappointed and relieved to have her step back away from him.

"There you go. That should do the trick. But I would still avoid diving and getting it completely wet," she warned.

Jonah nodded. "Thanks."

"Come on, you two! Get a move on!" Tristan yelled before diving into the pool with a swimmer's grace. Ava got up to do the same.

Jonah smiled and picked up his waterproof camera, making his way down to the shallow end. He took his time in sitting at the pool's edge before gently lowering himself into the water. His ribs pinched, and he grimaced, sucking in air and waiting for the pain to subside. He opened his eyes to find Ava watching him from the other end of the pool, concern thinly masked by a wary smile. Jonah braced himself and gave her a reassuring thumbs up.

Once the pain subsided, relief washed over him as his body finally had a chance to cool. The water almost padded his body against the pain, and he could move with much more ease inside the pool. Jonah reached for his camera perched on the pool edge and panned around with it, trying to find something of interest to shoot. He stopped dead when through the lens he saw Ava climb out of the pool. Without even thinking, he took the shot. Then he panicked and looked around for a witness. An older man in his seventies stood at the side of the pool with of group of other men his own age. The man gave Jonah a knowing smile and a subtle nod of acknowledgement before turning back to his group. Then Ava dove into the pool.

Jonah sighed and wiped the back of his cool, wet hand against his forehead. "That'll teach you to be a perv," he muttered.

"Yo, Jonah! Are you going to stand there all afternoon, or are you going to take some shots of me being awesome?" Tristan demanded.

"I've been trying to find something more appealing to photograph!" Jonah yelled back.

"What could be more appealing than me? I'm an Adonis!" Tristan raised his outstretched arms.

"Do you want to drown him, or should I?" Ava suggested as she splashed her brother from behind.

"Oh, it's like that, is it?" Tristan asked with a mock hurt before grabbing his sister in a headlock and dunking her. Jonah laughed and settled on photographing their tomfoolery.

His attention was then diverted to the group of elderly men to his left. They dove into the pool, one by one, and spaced themselves out perfectly. Once each man resurfaced, he began the butterfly stroke. At first, Jonah was amazed by the perfection of their swimming. He'd never considered himself to be an ageist, but their strength still impressed him, and he admired the way their chests seemed to rise out of the water without effort.

They continued swimming in synchronicity, and Jonah suddenly felt uneasy. Something about their perfect unison as their bodies rose and fell with each stroke seemed highly unnatural. Jonah glanced at Tristan and Ava, who still played around in the pool, oblivious to his discomfort. When he turned his attention back to the men, he raised his camera, hoping he wouldn't draw attention to himself. They seemed far too focused on their swimming to notice anyone else, even though there weren't many other people at the pool. Before long, Jonah was in the photographer's zone, snapping photos in rapid succession. Wanting to capture their synchronicity from an intriguing angle, he partially submerged his camera, aiming to get a shot with half their bodies above the water and the other half below. Concentrating, he tried to line up the shot as best he could. It was quite a challenge with having to keep his broken arm above the water.

After a few minutes, he felt rather pleased with the afternoon's work before realising he had yet to take any photos of Tristan. He aimed his lens at his friend, who was now doing laps in the lane behind him.

WHEN IT WAS time to hit the showers, Jonah was relieved to find it much easier getting out of the pool than it had been getting into it.

"Try not to take all night, okay, guys?" Ava pleaded as she headed off to the ladies' showers.

Tristan and Jonah nodded and headed off in the other direction. "So, did you get some awesome action shots of me?" Tristan asked with a wink.

"I haven't scrolled through them yet, but I'm sure I was able to make you look like an Olympic swimmer," Jonah said with a laugh.

As always, Tristan took his time. Jonah was forced to listen to him sing in the shower while he sat showered, dressed, and got ready to go—with injuries. So he killed the time by scrolling through his shots of the day and glanced at the first photo with a new wave of appreciation. Ava. His thumb hovered over the delete button before he thought twice and skipped to the next shot. A laugh escaped him as he flipped through the playful shots of Tristan and Ava. But the laughter died in his throat right there. The all-too-familiar sense of foreboding swept over him as he came to the first shot of the men swimming.

The photo displayed just how in synch they had been. If Jonah hadn't taken the photo himself, we would have sworn it was a fake. An above-surface shot, the photo clearly showed that each man was the exact distance apart from the next, each at the exact same point in their stroke, and all were perfectly aligned. Shaking his head in disbelief, he flipped to the next shot and swore out aloud. He struggled with one arm to prevent his camera from toppling to floor.

"Are you okay?" Tristan yelled.

Jonah couldn't answer as he steadied himself and looked back at the image. He didn't glance up as Tristan approached with a towel around his waist. Still without looking up, Jonah handed him the camera, then took a deep breath and waited for a reaction.

"You've got to be shitting me!" Tristan yelled. "Is this the only shot like this?"

"I don't know, to be honest. I hadn't managed to get past that one," Jonah said. He stood up and leaned in for a look as Tristan skipped through the remaining photos. They shook their heads in unified disbelief, but their silence was broken by a voice yelling through the entryway.

"How long does it take to have a shower, you two?" Ava moaned. "I'm a girl, and I'm still always ready before you."

"Coming!" Jonah replied as he gathered up his things while Tristan scrambled to get dressed.

Exiting the change rooms, they found Ava leaning against the brick wall with her arms crossed over her chest and her head tilted to the side in curiosity. Jonah followed her gaze.

"There's something not quite right about those men," Ava said. "Is it actually possible to be that in synch…"

"Maybe this will explain it," Jonah stated and handed her the camera.

She looked up at him, confusion flashing across her face, before glancing down at the photo on the screen. Then she gasped. "Holy crap!"

Tristan and Jonah both nodded with wide eyes.

"But… what? How?"

"Stuffed if I know," Jonah replied, then turned to face the men as they kept swimming, oblivious to their audience.

"I mean, from here, you can't tell anything's out of the ordinary," Jonah explained, as much to himself as to the others. "When I was taking the shots, I didn't see it, either. But the camera picked it up."

"Dude, don't stare at them. They'll know that we noticed," Tristan whispered, turning his back to the pool. He grabbed the camera from Ava as she indiscreetly tried to peer around him.

"This is unbelievable. They have fish tails. For real. Half man, half fish. So what, does that make them mermaids? I thought mermaids were chicks. Hot chicks."

Ava rolled her eyes. "I can't say I've ever encountered one before. But you know who probably knows more about them than we do? Dad."

"Well, let's just get the hell out of here before they notice us." Tristan took off for the carpark, failing in his attempt to hide how eager he was to leave.

Before stepping through the exit, Jonah paused. The hairs on the back of his neck stood on end, and he turned back towards the pool. His breath stopped in his throat. The men had stopped swimming. Still maintaining their perfect spacing, they now faced him, bobbing in the water. Jonah's gaze fell on the one who'd acknowledged him earlier. They stared back at each other for a few moments, unblinking, before the man gave a short nod in Jonah's direction. Jonah had to force himself to turn and catch up with the others.

"You all right?" Tristan asked. Jonah nodded but said nothing as he got into the car.

"I wish it would just bloody rain or something," Ava moaned, fanning herself with her hands. "Anything just to break this damn humidity. It's not even summer, for crying out loud."

"Well, judging by those clouds, I don't think you'll have to wait long. They're starting to look nasty up ahead." Tristan pointed, and Ava's gaze followed his.

"Hmm, you're right. We'd better get a move on, then." They both climbed into the car.

Jonah was already on his phone, checking for weather updates. "They've issued a severe storm warning."

Tristan nodded and started the car. "By the looks of that green tint to the clouds, I'd say we'll be in for some hail, too."

They'd only been driving for about ten minutes when the storm clouds moved in at a rapid rate. Ava and Jonah looked out the windows at the dark, ominous storm swirling overhead.

"Dude, that looks nasty. I hope it holds off until we get there," Jonah stated.

"You and me both," Tristan replied.

A fierce torrent of rain pummelled the car, and they realised they'd spoken too soon. Ava pulled back from the window to watch the large raindrops hurl themselves violently toward her.

"Are you okay, man?" Jonah asked Tristan, almost having to yell to be heard over the noise.

"Yeah, just trying to see better," Tristan replied, a deep frown across his forehead as he concentrated on the road ahead.

Lightning lit the sky with a massive clap of thunder, making them all jump in surprise. The rain only pelted down harder, and Tristan made an executive decision. "I'm pulling over."

"Is that safe in this?" Ava asked.

"It has to be safer than me trying to drive when I can't see a damn thing," her brother replied.

"You guys know how much I hate storms," she added in a weak voice.

"They say the safest place to be in an electrical storm is the car," Jonah said, hoping to make her feel better.

"Is that true?" Ava asked. "Or is that just one of those things people say to make you feel better about being stuck in a car during an electrical storm?"

Jonah shrugged. "How should I know? I'm just trying to make you feel better about being stuck in a car during an electrical storm."

Ava smiled. "Well, thank you for trying."

Tristan turned the engine off, having settled them on the side of the road. He left the headlights on for visibility should other traffic pass. The sky lit up again, this time with simultaneous hot-white flashes. The car shook with the rolling thunder that seemed to bang right over their heads.

Ava moved into the middle of the back seat and leaned forward with a white-knuckled grip on the front seats. Even Jonah wondered if they might not be as safe as they'd hoped. He attempted to yell this, but Tristan gestured that he couldn't hear a thing over the deafening noise. Instead, Jonah looked out his window, gripping his seat as the car shook.

A massive fork of lightning struck less than a hundred meters away with a force that raised the front of the car off the ground. Jonah and Tristan braced themselves against their doors and turned to look at Ava. Her face was contorted in a scream that appeared silent, her voice only drowned out by the din of the storm.

Jonah tried to peer out the windscreen toward where the lightning had struck. The sky now resembled a strobe light, and the earth itself felt like it shook without end. Squinting, he tried to peer into the distance. He swore something moved up ahead and nudged Tristan, pointing to his own eyes then out the windscreen. Tristan nodded and leaned forward to join him.

Ava forgot her fear as the boys' switch in attention distracted her. It was hard to see anything through the brief glimpses of visibility granted by each flash of lightning. All they could see was a large plume of smoke rising from the spot where the bolt had hit.

Tristan gestured to Jonah as if to say, 'What am I supposed to be looking at?' Jonah shook his head. He was certain he'd seen something out there.

Ava frantically tapped them both on the arms and pointed at the windscreen. Puzzled, Jonah studied the darkness in front of them, and his attention fell on the raindrops pelting the glass. He gasped and nudged Tristan to show him.

Tristan's eyes widened in disbelief, and he leaned in for a closer look while raising his hand up to touch the glass.

Rain pummelled the windscreen, while the raindrops already there appeared to be moving in reverse, as though some invisible force plucked them from the car. The sky thundered, and the trio found extended visibility as the lightning flashed over and over in rapid succession. They froze in awe.

The lightning illuminated the curtain of rain as it fell from the clouds onto the front of the car. The rain hurtling in reverse off the car could now be traced to a figure walking toward them in the distance, lit up by the quick flashes in the storm. The rain droplets appeared suspended in the air, circling around the man like a twister.

The stranger was now in clear view of the headlights, wearing what looked like a white sheet. In stunned silence, they watched him walk toward them. The rain spiralled around his head before disappearing into the sky. Raising his right arm, the man waived dismissively at the clouds so full and spilling rain, which rapidly dispersed and cleared. As if on cue, a brilliant, dusk sky emerged.

The instantaneous stillness and quiet seemed overwhelming after the deafening din of the storm. Jonah, Tristan, and Ava slowly leaned back into their seats as the stranger approached.

"Lock the doors," Jonah ordered, and the others were quick to comply.

The man stopped about a metre or two in front of the car. Illuminated by the lights, he was clearly a handsome man. He appeared to be in his late forties to early fifties, with olive skin and thick black hair with a slight wave to it that framed his face. Jonah thought he detected a hint of grey. The stranger had a fit and muscular though slim appearance. He stared at them with an intense gaze, and they stared back.

"What the hell is he wearing?" Tristan asked through his teeth.

"It looks like a toga," Jonah replied, attempting the same stillness as he spoke.

"Who the hell gets around in a toga?"

"I guess he does."

"I hope you two don't intend on starting a career in ventriloquism!" the man called out with a bemused smile. The surprise of his voice stunned them into silence again.

The man shook his head and walked around to Tristan's side of the car. Jonah leaned back as Tristan pushed himself away from the window. After a few moments of standing outside, the man bent over to peer in at them. With eyebrows raised, he lifted his hand slowly in what would otherwise have been a comical gesture and rapped three times on the glass.

Tristan and Jonah stared back at him with wide eyes.

"Wind the window down," Ava hissed, nudging her brother. Tristan glanced at his sister before leaning forward to manually roll down the window, moving slowly with caution.

"So, how did you enjoy the storm?" the man enquired, flashing them a charming smile. Tristan just stared at him incredulously.

Jonah slowly peered from behind his mate's shoulder. "Can we help you?" he asked.

The man nodded. "Yes. We're going in the same direction, and I would like a ride, thank you." He gave a polite nod.

"How do you know we're heading in the same direction?" Ava asked.

"I would think it was fairly obvious, given the direction your car is facing," the man stated.

"Sorry, mate, but I have seen too many horror movies to give a stranger a lift. Do you want us to call you a cab or something?" Tristan offered.

"That would all be well and good, if I was in fact a stranger." The man paused, letting his statement hang in the air.

"Oh... kay. So then, who are you if you aren't a stranger? Considering I'm certain I've never seen you before."

"You haven't seen me before. But I have seen the three of you. Many times. Especially you, Jonah," he declared. Jonah balked.

"All right, guys. Can we just go, please?" Ava asked.

Tristan started the ignition. The man placed the palm of his hand flat against the bonnet of the car, and the engine died. "What the hell?" Tristan exclaimed and tried again. Nothing happened. He swore and banged the steering wheel.

The man let out a throaty chuckle.

"I'm glad you're so amused!" Tristan yelled. "Tell us who you are before I call the cops!" He grabbed his phone from the console.

"I am Zeus," the man stated with a courteous nod.

The trio just stared at him.

"Right..." Tristan said, turning his head toward the back seat while he stared at the man. "Ava, I think this is right up your alley..."

The man who called himself Zeus cut in before Ava had a chance to say anything. "That won't be necessary. I have no need for any psychological assessment, thank you."

"Hang on," Ava added. "How did you know I'm a psychologist?"

"I know you're a psychologist the same way I know Tristan is a music journalist and Jonah is a photographer."

"Dude, he knows our names," Tristan whispered to Jonah.

Jonah could only nod. He had the sensation that he had in fact seen this man before; he just couldn't place where and when, and he realised that was the most unsettling part.

"Okay, look," Ava started. "Whoever you are—"

"I told you, I am Zeus."

She sighed in frustration.

"Okay, then," Jonah intervened. "I'll play along. Zeus who?"

The man stepped back from the car and held his hands out to the side in a grand display. "Zeus!" he exclaimed, seemingly amazed by their lack of recognition. "King of the gods of Ancient Greece, Commander of Weather, Wielder of Lightning!" He paused to shoot Ava a wink. "And other weapons of greatness."

Jonah glared at him.

"Yeah, right, and I'm Batman," Tristan scoffed.

Zeus shook his head. "No. You're not. But you would have liked to be. You have ever since you were a boy, and while you'd never admit it, you're quite put out that your Batman watch hasn't worked since your encounter with Charon." Then the man stood fully and waited patiently for the stunned silence to break. "Look, do I have to prove it to you further?" he asked, his jaw visibly clenching.

"That you're Zeus—the god?" Jonah answered, not oblivious to how ridiculous that sounded. Zeus nodded. "How do you think you've proven this so far?"

Zeus rubbed his forehead in frustration. "Was the storm not proof enough of my power?"

"The storm? You have *got* to be kidding me," Jonah exclaimed. "We're in Brisbane. That's how storms are here."

"Yes, but that one I created. That was me!" Zeus bellowed.

"Of course it was," Jonah said wearily, leaning back into his seat and wishing they could just leave already.

"What other proof have you given us?" Ava asked from the back.

"I ended the storm." The man called Zeus motioned to the sky, then threw his hand toward the car's bonnet. "I stopped the engine in your car!"

"Pure coincidence," Jonah said. "Cars play up all the time. Who's to say the lightning strike that hit over there didn't mess something up with the electronics?"

Zeus roared in anger, making Tristan, Jonah, and Ava jump in startled unison. "How could you not know who I am? How could you turn out to be such imbeciles?" he yelled, then turned and thrust his arm out towards a giant gum tree. A bolt of blue-white heat shot from his hand and hurtled into the tree. The eucalyptus in the tree ignited, engulfing it in flames.

"Okay. I would say I'm convinced," Ava squeaked. The boys nodded.

Jonah leaned over Tristan to call out the window, clearing his throat nervously when he saw the residual fury in Zeus' eyes. "Um, so, slight problem. The car won't start, remember? You broke it…"

"Do you want him to blow the bloody thing up?" Tristan hissed.

Jonah sat back in his seat and stared out the windscreen. Zeus' fury seemed to dissipate almost as quickly as it had risen. He smiled jovially and stepped forward again to heartily tap the bonnet twice. The engine roared to life, sounding better than ever, and Tristan reached behind his seat to unlock the back door.

"Are we seriously letting him in?" Ava whispered fiercely, scooting over to the other side of the back seat behind Jonah.

"Do you really want to be the one to argue with him after *that* display?" Tristan asked from the corner of his mouth. Ava folded her arms.

Zeus climbed gracefully into the back, full of charm. "So, I believe we are off to your parents' house, then?"

Tristan just nodded as he slowly guided the car back onto the road.

THE DROVE IN silence for a while, trying to find an ounce of reality to which they could grab hold. Jonah gazed out the window and marvelled at how crystal-clear the early-evening sky appeared now that the storm had passed.

Once he relaxed a little, Tristan managed to steal a few glances through the rear-view mirror at their new passenger.

"If you have a question, Tristan, it is best just to ask it," Zeus commented without looking away from the window.

Tristan remained silent for a moment, and Ava and Jonah only watched him with curiosity. "So, you say you're Zeus," he started. "Well, shouldn't that mean you should look significantly older? You know, with a beard only rivalled by Santa?"

Zeus just smiled. "I have the luxury of appearing however I wish. Back in the time of Ancient Greece, older men were considered to be wise, educated, and authoritative. I find, now, that the heavily bearded, dominant, and almighty-god stereotype isn't as widely accepted. For all intents and purposes, I need to appear more approachable. So, I went for a slightly younger, fresh-faced look. I incorporated a touch of grey still to indicate that I am, in fact, old enough to know what I'm doing."

"So, what's with the dress, then?" Jonah asked, purposefully adding that little jab.

Zeus either didn't pick up on it or chose not to retaliate. "It's a toga. Given your love of ancient history, I know you are well aware of this. Besides, I like the way it's designed to let everything... hang... naturally." Zeus winked at Ava.

She pulled a face of disgust and tried to inch closer to the door.

"What did you just say?" Jonah turned around with a fierce gaze before thinking better of it and turning to Tristan instead. "Did you hear what he just said?"

Tristan just shrugged. "Dude, he's a god. Do you really want to have a go at him?"

Jonah shook his head before turning to scowl out the window. Zeus laughed, then ran his hand along the length of his toga. As he did so, the toga became a pair of jeans and a t-shirt, making him appear even younger still.

Music blasted through the car as Tristan's phone rang in the console. Jonah glanced down at it. "It's your folks," he stated.

"Can you answer it for me, please?" Tristan asked. "Mum's probably stressing about where we are after that storm." He slowed down to navigate the debris scattered all over the road.

Jonah picked up the phone. "Tristan?" Mallory asked. "Where are you guys? Did you get caught in the storm? Are you all okay?" Her voice came through with a mixture of concern and relief.

"Hi, Mallory," he said when he could finally get a word in. "This is Jonah. Tristan's just driving at the moment. We did get caught up in the storm, so Tristan pulled over until it passed."

Mallory let out a huge sigh. "Well, that was very sensible of him. How far away do you think you are?"

Jonah took a quick look around. "Well, I'd say five, maybe ten minutes normally, but there's a fair bit of debris on the road. It might take us a little longer."

"Okay, well, just drive safely. There's no hurry. We'll just see you when you get here."

"Oh, one more thing. We have an extra person with us."

"Not a problem. The more the merrier." Then Mallory hung up.

"The more the merrier my ass," Jonah muttered.

CHAPTER FOURTEEN

AS THEY PULLED into the driveway, the front door swung open. Mallory Carter stepped out onto the porch, her hands clenched together against her chest. Ava, not hiding her eagerness to get out of the car, was the first to reach her, followed by the boys. Zeus sauntered towards them, looking around at the neighbourhood.

"Come in, come in. You must be starving," Mallory said, hugging her daughter.

"You know me, Mum. I'm always starving." Tristan patted his stomach as he leaned over and kissed his mother's forehead before walking inside.

"Tristan! Aren't you going to introduce me to your guest?" she called out.

"They can do it," he yelled, making his way through the house. "I'm getting some beers!"

Mallory shook her head and turned toward the approaching stranger. The smile on her face froze. Jonah noticed the change in her immediately and exchanged confused glances with Ava.

"Hello, again," Zeus said with a charming smile, stepping past her and into the house.

Jonah's mouth fell open. "You know him?"

Mallory looked from Ava to Jonah and back again. "Well, off you go. Dinner isn't going to stay hot forever." She ushered them towards the door, but before they could enter, a voice called out from within.

"Where are you all? Tristan just informed me we have a—" Alex Carter's jovial voice cut short as Jonah assumed he'd run into his houseguest. Mallory stepped in front of Ava and Jonah and hurried inside to find her husband; the others followed at her heels. They found Alex standing in the living room, looking stunned as he gazed up at Zeus.

Zeus seemed completely unaffected by the reactions he caused, and with a smile, he extended his hand to Alex. "Wonderful to see you again, Alex." He shook the older man's hand within his own powerful grasp. "Dinner smells divine. I can't wait to eat." Then he walked on into the dining room.

Jonah caught the silent conversation Mallory and Alex shared, their eyes locked. Their ability to communicate this way had always amazed him. Finally, Alex gave his wife's shoulders a reassuring squeeze and turned toward the dining room. He seemed to only just realise Ava and Jonah were still standing there.

"Well, come on then, you two. Since when do either of you need a written invitation for dinner?" he chided.

They followed him into the dining room and sat on either side of Tristan, who lounged back in his chair, legs stretched out under the table, with a beer in his hand. Zeus had seated himself at the other end of the table and now watched them all with a bemused patience. Unimpressed, Jonah turned his attention instead to the cold beer Tristan had placed in front of him.

Ava cleared her throat. "Mum, do you need a hand?"

"No thanks, love. I'll be out in a minute."

Then Alex stepped out of the kitchen, wearing his most hospitable smile. "Can I get you something to drink?" he asked Zeus.

"I am partial to wine, thank you."

"Red or white?"

"You choose." Zeus gave a courteous nod.

Alex returned the gesture and turned to his daughter. "I'm easy, Dad," she said. "Whatever you open will be fine." Jonah couldn't help but notice how rigid Alex's smile had become. Ava turned to her brother. "Are you not in the least bit concerned about this?" she hissed.

Tristan shrugged. "What's the point of getting all worked up? Whatever it is, it'll play out, regardless."

"Jonah?" Ava asked.

Jonah didn't meet her gaze but only shrugged and picked at the label on his beer. He knew if he looked at her, she'd see he knew something. He wasn't ready to start explaining how familiar Zeus seemed—that Jonah was certain he'd seen the god before, a long time ago.

"Here we are!" Mallory entered with the first round of plates. Jonah thought she'd attempted her best Stepford-Wife impersonation. Alex set down the wineglasses before heading back into the kitchen to grab the remaining plates.

"Thank you," Zeus said, admiring the meal placed before him. He raised the glass to his nose and inhaled; a joyous smile spread across his face. He opened his eyes to see everyone staring at him. "Please, sit down and eat. It would be a shame to let it go cold," he declared, gesturing at them to continue.

Everyone dug in except for Jonah, who pushed the food around on his plate. Zeus' presence made him feel particularly anxious, and nerves made his stomach churn, destroying his appetite. In all the years he'd eaten at the Carters', not once had he experienced a silent meal.

Once Zeus had finished eating, the others all put down their cutlery, finished or not. Jonah got up without a word, and Tristan and Ava helped him clear the table. As he passed Alex and Mallory, he couldn't ignore the worried expressions threatening their smiles.

Zeus, still oblivious to the effect he had on them, complimented Alex on his wine selection. "It's been a long time since I've tasted such a nectar. You have no idea how immensely this pleases me."

"No trouble at all," Alex replied, the perfect host.

Once everyone had taken their seats again, Alex cleared his throat. "Now that we've eaten, I would like to clear up a couple things. First"—he turned to face Tristan, Ava and Jonah—"we apologise if our reaction to your guest appeared less than hospitable. It's just that we used to see quite a lot of this man, back when you were children." The three of them stared at him in surprise. Alex turned back to Zeus. "Though what I cannot understand is how you can be sitting here before us, not a day older than you were fifteen years ago."

Jonah thought he might choke. Zeus nodded sagely, considering the tabletop. "I'm not who I said I was fifteen years ago…"

"And who exactly was that supposed to be?" Jonah interrupted from the other end of the table.

Zeus looked straight at him. "After the accident that killed your parents, you moved in with your aunt. I posed as a social worker and visited both your aunt, when she was here, and Mallory and Alex about once a month or so. I did this until you were eighteen, when I felt the guise was no longer applicable."

Jonah was speechless.

"But that is not relevant at the moment." Zeus turned his gaze back to Mallory and Alex. "My name is Zeus. I am the chief deity of the Ancient Greek pantheon."

Alex and Mallory just stared at him, letting the information sink in. "The storm… That was *you*?" Alex asked, leaning forward over the table.

Zeus nodded. "I have been… away… for many years now. It takes a great deal of energy to return to the mortal realm. The storms I create produce the energy necessary for me to do so."

Once again, a brief silence followed until Alex began to applaud. "Marvellous!" he declared. "Absolutely marvellous!"

"Are you bloody serious, Dad?" Tristan asked.

"Watch your language, young man. You are in the presence of a god." Alex offered an embellished wave toward Zeus, and Tristan just shook his head. Jonah also had a hard time swallowing Alex's instantaneous acceptance.

"Mum?" Ava looked at her mother.

Mallory frowned slightly as she studied at Zeus. "Ava, I don't know how I know, but he is who he says he is. I can feel it."

Ava, Tristan, and Jonah exchanged looks, confused and unsure what to think. Alex and Mallory Carter had always been the smartest, most rational, most logical people Jonah had ever known. Yet their acceptance of the scene unfolding before them left him feeling nothing short of bewildered.

Zeus sipped his glass of wine and waited for everyone to process his news. Alex sat still, shooting Zeus excited glances from the corner of his eye. Mallory sat just as still, shooting worried glances at the other end of the table. Tristan leaned back in his chair, one arm flung over the back as he gazed up at the ceiling. Jonah glared at Zeus, anger gnawing at him, though he was unsure why, while Ava's brow furrowed in agitated concentration. She was the first to break the silence.

"Okay. So, I don't think I can buy into the whole god story right this second, despite your display earlier. Regardless of that, why were you keeping tabs on Jonah all those years? And what the hell are you doing here now?" All eyes turned to Zeus.

"As for your first question, now is not the time for that to be answered. As for your second question, surely you cannot be surprised. You had been told I was coming, after all," Zeus said.

Ava frowned, her mouthing popping open a little, like she tried far too hard to figure out what Zeus was talking about. All eyes were now on her, except for Jonah's. He watched Zeus stare at Ava and give her a small nod. The man calling himself a god almost seemed to read her thoughts before confirming for her that she was on the right track.

"Caitlyn?" she whispered. "You're the man who appeared in her dream?" Zeus nodded. "You bastard!" Everyone but Zeus looked at her in surprise. "Do you have any idea what you've done to that girl? What you've put her through? Put *me* through?"

Zeus raised his hands in defence. "Ava, I assure you, I did nothing to those girls. Caitlyn and the others like her come from a long line of Oracle tradition, originating at Delphi. But again, we are getting side-tracked with details best explained another day. We have more pressing matters to discuss and very little time," he replied with a dismissive wave of his hand.

"I don't care about your pressing matters," Ava yelled, jumping to her feet. "All I'm interested in is how to help Caitlyn before you destroy her completely!"

Zeus was out of his chair faster than a blink. He leaned down, banged his fist angrily on the table, and roared, "Sit down!" The lights flickered, and the air itself audibly crackled with electricity. "You will listen to what I have to tell you, and you will not interrupt me again! Do you understand?" He stared her down, fury flashing in his eyes.

Once again, Zeus' anger dissipated as quickly as it had appeared, though he still leaned on the table with his head bent low. Without thinking, Jonah leaned forward and touched Ava gently on the arm, wanting to make sure she was okay. She gave him a half smile of unconvincing reassurance.

Zeus raised his head, gazing at each of them before speaking. "I cannot understand how my being here is so hard for all of you to comprehend, especially after everything you have witnessed in recent days. However, there is no time to ease your mortal minds into it. I must push forward, regardless of your conviction, for it has no effect on the gravity of the situation. Events will continue to unfold, either way." He paused, considering the best way to proceed. "Alex, am I right in saying you have identified the entities encountered thus far as the Fates and the Erinyes?"

Alex nodded, trying to conceal his pride. "That's right. As well as identifying the Oracles, Charon, and the potential influence of one, and possibly more, of the Muses," he added.

Zeus nodded, obviously pleased by this confirmation. He stood, frowning down at the table in front of him before turning his gaze to the far end of the table. "And am I correct in saying you three had another encounter today?" Jonah, Tristan, and Ava gave a simultaneous nod.

"Really?" Alex asked, sounding disappointed to have been kept out of the loop. "Why didn't you tell us?"

"Gee, I don't know, Dad. Perhaps we got side-tracked by almost getting electrocuted in a storm," Tristan retorted. "Or by having a god over for dinner."

"If I had intended to strike you down, I would, in fact, have done so," Zeus stated. Tristan turned to Jonah and rolled his eyes. "Jonah," Zeus continued, "we have heard very little out of you this evening. Would you care to elaborate on this afternoon's encounter?"

Jonah stared back at him for a few moments before diverting his attention towards Alex and Mallory. He filled them in on what had happened at the pool. It felt like it had happened days ago, not a matter of hours. Alex and Mallory couldn't hide their bewildered expressions as they scrolled through the photos he had taken. Feeling Zeus' intense stare, Jonah looked up, frowned in discomfort, and averted his gaze again.

"I must say that, without having to revert to some books, I can't honestly determine who or what they are," Alex said with a mixture of confusion and excitement.

"Could they be some kind of merfolk?" Mallory wondered aloud.

"You mean like mermaids?" Tristan piped up. Mallory nodded. "Awesome. Just our luck to encounter dude mermaids. How come we couldn't find the hot, female variation? You know, with the little seashell bikinis?" He almost sounded disgusted.

Jonah couldn't help himself and burst out laughing at his mate's dramatic languishing. Even Zeus himself appeared amused. "Because they weren't merfolk," the god said.

"Though I see how it was the obvious assumption." Zeus offered a jovial nod of appreciation towards Mallory.

"So, who are they?" Alex asked.

"They are called the Abgal," Zeus declared, moving around the table. "Their origin is Sumerian, from the ancient lands of Mesopotamia. The Cradle of Civilisation."

"Does that mean they predate even you?" Ava enquired, her question also a half jibe.

Zeus seemed oblivious to the cloaked insult. Instead, he only nodded. "They are a form of demigod and are known to be extremely wise. Half man, half fish, they have evolved over centuries the ability to conceal their true form. This enables them to move amongst mortals undetected. The Abgal are dedicated servants to the god Enki. They were responsible for teaching mankind the sacred laws and morals of civilisation, among other things. There are seven of them in total: Adapa, Uan-dugga, En-me-duga, En-me-galena, En-me-buluga, An-Enlida, and Utu-abzu—"

"Repeat that five times fast," Tristan muttered, and Jonah grinned. Alex gave them both a sharp glance.

Zeus didn't seem to notice. "They are protective guardians, and the fact that you saw them today—all seven of them—was in no way an accident. It certainly confirms the fact that things are far more ominous than we had originally suspected."

"Guardians of what?" Mallory asked.

"What ominous things?" Jonah demanded.

Zeus took a deep breath, opting to answer Mallory first. "They are guardians of the Tablet of Destinies. This was entrusted to them by the god Enki many centuries ago." He turned to Jonah. "The fact that they made themselves known to you means the security of the Tablet has been compromised."

"Compromised by whom? How? Where? Why?" Alex asked with obvious enthusiasm.

"By the Fates. I can't say much more until I have spoken to the others. There are a lot of whispers at the moment… but very little is known for sure."

"Hang on, the Fates—the women with the red hair we've been seeing?" Ava asked. "I take it their possession of the Tablet of Destinies is a bad thing."

Zeus nodded, the corners of his mouth drawn in a morose frown. "If the Fates gain possession of it, they have the power to rid the world of mankind. Permanently."

Everyone stared at him in horror. "Well, can't you stop them?" Ava asked. "I mean, you are a god, after all. Aren't you?"

With a long sigh, Zeus gazed down into the wineglass, turning it on the table in front of him. It surprised Jonah to see that the god appeared to struggle with the concept of existing limitations to his powers.

"Perhaps I can be of help here," Alex offered. Zeus nodded without lifting his gaze. "The Fates are primordial in origin. This means they have existed since the very beginning. Long before gods and man came about. Therefore, they exist above and beyond both."

"What does that mean, exactly?" Jonah asked, struggling to remain patient.

Alex looked to Zeus, who still only gazed into his wineglass. "Gods exist because man exists, and vice versa. They rely on the mutual belief in each other to sustain that existence. What makes the Fates such a dangerous force is that they will continue to exist, regardless of what happens to the human race. Or their deities."

Zeus finally raised his head and gazed around the table, ensuring each of them now grasped exactly what was at stake for all of them.

Jonah cleared his throat. "So let me see if I have this right. The Tablet of Destinies was hidden. Now it isn't, and the Fates know this and are trying to get their hands on it. If they do, they will use it to destroy all mankind and gods alike. Is that pretty accurate?"

Zeus and Alex nodded in unison. Tristan swore softly under his breath while Mallory reached for her husband's hand where it rested on the table.

"Well, you have some kind of plan, right?" Ava asked. "Why else would you be here?"

"In a manner of speaking, yes," Zeus finally answered. "But before I explain anything further, I need to gather the other gods."

"There are more of you here?" Alex asked, losing all ability to withhold his delight despite the dire circumstances.

Zeus nodded, a small smile tugging at the side of his mouth. "Of course. There are a number of us, actually. Or at least there will be. Right now, three have returned to this plane, awaiting my word."

"For what, a written invitation?" Tristan joked.

"Essentially, yes," Zeus retorted, ignoring the jest. "I was fairly certain the situation would be overwhelming enough for you all with only one of us. So it was decided that I would approach you first before collecting the others."

"By all means, go and collect them!" Alex exclaimed. "May I ask who they are?"

"You will just have to wait and see," Zeus teased. Still standing, he looked around at the others, as if he made some calculation just by the sight of them. Before he could do or say anything, loud voices talking over one another echoed from the lounge room.

Everyone dashed from the table to find out what was going on. Confusion turned to awe as, once in the room, they realised nobody was actually there. Instead, the television blared, along with the radio and the computer.

Ava stepped forward to turn them off. Jonah reached out and gently grabbed her, telling her silently to leave them on. As he moved closer to the television, the station automatically changed from one news report to the next. There was barely enough time for Jonah to catch what was being said before it switched again. Mallory and Alex moved towards the stereo, bending down so their heads were closer to each side of the speakers, their faces mirroring each other's grave concern. Tristan and Ava glanced at each other before moving towards the computer. Open windows alternated between live news coverage, YouTube clips, and updated news bulletins.

The noise intensified when each of their phones suddenly buzzed and beeped all at once, also displaying news updates and footage. Jonah turned to see what Zeus made of the racket, but the god just stood in the middle of the room. He folded his arms tersely across his chest and stared up at the ceiling, completely unreadable. Annoyed by the god's apparent lack of concern, Jonah turned his attention back to the television to try making sense of what was being said.

"...Authorities the world over struggle to determine the cause of the deaths of thousands of prison inmates. The official statement was originally suicide. Yet given the significant number of deaths and the varied locations, this explanation seems insufficient. We can only assume there is something far more sinister at hand..."

Over by the radio, Mallory motioned for him to listen.

"...In another bizarre turn of events, a large number of boats have vanished into thin air. The first known disappearance occurred only two nights ago, after a ferry broke down in the middle of the Brisbane River. The only known witness to the event, ferry driver Simon Colt, told authorities he received assistance from another ferry shortly after the breakdown. According to Mr Colt, all one hundred and twenty passengers had transferred to the new ferry while he stayed behind. While Mr Colt insists there was nothing untoward about the second ferry driver, neither the driver, the ferry, nor any of the passengers have been seen since.

"Following this initial disappearance, a multitude of boats and ships have been reported missing, including three large naval ships and four ocean liners. Despite thorough search efforts, the vessels seem to have vanished without a trace, taking their passengers with them..."

Shaking his head in disbelief, Alex turned off the radio. The Jonah joined Alex and Mallory in returning to the television as it jumped to another station.

"... Police are imploring the public to come forward if anyone has any information about the mysterious woman. The woman in question has been linked to a startling number of suspicious deaths in a matter of days. The increasing frequency of incidents has authorities in a tailspin..."

Tristan swore, and everyone turned toward him. A YouTube clip played in a loop on the computer—footage shot from land and submitted from someone's phone. The camera aimed up at a huge cruise ship as it pulled away from the dock. Passengers smiled and waved to friends and loved ones on land. The footage skipped forward until the ship had begun its voyage out towards the ocean. Then it shimmered. *"That's weird,"* the owner of the phone commented before a strange hum sounded. It was low at first but steadily climbed higher in pitch and volume. Then the cruise ship vanished. A brief, stunned silence followed as the crowd struggled to process what they had just seen. Then the shouts and screams started. This was soon followed by the rapid onset of hysteria and confusion before the footage cut back to the beginning.

"Unbelievable," Alex murmured, leaning closer to the screen, as if he would be able to somehow see more.

Zeus took a deep breath, closed his eyes, and exhaled sharply. He thrust his fingertips outwards, sending sparks of blue light towards all the electronics. The room went silent when everything immediately shut off.

"I take it misplacing the remote control has never been an issue for you?" Tristan asked with a grin. Mallory playfully slapped her son on the arm, and Jonah chuckled.

Zeus simply raised his hands, looking as though he were about to present them with something. He inhaled deeply and closed his eyes. They braced themselves for what they assumed would be more fireworks. Instead, Zeus let his breath out slowly and, to everyone's amazement, began to vibrate. As the speed of his vibration increased, the room itself moved with it.

Jonah had to close his eyes as the sight of his own hands shaking so quickly made him nauseas. Despite that, he was still all too aware of Ava's hand firmly gripping his forearm. He opened his mouth to call out for Zeus to stop, but before he could form the words, an odd hum filled the air around him. A bright flash shot across the room, and Jonah flung his free arm up over his eyes.

It was over almost as quickly as it had started. Jonah lowered his arm again, and his mouth fell open in a mixture of confusion and amazement.

They were no longer in the Carters' living room.

CHAPTER FIFTEEN

"**A**WESOME!" TRISTAN EXCLAIMED in appreciation of their new surroundings.

Jonah, feeling light-headed, looked at Zeus and caught the god's failed attempt to hide his pride. He turned to Ava, wanting to make sure she was all right; she stared up at him in wide-eyed bewilderment—a look he was fairly certain mirrored his own.

They now stood on an interior balcony inside the most extravagant nightclub Jonah had ever seen.

"It looks like *The Moulin Rouge* and *The Great Gatsby* got together and had a gothic love child…" Ava stated, clearly as impressed as the others—a feat in itself.

Jonah smiled at her astute description before turning to admire the scenery. As much as he didn't want to give Zeus the satisfaction, he had to admit it was impressive. Ambient music pulsated through the club, and everywhere he looked he saw people—standing with cocktails, lounging, dancing, or simply admiring the entertainers on display.

The group spread out along the balcony railing, all vying for a better view of the enticing spectacle playing out beneath them. Jonah gazed around the room. Enthralled, he watched a couple of fire-twirlers on a raised beam and a man juggling knives on one end of the bar. His attention then turned towards the dancers on platforms. They were spectacularly dressed in 1920's flapper-style outfits, their headbands bejeweled and feathered, their dark, smoky eyes and ruby-red lips adding an extra edge to the room. Bare-chested men in leather pants circled the room to collect empty glasses, and a bald-headed man sat in an illuminated alcove, stroking a peacock. Tristan's voice interrupted Jonah's engrossed observations.

"Now, Zeus, it's not that I'm not appreciative... but what are we doing in a nightclub..." He stopped talking to ogle a stunning, corseted woman walking beneath them. Once she had stepped out of view, he added, "And where are we? Because I think I would like to come back..."

"London," was all Zeus said.

"Why did you bring us all the way to London to go to a nightclub?" Ava inquired.

Zeus didn't reply but simply held his finger to his lips, gesturing for them to be quiet as a smirk played across his face. He redirected their gaze back to the scene below them. The others curiously stared down and tried to follow his gesture, hoping to see what it was he expected. Their anticipation grew as the ambient music faded out, and Marilyn Manson's cover of 'Sweet Dreams' played.

Tristan slapped Jonah on the back in his enthusiasm for the song choice, then turned back towards the club. Jonah couldn't resist returning the smile, easily caught up in his mate's fervour. Across from them on the far side of the club, a shimmering, beaded curtain of Swarovski crystals parted slowly, as though drawn by invisible hands. They leaned forward to see who would walk through, and Zeus stood back slightly, still within full view, his arms folded across his chest.

Then out she stepped.

The woman's appearance was just as dramatic as the nightclub itself—slim but with curves further accentuated by the black leather corset binding her tightly and the long, flowing black tulle and organza skirt covered in tiny silver crystals. The effect was intense; she looked like she had reached up into the starry night sky and draped herself in it. The leather platform-stiletto pumps in which she effortlessly moved created the illusion of lofty height. Her tousled black curls piled delicately upon her head, random tendrils escaping the twin crystal headband she wore, opting instead to gracefully frame her delicate face. With eyes sparkling in playfulness, her sensual mouth curled upwards to one side, forming the smirk of someone perfectly aware of her own effect on those around her.

As she walked, heads of both men and women alike turned in her wake. Sexuality emanated from her; everything about her was seductive, yet there was nothing arrogant in her demeanor—nothing forced, nothing tasteless. In silence, everyone watched her until she passed under the platform and out of sight.

"Are we enjoying the scenery?" the woman enquired, suddenly appearing behind Jonah and his group. They jumped, startled by the impossibility of her rapid ascent. She ignored their stunned silence and stepped towards Zeus, who met her with his arms outstretched in greeting.

"Inanna! I'm pleased to see you are your usual, vibrant self," he exclaimed. They clasped forearms and kissed each other on both cheeks.

"Now, Zeus." She leaned back to look at him, still firmly grasping his strong forearms. "I have to admit, this more youthful, modern look is very becoming on you. Not that I didn't think you were the most handsome of the gods in your previous form."

Zeus flashed her a brilliant smile. "Apparently, togas are very last-season." He winked, then released their clasp and turned to face their awed onlookers. "This is the goddess Inanna," he announced before turning back to the her. "And Inanna, please meet Jonah Sands and Alex, Mallory, Tristan, and Ava Carter."

Inanna nodded politely and smiled at each of them, taking a few extra moments to run her gaze over Tristan and Jonah. Jonah felt a flush rise in his face at her obvious approval of them. Tristan, on the other hand, took on his most masculine stance and grinned, clearly relishing in the attention. The goddess smiled a slow, sensual smile, then turned to Zeus and whispered something low to him.

Now that Inanna's attention no longer remained on Tristan, Jonah noticed his friend turning back toward the stage and the new song playing. But Jonah himself was far more focused on Zeus. The god turned his back on them as he spoke to Inanna. She was silent but clearly listened intently; her gaze flickered between Zeus' face, to Jonah, and then back again. The playfulness she had displayed earlier had dimmed somewhat, and she now expressed a serious-looking concern.

Annoyed by the fact that they were obviously discussing him, Jonah attempted nonchalance and turned his attention to Ava. She said nothing but attempted another reassuring smile, also aware that Jonah was the hot topic of conversation. Finally, Zeus cleared his throat and turned to face the group.

"We're done here. Time to head back," he announced.

"You mean, now that you've wrapped up your little secret meeting over there?" Jonah questioned. He felt Ava's hand on his back—a gentle warning he chose to ignore.

Zeus clenched his jaw and stared hard at Jonah, who only stared back, unflinching. The god appeared to consider whether or not to retort. Inanna placed her hand on Zeus' back, unconsciously mirroring Ava's stance to keep the peace. He turned his head ever so slightly to acknowledge her before facing forward again and closing his eyes. He raised his arms, and Jonah braced his stomach as the world around him rapidly vibrated again.

JONAH SENSED THEY were no longer in the club, primarily due to the sudden absence of noise. Regardless, he kept his eyes firmly shut until the wave of nausea passed.

"Dude, I swear that was even worse than the last time," Tristan moaned, bracing himself against the wall. Jonah slowly opened his eyes to see they had returned to the Carters' lounge room, all looking slightly ill—except for Zeus and Inanna.

Zeus stood in what Jonah now referred to as his god stance—legs slightly apart, arms crossed authoritatively against his chest, and a frown etched across his brow as he waited for them to recover. Inanna strolled around the lounge room, touching objects that drew her attention. She spoke without looking at them. "You feel nauseous because you're mortal. Your bodies are too firmly fixed to the physical world. Therefore, teleporting you even for relatively short distances disrupts your physiological and chemical makeup."

"What does that mean, exactly?" Alex queried.

"Well, it means that doing so is not without consequences. For you."

"What kind of consequences?" Ava asked slowly.

Inanna turned to face them, her attention drawn instantly to Mallory. "Well, that would be one, for starters."

They turned to see Mallory sitting on the couch, oblivious to the fact that her nose had started bleeding. She touched her upper lip and looked surprised to find blood on her fingertips.

"Mum!" Ava exclaimed and jumped for the tissues on the coffee table. Alex turned his wife's face towards him as he put his other arm protectively around her shoulders.

"I'm fine. It's only a little bloody nose," Mallory remarked, trying to put them at ease.

Yet Jonah saw the look of surprise darting across Zeus' face and instantly knew there was more to it. "Why is her nose bleeding?" he asked in a low voice.

Zeus looked to Inanna, who stared back at him with concern before giving him a small shrug and a slight shake of her head. Zeus cleared his throat. "Well, like Inanna said, your bodies aren't equipped to handle teleportation. Doing so incurs damage to your physical selves, which is why your nausea was worse the second time around."

"So you didn't think warning us beforehand was worth your time?" Jonah muttered through a scowl. God or not, Zeus certainly rubbed him the wrong way.

"We didn't have the time to get into it. There would have been too many questions. You saw and heard all those updates. You know what's going on. So you just have to accept that there are going to be decisions I will have to make that I won't be able to run by you. Deal with it," Zeus growled.

"Deal with it? Deal with it?" Jonah raged, stepping aggressively toward the god. "I don't care who the hell you are, but you have no right coming here and treating us like mindless puppets. If our lives are going to be at risk in any way, then you damn well better *make* the time to explain yourself. Or—"

"Or what?" Zeus cut in with a low, menacing tone, daring him to continue.

Jonah said nothing but didn't back down. Instead, he maintained his stance and steely glare, noting the Carters' complete surprise when the room fell deadly silent. Zeus gave off bursts of visible, electric sparks, like static.

"Now, now, gentlemen," Inanna cooed, moving toward them. She forced them apart enough to allow herself to step between them and intersected Jonah's gaze. "Fighting amongst ourselves is something I will not tolerate. I understand your concerns, so sit down, and I will answer any questions you have," she promised, giving him a gentle push.

"Whatever," Jonah muttered as he turned and strode towards the couch. "Wouldn't want him to short-circuit or anything."

The Carters sat and stared at Jonah and his uncharacteristic behaviour. Inanna turned towards Zeus, who still sparked, and forced him to meet her eyes. She gently lowered his arms from their tightly crossed position over his chest. Once she had his undivided attention, she whispered so softly, the others couldn't make it out. Zeus closed his eyes, and she ran her hands from his shoulders slowly down to his fingertips. The sparking ceased, and he opened his eyes to look up at the Carters—avoiding Jonah's gaze.

"I apologise that I did not forewarn you all. Mallory, how is your nosebleed?" he asked with genuine concern.

She lowered the tissues from her face. "I honestly think it's been stunned into cessation."

Zeus gave her a small smile. "A silver lining, nonetheless."

"Is this the worst we can expect?" Alex asked, his arm still firmly around his wife.

Zeus sighed and rubbed the bridge of his nose. "Inanna can probably explain it better." He stepped aside and gestured for her to continue.

"In all honesty, we would have anticipated you could undergo a number of instances without experiencing anything more than nausea, the very worst-case scenario being a severe headache not unlike a bad hangover. To experience a nosebleed after only the second transition was completely unexpected. If Zeus had thought for a moment there was any chance of this happening, I am sure he would have advised you." Inanna paused, directing her gaze at Jonah, which he ignored. "However," she continued, "it has been a great many centuries since we have performed such tasks in this realm, and while we knew the distance travelled played a significant role, there are a number of other variables we hadn't taken into consideration."

"Like what?" Tristan asked.

"Well, for example, environmental disturbances, the increase in radiation, altered magnetic fields…"

"What is the worst possible outcome if we continue to do it?"Ava interjected.

"Death," Inanna said bluntly, seeming annoyed at having been interrupted. "Yours, not ours, of course. Most likely it would be the result of a massive brain hemorrhage."

Mallory and Alex gasped. "Does this mean… Will I…" Mallory managed to squeak.

"No." Zeus stepped toward her. "You would probably have passed on already if that were the case. However, the fact that you did have a nosebleed means you won't be accompanying us on any further trips." Mallory nodded meekly.

"How about none of us accompany you?" Jonah proposed.

Zeus opened to his mouth to snap a retort but was instead halted by Inanna's hand on his arm. "Obviously," she replied instead, "when there are other options, we utilise them, despite the time it may cost us. Essentially, having you with us when we teleport is like supplying us with batteries. Your individual magnetic fields enable us to move faster and more precisely. But that's not to say that, in a little time, we won't be able to do so with just the two of us. And even solo."

"Batteries?" Ava scoffed. "Nice."

"What do you mean by 'in a little time'?" Tristan asked.

"Well, we aren't at our full capacity of power just yet. Unfortunately, it takes time for our abilities to completely transition when we cross over."

"Which is probably lucky for you," Tristan murmured to Jonah, who just ignored him and kept scowling.

"How many more of these 'retrievals' still need to occur?" Alex enquired.

Inanna and Zeus stared at each other, as if having a telepathic conversation. "A few," answered Zeus. "However, we may only need to retrieve two more using the teleportation. Once we have them here, we may be able to utilise a different method." He stared at Inanna, and her eyes lit up as she realised what he was thinking.

"Of course. I think we could pull that off, and we probably won't lose any time, either. That means we can also afford to leave the retrievals until tomorrow, allow time for some recuperation," she suggested. It was more of an olive branch extended to the group to obtain their compliance than any real desire to accommodate them. Much to everyone's relief, Zeus nodded.

"And here I was, thinking time was of the essence," a voice said from the hallway.

CHAPTER SIXTEEN

ATROPOS STEPPED INTO the doorway, her slender arms folded casually across her chest. Zeus and Inanna quickly placed themselves between her and the others. "Atropos," Zeus growled.

"Wondering how neither of you managed to sense my presence? Hmm… you must be far weaker than you had anticipated," she mocked. "I have been grounded far longer, not to mention my powers have strengthened the more I've used them, and I've put them to good use" She paused, lifting her delicate chin towards the gods as a small smile played on the corner of her mouth. "And, of course, there are three of us." Clotho and Lachesis stepped out from either side of the entryway and stood slightly behind their sister.

Now that Jonah saw the sisters together, he noticed the subtle differences in their appearances. Surprised, he realised it was from a complete lack of fear that he had been able to notice anything at all. He glanced towards Ava, whose previous encounters with the Fates had also been terrifying, only to find her expression mirroring his own. Turning back to where the stand-off continued, he wondered what the hell was going on.

"What matters of chaos have you removed yourselves from in order to grace us with your presence?" Inanna asked haughtily, her hands placed firmly on her hips, demanding full attention.

Irritation and boiling resentment flashed across Atropos' face. "Inanna, I am offended that you would not think us polite enough to welcome you back," she replied with feigned sincerity. Her sisters smirked.

"Well now, that is very courteous of you, Atropos. Now, will you reveal the real reason you are here, and then kindly leave?" Inanna demanded regally.

Zeus simply stood there, and while Jonah couldn't see his face, he sensed the god's scowl served as a warning to each of the redhaired sisters.

"Pace yourself, Inanna. There will be plenty of time for power struggles. We have no ulterior motive. At least, not any on which we care to act today. We simply wanted to show you all how... simple... it is for us to welcome you here, in this house. Well, any house, really. I like to think we are rather considerate that way." Her sisters turned to leave.

Atropos smiled eerily at Zeus and Inanna before following her sisters, but not before one last dig, as she turned her head back towards them. "If you think you can prevent us from possessing the Tablet of Destinies..." She shook her head and clicked her tongue in disapproval before turning her back to them completely.

Then they were gone.

Zeus turned to Inanna. "We cannot wait until tomorrow." She simply nodded, and they both turned to face the group, waiting for the argument. There was none. Zeus stared hard at Jonah, who returned the gesture and would not let the god read his emotions.

"I feel fine, now. I'm sure I would be okay to go again," Mallory offered to resounding shouts of protest from everyone, gods included.

"No, honey, we aren't risking it," Alex said gently to his wife, seeing her startled and slightly offended reaction to their forceful rejection. She looked up at him and smiled before leaning her head on his shoulder.

"So, how will it work this time? I don't want Mum left behind on her own after those bloody psychotic chicks made it perfectly clear they'll pop in whenever they damn well feel like it," Tristan stated.

"Tristan, watch your mouth," Alex exclaimed in alarm.

"Why?" he asked.

"Well… I don't know. What if they can somehow hear you?" Mr Carter replied. Tristan and Jonah glanced quickly about the room.

"Somehow, I think that if they could, they would have found that to be a compliment," Tristan scoffed.

"You're probably not wrong," Zeus replied. "However, I do agree. Inanna, I think it would be wise if you stayed here with Mallory and Alex. I will take the others with me to collect Enki and Isis."

"Enki and Isis," exclaimed Alex, almost jumping off the couch in his excitement before looking at his wife. Jonah felt bad for him, as he was clearly torn between his devotion to his wife and wanting to meet two of his favourite deities.

"Don't worry, Alex. We will bring them straight back here. You won't miss out on meeting them. In fact, I will probably have them spend the night here," Zeus advised.

Alex gasped. "Enki and Isis! Can you believe it? And under our very own roof." He turned to Mallory, who smiled at him before planting an affectionate kiss on his cheek.

Jonah couldn't help the smile spreading with warmth across his face at Alex's childlike enthusiasm.

"So the three of us are to go with you, then? Will that be enough... ah, well, battery power for you?" Ava asked as diplomatically as she could.

"It will have to be," Zeus remarked. "There is no other way." He turned to Inanna for confirmation.

Absently running her fingertips across her full lips, she paused. Jonah didn't know whether they should wait for her to speak or not. Finally, she reached up and unhinged the clasp of the long silver necklace hanging around her neck. She walked toward Ava, who blinked and took a small step back when the goddess encroached upon her personal space. Inanna reached her arms around Ava's neck and re-clasped the necklace at the back.

Ava fingered the eight-pointed star hanging from the necklace and looked up at the goddess, awaiting an explanation.

"The eight-pointed star represents Venus. My talisman and, in a manner of speaking, my essence. It will give you an extra kick."

"How come she gets to wear it?" Tristan asked, playfully trying to touch it as Ava fended him off.

"Surely you aren't suggesting I would place it around the neck of a man, are you?" Inanna asked incredulously.

Tristan paused mid-grab as he looked at the serious, unsmiling line of Inanna's mouth. He cleared his throat. "Uh... no?"

"Well, now that that's settled, we should go," Zeus said, beckoning Ava, Tristan and Jonah toward him. He leaned into Inanna and said in a low voice, "Be on alert. We don't want to underestimate the sisters, and you aren't at your full capacity yet."

"I will be fine. We will be fine. And what would they gain by returning again so soon?" Inanna shrugged before giving him an encouraging shove towards the others.

Ava stood between Tristan and Jonah, all three of them now facing Mallory and Alex on the couch and Inanna standing behind them. Jonah smiled at the excitement and anticipation on Alex's face and the worry and anxiety on Mallory's.

Ava blew them a reassuring kiss before grabbing ahold of both Tristan and Jonah's hands. Jonah looked down—a surge ran up the length of his arm, a direct current to his heart—before forcing his gaze forward again. Zeus stood behind them. As everything shook violently around him, he saw Mallory and Alex blow them kisses in farewell.

Jonah closed his eyes and braced himself.

He doubled over, propping his hands against his legs as simultaneous waves of nausea hit him. When they subsided, he slowly picked up on the sounds around him. He sensed quite a lot of people, but they seemed to be talking in hushed tones—reverent, even. Everything echoed, giving Jonah the impression they were in a long, open space.

He forced himself to take a deep breath, then opened his eyes. Surprised, he found Ava standing casually next to Zeus. She clearly tried to determine where they were based on the little information provided by the stark white passageway in which they stood. She turned to Jonah with a smile.

"It must be Inanna's necklace," she said. "I feel fine. Not sick at all!"

"Yeah. It's bloody brilliant to be some people." Tristan moaned and slowly paced, his hands behind his head as he tried to walk off the nausea. All Jonah could muster was a quick smile in response, as he didn't quite trust himself to open his mouth and not be sick.

"Okay. I give up. Where are we?" Ava asked Zeus.

"Berlin. The Pergamon Museum."

"I have always wanted to come here," Jonah exclaimed. He stood up again in his excitement, struck with both realisation and nausea. "Ishtar's Gate!" Ava and Tristan looked at him blankly. Zeus nodded, then closed his eyes and tilted his head, frowning in concentration, as if he were trying to hear.

Ava gestured impatiently for Jonah to elaborate further. "Ishtar's Gate is one of seven gates that were part of the wall of Babylon, which in turn was one of the original Seven Wonders of the World."

"So how did you know this gate is the reason we're here?" asked Tristan as he came to a slow stop in his pacing.

"Well, Zeus said Enki was one of the gods we needed to retrieve and, like Inanna, he's from the Mesopotamian pantheon. Babylon was a great city of Mesopotamia, so it's only logical to assume that, if he's waiting for us here, that would be where to find him."

"Oh. Naturally…" Tristan exclaimed with feigned understanding.

"This way," Zeus announced and walked past them at a rapid pace.

Ava, Tristan, and Jonah glanced at each other before hurrying after him. He was already some distance ahead and hard to keep track of amongst the crowd. Jonah stole longing yet fleeting glances at the displays while he scurried past them. They rounded the corner and momentarily forgot about pursuing

Zeus as Ishtar's Gate loomed up before them. Even Tristan gaped in awe at the deep blue stone, the golden depictions of animals, and the magnificence of the arch.

"Wow," Tristan whispered.

"Can you imagine seeing that rising up out of the desert at you?" Jonah asked, mesmerised.

"It's so beautiful," Ava whispered.

Tristan broke the spell by nodding at Jonah, then jerking his head toward where Zeus embraced a man they assumed to be the god Enki. The trio slowly made their way to the pair of gods, not wanting to intrude on the reunion.

Enki was similar to Zeus in height and build, though with a slightly more olive complexion. His raven hair fell in long waves, resting just below his shoulders. He wore a plain, white linen shirt, loose-fitting, quite long, and cut in a V at the front over a pair of matching pants. A simple pair of sandals covered his feet, and he radiated calm. As he turned in anticipation at their approach, Jonah was surprised to see that the god's eyes were the same stunning blue as the wall behind him.

Introductions were swift, as Zeus made no secret of the fact that he was eager to move on as soon as possible. Enki walked through the barrier and up to the Ishtar Gate and placed his palms flat against the wall before leaning his forehead against it. Jonah looked around them, surprised to hear no alarms sounding or see any security come running.

Zeus stood back respectfully as the other god whispered for a few moments, his eyes closed. When he was ready, Enki stepped back and looked up at the wall's beauty, his eyes full of sadness, as if he said farewell to a beloved friend. He then turned to Zeus and nodded.

Zeus turned and hurriedly made his way back to the passageway in which they had arrived, and Enki effortlessly kept up the rapid pace. Jonah, Tristan, and Ava were forced into a semi-jog in order to keep up. Jonah clutched his sore ribs, ignoring the concerned glances Ava shot his way. They had barely staggered into the passageway before Zeus vibrated again. Jonah felt the wave of nausea hit him, now stronger than ever. He felt himself falling forward and instinctively reached out to brace himself for impact. He landed on his hands and knees in what felt like sand before his stomach heaved violently and the nausea finally won over.

"Oh, dude, that's brutal."

Jonah opened his eyes. He wiped his mouth with the back of one hand and nursed his tender ribs with the other. Looking beside him, he saw Tristan lying on his back in what was indeed sand, grinning up at his mate with amused disgust. Jonah was fairly certain he detected a hint of green in Tristan's face, too, under the bright light provided by the full moon. "What the hell?" he exclaimed in belated surprise. "Nighttime?"

"Apparently," Tristan said and slowly raised himself up onto his elbows.

"There you two are," Ava said, approaching them with a cheery smile. "I think we got a little thrown apart that time. Probably on account of the rush. How beautiful is this place?"

"I am unable to comment, on account of throwing my guts up. Sorry," Jonah moaned, the memory of it making him dry-heave.

Ava shot him a pitying frown as she toyed with Inanna's talisman. They all looked up to see Enki and Zeus come from behind some trees to their right, walking along the sand. The gods, engrossed in their conversation, moved across the beach in front of the trio, then passed them completely before disappearing around more trees.

"Do you lot need a written invitation?" Zeus called out.

Ava and Tristan both smiled, while Jonah just rolled his eyes in annoyance. They quickly hurried after the gods. When they stepped out from around the trees, Jonah couldn't believe how far ahead of them the gods had travelled; he could barely make them out. He shook his head and picked up the pace with his friends.

When they finally caught up, Zeus and Enki were speaking in low voices, frowning at each other. "Something's not right," Ava stated.

"How do you mean?" Jonah asked, suddenly feeling quite worried.

Ava shrugged. "I'm not sure. I just feel uneasy, like something bad's going to happen."

Jonah wanted to reassure her, but watching the gods' concerning conversation didn't make him feel much better, either.

Ava stepped toward the gods and cleared her throat. "Is something the matter?"

"We don't know," Zeus said. "We can just feel…"

"…a shift," Enki repeated. "In energy, so to speak."

"Alrighty, then," Tristan replied, pulling a face at Jonah.

"So, maybe we should get this final *retrieval* over and done with already so we can go home," Jonah prompted.

Enki and Zeus nodded in unison. "It's just over these rocks," Zeus said, then turned and strode toward a natural rock wall jutting from the beach and looming out over the ocean. Luckily, the sand rose up against it at their end, providing a much easier means of getting over that wall. Ava and Tristan matched Jonah's pace. His pride prevented him from accepting their help despite the pain.

Fortunately, the other side wasn't as steep, and the luminous full moon provided ample light for them to see their way down safely. Tristan nearly bowled Jonah and Ava over when he stopped short. "Oh, come on! That just isn't fair," he exclaimed. Zeus and Enki stood in front of them, seemingly having appeared out of nowhere. "Are you sure the two of you aren't bloody ninjas?" he asked. The gods smirked at this, then turned to face the water.

Jonah joined them, Ava and Tristan trailing behind. With the gentle waves heaving and rolling, it took him a few moments to see her, but once he laid eyes on her, he couldn't believe he had missed her.

"Is that…" Tristan stepped forward, suddenly transfixed.

Zeus nodded. "Isis."

She was a fair way out in the dark waters. Jonah assumed the tide was low but then reminded himself that she was, in fact, a goddess. Her bare back was exposed from the hips up, the rest of her body cloaked by the darkness of the sea. Her long, straight black hair was pulled across one shoulder, and the moonlight illuminated her skin. She turned her head to the side for a moment, acknowledging their presence before tilting her head back and submerging herself. When she reemerged, she faced them and approached the shore.

Tristan let out an audible moan of anticipation before Ava whacked him. Much to Tristan's disappointment—Jonah was sure—as Isis rose out of the water, a sheath of white wrapped itself around her.

Zeus and Enki stepped forward to greet her, not only out of awe but what seemed to also be a great deal of reverence. The others looked on, completely captivated by her presence. Isis' demeanor differed vastly from Inanna's. While Isis was also exceptionally beautiful, she wasn't nearly as overtly sexual. She carried the same grace, but there was also something regal about her—calm yet authoritative, but also soft and nurturing.

As she returned the gods' greeting, her gaze drew past them towards Tristan.

He stood completely still, transfixed.

When respectfully able, she walked toward him. "I am Isis."

Tristan nodded and swallowed thickly. "I'm Tristan," he managed to get out.

"I know."

Despite Tristan's uncharacteristic silence, Jonah couldn't help but note the intensity of Isis' piercing green eyes lined heavily with black kohl. The goddess certainly was captivating.

Jonah exchanged confused glances with Ava, wondering if this goddess had somehow bewitched his mate. Even Zeus and Enki seemed a little bewildered, though they tried not to show it. He turned in alarm when Ava gripped his forearm, her fingers digging into his skin. She stared up at him with wide, panicked eyes, opening her mouth without the ability to speak.

"Ava?" Jonah turned quickly to stand in front of her and grabbed her other arm. His startled shout broke the trancelike state Isis' appearance held over Tristan and the gods, who all now hurried Ava's way to see what was going on. Jonah flinched when Ava's grip tightened further, her face now a deep red, as though she were choking.

"Ava? Ava can you focus on me?" Enki asked as he stepped up beside Jonah. With obvious difficulty, Ava swung her gaze from Jonah's face to Enki's. Slow convulsions overtook her body, and her wide eyes pleaded silently for Enki's help.

"What the hell's happening to her?" Jonah demanded.

"The necklace!" Zeus exclaimed. Inanna's talisman had illuminated on Ava's chest, then let off a brief, dull flash. Ava jerked violently before a second flash appeared, lasting a split-second longer.

Enki placed his hand on Jonah's chest and tried to push him back, but Ava's firm grasp prevented it. The amulet flashed a third time—a mere blink of light that now encompassed Ava entirely. Only Tristan and Jonah seemed surprised when the light took on Inanna's form—or, at least, some type of holographic version of the goddess.

"Inanna," Zeus shouted. "What's happened?"

Inanna's strength drained visibly as she tried to push through. Her image flickered in and out, restricting them to only snippets of what she was trying to say.

"…came…couldn't…hurry…" With a final, bright flash, she was gone.

Ava relinquished her grasp on Jonah's arms and collapsed in a heap. Jonah and Tristan quickly knelt by her side, but she stared up at the sky, dazed.

"Get her up quickly," Zeus barked. "We have to go."

Jonah and Tristan grabbed Ava under the arms and hoisted her up. She swayed unsteadily, and Enki stepped behind her for stability. Zeus and Isis closed their ranks, preparing to leave.

Jonah's heart pounded fearfully against his chest. He tried not to fill in the blanks left by Inanna's message, for he could only think the worst. He closed his eyes and braced himself for the transportation.

CHAPTER SEVENTEEN

WHEN JONAH OPENED his eyes, he was halfway up the Carters' driveway. He turned around to see Enki and Tristan assisting Ava to her feet again. Isis and Zeus were a few metres down the street, looking disorientated. Panic and fear completely overrode any nausea, and Jonah turned back around and bolted towards the front door.

"Jonah, stop!" Zeus shouted.

Jonah ignored him, willing himself to go faster. He heard the sound of Tristan pounding up the driveway after him as he ran into the house and headed straight for the living room. He'd taken two steps inside before his brain registered the scene in front of him and he stopped. All the air in his lungs seemed to escape him, and his chest tightened. Falling to his knees, he realized his fears had been confirmed. Tristan skidded to a halt behind him. There was a brief pause, and Jonah closed his eyes in the hopes that when he opened them, it would have all been a dream. The gut-wrenching bellow that sounded from his best friend clarified the reality of it.

Tristan lunged past Jonah towards the middle of the room. There Mallory sat, on the living room floor, her husband sprawled out before her as she cradled his head in her lap. Alex's eyes, now devoid of life, stared past Jonah's shoulder. Tristan half stumbled, half knelt beside her as he leaned over his father's body, his agonised howls filling the room. Jonah felt a sudden rush of air against his back; Zeus and Ava were a mere blur as the god delivered her to her family before respectfully stepping aside.

Ava's grief came out in semi-restrained whimpers, and the pain of such noises pierced Jonah's heart. She sat on the other side of her mother and bent forward to place a gentle kiss on her father's forehead. Leaving one hand on the top of his head, she wrapped her other arm around her mother.

Jonah felt the hot tears stream down his face as he watched Ava's back heave with the sobs she struggled to keep silent. Mallory looked up from her husband, and her eyes met Jonah's. She cried silently, like Jonah, made no attempt to brush aside the tears. Though their shared glance was only momentary, Jonah saw her heart breaking—through her eyes. It was as though a piece of her soul had splintered off, leaving her irrevocably changed. He then felt his own grief clench around his heart, but he refused to let it take hold. For the first time since he had met the Carters so many years ago, he felt as though he were on the outside looking in. It seemed he shouldn't be allowed to feel the weight of this loss as heavily as they did. Instead, the only other option was to be strong for them. He wiped away the tears with the back of his hand and took a deep, shaky breath. At the sound of a murmured voice, he turned to see Inanna for the first time since returning to the Carter house.

The goddess sat slumped with her back against the wall and her graceful legs stretched out, idle hands resting in her lap. Jonah found himself surprised to see that tears stained her cheeks, also.

"This is not your fault, Inanna..." Zeus said, kneeling beside her, and took her hand in his.

"I tried to stop them, but I wasn't strong enough," she muttered. "I am *so* sorry." Zeus let out a small sigh and moved the hair from across her face.

Enki and Isis walked around either side of Jonah and approached the Carters with nothing but reverence. Enki bent down on one knee. "May we?" he asked Mallory in a soft voice. With a confused stare, Mallory gave him a nod. Ava and Tristan looked up to watch.

Enki turned to Isis, who stood behind him and nodded as well. She knelt beside him and looked down upon Alex's body. Isis placed one hand on the crown of his head and the other across his throat. At the same time, Enki placed his hands against the middle of Alex's chest and on his lower abdomen. In unison, they bent their heads and closed their eyes. After a few moments, a white glow emanated from their palms. The bright light pulsated for a moment before stopping. The gods tried again, but Jonah sensed whatever they were trying to do just wasn't working.

Isis looked at Inanna and Zeus, then offered a small shake of her head. "It cannot be done," she said, her voice heavy with sadness. "There is no essence left. He is gone."

Enki looked up at Mallory. "I am sorry for your loss," he said and bowed his head. Arising from his kneel, he walked to Inanna, crouched down beside her, and planted a kiss on her forehead. Isis merely stared down at Alex.

"Are you Isis?" Mallory whispered.

The goddess looked up. "Yes, I am."

Mallory nodded, and the tears welled in her eyes again. "Alex was so looking forward to meeting you. I haven't seen him that excited in years."

Isis placed her hand over Mallory's before reaching down to close Alex's eyes. Then she picked up his hand, whispered a prayer, then placed Alex's hand back on his chest. "In my culture, we believe death is only the beginning. You will see each other again." Mallory nodded with a small smile, and Isis rose again to her feet.

Jonah looked at the Carters, the only family he'd ever really had—now minus one member. And for what? He looked up at Zeus talking with Isis while Enki helped the still weakened Inanna to her feet.

"This is all your fault," he growled. Everyone turned to him in surprise.

Zeus took a couple steps towards him. "Just how, exactly, is this all my fault?" he asked, his voice both calm and dangerous at the same time. Jonah took two angry strides forward to stand right in front of the god.

"Jonah, please…" Ava said in a meek voice, but to no avail.

"You're a god," Jonah yelled. "You should have known!" He threw a hard punch into Zeus' abdomen. Zeus didn't flinch or retaliate. "You knew what they were capable of." Jonah punched again, embracing the physical pain it caused him. "You should have *stopped* them! You should have *protected* him!" He slammed his fists into Zeus with every accusation. "You should have saved him!"

Realising his blows had no effect on the god, Jonah drew his fist back for a tremendous swing towards Zeus' head with as much furious momentum as he could muster. A shockwave of pain ricocheted up his arm, and Zeus' hand engulfed his fist to stop it in its tracks.

"Never the face," Zeus stated. Jonah stared at him, too stunned to say anything. With the thumb and forefinger of his free hand, Zeus flicked Jonah's bruised ribs. The small movement had enough force to send Jonah hurtling backwards before landing hard on the couch. He yowled in agony.

"Stop it!" Ava screeched. "You know he's injured." She ran to Jonah, who now tried to hide the tears stinging his eyes. Zeus immediately looked ashamed by his excessive use of force, and he approached Jonah, who lay sprawled on the cushions. The god offered his hand to help Jonah to his feet.

"Piss off!" Jonah spat through clenched teeth. In a single, impatient movement, Zeus leaned forward and yanked Jonah up by his good arm, causing him to once again howl in pain.

"Will you stop hurting him?" Ava yelled.

"Will you both be quiet?" Zeus roared. Small bursts of electricity sparked off his form. Still holding Jonah by the arm, he placed the palm of his other hand flat against Jonah's injured ribcage. He closed his eyes, and Jonah froze, stupefied, when his pain subsided. After a few short moments, Zeus released him, grabbed the cast around Jonah's broken arm, and twisted. The cast split open and fell to the floor.

Jonah didn't bother to protest as Zeus performed the same hands-on ritual with his arm. When the god finished, he relinquished his hold on Jonah and stared him straight in the eye.

"I apologise for harming you. It was wrong and inappropriate."

Jonah could only muster a brief nod in his surprise. Zeus seemed satisfied by the gesture and turned to join Enki's side.

Ava wasted no time stepping into the space Zeus left behind. "Are you all right?" she asked. with her usual heartfelt concern.

Jonah gave her a small smile. "I'm fine. I think he just healed me. But you shouldn't be worrying about me. How are you?" He placed his hands on her shoulders to more easily gaze at her face. He knew he would find the truth there, regardless of anything she actually said.

"I'll be fine. We'll all be fine," she replied without an ounce of conviction. She bit her lower lip and blinked away the tears. The intensity of Jonah's gaze proved too much for her, and she broke into sobs. Without a word, Jonah enveloped her in a protective hug, knowing there was nothing else he could do. To distract himself from his own grief, he focused on another whispered conversation between Zeus and Enki. Zeus give Isis and Inanna a subtle gesture to join them before recommencing in his hushed tones.

"Enough," Jonah stated, his voice firm and just loud enough to get everyone's attention. The gods ceased their whispering and turned toward him. "No more private conversations about matters that concern us all."

There was a brief pause before Tristan stood beside Jonah and his sister. "I'm with Jonah. Enough. If you want us to trust you, then you have to start trusting us, too," he declared.

"We need to know exactly what we're up against if we don't want to lose anyone else," Ava said, pulling back from Jonah to face the gods.

Much to their surprise, the gods didn't seem to be in the least bit angered by their outburst. Instead, they looked as though they wondered why the trio hadn't taken this position sooner.

Zeus nodded. "There is a matter we need to address first." He cleared his throat, giving away a rare moment of indecision.

Isis touched him on the arm as she stepped past him, then knelt in front of Alex's body once again. She picked up Mallory's hand, which rested above her husband's still and silent heart, and held it with both of hers. "Mallory, I am sorry, but we have to take Alex, now."

Mallory stared at her for a moment, clearly trying to process the information, and Isis waited patiently. "Yes. You're right. We have to call someone. I need to make arrangements. A funeral. Yes, I will—"

"Mallory," Isis gently interrupted, "there isn't going to be a funeral right now." Mallory looked around the room, unable to register what Isis said.

"What are you talking about?" Tristan asked. "We're having a funeral for Dad. Of course we are." Isis kept her gaze locked on Mallory, reassuringly stroking her hand.

Zeus, with renewed confidence, stepped in. "For reasons that have yet to be explained—but will be—we need to take Alex's body somewhere he will be safe."

"Safe from what?" Ava asked, clenching her fists. "The Fates? What more can they *do* to him?"

"We have only heard whispers," Enki said, "but it would appear at present that even the souls of men aren't safe from the Fates. Alex's soul is still connected to his body. That connection will weaken to the point where he can no longer sustain it, and he will be forced to move on. We need him secured and protected before that happens."

"What's so wrong with letting Dad move on?" Ava protested.

"Because his soul won't get very far," Enki replied. "If these whispers are true, the Fates are intercepting souls as they try to move on. Why? We are uncertain, but I am sure you will agree we must keep your father's soul safe from them."

"I... I... I don't understand what's going on," Mallory said, her eyes darting around the room. "I'm sorry. I just... I can't. It's too much."

Tristan knelt beside his mother, placing his arm around her shoulders. "It's okay, Mum. We'll take care of it."

"Please," Zeus implored him, "we will talk about this further, but time is a luxury we just don't have right now."

"We promise we'll have a proper farewell when this is over," Isis swore. "In the meantime, he will be safe where we take him. He will be protected by all the gods."

Mallory smiled sadly. "He would get such a kick out of knowing that." Isis nodded with a kind smile. After a few seconds, Mallory bent down and placed a lingering kiss on her husband's mouth before gazing upon him. It seemed as though she tried to burn every minute detail of him into her memory. Finally, she looked up at Zeus and nodded.

Seemingly relieved, Zeus turned to Enki, who stepped forward. "We just need you to move away from him," he instructed, and Jonah and Tristan assisted Mallory to her feet. Mallory's children took their place on either side of their mother, protective arms around her. Jonah stood awkwardly to the side as Enki took his position on the floor where Mallory had sat.

"Jonah?" Mallory called to him quietly. He looked up at her. "You're his family, too. You are our family." She gestured for him to join them in their shared grief. He stepped toward them, emotional and relieved. Tristan threw his spare arm around Jonah's shoulders and reined him in tightly. As Jonah patted his best friend firmly on the back, he was glad to no longer have bruised ribs.

Isis and Enki placed their hands over Alex's body just as before, then looked to Zeus for final approval. With a swift nod from the god, they lowered their heads and began an almost silent chant. Alex's body slowly rose off the floor.

Jonah felt the hot tears flow from his eyes, and this time, Tristan patted Jonah's shoulder hard. Jonah glanced quickly at Mallory, her eyes closed and her arms wrapped tightly around the waists of her children.

Ava had one hand on her mother's shoulder, the other placed delicately across her mouth as she openly cried. Suddenly overwhelmed by the sight, Jonah seemed to feel her grief on top of his own. He averted his gaze back to Alex, trying not to think about the fact that he had just lost a father for the second time.

A slight hum rose around them, and a haze enveloped Isis, Enki, and Alex's body. Then they were gone.

CHAPTER EIGHTEEN

NOBODY MOVED FOR what felt like an eternity. It seemed as if, by doing so, they'd admit to themselves that Alex was really gone. Surprisingly, Mallory was the first to break the reverent silence.

"Now, start talking," she said, quietly. Her tone, though, left no room for debate.

Zeus nodded and gestured for them to take a seat on the lounge. He then turned to Inanna, who got to her feet, her legs shaky as she steadied a hand against the wall for balance. As Zeus tended to the goddess, Ava removed the necklace from around her own neck and silently handed it back.

"Thank you," Inanna said, to which Ava responded with a sad smile before taking a seat beside her mother. Inanna took a deep breath, clasped the necklace around her neck, and closed her eyes, as though its return had revived a little of her strength.

As the group settled, she slowly replaced her elaborate outfit with a simple black sheath, not unlike Isis' own garments.

"Ready?" Zeus asked. Inanna nodded, looking energised now, and together they turned to face the expectant group. Zeus stared at the wall behind them, and Ava, with her astute intuition, felt he was trying to separate what to tell them from what to keep under wraps.

"No more secrets, remember?" she prompted.

That brought a small smile to the god's lips. "Ava, I am sure you can appreciate that when information of a sensitive nature is about to be divulged, it does not hurt to pause and consider the most sensitive approach." Ava had to concede he was right and gave him a small nod.

"Our concern," Inanna added, "is that we don't want to overwhelm you when so much has happened in such a short amount of time. As mortals, your capacity for life-altering events is limited."

"Well, it hasn't seemed to concern any of you up to this point," Jonah snapped. "So how about you just let us decide what we can and can't handle?"

Inanna shrugged, then gestured for Zeus to continue.

He cleared his throat and stroked his stubbled chin. "How much do you know of your ancestry?" he finally asked with a direct glance at Mallory, who could only gape at the unexpected question.

"Not a lot, to be honest," she replied, sounding more apologetic than upset. "I know I'm a third-generation Australian, but prior to that, all I know is my family originated in Europe somewhere. No one ever really talked about it."

Zeus opened his mouth to speak but was interrupted by a brief flash as Isis and Enki reappeared. Isis approached Zeus and whispered in his ear.

"No secrets," Jonah growled.

Isis turned, her eyes holding annoyance and understanding at the same time. She looked helplessly at Zeus, then said, "I don't think the Fates have gone very far. They aren't here specifically, but we definitely felt they were near, both when we left and when we returned."

Zeus stroked his beard again. "The three of you go around the whole perimeter of the house. I want two protective barriers up. One directly encompassing the house and the other around the property itself."

"Do you think it will keep them out?" Inanna asked.

"No, not entirely," he admitted. "They are the Fates, after all. If they want to get in, they will get in. At least, this way, we should get a warning—a chance to protect ourselves." The three gods nodded and left the room. Zeus sighed and faced the others sitting on the couch.

"Mallory, your family line was initiated in a place known as Troy, by the union of a Greek and a Trojan." He paused to see how they processed the initial information. They stared back at him in varying states of confusion and surprise.

"Troy? As in *Troy*?" Jonah asked. Zeus nodded.

"Dude, where the hell is Troy?" Tristan whispered.

"It was where Turkey is now," Jonah whispered back, half wondering why they were whispering. Tristan nodded, though Jonah knew his mate well enough to know he was now trying to work out where Turkey was located.

Mallory took a deep breath. "Go on," she prompted.

"Well, the union wasn't between just any Greek and just any Trojan…" Zeus paused again, the weight of his response hanging heavily over them.

Jonah impatiently rattled names of historically significant Greek and Trojan men out aloud. "Agamennon, Menalaus,

Odysseus, Hector, Paris, Ajax, Patricles, Achilles—" He stopped when the smirk lifted the corner of Zeus' mouth.

"*Achilles?*" Tristan repeated, this time in awe. Even Ava and Tristan knew the name well enough to be impressed by the revelation.

"Hang on. Didn't Achilles die in the battle of Troy? Wasn't he killed by Paris?" Jonah asked.

"That is correct," Zeus replied "He did… but not before he'd conceived a child. He never knew."

Jonah tried to mentally retrieve what he knew about Achilles. The others just watched him. "If I remember correctly, wasn't his mother Thetis a seer? If she could foresee his demise, why couldn't she also foresee a child?" Jonah asked.

"What do you mean?" Ava said. "She predicted his death?"

Jonah looked at Zeus, who regally gestured with a flip of his hand for Jonah to explain. "Well," Jonah started slowly, "from what I recall of the story, Achilles visited his mother to discuss whether or not he wanted to go to battle with Troy, as he had no interest in the cause and wanted her opinion. She, in turn, revealed to him the prophecy she had seen. If he stayed, he would live a long, happy life with many descendants who would cherish his memory—until they, too, faded from history. Then any trace of their existence would all but vanish with them. On the other hand, if he went to Troy, he would die there—but he would be remembered for all eternity as one of greatest warriors the world had ever known."

Zeus couldn't help but smile, admittedly impressed with Jonah's response.

"But that still doesn't answer my question," Jonah continued. "If she could see all that, why couldn't she see the child?"

"How do you know she didn't?" Zeus replied, letting the question hang in the air.

"All right. I'm clearly not following here," Tristan said.

"As Jonah correctly explained," Zeus said, "she told her son the consequences of going or staying. What she'd seen and didn't tell him was that, if he went to Troy, he'd conceive a child there. This child would be both Greek and Trojan."

"Why wouldn't she have told him that?" Ava asked.

"She told him exactly what he needed to hear in order for him to go. She appealed to his ego, to the warrior in him that wanted immortality, so to speak." Zeus gazed at their shocked expressions. "I suppose it does seem unmotherly by today's standards, encouraging your son to pursue certain death," he continued. "She saw enough within her visions to know how imperative this union, and the consequent new life, would be. She feared that if her son became aware of this, he would prevent the conception entirely, knowing he'd chosen his path and would not live to see the end of the war."

"Well then, who was the mother of the child?" Ava asked.

Zeus looked at Jonah, apparently giving him another chance to work that one out, too. Jonah sighed in frustration, aware that Achilles had liked women as much as they'd liked him, and wondered how he was supposed to know who it was.

"You're thinking too broadly, Jonah. Remember, the conception happened on Trojan soil," Zeus gently prompted.

"Brisaius..." Jonah whispered. Zeus nodded.

"And just who was she when she was at home?" Tristan asked drolly.

"She was a priestess of the god Apollo and beloved cousin of the two Princes of Troy, Hector and Paris," Jonah explained.

"So, how has this managed to be omitted from history?" Mallory asked. "Surely her pregnancy didn't go unnoticed."

"Good question, Mallory." Zeus smiled. "Once it was clear that not only had Troy fallen but that Achilles was killed by

Paris, Brisaius fled the city with the other survivors. Now, keep in mind she was a priestess of Apollo and therefore expected to maintain a virginal, pure status. So when her pregnancy began to show, the downtrodden people of Troy saw it as an immaculate conception. A gift from the gods and a sign directly from Apollo himself. A sign that all would be well. For why would a god give them his child if they were not meant to survive? It never occurred to anyone that the father was mortal and most certainly not a Greek. Brisaius never told another living soul the truth."

Tristan let out a low, impressed whistle. "So what you're saying, essentially, is that I'm basically like a freakin' Greek god?"

Ava jumped in before anyone else could. "I'm pretty sure he's definitely *not* saying that."

"Ava, I'm pretty sure it was *implied,*" Tristan retorted, as though his sister were a child who couldn't understand the grownup conversation. Jonah chuckled while Ava responded in the usual way to her brother's antics; she rolled her eyes. "Hold up," Tristan said, momentarily distracted from his new, self-appointed status. "If Brisaius never told anyone the truth about her child's father, how do *you* know?"

Zeus stared at him, looking somewhat bewildered that he needed to state the obvious. "Because, Tristan, I actually *am* a Greek god."

"Ahh…" Tristan nodded slowly. Jonah's heart ached when he thought of Alex and how much of a kick the man would have gotten out of this revelation.

"While our ancestry is obviously impressive," Mallory said, "I have yet to understand how it has anything to do with the current state of things. Or how it involves my children."

Zeus paused, and once again, Jonah felt as if the god still withheld something from them. "All I am prepared to say, for the moment, is that both Tristan and Ava have inherent genetic capabilities they may be able to utilize, therefore making them invaluable for what lies ahead."

"What *capabilities*?" Ava asked.

"Does that mean I get god powers?" Tristan asked eagerly.

A hint of a smile pulled at the corners of Zeus' mouth. "I think these questions will be better explained tomorrow, once we've gathered the rest of the Alliance. Not because I wish to withhold information from you, but there are some things that must be permitted to unfold as they will, without interference."

"What about me? Am I irrelevant in all this?" Jonah asked, surprised that he wasn't in the least bit relieved by the concept.

"You are most certainly relevant, Jonah," Zeus said. "However, it would be best if I explained it to you once you show me those photographs you're concerned about." Jonah stared at the god, his forehead clenched in concentration as he tried to work out how on Earth he could be connected to the site beyond having taken the photos.

At that moment, Isis, Inanna, and Enki walked back into the room. "Done," Enki announced.

"How is it?" Zeus asked.

"It's impressive, if I do say so myself," Inanna replied, evidently rejuvenated after retaining her necklace. Zeus nodded.

"What now?" Mallory asked even as she stifled a yawn.

"Rest," Zeus said. "Inanna, Enki, and Isis will stay here with you tonight. I will return to Jonah's with him to view these photos. We will return first thing in the morning."

Jonah inwardly groaned at the thought of having to spend time with the god—alone. He didn't know what it was about Zeus that grated on his nerves so much.

"What if... they... come back?" Mallory asked softly, her eyes coming to rest on the spot where her husband had passed.

Isis walked towards her and put a reassuring arm around her shoulder. "I think they have made their point. In saying that, we will not err by underestimating them again. We have a very strong, very magical boundary in place. Plus, you will have three gods here to protect you."

Mallory didn't appear to be in the least bit reassured, but she nodded and gave the goddess a small smile.

"Any more questions before we take our leave?" Zeus enquired, looking to both gods and mortals alike. When there appeared to be none, he headed out of the lounge room toward the house's entryway.

"Actually, I have one," Jonah said. Zeus simply nodded, indicating that they were all listening, though the muscles in his jaw clenched visibly. "Why are you in charge?"

"*Jonah*," Mallory scolded.

"No—think about it," he added. "It's the basic timeline of ancient history. Mesopotamia, Egypt, then Greece. Which makes you the youngest god here. So how did you end up calling the shots?" Admittedly, his questioning made him feel somewhat smug. At least, until he saw the scowl Ava directed at him, leaving him feeling childishly inappropriate. He pretended to ignore her as he stubbornly awaited a response.

Zeus blinked and cocked his head, apparently stumped by how to answer the accusation only loosely disguised as a question. Enki came to his rescue. "It is a matter of descendancy. This is why Zeus takes the lead in this particular matter."

"Descendancy?" Tristan asked. "You said we descended from Achilles."

Enki nodded. "Yes, that is correct. But who do you think, in turn, *really* sired Achilles? It wasn't Peleus, like history tells you." Everyone glanced at Zeus, who nodded in confirmation. "Therefore," continued Enki, "as the patriarch of both the Greek pantheon and the line of descendancy, it was only logical that Zeus would take the lead."

"That's that, then," Ava declared, rising from her seat. "Mum, how about you and I go into the kitchen and I fix you something to eat?"

"I couldn't eat. A glass of wine might be nice, though."

Ava rubbed her mother's back and nodded. Jonah also rose and bent to wrap Mallory in a massive hug, suddenly afraid to leave them. She hugged him back tightly, her surrogate son, before releasing him and placing her hands on either side of his face.

"Be careful, Jonah," she advised with a patient sternness. "Don't let your stubbornness put you in harm's way."

He couldn't help but give her a wry smile, aware that she was referring to the way he kept butting heads with Zeus. Then he turned to Ava, her eyes reflecting her mother's sentiments, before hugging her in the same manner.

"Call me if you need anything, even if you just need to talk," she told him.

He nodded. "Same goes for you." Jonah and Tristan then embarked on a silent hand-clasp-turn-hug before Jonah faced Zeus again, surprised to see the concern on the god's face.

"We'll be okay," Enki reassured Zeus, and the two gods clasped each other's forearms in farewell. Zeus then gestured to Jonah, who followed him reluctantly out the door.

Jonah didn't know if he'd actually heard it or just imagined the silent wish in Ava's voice, but before the front door closed behind him, he thought he heard her whisper, "Please don't let them kill each other..."

THE TRIP BACK to Jonah's was conducted in silence. But he was so caught up in his thoughts, he didn't notice whether or not any tension existed. Zeus himself seemed just as preoccupied.

Once home, Jonah walked straight into his study and turned on the computer. He wanted Zeus to find whatever it was he was looking for in the photos so Jonah could go to bed. He was far too wired right now to even contemplate sleep, but he also wasn't up for making small talk that would inevitably lead to an argument.

Zeus stood behind Jonah, who sat at the desk, in his usual god-like stance. "It says you have new mail," he announced. Jonah turned and looked pointedly back at him, biting his tongue before swiveling back around and opening the email. It was from Sydney.

Jonah leaned forward, eager to see what the man had discovered.

> *Jonah,*
>
> *I don't know what we have stumbled upon here, but I fear no good will come of it. I think I've successfully translated most of the hieroglyphs. Despite the appearance of a few symbols I've never seen before, when noted with the ones both prior and following, I think I was able to make an educated deduction.*
>
> *The first section tells about the retreat of the gods of old:*
>
> "…And like all things, the time had come to pass where the many gods of old chose to step aside for the few gods of the dawning era…"

The second part talks of prosperity:

"…and all the great prophets, both of the old world and the new, foresaw the end. A time when the three sisters would rise against them and bring about the age of nothingness…"

The third part talks of a meeting of the old gods:

"…Knowing they must retreat, the gods had walked the mortal realm too long to leave the safety of man to the gods of the new era. And so, the gods of old united themselves together, and an alliance was formed… that would see them called forth, back into the mortal realm, if the three sisters should rise…"

The last section, however, I cannot entirely decipher but only make an educated guess. There are far too many unknown hieroglyphs, to the point where it almost looks like gobbledy-gook. From what I can gather, it talks of a binding spell the alliance cast on the Fates to prevent them from working beyond the natural order of things. It seems the binding spell was kept in a seal and tightly closed with very ancient and very powerful magic. Therefore, breaking the seal would break the curse binding the Fates' powers.

There is also mention of a secret prophecy, though I can hardly make it out. Just that it had only been revealed to the gods. Though what it was about, I'm afraid I cannot decipher.

*I hope this is of some help to you. I would recom-
mend keeping this to yourself for the moment, with
everything I've seen on the news of late… What have
we gotten ourselves into?*

*Regards,
Sydney*

Jonah sat back in his chair and let out a deep breath.

Zeus stared at the email, and Jonah turned to look up at him expectantly. He cleared his throat to pull the god back to reality. Zeus merely turned and offered Jonah a blank stare.

Exasperated, Jonah made the first move. "So, you were there. In the tomb?" Zeus nodded, but he didn't seem ready to divulge anything else. Jonah tried a different tactic in the hopes of getting an actual answer. "Is Sydney's decipher of the hiero-glyphics accurate?"

Again, Zeus nodded. "For the most part."

"For the most part? Right. Well, what of the last part that he couldn't decipher? I'm sure you know what it actually says."

Zeus frowned. "Pull up the photo you took of the last sec-tion," he instructed.

Jonah eagerly did as requested, not even batting an eyelid at the command. Zeus loomed over Jonah's shoulder, spreading his hand out across the monitor, running his fingers across the symbols, as if he were reading brail. He paused briefly over a section, and Jonah tried to glance at him without being too ob-vious.

Admittedly, the god's new expression fueled Jonah's curi-osity; Zeus looked like someone who would have been happy to be proven wrong, only to be proven right—and that being right wasn't a good thing.

The god closed his eyes, letting his hand fall from the monitor. He turned and paced across the room. Jonah wasn't entirely certain he now wanted to know what the hieroglyphs said. A notification alert sounded from the computer, and he turned to see Ava had sent him an IM.

'Hey. Just thought I'd check in to make sure you haven't managed to piss off any gods lately...'

Jonah smiled, and quickly responded.

'I am nothing if not a slow learner! Everything's fine. At least right now. I think. Zeus is wigging out a little over these photos. How are you? How's everyone holding up at your end?'

'Why? What's with the photos? Tristan's retreated to his room and has plugged himself into his music, and Mum is sitting with Isis and Enki. Talking to them seems to be helping her a lot. I think I'm going to try to have an early night. I just wanted to check in on you first.'

'Don't worry about me,' Jonah typed back. *'I'll be fine. Tristan just needs his own space for a while. You know how he gets. Music is pretty much how he deals with everything. Don't know what's up with the photos yet, but hopefully I'll have something to share by tomorrow. I think an early night sounds like a good idea. Don't hesitate to text me or something during the night if you need me, okay?'*

He turned back to face Zeus, startled to see the god had stopped pacing and now stood in the center of the room, just staring. The blankness in his eyes unnerved Jonah.

"Uh… have I done something wrong?" he managed to murmur.

Zeus stared at him a moment longer before letting out a long sigh, gazing past Jonah to the image still on the monitor. Then he slowly walked approached him again, reciting aloud, " *To- gether, they forged the most powerful binding spell ever cast, to bind the Fates to the rules of Nature. So immense was the power they used, the gods of old were greatly diminished, and the Alliance fell into a deep sleep. That sleep would endure the ages—until a time when the world would call on them again.* "

Zeus now stood beside Jonah and looked down at him as he recited the last passage by heart. " *The great Oracle spoke her last prophecy and foretold of the coming of a descendant, a mortal born with the power to save mankind. If he falls, so too shall mankind fall. Look for the man born of the god Zeus, for he will be named Jonah—Saviour to All.* "

The ensuing silence was deafening as Jonah tried to process what he'd just heard. It took him three attempts to form a question out aloud. "So… it's saying we're… related… somehow? Like, metaphorically your son?"

Zeus shook his head. "No. It says, Jonah, I am your father. Literally."

CHAPTER NINETEEN

THE NIGHT PASSED slowly as both gods and mortals alike pondered the events of the day—what it meant and what would happen next.

As Jonah saw the first hint of light creeping up over the horizon, his phone beeped. He was grateful for the intrusion, picking it up to see who it was. Tristan had sent one of his typically disjointed texts.

'Dude. Everyone's up over here. Mum's cooking up a storm. Heads up, I'll eat it all if you don't get over here.'

Jonah smiled and texted back.

'Let's hope Zeus is a morning person. Far too early for a short-out.'

He decided he needed a quick shower to prepare himself for what was bound to be another day of insanity. He made a conscious effort to push out any thoughts of Zeus' revelation from his head. Jonah needed a coffee and to talk it out with Tristan and Ava before he could wrap his head around it. Even then, he still didn't feel it was the right time to bring it up after Alex's death. That thought alone brought a sharp pang of loss, and Jonah sighed, intrinsically knowing this was only the beginning.

AVA NURSED A cup of coffee as she stood with her back up against the doorframe, anxiously watching Enki and Tristan carting their mother's vintage, full-length mirror into the back yard. Isis stood regally, directing them into place, while Inanna pedantically placed white candles at regular intervals, forming a circle. Sensing movement from behind her, Ava turned to see her mother approaching.

"Hey, Mum. Did you manage to get any sleep?"

Mallory replied with a small smile, "I couldn't sleep any more than you could, sweetheart." Ava smiled, knowing how much alike they were. "What's happening here?" Mallory asked, looking past her daughter.

Ava shrugged. "No idea. They were already out there when I showed up. I'm assuming it has something to do with retrieving the other gods."

Mallory nodded, her gaze absently fixed on the scene before them as she leaned against the opposite side of the doorframe.

JONAH PULLED A clean shirt over his head, revelling in how great it felt to be able to do so without having to flinch in pain. He paused when he stepped into the lounge room, noticing the sliding door was wide open, the sheer curtains billowing with a gentle breeze. Cautiously, he looked around for an intruder—

or worse, the Fates. Jonah tentatively approached the door before yanking the curtains aside, almost ripping them from the railing as he tried to ensure he wasn't taken by surprise. Doing so nearly made him fall out the open door, and once he'd regained his balance, he found himself staring at Zeus.

The man who only a few hours ago had professed to be his father stood right in the middle of the yard. Naked. Arms outstretched, fingers splayed, he tilted his head slightly back. Jonah was grateful that the god at least had his back to him. He opened his mouth to speak, but before he could utter a sound, Zeus beat him to it.

"There is nothing quite like the sensation of the rising sun on your skin," he announced. Jonah pondered this with confusion. "As a god, I am hypersensitive to these things. Our senses are much more astute then those of mortals."

Jonah just nodded slowly before remembering Zeus couldn't actually see him. "Uh, yeah, I guess that makes some sense," he muttered, trying to find some other focal point on which to rest his gaze.

"Plus, I also like the quiet. It's nice to have time away from the relentless chatter of the world." Jonah didn't even attempt to answer this time. Zeus lowered his arms and started to turn around.

"Woah! Not cool, man!" Jonah shouted. "I'll wait for you in the car. And make sure you have some bloody clothes on." His hand hovered instinctively over his eyes as he tried to maneuver his way back inside the house, the sound of Zeus' boisterous laughter following him.

LACHESIS PLACED HER palm flat against the bark of the tree in front of her. "So tall. Ancient," she murmured. She could feel the lifeforce slowly resonating up and down the tree, like it had its very own heart, pumping the sacred energy up to the branches and then back down into the earth. Sighing, she rested her head against the trunk beside her hand.

"It's their fault there aren't as many as there used to be. You know this," Atropos said from behind her. Lachesis turned slowly before she leaned back against the tree and faced her sister.

"You look concerned, sister," Clotho added, joining them. Lachesis turned her gaze to the ground, unsure how to best express her concerns.

"Come, now. What is it?" Atropos prompted with a stern frown.

"I'm not entirely convinced we did the right thing in taking Alex Carter's life. You know it wasn't yet his time."

"His time is when we say it is!" Clotho barked. Lachesis turned her head, her gaze drifting off deep into the forest. "Why would you feel remorse now?"

Her sisters waited, knowing she would continue only when she was ready. Eventually, she replied, "It's not remorse. I'm just concerned that, in having done so, we have unleashed a force we know nothing about. What if we have underestimated him? Underestimated the prophecy?"

Atropos moved closer to her sister and placed a hand on her shoulder, half reassuring, half commanding. "We have nothing to fear. He is a mere mortal, despite his ancestry. And we are the Fates."

ZEUS WATCHED JONAH make his way up the Carters' driveway, his hands thrust into the front pockets of his jeans, shoulders hunched up, and his gaze aimed downwards. He felt a genuine sense of guilt for the part he'd played in the burden his son now carried—the burden, he knew, which would only grow greater and more difficult to bear.

"Jonah," he said. Jonah just threw a brief glance at him and continued walking. "Jonah!" Jonah stopped and turned around. "Jonah, I am sorry you had to find out. Now. On top of what happened yesterday... I—"

"Look," Jonah cut in, "I appreciate that. I do. But you're just going to have to give me some time. I need time."

Zeus stared at him for a moment, wanting to respect his son's wishes, but he was acutely aware of how much his son still didn't know. There was so much he needed to know. Instead, the god conceded with a small nod and followed Jonah up the driveway.

FOR THE FIRST time in his life, Jonah approached the Carters' house with a sense of trepidation. It pissed him off that his safe haven, his refuge from all that had ever ailed him, had been tainted. At this point, he thought this seemed to sum up his life in general. He still struggled with the knowledge that Zeus was his father. Who could be expected to wrap their mind around something like that? Could it even be true? Was there a way to know for sure? Jonah pondered the likelihood of potentially DNA-testing a god, then Ava appeared at the front door.

"I was wondering when you were going to make an appearance."

He smiled as he approached her, noticing the angle of the slowly increasing daylight hitting her skin, which appeared to illuminate her from within. The aura of light surrounding her only made her all the more beautiful. Jonah felt his face flush, and he ducked his head as Zeus stepped ahead of him.

"Good morning, Ava. Have the others started?"

She nodded. "Started what, exactly, I don't know… but they're all out back," she replied.

Zeus turned to Jonah. "I'll send Tristan out. I imagine the three of you will need a moment to talk." Jonah looked at him in surprise. Zeus gave him a quick nod of approval before stepping inside.

"What's all that about?" Ava asked. "And hang on. How come you're not at each other's throats this morning?"

Jonah sighed and leaned against the balustrade. "Well, it's amazing what being pain-free can do for a person's constitution," he replied.

Ava smirked. "This is true. But that's not what it is, is it?"

Jonah shook his head. "It's ridiculous how perceptive you are." She only responded with a shrug. "You're right, though," he continued. "We should wait for Tristan." Actually, he was just buying himself more time, unsure how to tell them about Zeus' revelation. He didn't get much time, as Ava turned her head at the sound of her brother's jeans scuffing together down the hall.

"Dude! Zeus advised me my presence was required," Tristan said, stepping past his sister to greet his mate.

"It is," Ava cut in, "so come on, already. What's with the secret squirrel business?"

"There actually *is* something?" Tristan asked with mocking sincerity. "I just thought Zeus was intimidated by the way the goddesses keep eyeing me off."

"Well, when we got back to my house, Zeus wanted to see the photos I'd taken at the site," Jonah began. "But we also had an email from a colleague of mine in response to my query on the hieroglyphs." He told them what he recalled about the translation, hesitating on the final passage. Only silence met him as Jonah let the revelation of his parentage sink in, wondering what any of them could possibly say next.

"Let me get this straight," Ava said. "You're somehow part of some epic, end-of-world prophecy? How do we even know you're the Jonah they're referring to? I mean, there's more than one person with the name Jonah out there."

Jonah stared down at his feet. "Zeus confirmed it."

"Hold up!" Tristan burst out in his trademark excitement. "He told you he was your father?" Jonah nodded slowly, gritting his teeth through his mate's eccentricity. "Do you have any idea what this means?" Tristan added, seemingly astounded that neither of them had clued into this yet. "Dude! You had a total Vader moment. For real!"

"Huh?" Jonah said. Ava groaned.

"As in, 'Luke, I am your father'?" Tristan explained, watching Jonah's face as it slowly dawned on him, too.

A wry smile spread across Jonah's face. "I guess I did."

"Really? That's what you're both getting out of this? A Vader moment?" Ava's voice battled between laughter and gobsmacked irritation.

"Hey, Sis, when life gives you lemons… you know how it is," Tristan replied. Ava went to playfully punch her brother in the arm, but he dodged her assault. Jonah couldn't help but chuckle. It felt good, even if he knew it was fleeting.

"Ahh… music to the gods' ears…" came Inanna's melodic voice as she approached the doorway. The trio looked at her, their laughter fading. Inanna glanced at them individually before turning and walking back into the house. "We're ready for you," she called over her shoulder. They exchanged raised eyebrows and promptly followed.

As they stepped out into the yard, they found the gods moving into their allotted positions around the circle. Zeus, Enki, Inanna, and Isis stood at the cardinal points, and the others were instructed to stand in the spaces between them.

Tristan frowned, counting the empty spaces. "Four spots. Three of us. Who else are we waiting for?" he asked.

"Me, of course, dear," his mum stated as she took her place between Isis and Enki.

"Whoa, hold up! Is this such a good idea? Won't this cause epic nosebleeds and imminent death?"

Inanna gestured for Tristan to stand between herself and Enki. "No, Tristan. That was caused by a disruption of her chemical makeup, resulting from her force move through space and time. None of us are going anywhere, and though we will be tapping into your energies, the level of it won't even register to you."

"Huh?" He stared at the goddess blankly, even when she moved from her own spot to position him correctly.

"We can draw any excess energy we require from the elements and from the energy that surrounds us," Enki stated.

Everyone took their places, none of them immune to the rising anticipation. Even the gods showed small cracks in their calm facades as they stood firmly, feet slightly apart. The immortals slowly raised their arms, hands in line with their hips, palms facing out and fingers splayed. The mortals self-consciously mimicked their actions.

"Now, try to keep your attention focused on the mirror," Zeus advised quietly as they all stared towards the center of the circle.

Flames jumped to life from the candles at their feet, and the gods closed their eyes as one, chanting in hushed tones. The others tried to keep their gazes firmly fixed on the mirror, but it became increasingly difficult with the breeze picking up. This quickly grew into a fierce wind, periodically whipping at them. Strangely, the wind had no effect on the brightly lit candles.

Dark, ominous clouds appeared, and the unmistakable sound of thunder crashed above them. Their rapidly changing surroundings were quickly forgotten as Jonah peered at the mirror. The glass looked less… solid, appearing to pulsate with a vibrancy that made Jonah think of the cord the Fates severed. He shuddered.

A wave rippled outwards from the center of the mirror, as though touched by an invisible hand. Jonah leaned forwards, watching whatever was happening behind the glass. Zeus and Enki continued their chanting while Isis and Inanna changed their words and rhythm. Jonah could barely make them out but thought it sounded like a name.

He couldn't believe his ears when he realized it actually sounded like they said 'Marduk'. Before his own awe had the chance to overwhelm him, a hand shot through the mirror, startling the unsuspecting mortals. Slowly, the body attached to the hand pushed its way forward through the glass. It didn't seem an easy feat; the glass appeared to present a challenging barrier.

A young man finally stepped out of the mirror, looking just a little younger than Jonah. He had olive skin, long, wavy brown hair, and brilliant blue eyes, bearing a striking resemblance to Enki.

"The first couple off the mark are always the hardest to get through," he said with a wink. He wore the same style of loose pants as Enki, though he remained shirtless, leaving Jonah and

Tristan feeling somewhat inadequate in comparison to Marduk's athletic form. As the new god turned his back, Jonah saw the god's large tattoo of what looked like a cross between a snake and a dragon, travelling up the length of his spine, wings outstretched across his broad shoulders.

Marduk stood between Enki and Tristan, taking a few moments to correct his stance and posture, before closing his eyes and joining in the chanting with the other gods. The process was repeated, and each time, another immortal stepped out of the mirror with a little more ease than the last. The storm clouds swirled and thundered overhead, and the temperature plummeted as light snow began to fall, astounding only the mortals. The wind picked up, whipping over them a little more violently, and the gods positioned themselves into the circle, producing more power with each addition. Jonah had all but forgotten to focus on the mirrors; he'd been trying to hide his enthusiasm. After Marduk came Kali, Hades, Vishnu, and Set.

If only Alex could have witnessed this, Jonah thought, glancing at Mallory to see the same sentiment reflected in her eyes. When she met his gaze, understanding dawned on her, and she gave him a sad smile in return. The gods slowed their chanting, and the volatile weather subsided and cleared. After a few moments, the chanting came to a complete stop, erasing any evidence that there had been freezing cold, storming gales, or snow.

Isis broke the circle when she stepped forward with a chalice in her hand and stood in front of Enki. He held his thumb and forefinger over the top and squeezed them together until a single drop of blood fell into the chalice. He gave Isis a nod, and she moved around the circle, obtaining blood offerings from each of the gods. When she had finished, Isis added her own, then moved to the front of the mirror. She bowed her head, and everyone followed suit. After giving a few quiet words of thanks, she inserted the chalice into the mirror. The mirror's surface rippled as the chalice disappeared from sight, followed by a bright, brief flash of light. Then the glass was solid—once more Mallory's normal mirror. The candles all extinguished themselves.

The gods moved together, greeting each other joyfully, as though this were some kind of estranged family reunion. Unsure of themselves, Jonah and the others huddled together, watching.

"So I take it you know who they all are, Nerd Boy?" Tristan queried as he eyed the newcomers.

"I know *of* them," Jonah replied, "but who's to say the information we have in books is correct? None of them really look like they are supposed to look."

"And for years I've been telling you, man, you can't believe everything you read!"

"Said the music journalist," Ava retorted through her smile.

"Of course, there has to be an exception to every rule," Tristan said. He pressed his lips together, but a smirk still showed through.

Zeus positioned himself between both groups and cleared his throat for everyone's attention. "Shall we go inside to get better acquainted?" he suggested. Gods and mortals alike obediently turned and followed him into the house.

CHAPTER TWENTY

THEY CONGREGATED IN in the living room, as it was the only room large enough to comfortably contain them all. Once everyone had either taken a seat, found something to lean on, or simply chosen a place to stand, Zeus took the floor.

"The silver lining to recent events is us standing here with all of you," Zeus commenced with grandeur. "For some of us, it has been a very long time since we have seen each other. While it is a most pleasant reunion of the Alliance, we can't forget the dire circumstances which have caused us to gather. First, I think some introductions are in order." He paused to walk toward the wall and raise his arm, pointing at a portrait of Alex.

"I would first like to introduce you to Alex Carter. Regrettably, he fell at the hands of the Fates yesterday. A few of us had the absolute honour and pleasure of making his acquaintance, and I can say with absolute sincerity that he was one of the most genuine, intelligent, and honourable men I have ever encountered. His wisdom and enthusiasm will be greatly missed."

The gods bowed their heads and said blessings in their own tongue, while Jonah, Tristan, Ava, and Mallory sat in stunned awe. Mallory issued Zeus her first real smile since her husband's passing, unable to voice her appreciation of his gesture. Zeus appeared almost humbled in return before he cleared his throat.

"Next, we have Alex's kin. His wife Mallory and his children, Tristan and Ava." The gods acknowledged them warmly, the attention only making the Carters more uncomfortable. Zeus' small smile fell, and he gathered all seriousness into his features, walking toward Jonah to stand beside him where he sat. Then he nervously cleared his throat.

"This is Jonah Sands." He left an expectant pause. "My son."

Mallory turned to Ava in surprise. "I'll fill you in later," Ava reassured her mother, who seemed too confused and bewildered to argue.

The gods seemed excitedly pleased by the news, though not surprised. Jonah felt even more embarrassed by their enthusiastic shouts and cries, and Zeus couldn't seem to help but smile at their boisterous enthusiasm.

"More about these mortals later. Mortals, I might add, who have been more than accommodating, given everything that has been thrown at them the past few days. So, respectfully, I feel we should each introduce ourselves properly and completely, to leave no more room for unpleasant surprises."

The gods grinned at each other. Jonah glanced at Tristan, who shrugged, oblivious to what Jonah deemed an inside joke among the gods—one they'd soon be privy to, whether they liked it or not.

"Obviously, I will go first!" Zeus boomed with a grand bow. The other immortals threw good-natured jibes about his ego. "As you know, I am Zeus, Patriarch of the ancient Greek pantheon and head of the Alliance. I am..." He spread his arms wide before lightning sparked from his fingertips, spreading out and around his body until he looked like he stood in the center of a nebulous plasma ball. The room shook as thunder rattled above them, and Zeus' voice grew deep and ominous. "God of the sky, the winds, the clouds, and the rain. God of thunder and lightning, and the Almighty God of Battle!" He let the impressive, intimidating scene continue for a few moments before returning everything to normal in one grand sweep of his hands.

Applause and cheers rose from the gods; Jonah and the others couldn't help but catch their enthusiasm and join them. Jonah had to admit it was an impressive display.

"Zeus, shouldn't there have been a mention of women in there somewhere?" one of the gods yelled cheekily. Zeus just winked at Ava in response, who promptly stopped clapping and rolled her eyes. Zeus chuckled, quite proud of himself.

"Enki, you're up," he announced, then retreated from his beloved spotlight.

Enki, exceedingly humbler in demeanor, gracefully approached the centre of the room. He stood for a moment, surveying his audience, feet apart and hands clasped regally behind his back. The god was completely captivating but in a way entirely antithesis to Zeus.

"I am Enki, beloved Sumerian High God from the Mesopotamian lands. I am the oldest of all immortals." He spoke softly, unassumingly, and his voice carried a hypnotic quality. "As such, I do have a number of talents attributed to me. I am the god of water, plants, intellect, creation, wisdom, and medicine…" Jonah found himself mesmerised by Enki's shirt, which displayed images as if it were a porthole into another time. "I possess the secret and magical knowledge of life and immortality, and at times, I can restore life to the dead." The images changed as he spoke. "I am creator of the ordered cosmos and of the earth. I cultivated humanity and instilled the knowledge of civilisation and culture. My incantations are so powerful, they come to pass as I utter them. I am also responsible for what is referred to as the Great Flood. That was in response to the last time someone wanted to rid the world of mankind."

The images faded, and he took a humble bow from the waist. The applause was enthusiastic but respectful. Enki smiled modestly, as though embarrassed by their reverence. "Isis." He nodded politely towards the goddess, who, on par with his grace and debonair authority, stepped forward to take his place.

Isis was not oblivious to the room's admiration of her natural beauty, but she took it in modest stride. Jonah couldn't help but notice her cool, piercing, kohl-lined eyes fixed firmly on Tristan, who had turned an intense shade of pink and appeared to have trouble swallowing. Jonah raised his eyebrows at his mate's highly out-of-character reaction, and Ava shot him a questioning look. Jonah shrugged but made a mental note to hit Tristan up about it later.

"I'm a short and sweet type of orator," Isis began. "I am the matriarch of the ancient Egyptian pantheon. After my husband's murder, I instigated the first immaculate conception." Jonah discreetly looked about the room to find the gods purposefully gazing everywhere but at Set. However, Set seemed unaffected by the reference and only stared unabashedly Isis.

"I am an Earth and Mother Goddess, attributed to medicines, spells and charms, rebirth, and reincarnation. The ankh is my talisman, and I command the power of the star Sirius." She touched the center of her forehead with her forefinger, and a bright light radiated from it, as if she were the star itself. She gave them a moment to appreciate the beauty of the star's energy before returning to her former stance.

"Excuse me," Tristan asked with a new, astounding politeness. Isis turned her gaze upon him. "Uh… you mentioned the immaculate conception thing? Um. No disrespect, but is that for real?" Jonah and Ava struggled to contain their amusement, as did many of the other gods—aside from Set.

Isis smiled kindly. "As gods of old, we sometimes forget that people of the modern world may not be familiar with our histories. Long story short, Tristan, my husband Osiris was murdered, his body dismembered and scattered throughout Egypt. My position as Queen was precarious without an heir, so I retrieved the body parts and reformed him for a time with powerful magic. However, I was unable to recover the vital part of him required for procreation."

"What part was he missing?" Tristan asked, not thinking beyond his enthusiasm for listening to the sound of her voice. She paused kindly, and the others waited for the penny to drop. Tristan only looked confused.

"Seriously?" Ava said, unable to comprehend the effect the goddess had on her brother. "Think, Tristan. Which part of your anatomy are you most fondly attached to?"

When it finally hit him, Tristan swore under his breath.

"Please continue," Mallory said, sparing her son further embarrassment.

"I had to cast a powerful spell to impregnate myself with his essence, after which he continued on to the Underworld. I remained in the mortal realm and raised our son," Isis finished.

"Who murdered your husband?" Tristan asked, hoping to redeem himself.

"That would be me," said a deep voice from behind them. Everyone looked at Set, who leaned casually against the wall.

"His brother."

"Awkward…" Tristan muttered.

"Speak of the devil," Isis announced. "Set, why don't you go next?"

"My pleasure," he replied with an amused smirk before taking his time in stepping to the centre of the room, all too aware of how much time it took. His hair was long and black like Isis', and he was slim with broad shoulders. He looked like a young man on the brink of a final growth spurt before shaking off the last remnants of boyhood. His only clothing was something long and black, not quite pants and not quite a skirt. An armband of leather and lapis lazuli clung to his bicep, and his bare back revealed a tattoo of the Eye of Horus, centered within a line of hieroglyphs running from the base of his neck all the way down his spine.

"I am Set, god of the Ancient Egyptians of the desert, storms, chaos, and darkness. Though obviously, I am most well-known for murdering my brother in cold blood." He nonchalantly made his way back to his prior spot.

"Thank you, Set," Zeus stated, apparently trying to revive the momentum while the mortals stared at Set, dumbfounded and unsure of what to make of him. "Inanna. You're next."

"Of course," she purred and moved into the proverbial spotlight, her hips swaying beneath her dark brown curls. They bounced softly, making her ornate earrings tinkle against themselves. "I am Inanna, goddess of the Mesopotamian pantheon. I am the goddess of both love and war and am known for embracing sexuality as well as being feminine, independent, and self-determined. I have been known to bring speedy comfort for those suffering during warfare, as well as inciting confusion and chaos in those who don't obey me. Put simply, I can quite literally drive people mad. I am an expert archer and have been known to ride lions into battle." She paused a moment for dramatic effect, smiling secretly at the admiration beaming toward her from each mortal's face. She lightly touched her talisman before continuing. "My talisman is the eight-pointed star of Venus, and it is of great importance to me."

Before Inanna could make her dramatic exit from centre stage, another voice rose. "I'm next!" The new god made his way to the centre. "I am Vishnu, of the ancient Indus Valley pantheon, more commonly known as Hindu today," he said jovially. He was extremely tall, lending a certain awkwardness to his appearance. "I am the god responsible for preserving and protecting creation, and I am the all-pervading essence of all beings. I am also well known for my mercy and goodness. However, I have little tolerance for ego. Except, of course, in your case, Zeus."

Zeus nodded, and round of chuckling spread through the room.

"I never sleep, and I haven't for as long as I can remember," Vishnu added. "Also, an all-humanistic form isn't my natural state of being. However..." He paused, his skin taking on a vibrant shade of blue before an additional pair of arms sprouted from his torso. In his four hands, he now held a conch shell, a mace, a disc, and a lotus flower. "I usually reserve my true nature for battle. These represent my responsibilities as a god. The conch produces 'Om', the sound of creation. The disc, a chakra, symbolises the mind. The lotus represents existence and liberation, and the mace represents mental and physical strength." Vishnu gestured towards the gem hanging low around his neck. "This is my talisman, the kaustabha gem, which never leaves my person. It represents pure consciousness in all its manifestations. If it were to fall into another's hands, it would corrupt them completely."

"We wouldn't want that now, would we?" came a dry voice from the back of the room. All eyes turned towards the god as he effortlessly pushed himself off the wall against which he'd been leaning.

"We didn't see you back there, Hades," joked Vishnu.

Hades smiled slowly. "What can I say? I like to lurk."

It took Jonah a few seconds to realise he'd been scowling at Ava, whose eyes had widened approvingly while she watched the newly arrived god. Hades moved slowly, purposefully, in a manner Jonah thought rather predatory. He looked more like a rock star than a god with his black leather pants and simple, plain black tee. His arms, folded casually across his chest, boasted a number of leather bands and string bracelets, and his jet-black hair fell in waves around his face, not quite reaching his muscular shoulders. As he laid eyes on Ava's upturned face, he seemed momentarily sidetracked.

"Ava. Pleased to make your acquaintance," Hades said with a charming smile. Then he took her hand and bowed to kiss it. Ava blushed, and Jonah struggled to contain his annoyance.

"Get on with it, Hades," Zeus commanded. Hades shot Ava a wink, to which she responded with a small smile.

"As mentioned, I am Hades, god of wealth and the Underworld. The dark realm…" He paused when he caught Tristan's eye. "Tristan! I believe you have already been acquainted with my assistant Charon. I hear he made quite the impression on you."

"Yeah, mate. He was a real card," Tristan retorted.

Hades chuckled and paced the room. "Contrary to popular opinion, I am not an evil god, but I wouldn't attribute myself with overt goodness, either. If anything, I am neutral. My role is to maintain the balance of life and death and to oversee the Underworld in its entirety. I consider myself to be just and fair, but those who cross me—or, should I say, attempt to cross me—will face a wrath unlike anything they have born witness to before. While I am just, I am stern and unpitying. It might seem cold and cruel, but I find the ferocity of my nature has always served me well, especially in battle. As has my cape of invisibility." He flung his arms dramatically into the air before vanishing briefly from sight, reappearing to enthusiastic applause.

"Who's next?" Zeus asked, looking around the room.

"I'll go. I am Marduk, god of the ancient Mesopotamian era. I am quite an expert on the tablet of destinies, hence one of the reasons I became a part of the Alliance. I suppose you would say I am a *hero* god. Or at least that is what I'm told they called me. I am the god of torrential rain and extreme wind, magnificent tornados and destructive hurricanes. I am also a master of the magical arts. Like Inanna, I too am highly skilled with the bow. As some of you may have realised, I am affiliated with the dragon..." The room fell silent as the young man sprouted an extra pair of ears and eyes, and his skin rapidly morphed into tiny scales. They were metallic in appearance and coloured like an oil slick on the road. "These scales are better than any armour man could make. Very useful in battle. So, too, is breathing fire..."

"For real?" Tristan blurted.

Marduk smiled before turning his head away from them. He opened his mouth wide, and a torrent of flame erupted, though he was considerate enough to ensure nothing was singed in the process. He chuckled, returning to his human form while everyone cheered.

"I'm next!" announced Kali. Jonah found her to be the most intimidating of the gods; she commanded the room's complete and immediate attention. "I am Kali of the ancient Indus Valley pantheon. I am a mother goddess but a benevolent one, as I am also the goddess of creation, preservation, and destruction. I am the conqueror of time, and I represent empowerment and eternal energy." Her skin shifted subtly into blue, much like Vishnu's had. "I am master of the sword and have some rather… unique skills. I can dance into such a frenzy that absolute destruction ensues. However…" She paused, opening her mouth and baring her teeth, which Jonah found odd. Until the fangs descended.

"Are you a vampire?" Tristan shouted before he could sensor himself. Kali contemplated the ceiling for a moment, and Tristan just looked scared.

"I can't say I like that word for it, given how sensationalised vampires have become in the modern world. But for descriptive purposes, I suppose I am. I don't have any weaknesses or boundaries vampires are believed to face, nor do I survive on blood. Though I am certainly strengthened by it. In fact, I quite enjoy drinking the blood of my victims, which, given enough of it, turns my skin a deep shade of red." Kali staring wistfully at the far wall with a small smile before stepping distractedly aside.

Jonah exchanged a bewildered look with Tristan.

Before he could say anything, the Carter house shook with a massive boom. Mallory, Tristan, and Ava turned to Jonah, as though expecting him to know the cause. He shrugged, aware he only mirrored their alarm and confusion.

The gods all stood to attention, poised and ready for action and listening intently.

"What the hell was that?" Jonah asked. The gods ignored him, except for Kali. She simply raised her finger to her lips, signaling them to be quiet before returning her gaze to the ceiling.

Another shudder, stronger than the last, shook the house like an earthquake. Jonah and Tristan stumbled their way toward Mallory and Ava, who sat huddled together. When the shaking stopped and it seemed to finally be over, Zeus nodded to the other gods in silent confirmation. Jonah opened his mouth to demand an explanation, but Zeus raised his hand to stop him.

"It's the Fates. They're trying to break through the barriers we raised around the house."

Jonah looked down to find Ava had grabbed his hand, though she focused her attention on her mother. At the mention of the Fates, Mallory was now as white as a ghost.

"Should we go greet them?" Marduk asked, looking quite ready to jump into battle.

"No," Zeus said. "They know an alliance exists, but they do not know its members aside from the four of us they've already encountered."

"Our barrier is strong," Isis added. "It's already resisted two blows."

"Yes, but how many blows can it endure before it falters?" Kali asked.

Isis looked first at Enki, then at Zeus. "We honestly cannot say. But the Fates have to generate excessive energy to fuel such forceful attacks, and they won't be able to sustain it long enough to fully weaken our barriers."

"Once they've gone, we can reinforce it again as a safeguard against further damage," Enki added.

The gods all seemed content with that plan.

"So, what—" A third blast cut him off, more violent than the last. The force knocked Jonah and Tristan to the ground while most of the gods struggled to stay on their feet.

"Oh, come on!" Tristan shouted before picking himself up off the floor. "Shouldn't they have given up by now?"

Before Zeus could respond, an ear-piercing shriek shattered the momentary silence, ricocheting off the walls. Then it was gone, and no one moved.

After what felt like an eternity, Zeus finally nodded. "Enki. Isis. Go. See if there's any sign of them. Try to avoid being seen, and while you're out there, assess the damage to the barrier." Enki and Isis nodded, then vanished. Then Zeus frowned at the far wall.

"I don't think you have to be a god to realise they're seriously pissed off," Jonah muttered.

"Who cares?" Ava said. "That just confirms they can't get in." Her phone rang, and she pulled it from her pocket. "Hello?" Jonah watched a harsh seriousness cloud her features before she frowned in concern. "I don't understand," she finally said, then lapsed into silence again.

Jonah caught the movement of Zeus leaning over to whisper to Inanna, but he was too concerned about Ava to interrupt.

"Yes. Send it to me, and I'll take a look myself," Ava instructed, rubbing her forehead with her other hand as she ended the call.

"What is it, sweetheart?" Mallory asked.

"Caitlyn. The patient of mine I told you about? She's been having some… unusual… problems."

"You mean the Oracle?" Zeus said.

Ava ignored him. "Now, she's vanished, apparently."

"How do you mean, vanished?" Jonah asked, noting that Zeus didn't seem in the least bit surprised. Instead, the god nodded slowly to himself.

"Vanished," Ava continued. "Literally. That was my boss on the phone, and he said when Caitlyn didn't attend breakfast, the staff went to check on her. But they didn't find her in her room, either, and no one had seen her when they asked around. Long story short, they resorted to security footage. Which ended up capturing the exact moment she disappeared. My boss is sending it to me now." Her phone beeped, and everyone gathered around as she opened the clip.

Jonah found himself loving the way her hair smelled, then he forced himself to focus on the phone in her unsteady hand. He shuffled a bit closer so the others could also see. Ava pressed play on the clip, and the footage revealed an angled view from above in the facility's hallway.

"That's Caitlyn's room." Ava pointed to a door on the right-hand side of the hall, central to the shot. A shadow in the doorway was the first thing they noticed. Then it grew, slowly spilling across the hallway before Caitlyn appeared in the doorway behind it. She halted for a few seconds, then glided out into the hall, the tips of her big toes barely touching the ground.

"Oh, my," Mallory exclaimed.

Caitlyn drifted into the middle of the hall, her ominous shadow spilling across the wall in front of her. Her head swayed from side to side, as though she were either nodding off to sleep or having trouble holding her head up. The dark curtain of her hair covered her face. Then Ava skipped through the footage a little; Caitlyn stayed that way for three minutes before she rotated, still not touching the ground, to face the camera. She raised her head, and her hair and clothes blew backwards as though hit with a gust of wind. The white orbs of her eyes looked straight at the camera, her mouth moved soundlessly, and then she was gone.

"What the... Where did she go?" Jonah asked. Ava shook her head but only stared at her phone.

"She said something before she disappeared," Mallory said. "Can you turn the volume up?"

"It's surveillance footage, Mum. There's no sound."

"Play it back," Tristan said. "Maybe we can make it out." Tristan suggested. They huddled closer together, trying to lip-read on the small screen.

"Wake?" Mallory said. "Is the first word wake?"

"Or it could be where," Ava added.

"I think that's closer," Jonah agreed, "but what's the second word?"

"Dude, I suck at this charade-type crap," Tristan muttered.

"I'm stumped." Ava sighed.

"Can I have a look?" Hades' deep voice sounded from behind them. Ava handed him the phone. He took one brief look before handing back her phone.

"She said, 'We're coming.'"

CHAPTER
TWENTY-ONE

ESPITE HER PROTESTS, both gods and mortals alike refused to let Ava return to work on her own. It wasn't that she didn't believe they were in danger, just that she craved a moment's solitude to wrap her head around everything. She wanted to grieve losing her father, and she'd just watched a bunch of immortal gods she'd never believed in walk out of a mirror. Now, she had to contend with the news that she'd inherited powers from some ancient superhero's mother. Who wouldn't need a time-out?

Hades had offered to escort her, quickly followed by Jonah. But Zeus decided a two-god-minimum escort was required, and Marduk and Isis seemed the least intimidating options, given where they were going. So, prepared to pose as Ava's visiting cousins, they jumped in her car and headed to her workplace. Ava couldn't help but smile when both gods gazed out the windows in awe; Isis had even pressed her palm against the glass to watch the world go by.

"I take it things have changed since the last time you were here," Ava said.

Marduk turned and grinned at her from the passenger seat. "You must think we're quite strange, the way we're behaving. But yes, the world has changed a great deal since we last saw it. It's different for some of the others, particularly Zeus, but Isis and myself have had little call to return to this realm over the centuries. And in earlier centuries, the changes were much slower in coming. From what Zeus has told us, the world has undergone miraculous and rapid shifts within the past hundred years alone."

Ava nodded. "Even in my lifetime, there's been some pretty substantial changes, and I'm only twenty-nine. I can't imagine how it must feel to come from your time and suddenly be thrust into the world as it is today." Then she let the gods view the modern world from the car in peace and quiet.

Eventually, Isis asked, "Does anyone ever consider how the modern world affects the Earth? All this technology and hustle and bustle must be awfully taxing."

Ava glanced in the review mirror, meeting Isis' stare. "Of course we do. There are a number of things in place to try to reduce the impact of our modern lives. For example, people recycle more now, and carbon emissions are monitored, and—"

"Do you think it's enough, really?"

Ava sighed. "No. No I don't. But this is the world we live in. We can only do our best to make sure the footprint we leave behind is as small as possible." There weren't any more questions, but as they drove, Ava noticed something odd in the people around them. Other drivers pulling up beside them at stop lights seemed tense and particularly distressed to be stuck in traffic. Pedestrians on either side of the road either walked quickly, their heads down, or dashed in and out of stores. It seemed no one really wanted to be outside at all. Ava couldn't blame them, though it scared her to realise that even those who knew nothing of what was really going on could sense the change in the air. Their instincts told them something big was coming.

She was only too relieved to finally pull the car into the car-park of the hospital where she worked. Then she issued the gods a few brief instructions and guided them into the building. "Okay, so don't ask any questions. Leave that to me. Remember, you're just my cousins in town for a visit. You have no idea about Caitlyn or what's been happening." Isis and Marduk nodded, their brows set firmly in determination. "And lighten up. Visiting your cousin's supposed to be fun, not like you're going to a funeral."

"Ava!" Dr Fraser headed toward her down the hall. "Look, I'm glad you're here."

"Of course. Any news on Caitlyn's whereabouts?"

"No, nothing. It's like you saw in the footage I sent you. She was standing here one minute, and the next, she was gone. Not a trace of her. We checked all the other cameras in case there was some kind of glitch, but we've come up with nothing. As she was your patient, you know her better than anyone here. I was wondering if you could take a look at her room, her recent case notes, and see if you can come up with anything out of the ordinary or anything that's different since you last saw her."

"I'll get straight on it. Do you mind if my cousins take a seat here in the foyer in the meantime? It's cooler in here than it is outside."

Dr Fraser looked behind Ava, only now noticing she wasn't alone. Flustered, he gestured to the chairs lining the wall. "Yes of course."

Isis and Marduk took a seat, doing their best to appear nonchalant and disinterested. Ava cleared her throat anxiously before she started toward Caitlyn's room.

"Ava?" her boss called again, quickly catching up to her.

"Yes?"

He leaned in close, his voice dropping to a whisper. "Has any of this got to do with what happened between you and Caitlyn?"

Ava pulled back and looked her boss straight in the eyes. "Yes. I believe it has everything to do with it." She then turned and continued to Caitlyn's room, and though she didn't look back, she could feel the burn of Dr Fraser's gaze behind her.

When she reached the center of Caitlyn's room, she stopped and slowly turned around. Nothing looked out of place or out of the ordinary. Certainly nothing to indicate that Caitlyn had planned to leave; all her clothes and belongings were in place. Ava raised her head to the ceiling and noticed the vent in the middle looked askew. Frowning, she grabbed the desk chair and pulled it beneath the vent. Even when she stood on the chair, she could only just reach the vent and pushed it up with her fingers. It shifted aside, and instantly, Ava felt something on the edge of the hole. She strained, trying to lengthen her reach, until she finally felt it move toward her and fall to the ground. Ava hopped off the chair and bent to pick up the book. No, it wasn't a book at all, she realized. This was Caitlyn's journal.

Ava looked back up at the exposed hole in the ceiling and the chair below it. While she wasn't tall, she was a good deal taller than Caitlyn, and she'd still struggled to reach the vent while standing on the chair. So how could Caitlyn have possibly reached it? Then she shuddered at the memory of the things she'd recently seen Caitlyn do.

Sitting on the girl's bed, Ava stroked the cover of the journal. On one hand, it went against an innate girl code to read another's journal. On a professional level, she could justify reading it as a means to help her patient. Either way, Ava knew that any clue as to what happened to Caitlyn, if it existed, would be in these pages. Taking a deep breath, she opened the journal at the most recent entry, which was dated today. The writing was very messy, not adhering to the lines, and some sentences had actually been written over the ones before them. It was a mess, and Ava was baffled as she tried to pull any coherency out of it. After a while, she thought she'd worked it out.

It's late, and I'm trying to write this by the minimal light coming through the window. There doesn't seem to be a moon tonight, or if there is one, it's not shining down on us. I could turn on the lamp or the main light, but they're watching me closely here, and I don't want to draw any more attention to myself. I can't let anything or anyone keep me from my task. It's only a matter of hours now until it takes ahold of me for good. I'm scared. I wonder if I'll still be me. Or will I cease to exist except for in body? Or, maybe worse, will I still be aware but trapped inside myself, unable to control my body, locked within ... just a passenger? I have to force myself not to think too much on it, or I feel the panic clawing at me, wanting to take hold. It does make it a bit easier now to know what my purpose is and how important we are to the cause. It's up to us to let them know, to make them listen. I don't know if the others see the exact same things that I do or whether we each get a glimpse of the whole as we hold up our own small piece of the puzzle.

I feel it now, stronger than ever. The fog is starting to move over me. There's nothing to do now but let it take me. To fulfil my destiny. All I can do is hope to come out of it alive on the other side. But knowing how many will die, can I really hold onto that hope?

Hope. It's all we have, isn't it?

Ava closed the journal and stared at the wall. Despite her rational, logical mind pulling her one way, she had to take the journal entry in context with what she knew about Caitlyn and what was happening. As ridiculous as it seemed, on the other hand, Ava couldn't ignore what she had seen with her own eyes.

"How's it going in here?" Dr. Fraser asked, pulling Ava out of her thoughts.

Ava sighed. "I think I have something, but I'm afraid it won't make much sense to you." He took three slow, hesitant steps into the room, appearing torn between wanting to know more and not wanting to know anything at all. She knew the feeling.

"I don't think it comes as a surprise to you that none of this makes any sense to me, Ava. In fact, the little I do know goes against every rational and logical bone in my body. But at the end of the day, a patient for whom we're responsible has disappeared from within our facility. Regardless of how she departed, we need to ascertain where she's likely to go and if she's likely to pose a danger to anyone. Now, have you found anything that answers either of those questions?"

Ava looked down at the journal in her hand. "Like you said, it won't make much sense…" But she decided to tell him anyway and gave her boss a brief summary of what Caitlyn had written.

"She sounds as though she's suffering from delusions," he said. "And it sounds like she is—or wants to be—part of a group… a terrorist group? She talks of people dying and fulfilling her destiny. These all have to be manifestations of her delusion, considering the only people she has contact with are inside this facility."

Ava opened her mouth to speak, then paused. She hadn't considered it from his perspective, but now that he'd voiced it, she certainly could see how Caitlyn looked like a terrorist.

"I alerted the authorities of her disappearance. Obviously, we'll need to pass this information on to them, too," Dr Fraser added. He'd stepped toward the window and now gazed through it, his feet apart and his hands clasped behind his back.

"I don't think that's a good idea," Ava replied.

"Why on Earth not?" He whirled around to look at her. "What aren't you telling me?"

Ava couldn't exactly tell him the truth, but she had to say something. "I really don't think she's a terrorist, though I can see how it looks that way. I just think there's much more going on, here."

"Well that's evident. There are clearly others. They may have even helped her escape."

A shaky sigh escaped her. She was at a loss as to how to explain something completely irrational to such a rational man. Even then, she also knew Dr Fraser would definitely not be the last person she'd have to convince. "You're right in that Caitlyn is a part of something big. But it's not what you think. I don't have all the answers yet, but I know she isn't a threat to you, me, or anyone else. We need to let this play out."

"What?" He stared at her. "Are you saying we *shouldn't* look for her? Do you realise how irresponsible that is? We have a duty of care, not only to Caitlyn as our patient but to the community, in case she is, in fact, dangerous!"

"I know that. But you can't honestly tell me that you haven't noticed a lot of strange things happening the past few days. Something big is coming. I need to you to trust me on this."

"Trust you? I don't even know what it is you're proposing. How can—"

"Excuse me. Sorry to bother you both, but Dr Carter, you have a phone call."

"Take a message or tell them she'll call them back later," Dr Fraser commanded.

"But sir, they said it's urgent. It's Dr Aljoy—"

"It can wait." Dr Fraser snapped, clearly losing his patience.

"Do you know what it's about?" Ava asked with every intention of taking the call.

"Yes. He said they have a missing patient. She vanished from their facility."

JONAH SAT ON the back porch, looking out on the yard in which he'd spent so many happy hours playing. It seemed surreal that only a few hours ago, he'd witnessed a number of ancient deities step through a mirror and into their world. But then, nothing that had happened to him since he returned from Greece seemed real.

"Penny for your thoughts?"

He turned to find Zeus approaching, but for once, he didn't feel the instant desire to pick a fight with the god. Instead, he only felt relieved to not be alone. "I'm just taking a time-out to go over everything. So much has happened in such a short space of time. It's not going to slow down, is it?"

Zeus sighed and took a seat beside his son. "No, Jonah, it won't. I think you're smart enough to realise that nothing is going to be the same again."

"Hmmm…" Jonah gazed out across the yard.

"Something bothering you? Aside from the obvious, that is," Zeus prompted.

Jonah studied the god, unsure whether to voice his concerns out loud.

"Always better out than in, I say," Zeus stated, leaving Jonah to wonder if mind-reading was part of his gifts.

"I was thinking about the car accident I was in the day I got home. Why didn't the Fate kill me? I was right there. I get now why she looked like she knew who I was, but I don't understand why she killed the taxi driver and let me live. Especially since I'm supposed to be a part of same grand prophecy to stop them."

"You're assuming that was their first attempt." Now Zeus stared out at nothing.

"What are you talking about?"

"Exactly what I said."

Jonah launched himself to his feet. "What are you implying? I'm sure I'd know if someone's tried to kill me. It's hardly the kind of thing a person forgets." He turned on his heel and headed back inside.

"Do you really think that was the first car accident you've survived?"

Jonah stopped, his heart racing, and his mouth went suddenly dry. Now, he didn't want to know what the god had to say, wishing he'd never raised it the issue in the first place. But he ended up turning back to face Zeus again anyway.

"What do you recall about your parent's deaths, Jonah?"

"They died in a car accident. I was at home with our next-door neighbour, Mrs Morgan. I was there behind her when she opened the door for the policemen who came to notify us."

Zeus nodded. "That is what you remember. It isn't what happened." Jonah just stood where he was, torn between wanting to stay and wanting to leave. Zeus took his silence as permission to continue. "The Fates tried to take your life when you were just a boy, thinking that if they removed you from the equation, there would be no one to stop them in the future. Without you, the prophecy would become irrelevant. Obviously, removing you as a child would have been far easier than waiting until you were old enough to set things in motion." Zeus dipped his head and eyed Jonah with a raised brow.

Jonah couldn't bring himself to speak. Instead, on shaky legs, he sat back down beside the god.

"I can't tell you why they chose that day. Or that age. But I know it would have made more sense for them to kill a family of three in a fatal car accident. No questions, no contentions. Neat."

"I don't understand…" Jonah whispered.

"Look back, Jonah. What does your heart tell you?"

Closing his eyes, Jonah forced himself back to the day he'd tried for so long to forget. He pictured his parents—their smiles and laughter. Then, almost like he'd been shocked with a life wire, his memory flooded with the true recollection of it. "I was in the backseat of the car. We were going to the lake for a picnic. I'd been nagging them to take me for weeks so I could try out my new kite."

Zeus placed his hand on Jonah's shoulder. "What happened on the way to the lake? Remember."

The memories danced in the recesses of Jonah's mind, taunting him. "We were singing some song on the radio. Dad kept changing the words, making us laugh..." He paused, rubbing his head in frustration, and strained with everything he had to picture what happened next. "She was there. Atropos. In the middle of the road. Dad was laughing and didn't see her in time to stop, so he swerved. We hit some cars parked on the side of the road, and I felt like I was flying... and then... then..." He let out a frustrated groan.

"What is it?" Zeus asked.

"Then I only remember standing behind Mrs Morgan when she opened the door and the police were there. But that's obviously not right."

"Oh, but it is." Zeus removed his hand from Jonah's shoulder.

"Huh?"

"What you don't remember is that before anything could happen to you, you were removed from the car. You were taken back to your own home and placed there with Mrs. Morgan, neither of you aware that you hadn't been there the whole time."

"Uh... who could've done *that*?"

"I did." Zeus stared at his son, but Jonah had to look quickly away.

"So it's my fault," he muttered. "It's my fault they're dead." His chest tightened; now, he couldn't seem to shove the emotions of that day back down where they'd been for so long.

"How can you say that? Of course it's not your fault."

"Why didn't you save all three of us?"

"And leave a wrecked car without anyone in it? There are limitations even to my powers, Jonah, especially when I'm not solely in one realm or another. I could only save you. I don't expect you to believe me, but it's the truth. And there's something else you need to know."

Jonah glanced at him sideways, not trusting himself to speak.

"Your parents knew how important you were. Are. They knew before you were even born. They couldn't conceive, Jonah, but they desperately wanted a child. The Alliance knew it was time for the prophecy to come about, and we had to ensure you'd be raised by good people. Have a good life. So that when the time came, you would know what you were fighting for. They knew the dangers of loving you. Of raising someone so important. They died to protect you."

Jonah let out a shaky breath as hot tears stung his eyes. "What about Tristan and Ava? Is that just a happy coincidence for you?"

Zeus looked down at his hands. "Do you honestly think there is such a thing anymore?"

Jonah swallowed. "So, my aunt?"

"Not really your aunt. At least, not a blood relative. More like a guardian we placed here in case your living arrangements were ever compromised. If we'd been fortunate enough not to lose your parents, they would have moved onto this street themselves. Either way, you would have met Tristan and Ava. Your destinies are intertwined."

Jonah dropped his head into his hands. He couldn't believe what he was hearing, and yet, his heart told him it was all true. "So you're telling me that my whole life, even before I was born, has been planned and manipulated… just to be ready for what the Fates are doing now?"

Zeus cleared his throat and gazed up at the clouds. "Yes."

Jonah couldn't speak; the lump in his throat threatened to choke him. Without a second glance at the god beside him, he stood and walked away, not bothering to wipe the tears blurring his vision. It perfectly reflected his new view of the world.

BEFORE AVA HAD hung up the phone with Dr. Aljoy, her boss had already been calling around to other facilities. She didn't need to hang around to hear the outcome. After speaking to her friend and colleague, she knew these weren't isolated incidents; two girls exhibiting paranormal phenomenon suddenly vanished from both facilities, each leaving a single message. 'We're coming.' Anxiety clenched her stomach like a vise as she wondered how many others were out there.

Hurrying out to the foyer, she gestured for Marduk and Isis to follow her out the door.

"Why are we leaving?" Marduk asked.

"There's nothing helpful here. We need to talk to Zeus. He seems to know a lot more about Caitlyn's—and whoever else's—role as an Oracle than he's letting on. I need to find Caitlyn before the Fates do." Ava ushered them into the car before flooring it out of the carpark.

DEEP WITHIN THE Blue Mountains, the Erinyes—Alecto, Tisiphone, and Megaera—stood atop the formation known as

The Three Sisters. Each on their own peak, looking out over the mountain range, they sensed the shift in the vibrations drifting up from the world below. The Oracles had been called forward, and the Erinyes knew it wouldn't be long now. In unison, they closed their eyes and outstretched their arms over the mountains. Opening their mouths wider than any human could, jaws extending like snakes, they screamed, sending their high-pitched torment out over the world.

CAITLYN OPENED HER eyes and inhaled deeply. A smile spread across her face. She'd been wrong. The time she'd spent worrying about what she'd become once the Oracle took over was wasted. It relieved her to know she was no different than before she'd left the facility. She still had her own mind, her own will, her own body. There were differences, though; she felt whole, like every part of her from her organs to the smallest cell brimmed with life. It wasn't just her, either. She felt life itself radiating from all around her and moving up from the ground beneath her feet.

She looked around at the others just like her, all standing peacefully, waiting. Caitlyn felt connected to each and every one of them, as if gossamer-like cables ran from one mind to the next. Facing forward again, she looked up at the looming formation in front of them, closing her eyes as the momentous energy it released pulsated over them in warm waves. The sensation was like nothing she'd ever experienced before.

Uluru.

Caitlyn knew she had never been there before but couldn't shake the familiarity of the place, but it didn't matter. A light atop the rock caught their eyes. It grew brighter, its rays slowly expanding out over the edge of the peaks. It rotated, releasing a low-pitched hum. The larger the energy grew, the brighter it became, but Caitlyn refused to close her eyes. As the energy moved over her and the other Oracles, her vision swallowed up in the brightness, the voices whispered to her—to all of them. Concentrating, she listened to everything that was to come.

AVA HAD BARELY turned the car off before she'd leapt out and dashed for the front door. "Zeus! Zeus!" she called, storming from room to room.

"Ava, whatever's the matter?" her mother asked. She gently grabbed Ava's arm and led her into the lounge room.

"I need to speak to Zeus. He knows more than he's saying."

"And why does that surprise you? He is a god, after all."

"It doesn't. But I need to know where he's taken Caitlyn. Where he's taken all of them."

"All of who? Ava, you aren't making any sense."

"She's talking about all the Oracles." Zeus' low rumble of a voice preceded him before he entered the room and took a seat across from Ava and Mallory.

"Well?" Ava demanded.

"Contrary to popular belief, Ava, I don't know everything that goes on." Zeus scoffed, though his expression made Ava suspect he certainly liked to think otherwise.

"But you know what's happened to Caitlyn. You've known all along. She even dreamed about you, for crying out loud."

Zeus nodded. "My role was to prepare those destined for the life of an Oracle. Not all who are chosen are suitable. By visiting them in their dreams, by exposing them to their gifts a little at a time, I was able to separate those who showed great potential from those who didn't have the fortitude for what's to come. Once they've been selected, I can only make an educated guess as to what happens next."

"Well, then, let's hear your educated guess," Ava said. Then Tristan and Jonah joined them, and she was momentarily distracted by the redness of Jonah's eyes. He refused to meet her gaze.

Zeus cleared his throat and leaned back leisurely in his chair. "Part of exposing these people to their gifts is to prepare them as vessels for the Oracle. During this process, they feel like they are losing themselves to another force. They experience blackouts and lost time, often suspecting they've been taken over by something else. Their minds need to expand to make room for all the Source has for them. Those who aren't strong enough will lose their minds. Lose themselves to the Source. The others will move past this stage, and once the Source accepts them, that power becomes more like an embrace. They will feel more complete than they ever have. They are happy. It's then that the Source will reveal everything to them, and they will become true Oracles."

"And what of those who don't make it the whole way through?" Ava asked.

"Usually, they go mad. The strain on their psyche proves too much, but it can't revert to their purely human state. Many end their lives or are institutionalised for life."

Ava scowled at the god's nonchalant response. "How can you be so cold about it? These are people we're talking about."

Zeus stared at her. "I have to be cold, Ava. Do you know how many people populate this planet? Do you know how minuscule the chance is of someone's eligibility as an Oracle, especially in this day and age? That's the price of finding those who *can* do it. Now more than ever, the Oracles are essential.

If you truly understood what was happening around the world right now and what's yet to come, how many lives have already been lost and taken... You would understand that sometimes, you must risk the lives of a few in order to save many."

"Well, I'm not okay with that."

"Ava, how you feel—how any of us feel—is irrelevant," Zeus said, his voice much softer now. "You're still failing to see the bigger picture. The Fates are here to find the Tablet of Destinies and end mankind. For good. In the interim, they're killing as many as they can, and with each death, they grow stronger. Add to that the Erinyes and the rogue Charon, and they're taking souls by the thousands."

Ava huffed, crossing her arms in frustration. "Can you at least tell me if she's going to be okay?"

"Are any of us?" Zeus fixed her with a solemn frown.

"If the Fates gain power by taking lives, is it the same for Charon and the Erinyes?" Tristan asked. He seemed surprised, flustered, and a flush ran up his neck to his cheeks as Isis gave a small smile of approval.

"No, it's not. The Erinyes have enough of their own. And they don't have the capacity to plan anything like this. They exist purely to torment and kill the wrongdoers of the world, and unfortunately, they have more than enough victims to choose from. Their presence merely works to the Fates' advantage. As for Charon... well, that's a troublesome collaboration indeed."

"Isn't he supposed to be under Hades' control?" Jonah asked.

"Control? No. He and Hades have had an understanding for centuries, and Charon has never shown any discontent for his role as the Ferryman. Hades is in the Underworld now with Set, trying to find some answers."

Before anyone could say anything else, the room shook violently around them, and a roar engulfed them to echo off the walls.

"Is it the Fates?" Mallory yelled over the noise, trying to brace herself in the jolting chair beneath her.

"No!" Zeus helped her to her feet and led her to the wide doorway. "It's an earthquake."

Jonah helped Ava to stand, and they followed Zeus. Mallory and Ava squeezed safely between Jonah and the god, who looked past all of them with a frown. "Stay here until it's safe," he ordered, then turned down the hall, hugging the wall as he moved. Ava turned back to see Jonah leaning out into the hall toward where Zeus stood with Enki and Isis at the front door.

"DON'T EVEN THINK about leaving!" Ava yelled in Jonah's ear, grabbing his arm. Turning to see the horrified expression on Mallory's face, Jonah knew he would have to wait. The quake felt relentless, rumbling on without stopping. Amid the crashes from within the house and car alarms sounding outside, he found all he could focus on was Ava's hand on his arm. Part of him wanted to pull away while the other part was grateful for the contact. Wanting to distract himself from his thoughts, he looked back into the lounge room to find the other gods hugging the wall closest to him. He frowned at their calm, completely nonchalant expressions but supposed this wasn't their first earthquake.

When the roar finally died, Jonah realised how tense his body was. He slowly lowered his arms.

"Is it over?" Mallory asked.

Jonah nodded. "I think so. At least for now." He followed her and Ava into the hall toward the front door, carefully stepping over broken glass from fallen photos. When they stepped out onto the porch, Jonah found Zeus, Enki, and Isis standing at the end of the driveway.

"Oh, my God!" Mallory shouted behind him.

Jonah hurried down the steps then slowed, now facing the full extent of the destruction. Debris covered the ground as far as he could see, the houses lining the streets in varying stages of ruin.

"How can one earthquake do all that?" Tristan murmured, stepping past Jonah without waiting for an answer. Cries for help echoed up and down the street as people found themselves trapped in what was left of their homes, trying to free themselves from the rubble. Those who had already escaped stood in shock—some in stunned silence, others in tears as they looked at the hell around them. The gods dispersed toward the rising shouts.

"Can you hear that?" Jonah asked.

"Hear what?" Ava said.

Jonah scanned the street, trying to pinpoint the sound's location. He focused on a wreck of a house down the street, then took off at a run. He only vaguely registered Ava calling out to him before he reached the house. Stumbling over the rubble, he paused and listened for the shout again.

"Help!"

It came from the top of the staircase, which somehow still stood against the toppled second floor with a section of the collapsed ceiling rested against it.

"Hold on!" Jonah reached for the debris and pulled it up and away from the voice. Grunting with the effort, he finally managed to break through to the person trapped below. "Are you okay? Are you hurt?"

"Something's wrong with my leg. Other than that, I think I'm fine."

Jonah leaned over and moved a beam pinning the woman's legs. Her left leg rested at an unnatural angle.

"Jonah."

He turned to find Ava standing at the foot of the staircase, her mouth open in surprise. "Hey, can you give me a hand, here?" he asked.

"Uh, sure." Ava seemed to remember herself and hurried over. "Hi," she said to the woman. "I'm Ava."

"I'm Kat."

Ava gave the woman's hand a reassuring squeeze. "I don't think we should move you, Kat. Your leg's broken, and you might have other injuries." The staircase swayed when the ground shook again.

"Is it another earthquake?" Kat asked, her voice pitched high in panic. Her grip tightened on Jonah's arm.

"It's probably just an aftershock," he replied. "But it's a strong one."

"Get me out," Kat said. "You have to get me out. Help me!" She struggled against the rubble, eyes wide as she edged toward hysteria.

"We have to move her, Ava."

Ava nodded, unable to hide a frown of concern. "Okay, give me your belt."

"My what?"

"Your belt." Ava removed her own from around her dress. "We can't move her with her leg like that. We'll need to splint it first." Catching on, Jonah quickly took off his belt. Ava grabbed a plank of wood from the rubble and cleared a space beside Kat's leg. "I'm sorry, Kat," she said, "but this is going to hurt." The rumbling intensified.

"I don't care. Just get me out of here, please."

Jonah grabbed Kat's arm for support as she howled in pain. Ava worked quickly to strap the woman's leg to the plank of wood.

"Help me get her up," Ava commanded, and without question, Jonah gripped Kat under the arm with one hand and yanked her to her feet. Kat squeezed her eyes shut, the colour rushing from her face and leaving her skin a pallid, ashen grey. She moaned and swayed on her feet. Jonah grabbed her arm and draped it over his shoulder as he positioned himself beside her.

"Hold onto the railing," he told her, "but try not to put too much weight on it. We don't know how sturdy it is."

Kat gave a quick nod, bracing herself as Jonah all but carried her down to the bottom of the staircase. He turned back to find Ava still sitting on the stairs with an awed and partly accusatory frown.

"Ava? What is it? Are you okay?"

She stared for a moment before shaking herself out of it. "I'm fine. Just get her out into the street." Then she tentatively followed.

Her stare made Jonah's stomach knot with anxiety, as though he'd done something wrong. But he had no idea what. He tried to ignore it, focusing instead on helping Kat out onto the street. He turned back in time to see Ava step off the driveway just as the remaining section of Kat's house collapsed.

The other gods were in the process of turning the street into a makeshift refuge. Enki stood in the middle, his arms outstretched as he uttered incantations. Pieces of debris lifted from where they lay, weaved around the stunned residents, then formed themselves into beds and seats for the injured. Jonah couldn't believe that no one batted an eye at the sight.

"They're probably in too much shock to register it," Ava stated beside him. Isis and Marduk were already busily tending to the worst affected, while Inanna and Zeus directed the ever-growing crowd of people. Jonah led Kat to a makeshift bed and gently raised her injured leg. She squeezed his arm in thanks, and he gave her a reassuring nod before joining Ava and Mallory again.

"Will you look at that," Mallory said quietly.

He followed their gaze toward the Carter home. "Holy shit…"

The house stood relatively intact. Aside from some broken windows and a crack running up the length of the driveway and the front of the house, it still stood. It was the only one, as far as Jonah could see.

He scanned the street again, this time more uneasy than awed. "What Tristan said before about the level of destruction… Do you think he was on to something? This was the first earthquake I've ever felt, and it was bloody intense. But given the damage, you'd think everything was built from matchsticks and cardboard."

"I honestly can't say," Mallory replied. "It does seem excessive. Though it certainly wouldn't be the first abnormal occurrence we've witnessed recently."

"You can say that again." Ava glared at him.

"Spit it out," he told her. "That's two bloody dirty looks you've shot me. If you've got something to say, then say it."

"What's going on?" Mallory interjected.

"Jonah's been holding out on us," Ava said, folding her arms across her chest.

Jonah's jaw dropped, and he threw his hands up in confusion. "What the hell are you talking about?"

"How about what happened back there with Kat? Not even two minutes ago. Ring any bells?"

"Uh…yeah…" he said with slow deliberation. "She called for help, and we helped her."

"I never heard a thing," Ava said. "Not from where we were standing. She was too far away. I have no idea how you heard her. Or how you just threw debris around like pieces of cardboard. Or how you lifted the woman with one arm and carried her out of her house without breaking a sweat."

Jonah stared at her, running through the scene one more time.

"I'm going to see if anyone needs a hand…" Mallory said quietly, stepping away from the quarrel.

Jonah looked back down the street toward the rubble of Kat's home. He hadn't realised at the time how easy it had been to clear a path to her or how light she'd been in his arms. "Must have been adrenaline…" he murmured, more to himself than to Ava.

Her scowl softened when she studied him for a moment longer, and she seemed to finally believe him. "You really had no idea you could do those things?" She placed her hand on his shoulder, pulling him back from his thoughts.

He shrugged her off. "Do what? I helped someone. That's all." Then he stormed off, leaving her staring after him.

"WHAT'S HUFFY MCHUFFY'S problem?" Tristan asked, coming to stand beside his sister.

"I think he's just landed himself some superpowers."

"Wait, what? Seriously?"

Ava nodded, her gaze still fixed firmly on Jonah's back.

"Hey, Jonah," Tristan yelled, jogging after his mate. "Wait up! Will you be my superhero?"

CHAPTER TWENTY-TWO

Set looked around the dark, damp cavern while Hades untied the wooden boat from its mooring. "You'd think after all this time, you would have fashioned a more elegant way to enter the Underworld..." he said, climbing into the boat behind Hades.

"And lose the charm of floating down the river Styx? I think not." Hades pushed them out into the water, letting the current guide them forward.

As much as Hades enjoyed a sojourn to the mortal realm, the Underworld was his home. He inhaled deeply, his eyes closed as he revelled in the smell of damp earth and salty air. Most of all, he loved the quiet. While the mortal world grew larger and louder with each passing decade, the Underworld remained unchanged. Hades turned back to Set and found the god resting against the stern, his arms folded across his chest and eyes closed. Hades turned around again and remained silent. He'd known the Set long enough to understand the god's belligerent, flippant attitude was only an external persona. He was far more observant and intelligent than he let on.

The boat came to a jarring stop, and Hades grabbed the bow to save himself from tumbling over the side.

"And you haven't mastered steering yet, either?" Set barked, pushing himself up into sitting.

Hades ingnored him and raised his hand. He tried to extend his reach beyond the boat, but he met only resistance.

"Don't tell me you're barricaded from entering your own realm." Set tried to peer around Hades without rocking the boat.

Hades didn't answer, focusing instead on mapping the range of that resistance with both hands. With a guttural growl, he slumped back to the boat's seat. Then he opened his arms to settle his palms above the surface of the water and whispered his incantations. The river surged to the right, tipping the boat precariously to the left before pushing back toward them and gently guiding them to the rocky riverbank. Without a word of explanation, Hades stepped from the boat and held it steady for Set to do the same.

"Where are we going?" Set asked. "We clearly can't travel much farther."

Hades scowled in focused determination and heaved the boat onto the rocks and beyond the water's reach. "No one knows this place better than I do." When he turned to find a way in, Set walked silently behind him, keeping pace and prudently refraining from testing any more of Hades' patience.

THEY CLIMBED A steep embankment, sending small rocks tumbling down into the river below, and when they moved higher, they had to navigate the stalactites hanging from the cavern's ceiling. Only a few meters from the top, Hades placed both hands on the cavern wall, bowed his head, and weaved his magic. A section of the stone faded away, as though it had never been, to reveal a narrow tunnel. Torches lit themselves as the god of the Underworld led the way, the flames jumping high and sending shadows across the walls as they passed. With determined strides, Hades obviously knew exactly where he was going. Set had to quicken his pace to keep up.

"It's a daring move, blocking you from entering from Styx," he stated, careful to keep his tone neutral.

"And I don't doubt the other six rivers leading into the Underworld would fare the same," Hades growled.

"Who could have done this? Why?"

"Charon is the only being beyond the gods powerful enough to control the gates of the Underworld." Hades hissed the name, and the torches flickered, as though wincing away from his wrath.

"After all these centuries? It doesn't make sense."

"No. It doesn't." They stopped at the passage's dead end.

"Now what?" Set asked.

With a flick of his hand, Hades extinguished the torches, throwing them both into darkness. Set could barely make out the shape of the other god's hand upon the rock wall. A blue light cracked through the crevices of the stone, and this section of the cavern also disappeared. A multitude of moans echoed toward them, bouncing around the narrow tunnel. "Is it normally this loud in here?" Set asked.

Hades gave a curt shake of his head without turning around. He motioned for Set to stay where he was and took a cautious step forward. A short ledge extended over the abyss before him, then the stone dropped abruptly to the central cavern below.

Hades stared out into the heart of his domain. Each of the seven rivers entered the cavern from a different direction to congregate in the centre, vanishing under a rotating platform. Upon that sat a high-backed throne forged of iron and stone. A snarling stone dog topped the back of the chair, its eyes glinting with fiery-red rubies. The ends of the armrests were decorated similarly—a tribute to Cerberus.

Perched on the throne, wooden staff in hand, sat Charon.

"Traitor," Hades growled, taking a step forward before Set placed a firm hand on his shoulder.

"You'll give us away."

Hades clenched his fists at his sides, clearly fighting his urges. Only once he stepped back did Set remove his hand. "Keep close," Hades commanded, raising his left fist above them. Then he opened it and slowly lowered his arm, as though he'd grabbed an unseen thing from the air.

Set looked up to see a hazy shimmer in the stone overhead, and he blinked to clear his vision. "What..." Something caressed his skin, not unlike the gentle weight of spiderwebs.

"Move slowly, and no one can see you beneath my cloak," Hades advised gruffly. "It will protect you." Then he stepped out onto the ledge again, where Set placed a hand once more on his shoulder—this time urging him onward.

They crept along the ledge, hugging the stone wall to keep their feet from the precarious edge, mindful of each step while observing what happened below. Boats entered the cavern from dark tunnels, the passengers blinking and covering their eyes against the unexpected light. The closer the boats drew to Charon on the throne, the more the people's forms faded, their essence disappearing until they were mere shadows. Before they even knew what was happening, what little remained of them was yanked from their seats and absorbed into the aether. Then the empty boats returned the way they'd come.

The aether stretched the width of the wall behind the throne's platform, casting an eerie blue light across the cavern. It reached at least a hundred meters wide and rose past Hades and Set, far higher than they could see. The force of it writhed and stretched, the souls contained within trying futilely to escape, their gaping faces masks of horror and despair.

Set swallowed. "Are they..."

"Shades. Yes."

They watched boat after boat arrive to offload its cargo before leaving for more. "Is it always this busy?" Set asked.

Hades shook his head. "He's collecting souls before their time and disrupting the balance—" A tremor rippled through the cavern. The proceedings below them continued as though nothing had happened. "There are too many. I guarantee this is the source of the earthquakes and their severity."

Before Set could reply, one boat entered the cavern below but did not perform as the others. Instead of delivering its passengers to then fade away, this vessel continued untouched. There were only three passengers, each with cascading red hair.

"I should have known..." Hades hissed. Set swore, his protests drowned out as another tremor rumbled around them. Charon rose from the throne in greeting, aiding the three sisters onto the platform where he stood. "We need to get closer," Hades said, but Set stopped him.

"There's no need." He placed his finger to his lips and turned his ear toward the column below them. Closing his eyes, he focused his hearing on the small congregation, blocking out all other sounds around them.

"WELCOME, ATROPOS, CLOTHO, Lachesis." Charon greeted each with a kiss on her outstretched hand, his voice deep and gravelly. "I'm glad you could make it."

"I'm sure you are," replied Atropos as she stepped aside and walked around the platform, inspecting their surroundings. Her sisters stood where they were but also surveyed the grand cavern.

Hades' breath hitched when Lachesis turned and looked straight up at where they stood. There was no way she could see them under the cloak, yet Hades thought she seemed to know exactly where—and who—they were. But she turned around without a word to focus once more on the meeting between Charon and Atropos.

"Are you aware of the damage our little project has caused in the mortal realm?" Atropos said.

"Yes. An unfortunate consequence—"

"Unfortunate? I think not. It's a matter of greater effect with less effort, if you ask me. The more devastation, the better. It makes our end goal all the easier." Charon simply nodded, leaving his head bowed. Atropos continued to circle the platform. "How much longer will it take to collect all the souls we require?"

"A week or two at most, I should think."

Atropos clapped her hands, a small smile flashing across her face. It only succeeded in making her look all the more sinister. "Think of all the damage incurred over another two weeks. There will be no one left to fight us at this rate."

"The odds are certainly in our favour," Clotho stated, a hint of a smile playing at the corners of her mouth. They all turned to Lachesis, eagerly awaiting her contribution.

"In whose favour would it otherwise be? We're the Fates, after all," Lachesis conceded, avoiding meeting their gazes as she stared up at the aether.

Atropos turned from her sisters and back to Charon with a raised eyebrow, flicking her hair off her shoulder. "You're certain they'll fight?"

Charon watched the faces of the dead, contorted by fear and despair as they surged against their confines. "To get out of there? They'll fight till there's nothing left."

Atropos looked up at the tortured souls; the blue hue gave her grin a malicious edge.

Set opened his eyes, his mouth agape.

"What? What is it?" Hades hissed, grabbing Set's shoulders to brace the unsteady god.

"We have to get back to the others. Now."

Hades froze, stunned into a split second of silence at Set's uncharacteristic display of emotion. Lowering his hands, he led them back the way they'd come. His heart thundered in his chest, and he suddenly felt claustrophobic under the cloak. Not in all the time he'd known Set had he ever seen the god afraid. Yet there was no mistaking the fear in his voice now, and Hades hurried them out of the Underworld.

JONAH SAT ON the curb in a futile attempt to break away from the growing crowd. Dusk rapidly approached, and people had gathered the debris to make small bonfires up and down the street. So many people. He knew they weren't all residents of this section of the street; he'd watched them make their way here from either end all afternoon. Emergency services had arrived at one point on foot, unable to get their vehicles through.

Once they'd seen everything was under control and the injured tended to, they'd left blankets, water, and first-aid supplies before moving on to check neighbouring areas. Without having to move closer, he'd heard them telling Enki of the widespread destruction. They had their work cut out for them, and while this street was fortunate enough not to have sustained any fatalities, others had not been so lucky. Enki had assured the paramedics they could send any survivors here. Jonah refused to think about his ability to overhear their conversation in the first place.

Instead, he replayed the afternoon over and over in his mind. The way Ava and Tristan had looked at him left him uneasy, and for the first time since he'd met them, he felt excluded. Sure, Tristan made his usual jokes, but once Jonah relayed to him what had happened, he'd noticed a sudden caution in his mate's eyes.

He'd tried to tell himself he was being paranoid, but the fact that both siblings had kept their distance the rest of the afternoon did little to dispel his fears. Hoping to distract himself, he'd fiddled with his mobile, but there was no reception.

Out of the corner of his eye, he saw Zeus take a seat on the curb beside him. For a little while, they sat in silence, staring out at the bustling street. Jonah let out a long sigh. "I'm guessing you're here because you heard what happened."

Zeus cleared his throat and answered without diverting his gaze. "Why don't you tell me what happened?"

"I don't really know. I heard a woman cry out for help, and I helped her. It wasn't until after the fact that Ava claimed I couldn't have possibly heard her, that I shouldn't have been able to free her from the debris as easily as I did. If I play it back, I know it doesn't add up. I was definitely too far away to hear her. She was caught under *so much* debris, I could never lift it on my own. But I did." He paused, stealing a sideways glance at his immortal father as he tried to gauge the god's thoughts. Zeus' expression remained unreadable. "I keep telling myself it was just like one of those random stories you hear, when people suddenly have super-human strength to save someone, but…" Silence hung between them as Jonah debated whether to continue.

"But you know in your heart that wasn't it," Zeus prompted.

Jonah leaned back on his hands, looked up at the darkening sky, and nodded.

"What do you think really happened?" Zeus asked.

"Why don't you just tell me what happened?" Jonah snapped, returning his gaze to the earth.

"Because you need to think this out for yourself. I can only guide you."

Jonah frowned; this made him angry, despite knowing Zeus was right. But voicing his theory aloud would mean acknowledging the changes in himself—and so much had happened already in such a short amount of time. "I don't know how to put it into words… I don't know if it's a one-off thing, or if it's part of something bigger. I didn't feel any different. I still don't. I honestly have no idea what's happening to me. Or what to think." He placed his head in his hands and realised the afternoon's feats had caught up with him. His muscles ached, especially his arms, and he closed his eyes as a wave of fatigue washed over him.

Zeus reached out and placed his hand on Jonah's shoulder. "Whether you said it aloud or not, you've accepted your decendency. By doing so, you have released a part of yourself that had been locked away until now."

Jonah lifted his head and looked at Zeus with raised brows—partly fearful but mostly intrigued by the sudden prospect. "You mean, I actually do have superpowers now?"

Zeus let out a deep, boisterous laugh as he dropped his hand from his son's shoulder. "Not exactly. Any mortal son I've sired in the past has possessed talents and skills that far exceed those of his peers. Inhuman strength is almost always one of them. Bravery, too. Yet you're the first of my offspring to not have had full access to these skills from childhood. The chance to grow into them. So I honestly don't know what to expect. I only know that in the coming days, you'll find yourself able to do things you've never dreamed of. It will seem daunting at first, but the other gods and I are here to help you adjust."

"Is there any chance I can just stay the way I am?"

"Of course," Zeus said with a gentle smile. "You can denounce me as your true and legitimate father. But would you really want to? We don't know for certain what's coming our way just yet, but I guarantee you, we could use whatever edge you might bring to the game."

Jonah sat silently, circling his thumbs around each other as he tried to wrap his head around the revelation. "You realise that so far today, I've accepted that a Greek God is my father, I've watched a group of ancient deities walk through a mirror, I've seen a girl vanish into thin air, discovered my parents' death wasn't an accident, experienced an earthquake in a place where I'm pretty sure there's never been one before, and have been told I have superhuman powers. The day's not even over."

"It is a lot, yes."

"That's the best you can come up with?" Jonah scoffed. "It's a lot?"

"What would you like me to say, Jonah? That tomorrow will be better? It won't. In fact, there's a good chance it could be worse. Should I tell you everything will be okay? Because it likely won't be. So yes, that's the best I can do right now."

"Hey, everyone! Come listen to this," someone called from beside a large bonfire up the street. Without another word, Zeus and Jonah stood and jogged toward the rapidly growing huddle of people. Jonah weaved his way through the throng to find a man of about sixty standing in the middle. His shirt was torn, his feet bare, and his face was streaked with dirt. But his eyes were ablaze with enthusiasm as he twisted the dials on an old AM/FM radio.

"I just had it working. One second."

The crowd waited tensely as the crackle and hiss of the static jumped from the speakers. With the twist of a dial, a voice broke through the noise, and they collectively leaned forward to hear.

"...emergency broadcast... catastrophic... worldwide... fault lines... all cities bordering the San Andreas Fault down through Chile have been destroyed... unprecedented... tsunamis have wiped out Japan, Hong Kong, New Zealand, South East Asia, Iceland... Africa has split down the middle, from Libya to South Africa... incoming... fatalities... next broadcast is at 6am EST..."

The voice faded away in the static, and the older man turned off the radio. "Best conserve the battery," he whispered. A resounding silence hovered over the crowd until the shock of the announcement passed. Then the questions flew with panic-filled voices.

"What's happening?"

"What do we do?"

"Where do we go?"

"Are we safe here?"

Jonah caught Zeus' eye from the far edge of the crowd and made his way back toward him as Enki replaced the old man with the radio to attempt some damage control.

When Jonah reached Zeus, he found Mallory, Ava, and Tristan already with the god, their expressions all mirroring fear and bordering on the same panic.

"Did you hear that?" he asked. They nodded.

"I can't believe it," Mallory said, her arms wrapped around herself and her face contorted with grief and concern. "A worldwide earthquake? How is that even possible?"

"How is anything that's happened today possible?" Ava said. "I don't even feel surprised anymore..." She placed an arm around her mother's shoulders.

"But all those people? All those places? I can't believe they're just gone..." Mallory's voice shook, and she wiped a tear from her face.

Zeus stepped forward and grabbed Mallory's hand, holding it until she looked up at him with a sad but grateful smile.

"What do we do now?" Tristan asked, his hands shoved into the pockets of his jeans as he stared at the ground.

"For now, we can only wait," Zeus replied. "As soon as I know more, you will too."

Jonah met Ava's gaze and felt overwhelmed by the flood of unspoken questions she directed at him. He opened his mouth, then closed it again, wanting to reassure her but unable to find the words.

He was saved by a quick flash of light farther up the street, and they all turned to see Set and Hades hit the ground running. They slowed their pace to a brisk stride, and despite the fading light of dusk, there was no mistaking their grim expressions.

Zeus strode toward them, the others hot on his heels. The gods clasped forearms in greeting. "I take it things didn't go well in the Underworld," Zeus stated.

Hades and Set exchanged a glance before Hades spoke. "I still can't believe it myself." He shook his head. "If I hadn't seen it with my own eyes…" Then he relayed what had happened, Set interjecting where necessary. When they'd finished, a dark silence draped over the group, clouding them in despair. Zeus swallowed thickly, his bravado clearly shaken.

"I can't take any more of this. I just can't!" Mallory sobbed and turned to hurry away.

"Mum," Ava cried, rushing after her.

Jonah gazed after them, not really seeing anyone. He felt like his brain had reached its capacity for comprehension a long time ago.

"At least we know what the Fates are up to, now," Zeus murmured, gazing up at the night sky, as though the answers were somehow located amongst the stars.

"Yes, well, there is that…" Set replied sardonically, his hands folded against his chest while he sneered.

"How could you let that happen?" Tristan spat at Hades. "Aren't you the bloody god of the Underworld? How could you not have noticed?"

"In case your puny mortal mind has failed to see, we've been dealing with a crisis in your realm. I wouldn't expect an imbecile like you to—"

"Enough," Zeus warned, his voice dangerously low as small sparks flew around him. "I will not tolerate fighting amongst us. Did you not hear what was just said?"

"So, what are we going to do?" Jonah cut in, flinging a sideways glance at Tristan. He tried to mask his concern over his mate's uncharacteristic outburst.

"Right now? We rest, because over the coming days, we need to find a way to convince all these people not only of who *we* are but that they are about to go to war. Against an army of the dead."

Everyone turned to look out over the street, eerily quiet after the ruckus following the radio bulletin. Now, the survivors all lay on makeshift beds or curled up on the grass of front lawns, which had been cleared of debris to make room.

"Wait, how did…"

"My words can have a potent persuasion when the need calls for it," Enki interjected, appearing suddenly behind Jonah.

"I wish you lot would bloody stop doing that," Jonah said in a forced whisper. "Did you make them forget?" He felt as if speaking any louder would pull the crowd out of their silence.

"No. That wouldn't do us any good. I've just placed them under a certain acceptance. They know what they heard but without fear or concern. It just is."

"Sounds like a magical Valium…" Tristan quipped.

"I don't know what that is, but I will take your word for it," Enki replied solemnly. "It will lift, of course. It's not a permanent fix, but it will enable them to rest, to recover somewhat from the day they've had, and to prepare for what lies ahead. Whether or not they know what's coming."

"Right. The army of shades waiting to be unleashed upon us," Jonah said quietly, his attention on his sneaker as he scuffed the toe back and forth along the bitumen. No one said anything. After a few moments, he felt Zeus' firm grasp on his shoulder.

"You should get some rest."

"We all know there's no sleep for us tonight. We don't have the luxury of being magically sedated."

"No, you don't. But you should allow your body to rest, even when your mind cannot."

"He's right, Jonah," Enki added. "We don't know when you'll next get the opportunity to do so."

Jonah nodded. "Okay. I'll rest. On one condition."

"What's that?" Zeus asked, lowering his hand.

"I think it's time you told us everything you know about the Tablet of Destinies."

CAITLYN LIFTED HER foot off the edge of the ledge where she perched, holding it out over the crowd congregating several stories below her. She smiled sadly as their gasps of thrilled horror rose toward her. A lot of thought had gone into which building to select as her platform. It had to be high enough that the threat of harm to herself was real, yet not too high that no one could see her. It also needed to be central enough to draw a large crowd and timed exactly right for maximum impact.

Yet despite her planning, she'd stood there for well over an hour before anyone had noticed. Caitlyn had watched them all scurrying below her, each contained within their own bubble—hundreds of people coming and going, yet they all moved as though they were alone. Now, her presence on the edge of the building pulled them out of themselves; there was nothing like a stranger's unfolding tragedy to draw them from their thoughts, uniting them in their need to witness someone else's pain and misfortune.

A breeze gathered around her, caressing her face, and Caitlyn closed her eyes. She felt a surge course through her, not unpleasant but a reminder of the tether to others like her—the chosen. The Oracles. She no longer felt fear. Everything had happened for a reason and would continue for a reason—the good and the bad alike. It had led her to her purpose. Caitlyn lifted her face toward the sun, smiling as the warmth spread through her. Then she jumped.

CHAPTER TWENTY-THREE

JONAH LEANED BACK into the ground-level beach chair he'd found his legs stretched out in front of him and his arms folded across his chest. He didn't care if the gods thought him stubborn; he didn't want to risk lying down and falling asleep. Tristan's feet rested on the ground to his left, his face hidden in the shadows of the hoodie he'd pulled over his head before leaning against the three. Ava's head lay on a bunched-up jumper to his right, her hands tucked under it for support. Mallory lay beside her daughter, gazing up at the stars. The gods congregated around them, some sitting, some standing.

Marduk sat on an upturned box opposite Jonah, the light from the small bonfire in the middle of their huddle sending dancing shadows across his face. "It is known that I am the most knowledgeable about the Tablet. I've endured the most exposure to it. Though I don't want to bore you with the lengthy myths and legends. It's been a long day.

"Most people assume the Tablet of Destinies is a clay tablet, largely in part to false information we delivered centuries ago, when mankind first became aware of its existence. It is actually comprised of three discs, each with a hole in the centre. The largest, the outer disk, represents the past, the middle disk represents the present, and the smallest, innermost disk represents the future. They rotate in constant motion, sometimes in unison, sometimes against each other, but always in a continual state of flux. Whoever holds the tablet, god or man, has the power to influence the universe."

"This might be a stupid question," Tristan interrupted. "But why hide it? If the owner becomes all-powerful, can't they just kick the Fates' arses back to wherever they bloody well came from?"

"Tristan..." Mallory chastised.

"It's not a stupid question," Marduk replied gently. "While that does seem like the obvious answer, it's not that simple. The Tablet is primordial in origin, as are the Fates, and contains more power than a god can indefinitely sustain. The Tablet is worn across the chest, and if a mortal were to wear it, even for a short length of time, their soul would be become corrupted, their sanity destroyed." Tristan only gave the god a brief nod.

"The Tablet was originally possessed by Tiamet," Marduk continued, "a formidable, primaeval creature, who also created the Mesopotamian gods. My family. She was our Great Mother... and I killed her. Under her reign, there was only madness. We believe the immensity of the Tablet's power fed on the darkness within her, amplifying it until she was capable of only destruction. Yet with it, she remained stronger than all of us combined. We do not know why she passed the Tablet to her consort Qingu. But we seized the opportunity and went to battle, where I eventually slew Tiamet. I wanted to end the chaos, and my brethren needed a permanent home in the mortal realm. When I dismantled her body, I used the pieces to form the lands of Mesopotamia."

"What the hell is with these gods cutting each other up?" Tristan muttered, then Zeus shot him a glance, clearing his throat to silence him.

Marduk went on with his tale, seemingly unaffected by Tristan's outburst. "When I took possession of the Tablet, its power was clearly unsteady. So full of magic, it had haemorrhaged, fuelling chaos in those who bore its weight. The only way I could contain it was to lock it with my own magic and seal it within my chest. This granted me the title of Supreme Sovereign of the gods, though I did not shoulder the burden alone. Any time I felt the essence of the Tablet weighing me down—and I did, frequently—one of the other gods watched over it until I could regain my strength and sanity."

"What does it actually do?" Jonah asked. "We know the Fates want it so they can rid the world of mankind, but how does it work?"

Marduk bowed his head and shifted in his seat, as though unsure how to tell them. Zeus placed a hand on the god's shoulder, who then raised his head. "We believe the Fates' intent is to destroy mankind. In the hands of someone as powerful as the Fates, the Tablet could emit a pulse of primordial energy to sweep across the world at unfathomable speed, decimating the human race in a single wave. Complete annihilation of an entire species, and there would be nowhere to hide."

The gods turned toward their human companions, trying to gauge their reactions. Jonah, Ava, Tristan, and Mallory sat frozen in place, their expressions variations of the same horror. After what felt like an eternity, Ava broke the silence. "How can something like that only wipe out mankind and leave everything else?"

Enki replied, "We don't completely understand how. If we did, we could have spent all this time creating a failsafe. We believe the primordial gods, despite their madness, foresaw man one day posing a serious threat to the earth, and therefore, the magic was focused solely on the human race."

"You can see why it's imperative the Fates never possess it," Marduk finished, "and why they are going to such lengths in their pursuit of it."

"Do you know where it is now?" Mallory asked.

Marduk exchanged glances with the other gods. "No. We don't."

"What?" Jonah and Ava cried out together.

"You're telling us an object that can eradicate us all in a matter of seconds is missing?" Jonah yelled, and Enki held his hands up in defence.

"Not missing, no. We just don't know where it is."

"I'm confused," Ava stated.

Marduk took a deep breath in an apparent attempt to remain calm. "When we began our retreat as the new gods came into being, we knew we couldn't keep the Tablet with us. We would be the first place the Fates would look once our powers had weakened. The prophecy surrounding the Tablet's role in our future came about, and we formed the alliance. I extracted the Tablet from myself and gave it to Zeus. Each of us agreed the mortal realm was the best place to hide such power, and that was the last time I saw it."

All eyes turned to Zeus, who stood with his legs shoulder-width apart and his arms folded across his chest. He said nothing.

"So… where is it?" Jonah prompted.

"I have no idea," Zeus replied, holding Jonah's gaze, as though daring a challenge.

"How is that possible?" Mallory asked.

"All I can say is that I must have found a safe, secure place. But I don't remember where that is."

Before anyone could voice further protests, Hades added, "Zeus came to me in the Underworld and told me he'd become a liability. Once he'd confirmed Jonah's conception, he was concerned the Fates would discover he knew the Tablet's location and would then use Jonah as leverage. So I agreed to let him drink from the river Lethe."

"Okay," Tristan said. "So I know I'm the mythology dumbass of the group, but would someone please explain to me how drinking from a river in the Underworld has anything to do with the Tablet?"

"It makes you forget," Hades stated. "It's usually reserved for the souls to drink from, erasing all memories of their existence before they're reincarnated. However, in strong minds and in controlled amounts, it can be used to eliminate only specific memories."

"So let me clarify," Jonah said, jaw clenching in anger. "We have no idea where the one thing that could destroy us all is actually hidden."

"That is correct," Zeus replied, seeming to ignore Jonah's irritation. "But I have complete faith the location will reveal itself in good time. This is the safest way for everyone. And it also means the Fates themselves don't know where it is."

"And now they've decided to just build an army and kill everyone on Earth anyway until they get their hands on it," Ava finished. "What can *we* possibly do?"

"We fight back," Zeus replied, gazing defiantly up at the stars.

CAITLYN TOOK A moment to steady herself. While she'd survived the fall, her body still trembled from the impact. On one knee, with her hands braced against the footpath and her head bowed, she heard the shouts of disbelief from the crowd surging forwards. Raising her head, she found herself confronted by a myriad of smart phones; those onlookers, amazed by their good fortune of capturing the impossible on camera, struggled for the best angle.

"Are you okay, miss? Are you hurt?" a gentleman in a business suit asked, one of only a few to approach her with any level of concern. She gave him a smile and slowly rose to her feet.

"Maybe you shouldn't move," an old woman added. "You could be hurt. You *should* be hurt." The woman apparently couldn't stop looking from Caitlyn to the top of the building and back again.

Caitlyn accepted the man's arm as she steadied herself, then stepped onto the bonnet of a parked car beside her. Climbing to the car's roof, she addressed the crowd. "Now that I have your attention, I am Caitlyn, Oracle of the Alliance. I am only one of many throughout the world. Today, we come to you with a warning. The end is upon us, whether you choose to see what's happening around you or not. They're coming for us all. Our hope lies with the Three…" She barely registered the gasps and exclamations when her feet left the car, and she rose into the air, her arms outstretched. "Open your eyes, and you will see them." The crowd erupted when she disappeared.

Caitlyn smiled at the wall of warmth sweeping over her. For a brief moment, she remembered how it felt to be held in her mother's arms. Instinctively, she knew the other Oracles felt it too—and what it meant. Opening her eyes, she felt her smile falter when she thought about what was coming, and she said a small prayer for Ava.

JONAH OPENED HIS eyes, blinking as he tried to regain his bearings. Realising he'd fallen asleep in the beach chair, he rubbed his neck, sore from the awkward angle. The gods were gone, but Tristan was out cold, snoring softly into his hoodie. Jonah turned to find Mallory also asleep, the light of the fire reflecting in the tears still upon her cheek. He sat upright when he realised only the jumper remained where Ava had lain. Instantly alert, he scanned their surroundings for any sign of her. He peered through the darkness and saw her farther down the street, her back to him as she walked in the centre of the road. Careful not to wake anyone, he jumped to his feet and jogged effortlessly toward her, hardly feeling his feet touch the ground before he'd rapidly closed the gap between them.

"Ava! Hey," he called as loudly as he dared. She turned, wide-eyed at his sudden approach. Then he noticed the way she hugged herself and the wetness of her eyelashes. "What's wrong?" he whispered.

The corners of her mouth tugged upward in a reluctant smile. "Really?"

Jonah gave a coy shrug. "Yeah, I guess that's a stupid question. I just don't like seeing you upset."

She nodded, and he fell into step beside her. "I keep waiting to wake up and find this was all a bad dream. But at the same time, as crazy as it is, I know it's real. This is our reality now, and I hate not having any control over what happens around me. Tristan's withdrawn, even for him, and he's barely said a word aside from the odd crack. Poor Mum is really struggling. I don't know how much more she can take. And… and I just miss Dad so much—" Her voice broke off with a sob, and she clasped her hand over her mouth when the tears came.

Jonah spun her around by the shoulders and pulled her toward him to wrap his arms around her. She clutched at his shirt and cried against his chest, overwhelmed by the grief, fear, and frustration she'd grasped so tightly. He remained silent, stroking her hair as she cried it out. When she finally seemed ready to stop, he was suddenly aware of the intimacy of their embrace. He froze in place, unsure whether he should release her or stay where he was. It both relieved and disappointed him when Ava raised her head. Yet she didn't pull away or seem to mind that his arms were still around her. As she gazed up at him, her hands still pressed against his chest, he hoped she couldn't feel the uncontrollable thundering of his heart. Staring down at her, his fears faded into the background, and he found himself lost in her wide-eyed stare.

Ava was always the strong one—so determined, albeit stubborn. Jonah was certain he could count on one hand the number of times he'd seen her cry. While he admired her strength and her voracity, her vulnerability at this moment made his soul ache. "Dammit, you're so beautiful, Ava," he whispered. A fleeting look of surprise flashed across her face before she reached up, wrapped her hand around the back of his neck, and pulled him close. She paused, leaving the least amount of space between them, and Jonah pressed his lips against hers. All hesitation melted away. His racing heartbeat echoed in his ears as she kissed him back. His body sizzled where it met hers, and a heat radiated from his chest, spreading through him until he felt so light with elation, he might float away. When she gently pulled back, every part of him trembled in protest. Still, he opened his eyes to find hers and felt happier than he had in his entire life.

Ava smiled, letting out a shaky breath.

"Woah…" Jonah grinned. "That was—"

"Ow!" Ava doubled over, clutching her forehead.

"What's wrong?" Concern swiftly replaced Jonah's joy. Ava fell to her knees, and he knelt beside her, trying to pull her hands away so he could see. But she squeezed them against her head, as though her life depended on it. Helpless, he watched her face contort in intensifying pain, tears streaming down her cheeks. "Help!" he shouted toward the camp. "Somebody helps us!"

Immately, Enki and Isis appeared, flocking to Ava's side. "Ava, tell me what's happenening," Isis instructed, her voice calm and even.

"Voices. So many voices," Ava moaned through clenched teeth. "Please. Make them *stop*."

Jonah didn't know what to do but step back. "I'm right here," he told her, and as soon as he spoke, Ava's head flew back, her eyes opening wide to gaze up at the stars. "Oh, shit…" The beautiful eyes he'd stared into only moments before had been replaced by milky-white orbs.

"Bear witness, for I am Hephalion returned." The male voice came from Ava's mouth before she slumped into Isis' arms.

Jonah stared down at them, unable to move. "What the… Was that a man's voice? In Ava?" he stammered.

Isis and Enki exchanged knowing glances. Isis rose, stepped toward Jonah, and placed a comforting hand on his arm. He barely noticed, watching Enki lift Ava into his arms, her head rolling against his chest like that of a sleeping child.

"I take it something happened between the two of you?" Isis asked quietly.

Jonah pulled his gaze from Ava in surprise. "Why would you ask me that? What the hell's happening to her?"

Isis paused a moment, studying him. "Long story short, she's fulfilling her destiny."

"WHERE IS SHE? What's happened?" Mallory cried, shoving her way through the gods converged in the hallway. Tristan followed a step behind her. When she found herself faced with a closed door, she looked farther down the hall to see Jonah pacing, his hands behind his head, eyes darting as if unable to clear an awful memory.

"Jonah! Where's Ava? Is she okay?"

"I... I don't know. One minute she was fine, and the next minute... She's in there with Zeus, Enki, and Isis. She passed out, and they brought her back to the house to keep her out of sight. They didn't want anyone else to see her."

"What happened? What was she doing?" Mallory demanded, her voice trembling as she struggled to hold back her tears.

"I... uh..."

Jonah was saved from having to reply when the door opened, and Zeus filled the frame. "Come in. You can see her now."

Mallory hardly waited for him to step out of the way before she pushed into the room and dashed to her daughter's side. Tristan followed with Jonah behind him.

Ava lay on the bed, her hands resting on her stomach and her eyes closed.

"Is she…" Tristan started.

"Sleeping," Isis finished for him. "She regained consciousness, but the transition requires a lot of energy, and she needs to rest while it takes place."

"Transition?" Mallory said, her voice breaking. "Will someone tell me what the hell happened?" She glanced at Jonah, but he seemed particularly interested in studying the corners of the room.

"I believe you heard Ava's story about the prophecy she'd been researching concerning Hephalion," Enki said gently.

"Yes, but what does that—"

"Hephalion and Ava are presently one and the same."

Mallory stared at him, her face contorted in confusion.

"What are you talking about?" Tristan shouted. "One and the same? Are you saying she's possessed or something?"

Enki slowly tilted his head from one side to the other, like balancing scales. "Essentially. We think Hephalion may have always been there, locked deep within Ava's psyche, awaiting to be triggered."

"Triggered by what?" Mallory asked, her terror turning to fuming rage. The ensuing silence swelled to fill the room, and Mallory turned from one god to the next, her hands raised in question, mouth open in flabbergasted distress. "Well?"

Zeus cleared his throat but did not remove his gaze from the ceiling.

Jonah stepped forward, seeming to struggle quite a bit just to swallow. "I triggered it," he said, then finally met Mallory's gaze.

"Jonah?" she asked. "I don't understand."

He shifted his weight from one foot to the other and ran a hand through his hair. "I… uh… we kissed."

Mallory said nothing, her eyebrows raised as she pursed her lips in an attempt to contain the smile pulling at the corners of her mouth. Then the consequence of the kiss she'd always expected returned to her.

Tristan stepped forward. "You're saying she's like this because of you? Because you kissed my sister?" Jonah gave a hesitant nod. In a flash, Tristan's fist swung up and connected with the side of Jonah's face. The blow knocked him off balance, and he crumpled to the ground.

"Tristan!" Mallory cried in alarm, then grabbed her son by the arm and yanked him backwards. He broke free of her grasp and stormed out of the room.

"Jonah, I am so sorry," she said. "I don't know what's come over him." Zeus and Enki helped Jonah to his feet.

"It's fine, I deserve it," he replied. Enki held a hand to the rapidly swelling eye to heal it.

"That's where you're wrong, Jonah," Zeus said. "This is no fault of yours. It just is."

"What are you talking about?" Jonah scowled at the god.

"Hephalion was always meant to be triggered, here and now. It was Ava's destiny. It's been written in the stars since the day she was born."

Mallory took a seat beside her daughter. She gazed down at the calm expression on Ava's sleeping face, wondering how such a storm could be raging beneath her closed eyes. She could feel Jonah standing behind her; the anger and guilt radiated off him in waves. As she tried to think of something to say, some comfort to offer him, Jonah turned and stormed from the room.

CHAPTER TWENTY-FOUR

JONAH SAT IN the driveway, staring out into the night. He felt like he was drowning under the weight of his thoughts and tried to push the kiss to the farthest recesses of his mind. The moment was tarnished somehow, now that he knew it had been preordained—that their kiss had left Ava in her current state. Anger swept over his confusion like a wave of molten lava, and he felt his blood boil under the surface. The delicate twinkling of her earrings was the only thing that gave Inanna away as she walked toward him. The fact that Jonah's anger simmered the closer she approached annoyed him.

"May I join you?"

"You're a god. Do what you want."

Tucking the skirt of her sheath dress under her, she gracefully sat beside him. Her legs stretched out in front of her and crossed at the ankles, displaying her ornate sandals. They sat there in silence for a moment, allowing Jonah's mood to calm further.

"I understand how you're feeling," she told him.

"Somehow, I doubt that."

"Well then, why don't you explain it to me?"

Jonah scoffed. "I'm not interested in a heart-to-heart."

"Why? Do you have something better to do right now?"

He felt his hostility dissolve under her gaze, and as much as he wanted to hold onto it, he also wanted to quiet the thoughts hammering around in his head. "I feel like nothing in my life is real," he blurted. "Like nothing has been of my own choosing."

When he didn't continue, Inanna prompted gently, "How so?"

"Everything has literally happened for a reason, from my parents' deaths to my fake aunt to living near the Carters. Now I'm told that what I thought was a spontaneous moment with Ava was in fact also written into the plan somewhere. So, what? I've had no free will my entire life? Has no choice actually been mine to make? And I care about Ava, but how can that even be real? I feel like a pawn for someone who doesn't know what the hell they're doing." Jonah knew he sounded bitter but didn't want to force the blame on Inanna. He made himself take a deep breath.

"I can certainly see how you could feel that way, Jonah. Especially with everything you've gone through recently. Here's the thing about fate. Yes, everyone has a destiny, but not everyone fulfils theirs. History is rife with examples of people who fell short, and that's okay. Do you know why that is?"

For the first time, Jonah turned and met her gaze. An instant calmness washed over him. "No."

"Because it all comes down to the choices we make. Your free will. There is almost always more than one path to fulfil your own destiny… or not, depending on the decisions you make along the way. For example, the fact that you and Ava have never kissed before, despite wanting to, is only because you have chosen not to, for fear of hurting your friendship with her and Tristan. You cared about how it might affect your relationship with the Carter family as a whole if things work out."

"How could you possibly know that?"

"I'm a god," Inanna said with a smile. "And it's a pretty simple conclusion to draw." She paused for a moment. "Would tonight's kiss have happened if it hadn't been the first? Would Hephalion still have been triggered? I don't know. There's no way to know. You could have just as easily decided not to act on your impulse tonight, and then what would have happened?

"But Zeus said it was mean to happen here and now."

"Yes, in a way, it was. But I'm saying that if it didn't happen tonight, who's to say it wouldn't have happened another time, or at all?"

"This is making my head hurt."

Inanna chuckled, the melodic sound reminding Jonah of a windchime. "Look, Jonah, I understand you feel as though your relationships with those you care about is lessened somehow by the knowledge that steps were taken to ensure you formed them in the first place. But you haven't connected with everyone who's been placed in your life. Your aunt, for example."

"Fake aunt," Jonah stipulated.

"There was no guarantee that you would befriend Tristan and Ava. Or that Mallory and Alex would welcome you into their family the way they did. But that's how it happened. You've been extremely fortunate not only with the decisions you've made but with those made by those around you. What I'm trying to say is that the path of fate might lead you one way or another, but only you can decide what to do at each fork in the road. Rather than feeling out of control and oppressed by the thought of a preordained fate, think of this as more of a guiding hand. The decision-making is entirely your responsibility."

Jonah nodded slowly, letting it all sink in. "Thank you, Inanna. I actually do feel better."

She gave him a small smile and patted his arm. "I'm glad I could help." When the scuffle of sneakers sounded on the driveway, they both turned.

"Sorry to interupt," Tristan said, standing before them with his arms folded against his chest. His gaze flicked from his feet to Jonah and back again.

"Not at all, Tristan," Inanna replied. "We're finished." She smiled, gave Jonah's arm a squeeze, and gracefully rose to her feet. "No fists, please," she teased, then walked back into the house.

Tristan sat beside his friend, and Jonah leaned slightly away from him, unsure whether to expect another angry tirade. Tristan cleared his throat, paused for a moment, and cleared his throat again. "Look, man. I'm sorry I decked you."

"I deserved it. I kissed your sister."

"Bullshit."

"What?"

"I said bullshit. I'm not pissed off because you kissed my sister. Shit, I don't know what took you two so long. It doesn't take a genius to see you've been pining after each other for years."

"I don't pine."

"You kind of do, bro. But that's beside the point. Seeing my sister lying there like that was just the final straw after everything that's happened. The kiss just gave me the opportunity to lash out, and I'm sorry it was at you. I mean, it's been a really shithouse week."

"Yeah, shithouse pretty much sums it up," Jonah replied, unable to stop the chuckle bubbling up from his chest. Before he knew it, they were both laughing uncontrollably at the absurd insanity of the situation and the relief of knowing everything was fine between them.

Once they managed to calm themselves down, Tristan slapped Jonah on the shoulder. "Woah!"

"Woah, what?"

"This Hephalion dude… He's inside Ava, right?"

Jonah shrugged. "That's what the gods are saying."

"So… when you kissed my sister, you really kissed a dude…"

"What? No. It was definitely Ava."

"I don't know, man. I'm fairly certain you actually kissed a dude."

"You're full of shit." Jonah lunged at his friend, narrowly missing him as Tristan leapt to his feet. Then he jogged back toward the house, laughing, but pulled up short when he saw Vishnu leaning awkwardly against the front doorway.

"You're both needed inside."

Tristan and Jonah followed Vishnu into the house, exchanging glances when the sounds of a news broadcast blasted from the lounge room.

"It just turned on by itself again," Mallory said, "and it's flicking from one news report to another." She perched on the edge of the lounge. Tristan took a seat beside her, but Jonah felt too agitated and decided just to stand.

"In what can only be described as miraculous, a young woman fell ten stories from a prominent building in Brisbane's CBD and remained unharmed. Witnesses reported the woman

had stood atop the building for quite some time before finally jumping, and the incident was filmed by numerous bystanders. The woman responsible has been identified as Caitlyn Wiseman, who was reported missing from The Hills mental health facility earlier that day."

The sombre reporter was replaced by the footage of the jumping woman. "No way…" Tristan murmured. The woman in the footage got to her feet, then stepped up on a parked car to address the crowd. Tristan turned and looked up at Jonah, shaking his head in disbelief. Jonah couldn't respond. Instead, he left the room.

JONAH LEANED AGAINST the window frame, staring out over the back yard. It felt like forever ago that he'd stood down there and witnessed the arrival of beings about which he'd only ever read.

Ava softly moaned where she lay on the bed behind him. He turned, concerned by the frown etching across her brow. He waited for her to settle back into sleep before turning again to the window. The first hint of sunrise lightened the sky, and Jonah was surprised he didn't feel more tired; he'd barely slept over the past few days. In fact, he felt the opposite—wired and not surprisingly anxious. The combination of the news from the Underworld and Caitlyn's dramatic circumstances had left him feeling fearful and even more ill-equipped to deal with whatever was coming their way.

With daylight rapidly approaching, he knew the survivors lining the street outside would soon be bustling about, looking for answers and guidance. If the news reports were anything to go by, they could expect more people to arrive, and for what? An unconscious woman and two blokes who could hardly organise a barbecue between the two of them? Resting his head against the cool pane of glass, he closed his eyes and tried to rally the strength to go downstairs and face a new day.

"Hey."

With an inward groan, Jonah forced open his eyes and turned to the see Tristan enter the room. As his mate took a seat by the foot of the bed, Jonah noted Tristan's avoidant stare and knew there was only more bad news to come. "I don't want to know," Jonah stated.

Tristan sighed. "I know, mate. That makes two of us. So I'll just spit it out. The incident with Caitlyn was not isolated."

"What? You mean she's done it more than once?"

"No. I mean there are others out there claiming to be Oracles and repeating the same message. Admittedly, not all with the same dramatic flair, but the effect is the same."

"How many more are we talking about? Five? Ten?"

"Try more like a hundred worldwide. That shit is going viral like you wouldn't believe."

"Spreading the message everywhere at once."

Tristan nodded. "Welcome to the age of technology, crazy Oracle people."

"What the hell are we supposed to do?"

Tristan shrugged. "I have no idea, man. But I'm sure the powers that be downstairs will have a few suggestions. Whether we like them or not. We've been summoned for another chat."

Jonah bit his tongue and followed Tristan from the room, pausing at the doorway to look back at Ava. His heart ached, but he forced himself to keep walking.

IN THE DINING room, Mallory and the gods had gathered around the table. Everyone looked up when Jonah and Tristan entered.

"Good morning," Zeus greeted them jovially.

Jonah gaped at him. "Good morning? Really? What reality are you in?"

Zeus didn't let his son's attitude wipe the smile from his face. "The same as you, son. Only I choose to see the positive side of things."

"Positive? Are you out of your bloody mind? Have you not seen Ava lying upstairs? Or the people out there in the street? Or are you ignoring the fact that half the world has been decimated in either earthquakes or tsunamis?"

"I think half is probably an overcalculation—"

"What he means," Inanna said before Zeus could infuriate Jonah any further, "is that this news of the Oracles coming forward is good for us. I understand it's daunting for you, but they're spreading the word and drawing people to us. The more we can get on board, the better chance we have of fighting the Fates."

"Why do you say 'fight' and not 'defeat'?" Jonah asked.

"Let's not get ahead of ourselves," Enki said. "We have more than enough to deal with in the here and now. First things first. We know there are a lot of people out there who are scared, and the Oracles are giving them something to hold on to. Some hope in their darkest hour."

"So they're basically preying on vulnerable people."

"Not at all. You're misinterpreting me. All great prophets and oracles have come about during times of high duress and grave desperation. Unfortunately, mortals are more inclined to listen to them when they have nothing left to lose."

"And where are the Fates in all this?" Jonah asked. "I mean, they've been killing left, right, and centre for days now, but when everyone's just out there like sitting ducks... nothing?"

"Despite their power, they can't be in two places at once. We know they've spent time in the Underworld."

"You think that's the only reason they haven't attacked?" Mallory asked quietly.

"I'm saying we shouldn't grow complacent, but there is also little we can do to protect so many people with just the nine of us."

"Well that's just brilliant," Jonah muttered. "And what about all these Oracles coming out of the woodwork? Are they just people who happened to like Caitlyn's footage and decided to jump on the bandwagon, or what?"

"They're legitimate Oracles," Isis replied. "Just like Caitlyn. Though admittedly, their numbers are greater than we'd anticipated."

"What's happened to Caitlyn?"

Everyone turned to find Ava in the doorway, swaying slightly. Mallory, Tristan, and Jonah all jumped to her aid.

"Ava, honey, you shouldn't be up. You need to rest."

"No, I'm fine, Mum. There's no time to rest."

"The dude possessing you... he's gone?"

Ava looked up at her brother. "No. I don't think so. I can feel... feel something... inside. I can't quite explain it."

Feeling like an idiot just hovering in front of her, Jonah stepped back toward the table and pulled out the closest chair. "Here. Sit down." She gave him a grateful smile, and he forced himself to cast aside the fluttering it caused, then moved to the other end of the table.

Mallory and Tristan guided Ava into the chair, the gods respectfully silent until she was seated.

"How much do you remember?" Isis asked, placing a gentle hand over Ava's.

"Everything. At least, I think it's everything. I remember being with Jonah, and then I remember the most incredible warmth spread through me…"

Tristan and Jonah both cleared their throats and squirmed.

"Then there was this searing white heat that felt like it pierced right through the centre of my forehead and into my brain. I've never felt pain like that before. But I could see some distorted figure. I wasn't afraid at all, and he came toward me, gave me his hand… and I took it. After that, I… I thought I was falling into darkness. There were so many voices… I begged him to stop. But he pulled me closer, held me against him, and then… Then we were the same person. I know it sounds insane. I heard his voice come out of my mouth, but it sounded like my voice at the same time. And that… that's the last thing I re-member."

"Is he, you know, still in you?" Tristan asked.

Ava pursed her lips and frowned, looking to the gods as though the answer lay with them. "No… and yes… I don't know how to explain it. It's not like I *feel* another presence. Not like I'm possessed or something. But I feel… bigger."

"Bigger?" Jonah asked, wanting to understand.

Ava scrunched her face in thought. "It's not the best word to use, but I don't know how else to describe it. I still feel like I'm completely me but also more than myself. It's like I could only half see before. Like I was squinting through dim lighting. Now, everything's… brighter. Like you guys, for example. You're surrounded by the most beautiful colours. And you're all completely different."

"They're called auras," Kali said with a rare smile.

"Aura…" Ava said softly, as though tasting the word. "I've heard of them but never imagined they would look so beautiful."

"They don't always," Kali warned. "But the ability to see them will help you determine friend from foe. It could be of great use to you."

"Bloody hell!" Jonah shouted. "Does everything have to be about fighting the Fates?" He slammed his hand on the table.

"Yes," Zeus replied, raising his eyebrows at his son. Jonah lowered his gaze, knowing the god was right and hating the fact that Ava was suffering.

Ava raised her hands to her forehead and squeezed her eyes shut. Her family watched her with tense anxiety. The few seconds felt like much longer before Jonah quietly asked, "Ava?" He felt his shoulders lower with relief when she opened her eyes; he hadn't realised how tense he was.

"I'm okay. There's a lot of them out there, isn't there? Oracles."

"There are," Zeus replied. "Each one as important as the next. Including Caitlyn." He gave Ava a pointed look, and she nodded slowly, as if it all finally made sense.

"I can feel all of them. Their energies. I've never seen anything like it. A vibrancy extends from each of them, and I can feel every one running through me and back to them. Like they're both strengthening me and weakening me at the same time."

"I can help you learn to control this flow of energy," Kali said, walking around the table toward Ava's chair. "Soon, you won't feel weakened by them at all. If you're up to it, we can go back upstairs and get started."

"Can't it wait?" Mallory asked, placing a protective arm around her daughter's shoulders. "She needs to rest. To regain her strength."

"She won't be able to do that until she learns to control the Oracles' energies. You can come with us, if it will put your mind at ease. But only you. Too many people will be a distraction."

Mallory wordlessly accepted the compromise, then aided Ava from her chair and out of the room.

"We need to get back outside," Inanna said, standing as well. "It's going to be another long day, and there a lot of people out there who need us."

"Where do we even start?" Tristan asked, unable to hide the despair in his voice.

"We start by going outside and saying good morning," Isis replied kindly, placing her hand on his forearm and guiding him out of the room.

"You can help us carry out the baskets of food," Zeus instructed Jonah. "I'm sure everyone will be hungry when they wake."

"What baskets?"

"These," Enki replied, gesturing toward the coffee table groaning under the sudden weight of tall, woven baskets laden with apples, loaves of bread, and bananas. Jonah smiled at Enki and Zeus. He felt better knowing he had something to offer the crowd—less useless. Heaving a basket of apples off the table, he left the room with a renewed sense of purpose, followed by Inanna, Hades, Set, Vishnu, and Marduk.

ZEUS STARED AFTER his son, still smiling.

"He's grown to be a good man, your son," Enki stated.

"That he has. Not that I can take any credit for it, of course. Still, I feel an overwhelming pride."

Enki patted his friend's burly shoulder before he collected his own basket and left the room.

JONAH WASN'T SURPRISED how many people were already awake, despite the early hour. If it hadn't been for Enki's enchantments, most of them probably wouldn't have slept much at all. Their gratitude humbled him as they approached for something to eat. A small grunt caught his attention, and when Jonah looked over the top of the basket, he found a small, grubby boy trying his hardest to reach up and grab an apple. Jonah knelt. "What's your name?"

The boy ducked his head shyly, sussing the stranger out before answering. "David."

"Hi, David. I'm Jonah. It's nice to meet you." He held out his hand, and the little boy grinned, then placed his tiny hand in Jonah's and boisterously shook it. Jonah laughed. "That's one mighty handshake you have there, David. For that, I think you should get an apple." He handed one to the boy and made to stand before he felt a tug on his jeans.

"Excuse me, Mr Jonah. Can I please have one for my sister too?" David asked, turning and pointing to the girl waiting patiently on the curb, a spitting image of her brother.

"What's your sister's name?" he asked.

"Bethany. She's only little still. She's three. I'm four and a half," David replied proudly, his chest puffed out.

"Well, since you're being such a good big brother, I'm sure I can spare an extra apple," Jonah said, handing the boy another.

"Thank you!" David exclaimed, his smile lighting up his whole face before he turned and ran back to his sister. Jonah gave Bethany a wave, and she waved back shyly, her hand barely lifting from her lap. Yet when her brother handed her the apple, she grinned and clapped. Jonah watched the children sitting side by side and eating their apples in content silence, as though they devoured a couple of chocolate bars instead.

Jonah's breath caught in his throat as it dawned on him how self-centred he'd been. He'd only viewed the recent events by how they affected him and those closest to him, and then by how it made him feel. He honestly hadn't given much thought to how the normal people around him felt, of how scared they must have been, with no knowledge as to what lay behind what they experienced. While he'd viewed all the information of who he was and what was really happening as a burden—a heavy weight bearing down on his shoulders—he now realised how fortunate he was to know the truth. Sure, it was still daunting and terrifying, but it was a great deal less so than having to go through the past few days with no idea of what was happening or why.

He realised now that he had a great responsibility to everyone around him. He had to get his shit together and work out exactly what he was capable of and how he could help save them all from the Fates. And he had to do it fast. He strode toward Enki, who arranged some of the food baskets farther down the street.

"It never ceases to amaze me," the god stated.

"What does?" Jonah asked, frowning.

"That everyone is coming and getting something to eat, yet no one seems to notice the quantity of food remains the same."

Jonah looked at the god in surprise, then gazed down at the basket of bread in front of him. It was indeed still full despite the hands reaching for loaves. He looked back to where he'd stood at the basket of apples to find it, too, remained full despite him having handed out at least thirty apples. "Well I'll be damned…" he said quietly.

Enki chuckled. "If you're looking for Zeus, he's returned to the house for the water flasks. I'm sure he could use a hand."

Jonah thanked the god before he headed back to the house. He found Zeus in the dining room, loading up Vishnu with the flasks.

"You know, my extra arms would really come in handy right now…" Vishnu stated, winking at Jonah.

Zeus smiled. "Perhaps, old friend. But I don't know how the locals would take it just yet. What can I do for you, Jonah?"

Jonah hesitated, flicking a quick glance at Vishnu before looking back to Zeus.

"I need to get these flasks out," Vishnu announced, stepping around Jonah as he left the room, his awkward gait exaggerated by the uneven load.

"I was wondering if you had a second?"

Zeus, obviously sensing Jonah's seriousness, left the remaining flasks alone and turned to give his undivided attention. Jonah felt self-conscious under the steady gaze and found himself looking around the room. "Time is of the essence, Jonah," the god prompted.

Jonah cleared his throat and ran his hand through his hair. "I just wanted to say, uh, I'm sorry I've been such a dick."

There was a moment's silence before Zeus' boisterous laugh rang through the room. "No need to apologise. You're your father's son, after all."

Jonah gave him a sheepish smile. "It took me longer than it should have, but I finally realise that, while I'm at the centre of all of this, it's not about me. Not really. It's about all of us. I guess that makes me sound stupid and self-absorbed..."

"You've had to process a huge amount of life-altering information in a very short amount of time. I'm proud of you for handling it as well as you have. We've tried to give you as much space as possible while you worked through it, but I must say, I'm relieved you've had your epiphany sooner rather than later."

"Why's that?"

"Well, we think it's high time people knew the truth. So we're going to announce the Alliance."

"Woah, what? People aren't ready for that. They'll think we're all crazy."

"That's why having you on board is essential," Zeus said. "They will need a leader. One of their own. The Oracles have already pointed thousands of people in your direction, and they'll be expecting answers."

"I'm not ready for that—I'm not a leader!"

"Most leaders have said that at one time or another." Zeus chuckled.

"I'm so glad you find this amusing."

"Jonah, laughter is a way to hold onto the light when you are surrounded by darkness." He put his arm around his son and patted his shoulder.

"All righty, then..." Jonah didn't pull away. "So when are you planning this big announcement?"

"Once everyone has had the chance to wake up properly, eat something, and reflect on yesterday's traumas."

"You mean when they realise it's not all just a horrible nightmare?"

Zeus just grabbed more flasks of water and handed them to Jonah. "Make yourself useful and take these out for me."

Jonah gave his father a wry smile as he carted the flasks away, Zeus not far behind him. When he stepped out onto the driveway, it was all he could do not to drop everything. "What the…"

The number of people in the street had nearly tripled while he'd been in the house. He hardly registered Zeus' brief pause beside him before the god continued ahead. "Keep moving, Jonah. The water isn't going to carry itself."

Jonah hurried after him. "Are you not seeing this? Where did they all come from? What are we going to do?"

Zeus turned to face him. "We're going to remain calm. We knew with the Oracles' announcements that we'd see the arrival of more people. Remain focused on the task at hand."

Jonah nodded, mentally telling himself to man up, but he couldn't help from gazing out at the ever-growing crowd, wondering just how many more would join them.

CHAPTER TWENTY-FIVE

AVA LAY STRETCHED out on the carpeted floor, staring up at the ceiling, while her mother sat in a chair by the window. Kali sat cross-legged on the edge of the bed, looking down at her. Ava would have preferred to lie on the bed, but the goddess was adamant that the harder surface would be more conducive to their work.

"Close your eyes and focus on your breathing," Kali instructed. Ava closed her eyes and exhaled. "Now I want you to push all the sounds and images out of your mind and focus only on my voice."

"But—"

"No talking. Focus."

Ava closed her mouth, shifting in agitation. She could feel the goddess' gaze boring into her. When she finally stopped fidgeting, there was a moment's pause before the goddess spoke.

Kali's voice was lower, whispering, yet it sent a wave of vibrations through Ava. "I want you to focus on your root chakra. Think of the area near your tailbone. Picture a tiny pinprick of red light. As you focus on it, it grows larger, swirling in a clockwise direction. Feel the warmth radiating from it, spreading slowly outward and up to your sacral chakra below your navel. When the energy reaches this point, envision the same tiny pinprick of light. Only this time, its energy is orange. When you feel that warmth radiating outward again, see the energy travel up once more to your solar plexus chakra at your stomach..."

Ava felt as though her whole body relaxed into the floor while simultaneously floating in weightlessness. She thought she heard her mother say something, but it sounded far away. Then she realised Kali's voice had also grown muffled, as if Ava were underwater and could hear people talking above her. Yet it didn't alarm her. In fact, she felt quite pleasant as the chakra energy flowed through her. It was like an enormous snake warmed by the sun, sliding along her body, triggering the ancient energies within her.

She felt herself shiver, which she vaguely registered as odd since she didn't feel in the slightest bit cold. Her breathing slowed, but she didn't think she might fall asleep. Perhaps it was something else, like a trance. Ava wondered if this was what it felt like to be hypnotised. When the traveling energy reached her third-eye chakra, her eyes flew open. A powerful surge of energy coursed through her, making her draw in a sharp breath.

Kali's voice barely broke through, but Ava detected the urgent tone as the goddess commanded her to breathe. The energy swiftly continued up to Ava's crown chakra, and then her mouth opened wide in excruciating pain; her head felt as if it were splitting down the middle. An odd sound came to her from far away—high-pitched and reminding her of an old steam train's whistle. Then, with no emotion at all, she realised the sound came from herself.

She felt a shift inside her—movement. Logic told her it couldn't be the floor moving beneath her, so she must have been the one moving. When she felt the balls of her feet settle into the carpet and her hair falling onto her shoulders, Ava knew she stood upright. The pain in her head subsided, leaving her a little rattled, as if she'd fallen and hit her head. That, too, subsided when she forced herself to take a deep breath. A new, not-unpleasant hum radiated from the top of her head.

All she could see was a brightness, indistinguishable and yet all-encompassing. One by one, the images appeared—faces she didn't recognise but felt she knew. So many faces.

Then an image of Caitlyn found her; the girl stood amongst a crowd at the foot of Uluru. Her smile lit up her delicate features, and the white light approached them, strengthening and binding her connections to the others around her. Next, she saw Caitlyn jump from the building, then Caitlyn striding with determination down a city street, now devoid of traffic, replaced by the crowd of people following behind her.

Caitlyn gave a quick smile and a nod, as though she felt Ava's gaze upon her. More and more images appeared, all with a similar message, and Ava knew she was watching the Oracles. She felt a surge of new hope at the sight of so many people gathered around these Oracles. Suddenly, the prospect of an army of shades didn't feel quite so devastating.

JONAH STOOD IN the doorway, watching Ava in the chair. She gazed out the bedroom window, her back to him, and he admired the way her hair sat in a tussled heap atop her head, revealing her long, graceful neck. Her knees were drawn up to her chest, her arms draped casually around them. He longed to reach out and touch her. Ava ran her hand along her neck and turned to face him. "You can come in, you know."

Jonah gave her a small, hesitant smile and stepped into the room. He tried his best to look relaxed, but he'd never felt gawkier in his life.

"It's me, Jonah," Ava said with a reassuring smile.

He squinted and tilted his head from side to side.

"Nothing has changed," she added. "I'm still me, and you're still you." Her voice had a hint of pleading to it, and he wanted nothing more than to agree with her. Instead, he leaned against the wall beside the window and looked down at her.

"Everything has changed," he said. "You know it better than any of us. I know it hasn't been very long, but we've both changed already. We're still changing. Who knows the people we'll become by the end of all this?"

"I'll still be me. And you'll still be you. That won't change." The pleading in her voice had now been replaced by a steely resolve.

Jonah stared at her; he'd always thought she was beautiful, but now she looked even more so. A certain radiance surrounded her now that hadn't been there before. Like something—or someone—had flicked a switch on within her. A surge of despair hit him; his heart physically ached. With a long sigh, he diverted his gaze to the floor. "I came here because I wanted to apologise."

"You have nothing to apologise for."

"I do. Regardless of whether your... transition... was supposed to happen now or later, or ever... I shouldn't have kissed you. You were upset and feeling vulnerable, and I took advantage."

"It wasn't like that, and you know it."

He shook her off. "It is what it is, and I'm sorry for what you've gone through."

"Sorry? Jonah, look at me."

He kept his gaze fixed at his feet.

"Don't you dare ignore me!" she commanded, her voice trembling.

Jonah cautiously lifted his gaze and instantly regretted the tears welling in her eyes. He had to fight back the sting of his own.

"For the first time since this all started," she said, "I don't feel lost and scared. I know I'm exactly where I'm supposed to be. I understand the things that have happened to me, and to Caitlyn, and to the others like her. I'm not afraid anymore. At least, not of that. I'm grateful for that weight to have been lifted, to feel empowered to help us in whatever comes next. I don't feel like I'm just sitting here on the sidelines waiting for the next bad thing to happen."

"I guess it was meant to be, then. It was meant to set you on your path."

"What was?"

"Our... moment. The trigger."

"Jonah, that's not what I meant at all. I... it's just... I'm trying to explain to you that the consequences aren't dire. That kiss was—"

"Nothing," Jonah said, then pushed himself off the wall and stormed out of the room.

JONAH FOUND HIMSELF standing at the foot of the Carters' driveway, staring out at the bustling street. Yet he didn't truly see anything. The conversation with Ava had not gone according to plan, and he wasn't sure how it had ended so badly. His pride still couldn't get past Hephalion. He shook his head, trying to banish her from it.

Rising noise from a gathering farther up the street would be a welcome distraction, and he made his way toward the crowd to see what was going on. When he managed to step through, he found the elderly man with the radio standing in the centre. The man banged on the radio's exterior and twisted and turned the knobs, but they only produced static. He looked up at Jonah's approach, his mouth downturned and his eyes wide with disbelief and disappointment.

"It was working last night! I don't know why I can't pick up any signals this morning. There was supposed to be another broadcast, but there's nothing."

"What does that mean? Where did they go?"

"I don't know," Jonah stated, holding his hands up to the crowd. "But I can tell you that we'll have some answers for you soon. So if you could all please remain calm, grab something to eat and some water, I'll be back soon." He gaped at the crowd when it dispersed, jumping as a firm hand grasped his shoulder.

"Nicely done," said Zeus.

Jonah looked up at him, his eyebrows raised. "I didn't expect it to be that easy."

"Oh, it won't always be. You've promised them something they want. Answers. Now, we have to deliver. Then things will get intense."

Jonah swallowed thickly, wondering if all hell would ensue. "So where are we going to do this?"

"I say we make the Carters' driveway our platform, given that it's raised above the street level and will allow most people to see us," Zeus replied.

Jonah nodded, and they walked together toward the house, Zeus signalling to the other gods to join them. Jonah barely looked up to see Ava, Mallory, and Kali already standing in the driveway, and he turned his back to her as he faced the crowd alongside Zeus.

Before the god and his son could call the people's attention, Jonah felt Ava grip his arm. "Wait," she whispered. But she looked out at the crowd, her face ashen and her eyes wide.

"What is it?" Jonah asked, concern overturning his frustration toward her.

"That woman. Her aura... it's black." She pointed at the other side of the road, where a dishevelled-looking woman in a tattered white dress held onto the streetlight with one hand and languidly circled the post. She paused halfway around and tilted her head, eyeing them from beneath the dark, matted hair half-obscuring her face.

"There's another one." Ava pointed to their left, where an almost identical woman stood atop a makeshift bed. "And there!" To their right, a third sat atop the roof of a parked car, her head lowered as she twisted her tangled hair around her fingers.

"They look like the woman in Grommo's video..." Tristan stated.

"The Erinyes," Zeus growled, stepping forward. Before he could move again, the Erinyes' released a deafeningly high-pitched scream. The people closest to them were hurled backwards, as though a bomb had detonated, and the crowd erupted in panic, wanting to run but having nowhere to go.

Ava pushed past Jonah and ran out to the street. "Ava, no!" he cried and hurried after her. She ignored him, surging through the panicked and the injured and headed straight toward the Erinyes beside the pole. The creature smirked at Ava's approach and made no attempt to move.

Jonah tripped and landed heavily on his knee, but he couldn't take his eyes off Ava, afraid she was about to get herself killed. He called out to her again, and the Erinyes slowly closed her eyes before reopening them. Focusing her attention solely on Ava, the creature opened her mouth and let it fall impossibly far, all the way to her chest, to reveal a black, gaping hole.

Jonah waited in horror for the inevitable sound, but as the creature made its move, Ava threw her arms up as though to brace herself against the incoming impact. Instead of the Erinyes' ear-splitting screech, a loud, low hum sounded, and Jonah froze at the sight of an opalescent light shooting from Ava's hands. It rapidly spread out and up like a shield. Time slowed, and Jonah gaped up at her in awe, hearing only the sound of his rapid breathing echoing in his own ears.

At either end of the street, where the other Erinyes attempted to continue their attacks, similar shields had risen. Jonah realised with grateful relief that at least two other Oracles had joined them. The gods took advantage of these defences by half-carrying, half-dragging the injured out of the street. The hum increased in pitch, and Jonah looked back at Ava, who now leaned forward, as though trying to physically push the Erinyes away with her force. The Erinyes' jaw slackened and swayed side to side like an overstretched elastic band. The creature tried to lunge at Ava with no success. It raised its head to the sky and screeched with rage, but all its power had dissapated. Its feet shifted backwards, just a little at first but then with more force. It grasped for the pole as it was launched up into the air and held in place, kicking and screeching. Cracks appeared in its features, revealing a black smoke that spewed out in all directions. The fissures increased and intensified, the humming grew, and in a matter of seconds, the Erinyes erupted into nothingness, leaving only a trace of black smoke behind.

As the shields lowered, Jonah looked around to find the other Erinyes had met the same fate.

Then the world returned to him, the sudden volume of the people around him nearly deafening. Realising he was still on his knees, he looked down to see what had tripped him in the first place. It took him a moment to register, but once he did, his shoulders slumped in defeat. His hand rested on the leg of the little boy to whom he'd given those apples. His sister lay sprawled across him, her head on his chest. Jonah reached out to check their pulses, but he knew they were gone. They looked so peaceful—flawless but for the smudges of dirt on their faces. He found himself staring at the apple core still fixed in David's hands, and he recalled the sheer joy the siblings had shared in such a simple thing.

"Jonah?"

He felt Ava's hand on his shoulder, and he reached up to cover it with his own; he knew if he looked up and found sympathy in her eyes, he'd lose it. Instead, he stared straight ahead, catching sight of Zeus watching him from the other side of the street. After a moment, the god nodded, then turned back to the growing number of bodies behind him.

Forcing himself to take a deep breath, Jonah gave Ava's hand a squeeze, then released it. Without a word, he slid one arm under the little girl's head, the other beneath her legs, and lifted her to his chest.

"I'll be back," he told David, hoping that, somewhere, the boy could hear him.

He hardly registered the space on the block from which the destroyed home had been cleared as he walked toward it; nothing surprised him about the gods anymore. Instead, he tried to ignore the bodies he passed, spaced out evenly in rows, and looked for a suitable spot for the little girl and her brother. He found one near the rear of the plot, where a small tree stood, the sunlight streaming through the branches and causing leaf-shaped shadows to dance playfully across the grass. He laid her out carefully, straightening her dress and smoothing her hair before he placed her hands on her chest, encasing the remains of her apple.

Then he turned to see Tristan with the girl's brother in his arms. His mate opened his mouth and closed it again, but Jonah appreciated the sentiment all the same. Jonah arranged the brother beside his sister, and with a hand on each of theirs, he bowed his head. He'd never prayed before, and he felt silly when nothing came to mind, but he hoped that wherever they were now, they were together.

"Come on, mate. We're needed," Tristan said.

Jonah got to his feet. His legs trembled as he walked back through the deceased, more of them carried by the minute and laid to rest in growing rows. "How many are there?" he asked.

"I don't know, man. A lot," Tristan replied. "I honestly can't even think about it right now, so I'm just helping out where I can."

Jonah briefly squeezed his mate's shoulder, knowing Tristan was as horrified by the turn of events as he was. They went their separate ways to tend to the injured and the dead still lining the street.

"THE ERINYES ARE gone." Clotho spoke to her sister's back.

"They're flighty creatures," Atropos replied. "They'll return soon enough." She offered a dismissive flick of her hand, not turning her gaze from the view of the valley stretching below them as she leaned against the trunk of an ancient eucalyptus.

Clotho cleared her throat and tried again. "No. They're gone. For good. Dead, if you could consider them to have been alive in the first place."

Atropos turned slowly to face her sister with a thunderous scowl. "What do you mean for good? The Erinyes cannot be killed."

Trying not to squirm under the intensity of her sister's glare, Clotho gazed out at the beautiful horizon before her. "I mean exactly that. They opened their attack on the crowd as instructed, but…"

"But what?" Atropos growled, daring her sister to continue.

"It seems they were met with some resistance. They were… obliterated."

"Obliterated?" Atropos screeched, launching herself from the tree trunk before striding toward her sister.

"They were decimated. Reduced to nothing but black smoke. It happened in minutes. I can't see anything more than that, but there is no sense of them now. In any capacity. Their existence has ended."

"Impossible." Atropos paced the earth beside the tree trunk. "How did it happen?"

"The woman. Ava. She released her own protection when she approached one of the Erinyes. I don't think she knew what she could do, but regardless, the end result was the same."

"And she did this to the other two as well?"

"They suffered the same fate, yes. Two other forces were present. Not as strong as Ava's, I can sense that much. But their proximity to her only strengthened them."

"Oracles…" Atropos muttered.

"That would be my guess. But I don't know how. We've never seen Oracles with this kind of power before."

Atropos shook her head in annoyance. "The power comes from Ava herself. She's connected to them, and they to her."

"How is she so strong already?" Lachesis asked, sitting quietly in the grass and observing her sisters, half obscured by another tall eucalyptus.

"She's had help. I don't know from whom or what, but no mere mortal could do this. Not even one with her descendance."

"From whom? There's only Zeus, Inanna, Isis, and Enki, none of whom have that ability."

"There must be more of them…"

"If she can kill the Erinyes," Lachesis asked, "does that mean she has the same power over us?" She plucked a blade of grass and held it up for inspection, as though the dire circumstances were of no consequence.

"Don't be stupid," Atropos snapped. "Of course she can't. Neither she nor her precious Oracles combined could destroy us. We need that damnable Tablet."

CHAPTER TWENTY-SIX

JONAH WATCHED THE gods extend their hands toward the deceased, whispering their incantations. Devastated sobs rose around him from those grieving over the sudden loss of their loved ones and the trauma of the unbelievable experience to which they had just borne witness.

He'd intentionally stayed away from the Carters, preferring to be left alone with his thoughts, knowing the people surrounding him were too caught up in the moment to care who he was. A gentle hum rolled out over the crowd in waves, and the bodies laid out in the vacant block shimmered like the distant haze over a hot road in summer. Knowing what was coming for every survivor here, he wondered how the crowd would react to his announcement. Would it help them or only make matters worse?

The humming increased, and though he couldn't see the children from where he stood, he focused instead on the sight of the tree draping over them. Then, with a quick flash, the bodies were gone. The crowd erupted into sobs and moans.

"What just happened?"

"What did you do?"

"Where did they go?"

"What the hell is going on?"

The gods broke formation and moved to the footpath as a group. As though he'd known exactly where his son stood, Zeus found Jonah in the crowd with ease and gestured for him to join them.

Jonah's feet moved, heavy, sluggish, and leaden, and a massive weight lodged in the pit of his stomach. His senses reeled as he flicked his thumbs with his middle fingers, constantly scanning his surroundings. A deep shame filled him at the knowledge that he'd been unprepared for the Erinyes' attack. He'd just knelt there on the ground while Ava had been the one to take charge and save them. Perhaps Zeus had it wrong; perhaps the prophecy was wrong. Jonah was no hero. He was just a mortal—and a cowardly one, at that.

It surprised him, when he reached the god's side, to find Zeus' expression had grown as grim as Jonah's. Zeus turned to him and nodded. "Let's get this underway. But everyone be on the lookout. The Erinyes will not return, but that does not mean we are safe."

Their party nodded. Jonah glimpsed Tristan standing beside Isis, looking solemn, and Ava standing with Mallory behind the gods, holding her mother's hand in both of hers.

The gods stood silently, waiting for the cries of surprise and grief and outrage to subside. An eerie silence quickly rolled over the crowd. It surprised him to find he was so nervous. He stared out at all the expectant faces and wiped his hand across his forehead. Again, he doubted whether he could shoulder the responsibility bestowed on him. Jonah wanted to turn his gaze, but there was nowhere else to look except at his feet, and that somehow didn't seem any better. Fortunately, Zeus chose that moment to speak, and Jonah focused on him instead.

"You have all been through a tremendous loss. First your homes, and now, for many of you, loved ones. We are deeply sorry for this grave cost to you. In saying this, though, there will likely be more to come, and I cannot say with any conviction that each of you will come out the other side of this alive—"

Jonah cleared his throat, and the god stopped to glance sideways at his son. Jonah raised his brows and widened his eyes, trying to let his father know this lack of tact would not be appreciated. Zeus sighed. Then the crowd threw more questions his way.

"What's happening?"

"Who are you?"

Zeus returned his attention to the cautious, anxious people gathering before them. "What's happening," he replied, "is a small but powerful group of individuals have been instigating attacks over the past few days—"

"Terrorists?" an onlooker shouted.

"Not in your traditional sense, no. But I suppose they could be considered as such. They *are* capable of terrifying deeds."

"What do they want?"

"To kill as many of you as they can as quickly as possible."

"Don't bother sugar-coating it," Jonah muttered before Zeus shot him another pointed look. The crowd took a silent moment to process what they'd just been told.

"Why?"

"Who are they?"

"Because they are evil, and because they can," Zeus announced. "That's the only explanation I can offer you at this stage. As to who they are, they are the Fates, joined in legion by the Underworld entity Charon."

Murmurs grew and spread through the crowd. Zeus seemed to take this as a sign to proceed.

"We anticipated a long time ago that something like this would happen, so we formed an alliance to assist us when the time came. That time is now."

"What are you talking about?" another angry voice shouted.

Jonah's eyes darted from one face to another, his concern growing when he saw these people's grief swiftly churn to disbelief and anger. "This isn't working," he said, low enough for the group to hear him. He felt a hand on his shoulder and turned to see Vishnu behind him.

"Let him go," the god said. "This needs to unfold." Though unconvinced, Jonah turned back to face the crowd.

"I am the leader of an ancient alliance formed by gods of old. I am Zeus, god of the ancient Greeks—"

"Bullshit!" someone spat, and everyone turned to look at the man. "I don't know who this asshole is, but we don't have time for this shit." Murmured agreement rose full-scale. "Most of us here have nothing but the shirts on our backs, and a lot of us, like myself, don't even live on this street. We were directed here because there's nowhere else to bloody go, and no one knows what's going on! The last thing we need is some crackpot spinning some shit about gods and alliances—"

"Let me finish," Zeus growled, the tell-tale sparks jumping across his skin.

No one seemed to notice, and the instigator among them continued his tirade. "We just watched our family and friends get murdered by some... I don't know. Suicide bombers. And now you expect us to stand here and listen to this horseshit?"

"Enough," Zeus warned again, the sparks flying now. Those in the crowd closest to him tried to step away.

"Communications are down," the man continued, seemingly unfazed, "and without them, we have no way of knowing what's going on beyond this street. I mean, there were just three explosions, and there's no police, no ambulances, no fire trucks. Nothing! I say we go find someone else who actually knows what's going on." A few scattered cheers of agreement bubbled from the crowd, and the man glanced around with a proud, invigorated smile. Then he turned back to Zeus with a sneer. "You can stay here and play god all you want but—"

"Silence!" Zeus swung his arms out and brought them together in a thunderous clap above his head. The ground shook beneath them. Jonah hardly had time to steady himself before a bolt of lightning released from the god's clamped hands and shot straight at the man in the crowd. Time seemed to slow—a slight frown had replaced the agitator's sneer as he tried to comprehend what was happening. Jonah reached out to push Zeus aside, but he knew he was already too late. The lightning bolt crackled and speared the man through the belly before obliterating him, leaving absolutely nothing behind. In a chaotic flurry of terrified shouting, those closest to tried to run, despite being unharmed, while those on the outer edges of the crowd pushed inward for a better look.

"What the hell did you just do?" Ava screeched, yanking at the god's shoulder from behind. "You can't just go around killing people. You're no better than the Fates!"

Zeus shrugged her off, his gaze never moving from the crowd. Ava turned away, hiding her face with her hand, and Jonah could only glance from one of them to the other.

Then he stepped in front of Zeus, trying to force the god to look him in the eye. "Why?" he asked. "How is that helping?" When his father ignored him, he turned to the other gods, who all stood as steadfast as their leader. "Do none of you see anything wrong with this picture?"

"Enough!" Zeus yelled, stepping back around his son to once again gain a full view of the crowd before him. The ground and sky rumbled alike at the fury of his command. He didn't wait to ensure the people had stopped their scurrying before he spoke again, but there was no need; they froze in place as the god's voice rumbled so loud, it drowned out the thunderous clouds above them.

"Do not doubt me, for it will be at your peril. I have no patience and less tolerance for insubordination and trivial whining. We are not here to befriend you, to hold your hands, to make things better for you, or to cater to your whims. We are here because without us, you will die. We all will." He paused for a moment, using the stunned silence of the crowd as his cue to continue. "You only need to feel the tears on your faces to know the loss you've experienced is real. While you won't understand why or how it happened, you need to believe that this is just the beginning of what's to come. Unless we can unite as one. I don't care what your beliefs are—religious or otherwise—or if you've even heard of us. All you need to know is we are here, regardless, and we are prepared to fight alongside you."

"Against who? Against what?"

"Against those responsible for the people and the homes you can no longer see around you. And so much more. This is far greater than those of us affected here. Other people like yourselves the world over have also lost everything. Only you have the opportunity to do something about it." Zeus gave the crowd a sweeping glance; they had fallen motionless in a stunned, communal silence.

Jonah cleared his throat, looking to Zeus for approval. The god nodded and took a small step to the side. "Quite a few of you know me," he began. "I've spent more time on this street over the years than anywhere else. But for those of you who have come from elsewhere, my name is Jonah. I understand how crazy this all sounds, believe me. But we can't ignore the fact that there's something really wrong going on. We've all seen things we can't explain over the past few days, whether it was first hand, on the news, or via social media and the internet. You may have tried to explain it away as a hoax, anything else that made more sense than what you were seeing. But I know that deep down, you can all feel there's a larger truth to this. *I* know there is. I can feel it too."

The sight of so many eyes on him, so many faces upturned in awakened hope—however fragile—gave him a courage to continue he had not expected. "I know it's hard to comprehend that deities of another time have come back to save us—or to help us save ourselves. So for now, at least, don't think of it that way. Just think of them as men and women who are here to help. Men and women who can do things we can't. You don't need to fear them. *No* harm will come to anyone who decides not to join us." He turned his head briefly to meet Zeus' gaze and make sure the god knew Jonah meant him specifically. "I will make sure of it. But please understand, we can't win this war on our own. If we can't stand together as one and fight, then we'll all die."

"What's there to fight for?" a sweating man shouted from the crowd. "My home is gone, and now so is my wife!"

Jonah gave the man a solemn nod. "That's true, and I'm sorry. I'm so sorry for all your losses. But you're still alive, and homes can be rebuilt. Everything can be rebuilt. Our material possessions don't matter at all." He paused and offered the man a gentle frown of concern. "Would you want your wife to have died in vain, or would you rather make her death mean something? We've all lost someone we love, and the pain is unbearable. I know. But just because they've taken our loved ones away from us doesn't mean we have nothing to fight for. Our grief doesn't weaken us. It gives us the strength to fight back. For the memories of our fathers, mothers, husbands, wives, children, friends... we have to fight for the very right to exist. So who's with me?" Jonah cried.

For a brief moment, he felt incredibly foolish. But then a shout of support rose from those gathered, followed by a handful more, and soon the crowd was cheering for him where they'd previously been about to tear the place apart. Then he felt the hearty pat on the back from his father.

"I couldn't have said it better myself," Zeus stated, and Jonah couldn't stop the goofy grin of pride sweeping over his face. Then the god stepped back just before Tristan and Ava swarmed toward Jonah, both grinning.

"Nice one, mate. You should probably write that shit down in case it was a fluke," Tristan said, smacking his friend on the shoulder.

"Yeah, thanks for that."

"You nailed it, Jonah," Ava said, standing on her tiptoes to kiss his cheek. Then she pulled back, her cheeks flushing, before quickly turning and weaving back through the gods. Jonah only stared after her.

"Seriously, dude," Tristan said. "When are you two going to get your shit together? Didn't you just give a whole carpe diem speech? Practise what you preach, mother—"

"One thing at a time," Jonah exclaimed, raising his hands in defence. "I think we have a few more important things to worry about than my love life."

"If you say so…" Tristan murmured, distracted by Isis' beckoning hand.

Jonah watched his mate head off after her, bemused by the effect the goddess had on his usually unflappable friend. But his distraction was short-lived, overpowered by people in the crowd surging forward to shake his hand and ask questions— many of which he had yet to answer himself.

As though he sensed Jonah's overwhelm, Zeus stepped beside him once again. "Okay, everyone. We appreciate your enthusiasm, but we need to get organised…"

Jonah was more than happy to relinquish the lead, and before he knew what he was doing, he found himself at the tree where he had laid out David and Bethany only a short time before. The rapid change in mood made him dizzy.

Maybe Tristan's right. Seize the day.

The hand on his arm made him jump, and he turned to find Enki there with him. "I'm sorry to startle you, Jonah."

"That's okay. I didn't realise I was so out of it." Jonah glanced up, surprised to find the sun had shifted so widely in position. "How long have I been standing here?"

"A little while," Enki admitted. "But you looked peaceful, and you've barely rested since our arrival. We thought it best to leave you be. Still, we thought you'd like to know."

"Know what?"

"It's time to give Alex his farewell."

Without a word, Jonah left his post at the tree and followed the god.

CHAPTER TWENTY-SEVEN

L EAVING THE OTHER gods to organise the crowd into clearing the street, Zeus, Enki, Inanna, and Isis led the Carters and Jonah back inside the Carter house and into the lounge room.

"Take a seat," Isis gently instructed, and they all obeyed.

"You said we're going to farewell Alex?" Mallory asked, the slightest tremble in her voice. "Will we get to see him? His... body?"

"Yes," Isis replied. "We are taking you to where we have kept him. A sanctuary, if you will."

"I thought you said the Fates could take him for their army if you released his soul," Tristan said.

"That was the case, but not anymore," Isis explained. "Alex's soul has spent enough time in this sanctuary to resonate at a higher level than the normal mortal soul. The Fates, or anyone else wishing him harm, can no longer touch him."

"But we only have a small window," Enki added, standing. "So if we're going to do it, it needs to be now. Join hands."

The group repositioned themselves to form a small circle, each of them facing inward. Jonah swallowed thickly as he felt Ava's hand slide into his. Squeezing his eyes shut, he braced himself for the vibrations he knew would accompany their transportation. When they didn't come, he squinted through his semi-closed eyelids, then opened them wide in disbelief. He freed his hands without any resistance and stepped away from the circle, admiring their new surroundings. Vaguely aware of the others doing the same, he stepped toward an enormous stone wall behind the group. Jonah tried to see how high it rose, but the hovering mist above them made that impossible. Considering the wall extended in either direction as far as he could see, he was sure its height was just as vast. He touched the leaves on one of hundreds of vines spreading across the stone surface, jumping back when the plant moved away from his touch.

"Did we come *through* there?" he asked, turning around to see Zeus watching him.

"In a manner of speaking, yes."

"I hardly felt it this time," Ava said, stepping beside Jonah to admire the wall.

"We're no longer in the mortal realm," Enki explained softly and without condescension. "And we have to be quick. Time moves differently here." He turned away from them and the wall, and the other gods fell in line behind him. With a quick glance at Ava, Jonah gestured for her to go first, and they followed the gods.

It was all he could do to keep pace, finding himself distracted by this strange new place. He'd never seen anything like it. The grass was thick and lush under their feet, and he longed to take off his shoes. Magnificent trees ascended toward the sky, the branches swaying ever so slightly as the mist weaved and danced through the foliage. Shrubs and flowers of every colour decorated the grounds, the air filled with the buzzing of bees and the twittering of birds. Despite the mist, the light felt warm and bright, as though the sun beamed down on them through clear skies.

They hadn't walked for long before Enki stopped in front of two trees. They appeared to mirror each other, their trunks wide and dark and the thick, foliage-laden branches sweeping out long and low. Jonah knew if he raised an arm, he could touch one. Enki whispered something, his head bowed, and Jonah looked around to find the group now stood before a small stone door fixed between the two trees. A light passed through the surface of the door, filtering from the top to the bottom, and then the door swung slowly open. Ducking his head, Enki entered without hesitation, and one by one, the rest followed.

Given the entryway, Jonah expected to step into a dark room and was surprised once again to find this wasn't the case. Instead, they had entered a circular stone chamber, its walls vaulting up to a domed, latticed roof. Flowering vines weaved their way through the roof and down along the walls, their scent perfuming the air. Rays of light penetrated like soft spotlights. The same lush grass covered the ground here, too, and in the middle of the room sat a stone altar adorned with fine golden cloth and surrounded by flowering wreaths. On the altar itself lay Alex.

While everyone else hung back at a respectful distance, Mallory approached her husband first. He was dressed in a tunic and pants not unlike those Enki wore, though these were of the palest blue. His feet were bare, his hands folded across his chest. Mallory walked reverently around the altar until she stopped beside his head. She gazed down at him, running her hand through his hair. A smile graced her lips, which she then pressed gently to her husband's as she bent over him. When she straightened, she exhaled a shaky breath and gestured for the others to join her.

Ava and Tristan both kissed their father, while Jonah placed his hands atop Alex's. "Thank you so much. For everything," he said softly. Staring at the only father figure he'd ever really known, he felt the loss all over again. With everything that had happened, none of them had been given the chance to properly grieve, yet even now, Jonah felt it wasn't the right time for his own emotions. He looked up at Ava, seeing the tears streaming unabashedly down her face, and told himself he had to be strong for them.

"Thank you," Mallory said, placing her hand to her heart and giving the gods a sad smile. "Alex would have gotten such a kick out of this. We appreciate the opportunity to say goodbye to him in such a beautiful setting." The gods only nodded in acknowledgement.

"I wonder what Dad would think about everything that's happening," Ava mused.

"He'd be bloody loving it," Tristan said. "I mean, not the part about tons of people dying and the Fates wanting to kill us all, but the other stuff. You know, with the gods, and the Tablet, etc…" He shoved his hands in his pockets, apparently having decided the domed ceiling was more interesting.

"We know what you mean," Mallory said. "And you're right."

Jonah swallowed thickly as he clenched his teeth, trying to hold back the tears. He felt a hand clasp his shoulder and looked up to see Tristan beside him. Jonah tried to smile. Tristan threw his arm around his mate's shoulders, and that simple action released something in Jonah; a weight lifted, as though his friend's acknowledgement freed him to feel what the others experienced without shame.

Jonah grasped his friend's shoulders in return, and side by side they stood, their tears even further binding them.

He wasn't sure how long they stood there, but all too soon, Enki quietly told them it was time to go. Without a sound, the group followed him back the way they had come. Bringing up the rear, Jonah couldn't help but turn back for one last look at Alex. He could have sworn he saw a smile on the man's face.

Once he stepped through the door and back between the two trees, he heard a faint hiss. Jonah turned in time to see the door vanish, as though it had never been there. At Isis' prompting, those who had gathered for the farewell once again joined hands, and Jonah took a deep breath.

When he reopened his eyes, the group had returned to the Carters' loungeroom.

"Good. You're back," Marduk stated from the doorway.

"How much time did we lose?" Zeus asked and approached his fellow god.

"About two weeks…"

Zeus swore under his breath.

"Hang on, what?" Jonah asked but was ignored.

"We knew the risk," Inanna added. "It had to be done. It was the right thing." Zeus glanced at her and nodded.

"Hey," Jonah said, raising his voice and grabbing his father by the shoulder. "What do you mean we've lost two weeks?" Zeus stared down at him, his brows raised and nostrils flaring.

Inanna gently led Jonah back to the others and addressed them all. "Time is not the same in every realm. That's why we couldn't stay with Alex for as long as you may have liked. There's no way of knowing before you leave how much time you will lose, though we didn't expect it to be quite two weeks. The size of our group may have had a role in that."

"Is everyone okay?" Ava asked.

"A lot has happened in the time you've been gone," Marduk replied. "We've had multiple attacks from the Fates, but as more Oracles arrived, our boundary defences have grown stronger. In saying that, though, there are probably five to ten times as many people here now as there were when you left."

"What preparations have been made in our absence?" Zeus asked.

"Well, I'm pleased to say we're making progress. I don't know whether it was from having accepted our presence here or out of a need to do something about the situation in which they now find themselves, but the mortals have been on board since you left. All the rubble has been cleared and used for makeshift shelters, though those who *can* find relief in sleep usually do so wherever they can find the space to lie down. We even have a stockpile of weapons—"

"Weapons?" Jonah asked.

"Yes, Jonah," Marduk replied, unfazed. "How else did you think we're going to fight off the Shades?"

"Uh… honestly, I hadn't thought that far ahead…" Blinking, Jonah lowered his head, feeling stupid.

"A surprising number of mortals arrived with their own weapons. Mostly collections of hunting knives, swords, a few crossbows. Even more obscure items like nunchucks, throwing stars, a handful of boomerangs…"

"I've always wanted to try nunchucks!" Tristan exclaimed. Ava elbowed him in the ribs. "What? Don't tell me you've never wanted to try. You *loved* the Ninja Turtles when we were kids."

"Swords?" Jonah said. "Seriously?"

Marduk nodded. "Apparently, mortals enjoy purchasing replicas of weaponry from television shows and movies."

"Oh, so not real swords, then."

"You forget we're fighting Shades, not flesh-and-blood mortals. Fortunately for us, replica weapons will be just as effective in combat."

"And has any training taken place yet?" Zeus asked.

Marduk smiled. "Come and see for yourself."

The two gods exited the house, and Mallory, Jonah, Tristan, and Ava stopped behind them at the top of the driveway, gazing around in surprise. Zeus and Marduk continued down the street, as though nothing at all had changed. But nothing was the same.

Adjacent to the Carter home stood a long line of shanties, people milling in and out of them. On the opposite side of the street, the block had been completely cleared, and the crowd of people had been separated into large groups, apparently engaged in varying stages of training. At the centre of each group stood one of the gods, instructing and directing.

"Holy shit…" Jonah whispered.

"Dude. How many people do you think are here now?" Tristan asked, his mouth dangling open.

Jonah looked down one end of the street, then back up the other. "I don't know. Thousands?"

"And then some," Ava added.

FEELING THE UNMISTAKABLE sensation of someone's eyes on her, Ava moved her attention to a small group of about twenty people sitting together on the grass—all staring at her. Her initial unease gave way when she recognised Caitlyn amongst them. She dashed down the driveway and across the road, Caitlyn rose to her feet, and the women embraced.

"Are you okay?" Ava replied and pulled back, her hands framing the woman's face so she could get a good look at her.

"Better than ever."

"I'm so sorry about all of this."

"Don't be," Caitlyn said, sounding more confident than Ava had ever heard her. "This is exactly who I'm supposed to be. Exactly *where* I'm supposed to be. Where we're both supposed to be."

Ava couldn't help but smile at the sincerity in the woman's voice, at the bright exuberance in Caitlyn's eyes. She nodded, then shifted her gaze over the rest of the group still seated on the grass. "I take it you're the other Oracles?"

"Some of them," replied a young, red-haired boy of about eighteen. "A lot more of us around the world couldn't get here, but we're all connected. It's almost like they've joined us."

Ava gave him a warm smile, not quite understanding what he meant but not wanting to come across as lacking in her knowledge. "Well, I'm Ava—"

"We know!" exclaimed a teenage aboriginal girl, flashing a brilliant smile, her dark eyes wide with excitement.

"Oh." Ava let out a nervous laugh. "I'm sorry. It's a little strange for people to know who you are when you don't know them in return."

"Well let's remedy that," said the red-haired boy. "I'm Henry."

"I'm Mithea," said the girl. Ava smiled at each Oracle in turn as they sounded off their own names as if in a roll-call— Aubrey, Olive, Joel, Nicole, Faye, Tov, Dina, Evangeline, Hadi, Winnie, Kai, Monroe, Otto, Felix, Nadia, Izzie, Zia.

"And of course, you know me already," said Caitlyn with a wink.

"It's lovely to meet you all. Though I have to ask, aren't Oracles traditionally female?" Ava felt her cheeks flush, not wanting to offend but still remarkably curious.

"Traditionally, yes," Felix replied, "but apparently, modern times called for a change."

"Trust me," Tov added, "we were just as surprised as you are." The group exploded into laughter, and Ava, feeling more at ease, sat down amongst them.

"JONAH! TRISTAN!" ZEUS called, and with a quick sideways glance at each other, they hurried to join Zeus, Set, and Marduk. "Gentlemen, I'm sure it's occurred to you that you will have to actually fight at some stage, and I'm assuming you both have little to no experience."

"Well, I can vouch for Tristan's right hook," Jonah replied dryly.

"Yes. Well, punching a shade will have as much effect as shoving your fist into a body of water. But at least we know you have decent aim," Zeus muttered. Tristan could barely contain his sheepish grin. "Marduk and Set are our two most spirited and experienced fighters, each with strengths I think will serve you both. I expect you to do as they say. You'll find that, once taken seriously, your innate abilities will kick in, and you'll progress in leaps and bounds. Still, like anyone else, in order to do that, you need to train." Zeus nodded at the other gods, and without awaiting a response from either Jonah or Tristan, he walked away.

CHAPTER TWENTY-EIGHT

JONAH HURLED THE plank of wood to the ground in frustration. Looking at where Tristan worked with Set, he assumed by his mate's pointed gesticulating that Tristan wasn't faring much better. Around him rose the chants and grunts of those participating in the basic training—which was pretty much everyone—making Jonah feel even more like a bumbling fool.

Son of a god, my arse...

"Again," Marduk commanded, standing a few metres away, his feet braced shoulder-width apart, arms folded against his chest.

"You know," Jonah stated as he bent to pick up the wood, "that stance is just insulting. It's basically telling me there's no way you think I can actually hit you."

"You can't," Marduk replied, his expression blank.

Jonah lunged at him, grunting in both exertion and frustration. He barely saw the god move before he found himself stumbling into a heap on the grass. Again. "This is bullshit. Clearly, I don't know how to fight, so why am I not in basic training like everyone else instead of over here embarrassing myself for everyone to see? What kind of leader does that make me look like?"

"If you put as much focus into your training as you do into your complaints, maybe you would discover the answer."

Scowling, Jonah returned to his starting position. He turned the plank over in his hands and looked up when he heard Tristan swear.

At least it's not just me...

"When you're ready," Marduk instructed.

Jonah ignored him, instead finding himself glancing at Ava, who worked with the other Oracles and seemed to have bonded with the group. As if she felt his stare, she looked up and smiled—the first genuine smile he'd seen on her in weeks. The sight of it made his heart skip, yet he wondered how she could possibly be happy in the midst of all this.

A stirring breeze swept across his face. It carried a lingering scent he couldn't place, and his mind instantly withdrew to his childhood.

STANDING IN THE street in front of the Carter house, Jonah stood awkwardly with a cricket bat in his hand and a wheelie bin behind him.

"You gotta turn the bat around the other way!" Tristan called out, tossing the cricket ball from one hand to the other. Adjusting his grip, Jonah flicked a quick glance up at the Carter house, hoping Ava wasn't watching covertly from any of the windows. He focused on Tristan's long-winded wind-up before his mate finally hit stride and bowled the ball. Jonah dropped the bat, his hands flying up to cover his head as the ball pounded into the bin behind him.

"Dude! You didn't even try to hit it," whined Tristan.

"This is a stupid game. Why don't we do something else?"

"Uh-uh. No way. You said if I went with you to watch Indiana Jones, then you'd play cricket with me."

"Yeah, but you like Indiana Jones. I don't like cricket."

"Tough luck, bro. If you tried hitting the ball, you might actually enjoy it."

"Piss off..." Jonah called back.

Tristan laughed. "Getting annoyed, are we, mate? Good!" They faced off, Tristan tossing the ball in his hand while Jonah gripped the bat tightly, tapping it on the ground like he'd seen on the T.V. At least he knew he had it the right way around this time. Tristan started his run-up, but before he released the ball, he shouted, "Indiana Jones is a big girl, and so are you!"

Jonah glared at his friend as the ball bounced in front of him. He swung his bat as hard as he could. His glare morphed into stunned surprise when the vibration of the impact shuddered up the bat's handle and into his hands. Tristan's gleeful whoop bounced around the street, and the ball went flying into a high arc before crashing through the Carters' window. Jonah dropped the bat, and Tristan rushed to his side to thump him on the back. "Dude. That was awesome!"

"Tristan Carter!" Mallory yelled from inside the house. The boys grinned at each other and took off running down the street.

"YOU LOOK LIKE a man who's just had an epiphany," Marduk stated. Jonah flicked him a quick glance in response but said nothing as he shifted back to his starting position once more. He faced the god and slowly turned the wood over in his hands. Finally, he allowed himself to shift through the images he'd struggled to ignore for days—the look on Ava's face when she collapsed after their kiss; the lifeless bodies of David and Bethany; Alex's eyes staring at him, devoid of all life; Atropos' slow, smug smirk of triumph. Without giving any warning, he heaved the wood over his head and charged at Marduk. Yet the faster he ran, the slower everything else seemed to move. He registered the flicker of surprise in Marduk's eyes before the smallest hint of a smile replaced it. He felt the barely discernible shift in the flow of air around them. The wood in his hand no longer felt heavy but like a natural extension of his own arm. His feet deciphered any unevenness in the ground ahead without Jonah having to look, and they moved almost on their own to avoid the obstacles. And Jonah realised he felt the vibrations of the god standing before him, rolling off Marduk in waves.

As Jonah prepared to strike his first blow, Marduk's energy changed, alerting Jonah to the god's next move before he made it. Marduk had anticipated Jonah's first attack and stepped away to avoid it, only this time, Jonah altered his course at the last moment and swung his makeshift sword down toward the god's neck.

Marduk gripped the wood only centimetres from impact and stared at Jonah. "That's more like it. Again."

AVA SAT CROSS-LEGGED on the grass, surrounded by the Oracles seated around her in a circle. Kali sat opposite her, mirroring her position. "We've seen you have great strength, Ava," she said. "That much is certain. First, however, we need to you to learn how to control it. To focus it at will, not just in reaction. Only then will we test the strength of your powers."

Ava nodded and tried not to think about the group's eyes on her; she couldn't help the feeling of inadequacy plaguing her. The Oracles all seemed so at ease with what they'd become, as though it were the most natural thing in the word. Yet she still felt herself fighting against it, doubting her capability to embrace the all-powerful Oracle everyone believed her to be.

"Take a deep breath and release the tension from your body," Kali said. "Feel your shoulders drop." Ava did as she was instructed and found she felt less exposed with her eyes shut. "Now, without trying to rely on your memory, I want you to see in your mind's eye the Oracles seated around you, and I want you to tell me the order in which they're sitting, starting with Monroe."

Ava focused on her breathing the way Kali had shown her, but try as she might, she could only vaguely picture Caitlyn sitting at about two o'clock and someone beside her in a white shirt. With a sigh, she opened her eyes, but before she could speak, Kali said, "You're trying to *remember* where they are. Don't."

Ava shook her head in frustration. "I don't know how else to do it. I can't control what I see with my eyes closed."

"Yes, you can," Kali retorted, her voice firm but never deviating from its meditative hum. Ava exhaled slowly, trying to force the frustration out with it. Closing her eyes again, she let her mind go blank. "Good. Now imagine your third eye opening in the space just above the bridge of your nose, slightly above the brow line. As it opens, you'll be able to see your surroundings."

Ava concentrated all her energy on her third eye. For a while, nothing happened, but just when she was ready to give up again, she noticed the edges of her vision had started to lighten and blur, slowly disintegrating the blackness. It did not have the same clarity as with her eyes open—at least, not yet. She felt the smile spread across her face when she made out the group sitting around her, the joy in her voice unmistakeable as she rattled off every Oracle's name in turn.

TRISTAN STALKED BACK and forth, listening to Jonah's triumphant hoots as his mate progressed in strides. The competitive fire light up within Tristan's stomach, and not wanting Jonah to have all the fun, he turned to face Set, who stood with a bored expression and his hands clasped behind his head.

"Okay. You can let me in on the secret, now. How do I kick-start my superhero powers?" Tristan asked.

Set sighed. "There is no secret. You either have them, or you don't."

"Hang on, what? I either have them or I don't? Of course I have them. Don't I? I'm descended from Achilles. I've got superpowers, damn it!"

Set lowered his arms and shrugged. "We assumed you would, but perhaps they only touched your sister. Looks like you've lucked out."

"Piss off, mate. I've got them."

Set just raised doubtful eyebrows. Tristan dropped his piece of wood and leaned forward, glaring at the god. *I'll show you.* With a grunt, he launched himself at Set, and he had no more time to think before he was flat on his back with the god grinning down at him.

"Maybe you've got something after all…"

"Huh? I'm on my arse. What the hell just happened?"

"Looks like you've got speed on your side, even if you still can't land a shot. Mind you, it would also help if you didn't drop your weapon before you attack someone…"

"Speed…" Tristan said in awe, accepting the god's hand before being yanked back to his feet. "We're talking speed-of-light kind of fast, right?"

"Perhaps not quite that fast," Set replied, "but that was fast enough. Try it again. Only this time, don't run at *me*. Pick another target and see how quickly you reach it."

Tristan didn't have to think twice. He looked at Jonah sparring with Marduk. Grinning, he took his stance and launched himself toward his mate.

"What the…" Jonah groaned and pushed himself up into sitting, blinking around in a daze, as he seemed to just realize he was now on the ground.

"Dude, I'm the bloody Flash!"

THEY SAT SIDE by side on the curb, staring into one of the small bonfires Enki had conjured to line the street.

"Dude, what a day…" Tristan said with a groan.

Jonah nodded, rubbing his own shoulder. Despite their rapidly growing abilities, their bodies were still mortal. "Yeah, I don't reckon I'll be able to move in the morning."

Tristan chuckled. "At least, not as fast as me."

"Ha! Maybe not, but I'm pretty sure I'll be able to see you coming."

"Bullshit!"

"Marduk moves like lightning, and if I can see his next move, then I have a good chance at stopping you."

"That sounds like a challenge, mate. Let's just leave it a couple days, though. I don't think I'll be able to move from this spot for a while." Tristan hissed out a sigh and stretched out his legs.

Jonah grunted in agreement, but his focus was on Ava. She sat across the road, beside the tree where he had laid David and Bethany. Her legs were crossed, eyes closed, the backs of her open hands resting on her knees. "What do you think about Ava and the Oracles?" he asked.

Tristan followed his gaze and shrugged. "I don't know, to be honest. I mean, she's changed a lot recently, but who hasn't? Extreme times and all. But she looks happy, like she's found her place. Like a weight's lifted off her shoulders."

Jonah only nodded. He knew it was selfish, but he felt as though the closer she grew to the Oracles and to revealing her own powers, the larger the space between them became.

"Yeah, mate. I miss her, too." Tristan patted him on the shoulder and gave a knowing smile. Jonah chuckled at his mate's rare moment of perception. "What do you think she's doing over there?"

Jonah took another moment to watch her. "It kind of looks like she's meditating. Are people supposed to smile when they meditate?"

"Stuffed if I know. I tried it once and fell asleep."

Jonah laughed. "I want to find out how she is, but at the same time, I don't want to disturb her."

"Your call, bro. Either way, I'm sure she'll find us when she's ready to share."

Jonah frowned and returned his gaze to the fire, the sounds around him fading away.

CHAPTER TWENTY-NINE

A VA FELT A little lightheaded but held her position. It amazed her how quickly her mind's eye had opened under Kali's guidance. A tingling coursed through her, from where her tailbone rested against the grass, right up through the centre of her body before intensifying through her third eye and the crown of her head. The sensation had scared her at first, but she'd quickly grown accustomed to it, especially once her vision kicked in.

One by one, she met the other Oracles spread out over the globe. They showed her where they lived, what they looked like, their part of the world through their own eyes. Now, she viewed through the eyes of an Oracle named Genevieve sitting atop a deserted Eiffel Tower, watching the sunset. It was so beautiful, the golden oranges and pinks blending into the fading blue. Ava found herself caught up in the moment, and a smile warmed her face. Until Genevieve rose to her feet and looked down from the dizzying height at the people below. The scene was not unlike the makeshift camps lining the streets where Ava sat. People huddled together, shelters set up where they could find space. Earthquakes and floods had brought the same devastation, no matter where in the world the Oracles were.

Ava released a shaky sigh. They'd been so caught up in their own experiences, they hadn't given a lot of thought to those suffering elsewhere—she found herself saddened by the thought of those Oracles lost among the destruction after the worldwide quake. The loss of lives in general was hard to fathom, but now she was connected to the Oracles, she felt their loss as keenly as her own.

'Open your eyes.'

The command came from within her own mind yet was not her own voice. Ava complied, frowning in confusion. She looked around and saw Kali standing in the shadows, watching her. Ava moved to rise, but Kali stopped her *'Stay there.'* Not removing her gaze from the goddess, Ava settled back into position. *'I'm proud of how you're advancing, but I need to push you a little harder.'*

Ava nodded, feeling a hint of fluttering nerves in her stomach.

'I want you to close your eyes and focus on my voice. Now, like before, focus on your breathing and feel the energies of the Oracles flow through your chakras.'

Ava twitched as she felt the spark of energy run through her.

'You've shown you can see through the eyes of the Oracles,' Kali added, *'but now I want you to access their minds.'*

Ava's eyes flew open. "That's an invasion of privacy!" she shouted, causing those around her to stare. Despite the distance between them, Ava clearly saw Kali's frown at such a disobedient challenge.

'They are aware you can and will access their minds,' the goddess continued. *'Now close your eyes and start again.'*

Ava did as she was told, not willing to defy the goddess' orders. Inhaling deeply, she held her breath for a moment, then released. This time, she found she didn't need to concentrate quite as hard before she felt the energies travelling up her body, moving through the energy centres one by one. As each chakra activated, her awareness and focus heightened. The energies peaked at her third eye and crown, causing a momentary loss of breath; the sensation was very much like jumping into icy-cold water and feeling her lungs seize from the shock. It brought her to the edge of panic, and she gasped for air.

'Focus. Control your breathing,' Kali instructed. It took a few attempts, but Ava steadied her breath and found the images flickering across her closed eyelids—only they weren't her own but those of the Oracle Hadi. She'd entered a memory from when the woman was five or six years old.

How do I know how old she is? Ava hadn't meant to address this question to Kali, but the goddess picked up on her thoughts nevertheless.

'Because she knows,' Kali replied. *'Don't question the images that come to you. This will only stagnate the process. Keep your mind open and free of any misconceptions or judgements.'*

Ava swallowed thickly as she allowed the images to unfold. She watched Hadi run through the long grass, giggling as the blades whipped at her splayed hands. When the young girl fell to the ground and rolled onto her back, looking up at the cloudless sky, Ava smiled. The grass stood tall around her, and Hadi felt protected, hidden, as though she were the only person in the world.

'Now focus on Tov,' Kali instructed. Ava complied and found herself viewing a particularly hot and heavy memory

from last year's school camp. She quickly withdrew, feeling her face flush at the intrusion.

Okay. I can see their memories, she thought to Kali. *But what's the point of this? How are memories going to help us against the Fates and their army of shades?*

'Wait here.'

Confused, Ava opened her eyes to see the goddess walking quickly away before disappearing in the throng of people. While she waited, she found herself wondering how Jonah was doing. Then it occurred to her she could probably delve into *his* memories too, if she wanted.

"Don't you dare!" she said aloud, chastising herself and again garnering odd glances from those around her. Lowering her gaze to her hands, she couldn't help but berate herself further for even thinking such a thing.

"Are we interrupting?" Zeus's deep voice erupted from right in front of her, and Ava jumped in surprise. Despite his size, he managed to gracefully sit facing her, legs crossed to mirror her own.

"Uh. Am I in trouble or something?"

"Or something," the god replied. "Kali tells me you can now access the Oracles' memories."

Ava nodded. "Yes. But only the Oracles. I wouldn't dare try to—"

"We need you to find a memory," he continued. "An important memory."

Ava stared at him, her brow furrowed as she tried to work out what he meant.

'The Tablet...' Kali told her, though despite Ava's search, she couldn't find the goddess anywhere. *'You can do it.'*

"I thought you'd lost that particular memory," Ava said.

Zeus nodded. "We're hoping it's still in there, buried deep within my subconscious despite my inability to access it."

"And you think *I* can access it?"

"We hope so. I'm sure I don't need to tell you the importance of locating this particular memory—and what it could mean for us."

"No pressure..." Ava muttered, then closed her eyes and focused. Allowing the energies to traverse through her once more, she opened her mind to Zeus. At first, the images appeared in disjointed fragments—the warmth of the sun on his skin; the pleasurable heat of wine travelling down his throat; the touch of a woman, then another woman, and another and another. The visions flashed by with increasing speed—battles and blood and thunder roaring in her head.

'Slow them down,' Kali instructed.

"I can't!" Ava shouted, growing nauseous from the onslaught of images pelting her. Just as she was about to give up and open her eyes, she noted one image far different than the rest. She grabbed at it with her mind and willed it to unfold before her. By the way it flickered in and out of focus, it was obviously damaged. Ava hardly registered Zeus' moan, focusing instead on the certainty that she was on to something. Pushing her own mind forward, she dove deeper into the memory, trying to make sense of it. She saw a group of men, seven of them, all with the same face. The cries of a child were faint, as though listening from far away. The strongest part of the memory was the smell of the air just before it was about to rain. Her eyes flew open in time to see Zeus crumple to the ground, panting as though he'd undergone a great, physical task.

"Tell me you've found something," he gasped, his voice hoarse.

Ava nodded. "I know where it is."

JONAH HAD NO idea what time it was, just that it was late—or was it early? Either way, it was dark and relatively quiet—as quiet as it ever got with so many people around. Most of them had retreated within the shelters, and those who couldn't sleep sat quietly around the fires. He approached one of the shelters, where a bicycle leaned against one wall. Jonah had seen it there earlier and had intended to ask the owner if he could borrow it, but he had no idea who the actual owner was. He certainly wasn't going to disturb anyone at this hour just to ask, and he eased his conscience by affirming that he'd have it back before whoever owned it even knew it was gone.

His muscles screamed at him as he mounted the bike and started peddling, but he knew they'd loosen up. He'd feel better for it come the next training session. But that wasn't the purpose of this exercise. Their farewell to Alex had made him miss his own parents all the more. He hadn't visited them since he'd returned—there hadn't been time—but with everything that had happened, everything that had been revealed to him, Jonah needed to speak to them.

Their resting place wasn't far, at least by car, and he knew it would take an hour or so by bike. But even while he peddled, the road sped past him, and he found himself grinning at this new reminder that he was no longer a mere mortal.

In far less than the anticipated hour, he stopped at the cemetery's entrance. He'd half-expected the large, wrought-iron gates to be closed, surprised to instead find them wide open, as though they'd expected him. He got off the bike and leaned it against the wall, wanting to cover the rest of the distance by foot.

Taking the path he knew quite well through the cemetery, he scanned the gravestones around him. A figure rose from between two markers, and Jonah's breath caught in his throat. But when the old man saw him, he only nodded at Jonah before wiping his forehead with a hand clutching a bunch of weeds. Jonah quickly scanned the man's overalls and figured he must be a groundskeeper. He politely returned the nod before continuing, but then he wondered why a groundskeeper would be working at this hour. Something about the old man seemed familiar, though he couldn't put his finger on it.

He'd only walked a few metres when he saw the same man raking up leaves under a tree. Looking up at Jonah, the man paused and raised his hand to his hat, tipping it toward Jonah in greeting.

What the...

He was sure the man had not been wearing a hat a moment ago. Quickly turning around, he didn't expect at all to see the first man exactly where Jonah had seen him between the headstones. Despite the darkness, he could have sworn the men looked exactly the same.

He forced himself to keep walking anyway. Despite the eeriness, he didn't sense anything intimidating or dangerous about the men. Still, when he turned back around one final time, the sight of them both staring after him was certainly unnerving. It also gave him a sense of déjà vu, which his fatigued mind couldn't process. Deciding to just keep his head down, he picked up the pace and hurried toward his parents' graves.

"Hey, Mum. Hey, Dad. Sorry it's been longer than usual. You wouldn't believe the shit that's been going on around here..." A tingling sensation crept up his spine; he was being watched. Slowly, he turned and looked up. Not only were the two old men watching him from a distance, they'd been joined by five more, all identically dressed in overalls. Then it dawned on him who they were. *Why are the Abgal here?*

Knowing he'd get no answers, he instead tried to ignore them and took a seat at the foot of his parents' burial plots. He opened his mouth to speak but closed it again. Suddenly, words just felt inane; nothing he could say would come close to bringing justice to his experiences, to what they'd all experienced. Instead, he found himself thinking of the few years he *had* been fortunate enough to spend with his parents, with all the laughter and happiness and safety.

Thank you.

By the time Jonah stood up from the graves, he could no longer see the Abgal—and yet, he could feel their eyes on him from all around. It wasn't a threatening sensation, just more like a sense of protection. He briefly wondered why they'd bother to hide when he'd already seen them but shrugged it off and headed back to the cemetery entrance.

When he approached the gates, though, he realised exactly why. Atropos stood beyond the wrought-iron bars, arms folded regally across her chest. Jonah froze, every muscle in his body tensing.

"Relax, Jonah. I'm sure you've worked out by now that I can't hurt you. At least, not directly…"

"What do you want?"

"I want us to stop wasting each other's time. How many more lives must be lost? How many will you sacrifice for a battle you can't win?"

"I don't think you're actually concerned about the loss of human life." Jonah sneered as he looked her up and down.

Atropos shrugged. "I'm not, truth be known. No more than a mortal cares about the ants upon which they tread. The point is *you* care. How was Alex's farewell?" A smirk crept across the corners of her mouth.

Jonah swallowed thickly, his hands clenched into tight fists by his side.

"You know, I've never understood the mortal desire to hold onto the dead…" Atropos glanced past him to the cemetery. "You realise it's not really your parents in there, don't you? Not anymore. It's just dirt and dust. That's all."

"Tell me what you want, or—"

The Fate laughed. "Or what? What are *you* going to do to *me*?" Jonah frowned at her scorn but said nothing. Atropos let out a dramatic sigh. "I'm bored with this realm now. We're prepared to abandon our plans for war on one condition."

Jonah scoffed. "What's that?"

"Hand over the Tablet."

"Well I don't know where it is. And why would I give you the one thing capable of destroying us all in a heartbeat?"

A flicker of annoyance scattered across Atropos' face, but her recovery was smooth. "Just because it's capable of doing so doesn't mean we intend to use it for that purpose."

Jonah barked out a laugh of disbelief. "Really? Just what are your grand plans for it, then? I'm pretty sure it's not to let us all live happily ever after while you piss off back to where you came from."

Atropos offered another nonchalant shrug, but her eyes flashed when her mouth twisted up into a sneer. "No. Not all of you. There are far too many of you, after all. Even now. Just enough to continue the species. I'd even agree to letting you and your loved ones live. It would be your choice."

"What kind of twisted choice is that?"

"The only one you have, boy," Atropos spat, her patience suddenly snapped. "With barely a flick of our fingers, we have bestowed a staggering number of deaths already. Add to that those who will perish in this useless fight of yours, and how many of you do you think will be left? My prediction is none."

"Well I'd like to bet otherwise," Jonah stated, not feeling half as brazen as he sounded.

Atropos narrowed her gaze with a sneer. "Perhaps you should run along back to your gods and see what counsel they would give you. You have twenty-four hours to return here to me with your decision." Before Jonah could reply, she turned her back on him, and that mystical wind once more appeared. It sent her hair and dress whipping out around her, and in three steps, she was gone.

Jonah braced himself against the wall, his heart pounding in his chest as he swore. She might not have been able to lay a finger on him, but that didn't make her any less terrifying.

Jumping on his bike, he didn't even notice the ache of his sore muscles and sped back to the others.

CHAPTER
THIRTY

JONAH SAT ATOP the Carters' driveway, tapping out some unknown beat on his knees pulled up toward his chest. He knew he had to tell the others about the Fates' proposal, but he hoped at least some of them were getting some rest—or better still, some sleep.

Yet as he sat there, one by one, the gods appeared. Not one of them said a word as they sat around him. Then, with the approach of the new day's light glimmering across the sky came the Carters. Tristan looked dishevelled, his hair tousled, wearing the slightly creased, just-woke-up look. Mallory looked tired, the sadness she carried unmistakeable behind her eyes. Ava, on the other hand, looked as though she'd spent the past twenty-four hours at a day spa.

"Dude, I had the strangest dream that you were sitting on our driveway, summoning us about some message. I woke up asking myself, 'Why would Jonah just be sitting there like a knob?' Yet he we are."

"Good morning to you too."

"Do we need to take this inside?" Zeus queried, nodding toward the few people stirring out on the street.

"Yeah, probably a good idea," Jonah said.

The group got to their feet and went inside. They gathered around the dining table, and Jonah rehashed his conversation with Atropos. When he finished, Tristan let out a long sigh, sounding surprisingly loud and overexaggerated in the heavy silence.

"What was your read on Atropos?" Zeus asked, leaning heavily on the back of one of the chairs as though burdened by a great weight.

Jonah looked up, unable to hide his surprise. "Aside from the fact she's a scary, crazy bitch?"

"Jonah!" Mallory chastised.

"Look, honestly, I don't trust her as far as I could kick her."

"Why would we kick her?" Vishnu asked, looking from one god to the other for confirmation.

"It's a figure of speech," Jonah explained. "It means we can't believe anything she says."

"Her proposal's not an option, right?" Tristan asked. "I mean, putting the Tablet in her hands is exactly what we're trying to avoid, isn't it?"

"Exactly," Enki added. "We've known Atropos a long time, and she wouldn't just sit on all that power after all this time."

"She has no love for the mortal realm," Isis said. "So why would she agree to save it?"

"Surely the only reason she's made an offer at all is because they doubt their victory," Marduk proposed.

Zeus straightened. "The thought had occurred to me, but after Hades and Set described what they saw in the Underworld, I can't see how'd they be anything less than confident."

"The shades are essentially dead, aren't they?" Mallory asked. "They're souls. Not flesh and blood like us?"

"Correct," Hades replied.

"Well, we've been so concerned with their sheer numbers instead of focusing on how they'll actually fight us. What if the Fates have made this offer because the shades lack the power that would actually stop us?"

Zeus and Hades exchanged an unreadable glance. "I think it's worth investigating," Hades drawled in his deep voice.

"Do it," Zeus commanded.

"I'm going too," Set stated, turning and following Hades without waiting for an answer.

"Perhaps there's something we can do in the meantime," Inanna suggested.

"What's that?" Zeus asked.

"The Oracles. Their strength grows daily. Surely we could obtain a glimpse into what's to come?"

Zeus looked to Kali, who nodded slowly. "I think they're ready to try," she said, "though the Oracles' visions can at times be vague and easily misinterpreted."

"True." Zeus stroked his beard. "But if it gives us anything at all to work with, it's worth a shot. Perhaps set only half of them to working on it at a time, in case we need the others."

When Ava stood from her chair, Jonah noticed the confidence she'd carried around the past few days seemed to falter. As though feeling his stare, she turned her head to meet his gaze. A quick smile flickered at the corners of her mouth, but he'd known her too long to mistake the concern in her eyes. But there was no opportunity to ask if she was okay, as she was whisked away by Kali and Isis.

"Earth to Jonah…" came Tristan's voice.

"Huh? What?"

"Dude, snap out of it. We've got training."

With an inward groan, Jonah stood from the table to once more follow the others out of the house.

"WE'RE NOT GOING outside," Kali instructed as Ava turned for the front door. Instead, the goddess headed for the lounge room. "It's best if we do this somewhere private, without any distractions or influences." Ava swallowed thickly and took a seat on her father's favourite chair, hoping it would provide some comfort. "I'll return with the Oracles." Then Kali left the room.

Isis remained on her feet, pacing leisurely as if she didn't have a care in the world. "It's okay to feel nervous," the goddess said gently, not looking at Ava.

Ava cleared her throat. "I'm not sure why I'm feeling anxious. I've been nothing but confident since meeting the Oracles. I guess… I feel like I have a sense of purpose in all this chaos." She frowned, looking down at the arm of the chair, and placed her hand over where her fathers had once rested.

"Yet you hadn't considered looking into the future?" Isis prompted.

Ava shook her head and looked up. "Honestly? No."

Isis gave a kind smile. "It's a good thing you're not cavalier about it. Obtaining a vision should be taken seriously. Looking into the future for answers is daunting, especially at a time when the future has never felt so uncertain. You just need to remember you are not alone. While the burden is an enormous one, we've a lot of shoulders to carry it."

Before Ava could thank her, Kali entered with Aubrey, Olive, Joel, Nicole, Faye, Dina, Evangeline, and Monroe. Ava wasn't sure whether to be relieved or concerned that their confidence also seemed deflated, and she did her best to give them a reassuring smile.

"We need to clear a space," Isis said. The goddesses stood back, speaking privately while Ava and the other Oracles moved the coffee table and chairs to one side of the room.

"I want you to sit in a tight circle," Kali added. "You need to sit cross-legged with your knees almost touching the person beside you. Ava, sit in the centre facing north."

"Uh, north?" Ava asked, feeling foolish for having no handle on directions inside the house. Isis kindly pointed it out for her, and north saw Ava facing a corner of the room. It felt remarkably unnatural, and she shifted this way and that, angling to get comfortable as Isis spoke.

"Remember to pay close attention to what you see and hear. Even though you are all together, you'll each have a different experience of the prophecy. No two visions will be exactly the same."

Without waiting for her to settle, Kali walked them through the initial steps while Isis paced slowly around the circle.

"Everyone, close your eyes." Ava did as she was told, the sudden darkness heavy and thick. "Focus on your breathing. Inhale, hold it for four counts. Exhale. Inhale, and this time hold it for six counts. Exhale. Inhale, hold it for eight counts. Exhale…"

Ava knew she held her breath for increasingly longer periods of time, yet she noted no strain or struggle in her lungs. Her body felt lighter with every inhalation, as though she were a balloon slowly inflating with each intake of air. Her eyes relayed the sensation of being wide open, but as she looked from left to right, all she could see was darkness. Kali's voice faded away, muffled as if Ava listened to her from under water.

Holding her breath, she felt the energies of those around her shimmering in gentle waves, and it reminded her of her child-hood—playing with the bedsheets, flicking them above the bed and watching the air billow toward the other end. It made her smile, and Ava realised her lips were tingling. But this didn't concern her; she felt rather detached from her body—still con-nected to it yet somehow outside it.

A hazy fog drifted toward her, both pulsating and wispy at the same time. When it reached her, it thinned and spread out, forming fine tendrils wrapping and binding around each other like spiderwebs. Ava felt herself reaching out, wanting to touch the centre of one of these webs, yet she couldn't see her own hand move. The web seemed to anticipate her intention, and the section on which she focused illuminated to a bright white, dimming the neighbouring webs to a dull grey in comparison. The light filled her vision, pushing away the darkness, but still, she could discern no details.

She did *hear* something, though, too soft to make out but coming from both within her ear and outside her body, as soft as a whisper. Straining to listen, she forgot about trying to see.

"Listen to my voice, and I will show you what you need to see…"

"Who are you?" Ava asked.

"I am Hephalion, and I am you. We are one and the same, existing in different times and at once."

"I don't understand…"

"You have no need to. The brain cannot always understand what the heart already knows. We are the same, you and I. Two extensions of the one soul."

Ava knew he spoke the truth, and it felt as though she finally accepted a long-known certainty about herself. She focused again on the glowing web, Hephalion's whispers in her ears.

Then her mouth fell open in awe as the images spilled forth. They appeared in disjointed fashion, but Ava did her best to take note of everything flashing before her.

She gazed down into a wide valley. The ground shook below her, then cracked open to reveal the presence of some unseen force. The moon moved in front of the sun, and beneath that eclipse, shades spilled out of the crevasse. Ava heard a massive roar, then shifted her gaze to see a lion with a diagonal scar across its face. It opened its enormous jaws and roared again before hurtling toward her. She would have ducked despite knowing this was a vision, but the lion leaped and cleared her head in one swift motion.

When she turned around again to watch it land, the beast had vanished. In its place yawned the black mouth of a cave, a narrow river flowing past her. The water was smooth and dark, like the surface of a black mirror, the subtle movement of its current barely visible beneath the surface. Beside her on a large stone, in which a smooth groove had been worn away, there sat an ancient-looking wooden bowl with strange markings on the sides. Then everything vanished, and she now gazed upon twin vials of blood as long as her index finger, stoppered with aged cork.

Hephalion's whispers ceased, and the images were wrenched away from her, pulling her forward as though she'd been physically attached. Her ears filled with a swift, heavy rush, and Ava felt her head hit the floor. Her eyes flew open to the sight of everyone gathered around her.

"Holy shit…" she muttered.

Kali nodded. "We'd hoped as much. Take a moment to recover. Then we need to know everything."

Ava pushed herself up into sitting, her arms shaking beneath her weight. She glanced around at the other Oracles; most of them had gone pale, and a few sported bloody noses. Ava hoped the visions would be worth it. Olive shied away when their gazes met, and Ava frowned. She watched the girl for a moment, who'd suddenly engrossed herself in the carpet beneath her fingertips, and briefly wondered why Olive would avoid her at all. Then she quickly reprimanded herself for embracing such fatigued paranoia.

HADES AND SET moved silently through the secret tunnel leading to the Underworld's central chamber. Stopping at the wall, Hades placed his palms against the stone, but this time, it did not move aside. Lifting his hands briefly, he scanned the wall, searching for the cause, then tried again.

"Don't tell me we're completely locked out, now." Set sighed behind him.

"There's some resistance from the other side. A push-back of energy."

"The Fates?" Set asked, peering around Hades' shoulders for a better look.

"I don't think so. This doesn't feel like a barrier. More like trying to open a door when something has fallen against it on the other side." Hades spread his hands farther apart and leaned into the stone wall. Faint cracks of blue light spread outward from his touch.

"It's working," Set hissed. "Keep going."

Hades felt a shudder rise through his arms and into his shoulders, but he held the pressure. Finally, the stone wall dissipated to reveal what had held him back.

"This is not good..." Set whispered. He stepped out beside Hades onto the narrow ledge. "I wouldn't get too close."

Hades ignored him. Instead of the view of the central cavern below, which had met them during their last visit, they now faced the ether. Faces of the shades pushed against it, wearing contorted masks of despair.

"Has it ever grown to this size before?" Set asked, pressing his back firmly against the stone wall behind him.

"Never. Maintaining the natural balance keeps it at bay."

"How many souls do you think are in there?"

Hades didn't reply but crossed his arms over his chest and watched the shades.

"Gentlemen…" came a voice to their left. Startled, both gods turned to find Lachesis on the ledge beside them. "Don't worry. I'm not spying on you. I was actually hoping Atropos' ultimatum would prompt another visit."

"What do you want?" Hades growled.

"To help." She took a few steps closer. The ether's blue light shimmered upon her ivory skin, making her look eerily like an escaped shade herself.

"Help *us*?" Hades growled. "Do you think we're that ignorant? This has been your doing from the beginning."

"That's not entirely true. If the humans had taken better care of this planet and each other, we would not have been forced to take any action at all. How many thousands of years do you wish us to give them before we show them enough is enough?"

"How is this helpful?" Set asked.

Lachesis turned and stared into the ether for a moment, her expression fully unreadable in the eerie light. "My sister has become blinded by her hatred for both mankind and their gods. Whatever she has promised Jonah in exchange for the Tablet is a lie. Her only intention is to rid the world of the human race. There will be no exceptions."

"Why are you telling us this?" Hades demanded, his distrust hanging heavily with each word.

"Because I don't agree with her actions in their entirety. It goes against our sole purpose of maintaining the balance, of the role we play in the lives of the race she means to eradicate. Atropos sees the world without mankind as a world of freedom."

"You don't?" Set sneered.

"No. Not in the same way. Whether or not we approve of what the human race has done to themselves and this world, they give us purpose. Without them to mould and to guide—"

"You mean to toy with," Set spat.

The Fate ignored him. "We will become the most powerful entities in the universe, vain and purposeless."

"Let me clarify," Hades drawled. "You want to aid us merely to stave off your boredom."

"No, you fool. I do this because there always must be a balance. An order to things. This is who we are. If we turn against that, I'm afraid we too will lose all meaning. There may well come a time when the human race will drive itself to extinction, but it cannot be at our hands."

Hades glanced over his shoulder at Set, then back to the Fate standing before them. "I can't say I trust you. But I'm willing to hear what you have to say."

"Then listen closely."

JONAH RESTED HIS head against the stone wall at his back, waiting for Atropos to appear. He'd quickly searched the cemetery for the Abgal upon his arrival, and while he couldn't see them, he sensed their presence. He could only assume their insistence on remaining out of sight stemmed from Atropos' pending visit.

He let out a long sigh, trying to not let his impatience get the better of him. Part of him wished he'd let Tristan come with him, but he hadn't wanted to provide Atropos with an outlet for her revenge once he told her they would not accept her offer. Besides, if Tristan felt half as wrecked from their second day of training as Jonah did, his mate would be grateful for a few hours of rest.

Jonah then found his thoughts wandering to Ava, and he tried to recall when they'd last actually spoken. He wasn't sure if he was avoiding her, if she was avoiding him, or if they were both just so caught up in their new tasks that they didn't have the time. He knew she was busy searching for the prophecy, and while he hoped she was successful, he wasn't quite sure whether or not he wanted to know the future it held. He'd seen Ava and some of the Oracles emerge from the house just before he left, and aside from looking a little shell-shocked, they were hard to read. He told himself he needed to make a point of pulling Ava aside when he returned.

"One should be more alert when waiting alone in a cemetery..."

Jonah jumped, nearly falling over his own feet as he found Atropos beside him. "Shit. You sure like to make an entrance, don't you?" he grumbled, momentarily forgetting to whom he spoke.

Atropos smiled and walked around him. "Let's not beat around the bush, as you mortals like to say. Do you accept my terms?"

"No. We don't," Jonah replied firmly.

Atropos' smirk shrivelled into a thunderous glare. "I'll give you five seconds to reconsider the stupidity of this decision."

Her voice dropped dangerously low, raising the hairs on the back of Jonah's neck and arms.

"I don't need it. We won't ever accept your offer."

"You're a fool, Jonah Sands. You will regret this."

"No. I'm Jonah, son of Zeus. And you'll be the one regretting everything you started." He pushed himself off the wall and stormed past her, his heart thundering in his chest, leaving Atropos in a furious silence behind him.

SITTING AT THE Carters' dining table, Jonah pinched his nose, his eyes tightly closed.

"You all right, mate?" Tristan asked as he swaggered into the room.

Jonah opened his eyes and looked up. "Yeah. It just dawned on me that we declared war on the Fates tonight."

"It surely doesn't come as a surprise, does it?" Enki asked as he joined them, closely followed by the rest of the gods.

Jonah sighed. "No. I know it was inevitable. It's just more real, now. I know that sounds stupid, but I think everything finally just hit me."

"Was Atropos pissed when you shot her down?" Tristan asked.

"Oh, yeah. But I left before it got too ugly. I didn't want to give her any more ammunition to attack us."

"Things are going to move quickly from here," Zeus announced, coming to stand last at the table.

"Like they didn't already?" Jonah asked.

His immortal father only gave him a sombre nod. "Ava and a group of the Oracles are working together as we speak to look for anything that may help us. Once they have had the chance to rest and regenerate, they will connect us to the other Oracles around the world. Jonah will address the people, and the Oracles will broadcast it, if you will."

"Wait, what?" Jonah asked, blinking. "What do you mean address them?"

"Exactly that," Enki replied. "We may be the focal point of the Fates' attack, but that's not to say there won't be attacks elsewhere. There's no telling how large the army of shades has become. Everyone needs to be ready." The softness of his tone only amplified the gravity of the situation.

"About that army…" Set stated as he and Hades appeared in the doorway.

"Did you find anything of use during your visit to the Underworld?" Isis asked.

Hades and Set exchanged a look. "In a manner of speaking," Hades said. "Do you want the good news or the bad news first?"

Tristan scoffed. "There's good news?"

"Let's hear the worst of it first," Inanna suggested.

Hades cleared his throat. "The number of shades is incalculable." The statement received only a heavy silence in reply.

"He's not even exaggerating," Set explained. "The ether is all but bursting at the seams from all the souls crammed in there."

Jonah glanced at Zeus, who stood with his arms folded against his chest, gazing up at the ceiling. Finding no reassurance there, Jonah lowered his own gaze to his hands resting on the table in front of him. "Does that mean we're completely screwed?" he asked quietly.

"Not necessarily," Hades said. "There *is* the good news. We had a surprise visit from Lachesis in the Underworld."

"That's your good news?" Jonah asked with wide eyes.

"There seems to be dissension among the sisters," Hades continued, "and she's not happy with Atropos' grand scheme. Lachesis has disclosed some information that will be pivotal for our defence."

"How can we trust anything she says? It could just be a trap," Enki said, pacing around the table.

"Believe me, we were prepared to take anything she said with a grain of salt," Hades replied, "but I think she's told us the truth."

"Well, what is it?" Zeus grumbled.

"As you know, we weren't sure how effective any attack on the shades would be. We weren't confident in how to kill an entity not of flesh and blood—"

"Wait," Jonah interrupted. "You said beheading them or at the very least hitting them in the brainstem would kill them. Everyone's been training for head shots."

"Yes. Well. We had hoped that would work, based on the minimal information at hand. But we really had no way of knowing for sure."

"Well, that's bloody good to know!" Jonah shared an incredulous look with Tristan.

"On with it." Zeus growled again.

"We consecrate the weapons in the waters of the five rivers of the Underworld. Each has its own properties, but when combined, they have the potency to kill a shade. What's more, with a consecrated weapon, it doesn't matter where you strike them, just so long as the weapon pierces their... skin, for lack of a better term. It will kill them."

"Well, shit..." Jonah said, feeling the hint of a hopeful smile turn at the corners of his mouth. Still, he remained too cautious to allow himself much more optimism.

"How would we get all the weapons into the Underworld?" Inanna asked. "Not to mention to each of the five rivers. That would take up far too much time we don't have."

"We wouldn't have to," Enki said. "We could collect the water from the rivers and bring them back up. All we would need is the god of the Underworld's consent, and I'm assuming we have that already."

"You do," Hades replied with a solemn bow.

"That's settled, then," Zeus added. "Vishnu, Marduk, Kali, you go with Hades and Set into the Underworld to collect the water. Try to be as quick as you can." Without a word, the three gods left, leaving Tristan and Jonah with Zeus, Isis, Inanna, and Enki.

"This is awesome news, right?" Tristan asked eagerly. "I mean, we actually have a good chance now, don't we?" He glanced from Jonah to the gods and back again.

"It certainly does seem that way," Enki mused. "But is it too good to be true? Can we really trust her?" He turned to Zeus.

The god of thunder sighed. "I don't think we have a choice. If I were going to accept the word of any sister, it would be Lachesis. She's never shared Atropos' maleficence. If anything, she's always carried an empathy for mankind, perhaps because her responsibility bears allocating each person their lot in life."

"What have we got to lose?" asked Jonah. "It's not like stabbing a shade with a consecrated blade is going to turn them into some kind of amped-up super-shade, is it?" He laughed, the sound falling away quickly when only Tristan joined him in it. "Is it?"

"It's extremely unlikely," Inanna reassured him, "but we'd be irresponsible not to consider every possibility."

"Hades knows the Underworld better than anyone," Enki stated, "and if he's confident it can be done, so am I."

Zeus clapped his enormous hand on the other god's shoulder. "As am I. At least now Jonah can deliver some semblance of good news in his speech."

"Is that wise?" Jonah asked. "I mean, announcing our new plan of attack to the world. What's stopping the Fates from overhearing it?"

"You don't need to stipulate the details," Zeus replied. "Our Oracles will convey the specifics to the others later. I'm sure the very news that we *have* a plan will be enough for now to ignite the fires of hope."

Jonah cleared his throat. "Well, let's get this over with."

AVA HELD A hand up to her mouth, stifling a yawn. She felt both tired and exhilarated. While she had little idea of what her visions meant, the fact she'd had them at all awed her. Running back over them in her memory, though, only added to her confusion. On thinking of the wooden bowl, she felt lost and scared, fearful and desperate, as though something awful were about to happen. However, looking upon the vials filled her with trepidation, yet there was also a sense of hope. This categorising visions by emotional response was all so new to her, and she worried she wasn't doing it right—that she was missing some crucial part of the puzzle.

The sight of Olive pulling Isis aside distracted Ava from these memories. The girl looked up to see Ava watching her and quickly turned away to continue whispering to the goddess. There was no mistaking the worried crease in her forehead and her wide-eyed stare. Ava felt a flutter of nerves and wasn't sure if she wanted to know what they were saying, though she couldn't shake the feeling that whatever it was also affected her.

"Hey."

Ava jumped and turned to find Jonah by her side, her checks flushing hot at his sudden presence.

"Zeus needs us." He opened his mouth to say more before he seemed to think twice and closed it again.

"Lead the way," she replied with a tight smile. Walking a step behind him, she found her frustration reaching breaking point, forming hot, angry tears. She quickly flicked them away, not wanting Jonah to see her so upset. Nothing in their life had ever before made her feel so disconnected from him, and it broke her heart. If nothing else, he was her best friend, and it pained her to not have him by her side. More than anything, she wished she could make him understand she didn't regret their kiss, not for one second—but not because it had unlocked Hephalion and her powers. Ava loved him, and she always had.

CHAPTER THIRTY-ONE

"JONAH, HAVE YOU thought about what you're going to say?" Inanna asked as she walked fluidly alongside him, hooking her arm through his. Jonah looked over his shoulder to find Ava scowling, then he quickly turned around again. "Uh, sort of. I'm just going to be honest and hopefully not sound like a bloody idiot."

"Well, I suppose that's as good a plan as any," the goddess replied, and Jonah thought he detected a hint of humour in her voice. "We've set you up over here." Inanna gestured toward the Oracles, who sat in a circle, watching him, Ava, and Inanna approach with eager smiles and wide eyes. Isis and Zeus stood in the centre of their group, their heads bent together as they whispered.

Jonah loudly cleared his throat as they neared, and the two gods looked up at him. Zeus' slight frown surprised him. "Is everything okay?" he asked.

Zeus nodded. "We really need to get this message across as soon as possible. We may only have one shot, so you need to get it right."

Jonah let out a low whistle to avoid biting back.

"We need both of you to stand in here," Isis instructed. Two of the Oracles leaned away from each other to allow Jonah and Ava through. Jonah tried to avoid looking directly at Ava but couldn't help a few quick, sidelong glances.

"Zeus is right," Inanna said. "We likely only have one shot at this. The energy Ava and the Oracles must generate will be too taxing for them to repeat. At least, not as quickly as would be necessary if anything goes wrong."

"So basically, don't stuff it up," Jonah stated, shoving his hands in his pockets.

"You won't stuff it up." Ava turned to him, forcing Jonah to meet her gaze. "Just pretend you're talking to me or Tristan. Or even Mum. How would you tell us?"

Jonah stared at her for a moment and swallowed thickly. With a small smile, he thanked her and turned to the gods. "Let's do this."

"The pair of you need to stand in the centre of the circle," Isis told them. "Jonah, hold Ava's left hand with your right."

Jonah stood where Isis placed him, removing his hands from his pockets. He was suddenly all too aware his arms hung like dead weights by his side, and it took all his willpower not to wipe them on his jeans. Before he knew it, he felt Ava's hand grasp his with a reassuring squeeze. Immediately, he felt his anxiety receding like a tide, leaving in its wake a calm focus and clarity. The nerves didn't return even as he noticed the congregation of people gathering as close to the circle as Enki would allow. Feeling the firm grasp of Zeus' hand on his shoulder, Jonah turned.

"You'll do fine," his immortal father said. "Let them know we have a plan, but just remember not to explain what it is."

"Say something while saying nothing…"

Zeus only replied by giving Jonah's shoulder a final squeeze, then withdrew his hand and walked out of the circle to join the others. Jonah saw Tristan front and centre, his mate giving him a big thumbs-up, before Isis stepped in front of him and blocked Jonah's view.

"Ava, the Oracles will begin their chants to raise their vibrations. Once you feel the charge, you need to open your third eye chakra as wide as you can and connect to the minds of the other Oracles."

"All at once?" she asked quietly. "I've only ever accessed one at a time."

"I know, but we don't have time to expand your training." Isis nodded in what Jonah assumed was meant to be reassurance. "By utilising the Oracles' energies, you will find it much easier than you think. Just don't try to *control* the flow of energy. Let it move through you as a part of yourself."

Ava remained silent, and without thinking, Jonah returned the favour with a reassuring squeeze of her hand.

"Now, Jonah," Isis continued, "you won't notice anything different, so when we signal you to begin, just talk to the crowd before you here. Make sure you speak loudly and clearly."

Without waiting for confirmation, Isis turned and stepped out of the circle to join Zeus. The murmuring crowd fell silent as the Oracles bent their heads and chanted together. At first, it was so soft, Jonah could hardly make it out, but with each iteration, their voices rose. Beside him, he felt Ava stiffen, her breathing increased, and Jonah struggled against the urge to ask if she was okay.

The chanting grew louder, faster, though despite his best efforts, Jonah couldn't understand a single word of it; he couldn't even determine the language. Then, without warning, the cadence of their voices stopped, each Oracle throwing their head back to gaze at the sky, their eyes large white orbs. He didn't need to look to know Ava had entered the same state; he only had to glance at Tristan's gaping mouth. Zeus raised his hand in the air and nodded, and Jonah took a deep breath.

"My name is Jonah Sands, and standing beside me is Ava Carter. Many of you have heard of us by name only, with no idea who we are or why you've been told to seek us out. Now you can see we're just like you. We've watched one disaster after another hit everywhere around the world, helpless and scared, like all of you. We've lost count of the number of lives lost, becoming desensitised and numb to the ceaseless destruction. We've had people we loved and cared for ripped away from us, and we've questioned over and over why any of this is happening. Wherever you are, you're in the presence of an Oracle. I know that's new to most of us, including some of the Oracles themselves. The fact that they are here, that their presence lets you see us from the other side of the world, is something I still can't get my head around. But here we are.

"We don't have long, and I know you're all exhausted and still scared of what lies ahead. You've all heard the rumours of the coming war, and it is with great sorrow that I must confirm this unavoidable truth. But we *do* have a plan, one we strongly believe in, and we have every confidence that by pulling together mortals, gods, and Oracles alike, we can defeat the Fates and their army of shades. I won't go into specifics, as we don't know how accessible this communication may be to those who would use it against us, but trust that your Oracles will be well advised and will soon have all the information on hand. We will keep you all updated and informed.

"For now, please find some solace in the fact that you are not alone. We are all in this together until the end. So stay strong, stay safe, and look out for each other. Over and out."

Jonah released Ava's hand, severing the transmission, and his mouth fell open in a heavy sigh as the crowd before him erupted in cheers.

Tristan ran toward them, leaping over the seated Oracles before clutching his mate in a bear hug. "Dude, that was awesome! The over and out bit was a nice touch."

Jonah chuckled. "I didn't know what else to say. It just popped into my head."

"Well, it was perfect. And Ava, if only you could see what you looked like. I mean, if you think you're scary-looking first thing in the morning, this was totally some next-level—" Tristan dodged a swipe from his sister and laughed.

Despite her smile, Jonah saw the fatigue behind her eyes and in the way she swayed a little when she moved. He reached out and placed a steadying hand on her back. "Do you want to sit down somewhere?"

She looked up with a grateful smile, her face ashen. "I think I need to lie down, maybe. Have a little nap."

Jonah nodded, trying to hide his concern when she buckled and leaned into him to catch herself. Tristan rushed to her other side, and the two of them passed a shared look of concern over her head. "Let's take her back into the house," Tristan suggested, Ava too weak to agree. They passed Zeus speaking with Inanna, Enki, and Isis.

Inanna immediately broke suit and led the way for them through the crowd of people, those closest trying to grasp Jonah or pat him on the arm or back as he passed. He tried to hide his rising frustration at their difficulty in weaving through the throng, and it seemed like an eternity before they finally stepped into the house to guide Ava onto her bed.

"Can I get you anything?" Jonah asked her.

"No, thank you. I just need to close my eyes for a little bit."

Before he could say anything else, Ava was asleep. He and Tristan turned to Inanna in alarm. The goddess sat in the chair beside the bed, raising her hands in a reassuring wave. "She'll be fine. It took an immense amount of energy to do what she just did, and I imagine she will need to sleep for quite some time before she feels like herself. You two go. I'll stay with her for now."

Knowing an attempt to convince the goddess otherwise would be futile, Jonah looked at Ava once more, then he felt Tristan's hand on his shoulder. He let his friend guide him from the room.

When they reached the bottom of the stairs, Isis stepped out in front of them. Both men jumped, and Tristan blushed profusely.

"If you're looking for Inanna, she's upstairs with Ava," Jonah advised, throwing a glance back up the stairs.

"No. I was actually looking to speak with Tristan."

"M-m-me?" Tristan answered, the shade of pink deepening.

"I should probably debrief with Zeus anyway," Jonah replied, leaving them alone and trying to hide his amusement at his mate's terrified reaction.

TRISTAN STOOD WITH his hands shoved into his pockets, mentally smacking himself about the head as he looked around his old bedroom. He couldn't believe, out of all the rooms in the house, this was the first place he took Isis when she said she wanted to speak to him in private. Sure, he'd bring Jonah or Ava in there if they needed to talk, but Isis was a goddess—and the most beautiful woman he'd ever seen. He scratched at his stubble and glanced at the old band posters on the walls—The Cure, Stone Temple Pilots, Soundgarden, The Smashing Pumpkins, and Nine Inch Nails just to start. Oddly enough, he found himself wondering if she'd ever heard of them.

His heart nearly flipped in his chest when Isis took a seat on the edge of his bed, and he could only reprimand himself. *What is* wrong *with you? She's not the first woman to sit on your bed, so calm the bloody hell down, you moron!*

Seemingly oblivious to Tristan's internal struggle, Isis reached out to run her fingers along an old photo on his bedside table—Tristan, Ava, and Jonah when they were kids. The three of them were covered head to toe in blue for their school's swimming carnival, and all of them had taken home ribbons that day.

Tristan cleared his throat. "Yeah, um, my room doesn't look like this now. I mean, this room does, obviously, but I don't live here anymore. I have another room that looks, uh…"

"Tristan, there's something you need to know."

He fell silent, at first relieved she'd put an end to his rambling until he noted the seriousness of her slight frown and the way she seemed to look through him rather than at him. Pulling the desk chair out from under the desk, he straddled it and waited for her to continue. The goddess looked down into her palms, as though searching there for the answer to a troubling question, and finally looked up to meet Tristan's stare. The sadness in her eyes produced a heavy, sick feeling in the pit of his stomach. He tried to ask her what was wrong but found himself unable to speak.

"One of the Oracles came to me after their premonition session in the hope that I might provide some clarity to put them at ease. Unfortunately, my own attempts at divination have only confirmed what she saw."

"Okay..." Tristan said slowly, not wanting to hear anything further but knowing he didn't have a choice.

Isis looked down at her hands again before she continued. "It seems history is set to repeat itself. As you know, you are a direct descendant of Achilles." She paused, and Tristan gave a quick nod of acknowledgement. "A prophecy has come to light, not unlike the one presented to him before he left for Troy. Tristan, there's no easy way to say this, but if you go into battle with your friends, you will die. You'll be remembered as a great hero, but you will die. I am so sorry..."

Tristan swallowed thickly and averted his gaze, not wanting the goddess to see the tears of shock forming in the corners of his eyes. Clearing his throat, he willed himself to speak. "It's just a prophecy, right? I mean, I can take steps to make sure things play out differently... Free will and all that."

Isis shook her head. "I'm afraid not, Tristan. Not with this. I've tried every form of divination I know, hoping to find the cosmic loophole, but they all come back the same. The details may change, but inevitably, your path will end on the battlefield. There are only two choices, here. If you stay behind, you will live to struggle with condemning yourself as a coward. Or, if you fight alongside your friends, your fate will play out as I've seen it, and all will hear the story of your deeds."

Tristan exhaled shakily, gripping the back of the chair in tightly clenched hands. "Wow... Some choice, hey?" Isis didn't answer. "If the prophecy came from the Oracles, why isn't Ava the one telling me this?"

"While she was connected to them at the time, each Oracle's visions are independent of the next. In that state, they can only see what is revealed to them, not what others may be shown. In short, she doesn't know. The other Oracle and I are the only ones with this knowledge. And now you."

Tristan chewed his lip. "So, should I tell the others?"

"I can't make that decision for you," she said. "It's an awful burden to shoulder, and no one would blame you for wanting to share the load. I'm willing to inform the other gods on your behalf, if you wish."

Tristan shook his head. "Not yet. I... uh... Oh, shit. Mum!" He groaned. "How can I do this to her? She's barely coping with losing Dad. What will happen to her if she loses anyone else?" He buried his face in his hands, vaguely aware of the sound of Isis standing from the bed. Then he felt her cool hand on his head.

"Whether you decide to tell them or not, I am here for you. For whatever you need."

"I think I just need to be alone for a while."

"Of course."

Tristan kept his face covered in the darkness behind his hands long after he heard the click of the bedroom door closing.

JONAH STEPPED OUT into the crowd, curious to know why everyone moved together now in one direction. Making his way through the sea of people, he was relieved to find the gods sent to the Underworld had returned, each with a large urn of water before them. He and Zeus reached them at the same time.

"Perfect," Zeus said. "Now let's hope this works." Then he turned to face the crowd. "Listen, everyone! Before you stand five urns of water and our greatest weapon against the shades." Jonah watched the faces in the crowd glance dubiously at the urns, at the gods, then finally at each other. "Hades will explain their power to you." Zeus stepped aside.

"We have collected the magical waters of the Underworld," Hades began without hesitation, "each with their own essential property. The river Styx represents hatred. The river Acheron represents pain. The river Lethe for forgetfulness, Phlegethon for fire, and Cocytus for wailing. By consecrating your weapons in each, you will be armed with a tool quite capable of killing a shade, regardless of where you strike the blow. Jonah will demonstrate."

Jonah stepped forward, taking the offered sword from Hades' hands, and stepped up to the urn from Styx. When the blade pierced the water, it let out a low, fierce growl. Jonah was so startled, he almost dropped the sword into the urn, and he struggled to compose himself under the watchful gaze of both the crowd and the gods. He withdrew the blade and moved to the next urn from Acheron, gripping the handle tightly as howls of pain bellowed from the water. Many of those standing closest covered their ears. Quickly moving on to the urn from Lethe, he was surprised when only a cloud-like vapour rose upwards, hovering for a moment before disappearing. Feeling more confident, he plunged the blade into the urn from Phlegethon, quickly jumping back from the flame shooting up from the water and nearly singeing his eyebrows. Clearing his throat, he quickly moved to the final urn from Cocytus. This time, the water omitted a gut-wrenching wail of anguish and loss. It stunned him briefly, but he recovered in seconds, relieved to be finished. Finally, he stepped beside that final urn, raising the sword engulfed in a blue light encasing it from the hilt to the tip before it ignited. A white line of crackling fire rushed up the blade toward Jonah's hand.

He resisted the urge to drop the sword before the flame went out, leaving the wood blackened but slick, its surface reflective. An appreciative awe swept over the crowd, and Jonah couldn't help but feel like Arthur with Excalibur when he raised the sword high above his head for everyone to see.

With a goofy grin, he scanned the crowd for Tristan, who he knew would be thinking the same thing, but found him surprisingly absent. Lowering the sword as the crowd formed lines to anoint their own weapons, Jonah strode toward the congregated gods. "Have you seen Tristan?"

"He's back at the house," Isis replied, not meeting his gaze but choosing instead to focus on the urns.

Jonah found her disinterest a bit odd, but he left the gods to jog across the street and up the driveway. Tristan stepped from the front door as Jonah arrived. "Hey, mate. You missed the big display." His smile faded when he noticed his mate could barely look him in the eye, either. Tristan's red, glassy eyes made it seem as if he'd been crying, and Jonah instantly felt a pulse of fear in the pit of his stomach. "What's wrong?"

"Nothing, mate. I'm fine."

"Bullshit. Tell me what happened."

"I found a rip in my vintage Robert Smith tee."

"I'm being serious…"

"So am I. Do you know how much that shirt was worth? It was a limited release collector's item. There's no getting a replacement." Tristan stalked past Jonah, ignoring his mate's concern. "Now are you going to show me this consecration stuff or what?"

Knowing he wouldn't get anything until Tristan was ready to tell him, Jonah followed his mate back into the crowd, unable to shake the gnawing feeling in his gut that something was incredibly wrong.

AVA FOUND HERSELF standing alone, engulfed in a darkness so vast and immense, it gave her a touch of vertigo, making her feel like she hovered in space. The sensation eased as a glowing grey fog approached from behind her, entwining itself around her ankles. Watching it grow in density, Ava knew she must be dreaming, yet she felt completely alert and conscious.

The fog stretched out before her and seemed to beckon her to follow. Tentatively, she took a step forward, unsure of her footing when she couldn't see any surface beneath her. But with each step, her confidence grew, and her focus settled on the alluring fog. It didn't travel in a straight line but ducked and weaved as though navigating around invisible obstacles. Ava had concentrated so much on following the mist that it took her a few moments to realise she saw tufts of grass around her, faint at first but gradually growing more vivid with each new step. Now that she saw the ground beneath her feet, it seemed she now climbed a hill. The fog thickened, then Ava found herself standing on the hilltop and looking down into the valley below.

The fog itself moved around her before cascading down the hillside, but Ava didn't follow it this time. She didn't know why she was there. Then the ground trembled beneath her, and she stumbled to her knees, catching herself with outstretched hands disappearing beneath the fog. Her gaze was pulled to the small cave in the valley, which glowed when the thick white mist entered its small opening. A crack of blackness split from the mouth of the cave, and the ground opened up in a long, narrow crevice. The trembling continued, the crevice widened, and a sharp tingling ran from the base of Ava's spine to the back of her neck, accompanied by the sudden urge to run.

Before she could register what was happening, shades spilled from the crevice and cave into the valley—thousands of them, tripping and clawing at each other in their urgency to escape the Underworld. From her position atop the hill, they reminded her of scurrying ants, only far more terrifying.

"Ava! Ava, wake up…"

She opened her eyes to find Jonah sitting on the bed beside her, shaking her by the shoulders. Disorientated, she turned to see Inanna sitting casually in the chair by the bed. "What's going on?" When Jonah released her, she slowly sat up.

"You were having one hell of a nightmare. I could hear you from downstairs."

"I told you she was perfectly fine," Inanna said.

"That didn't look fine by a normal person's standards," Jonah snapped. The goddess only gave a nonchalant shrug.

"No, really, Jonah. I'm fine." She grasped his arm and looked from him to Inanna. "I know where the shades will enter from the Underworld."

Inanna gave a slow nod, a small smile playing at the corner of her mouth as though she'd expected the outcome. "Good. I'll get the others. Meet us downstairs once you feel able."

"ARE YOU CERTAIN about this?" Zeus asked, leaning forward on the dining table. Too much anticipation hung in the air for anyone to sit.

"A month or two ago, I would have just chalked it up to a bad dream," Ava replied, leaning over the table as well opposite Zeus. "But you've been telling me to trust my powers. My instincts. This is the first vision I've had where I actually knew where I was. It's not a coincidence."

"Is the place far?"

Ava shook her head. "Not at all. Maybe an hour's walk? Depending on pace."

"Wait, are you talking about Troll-Back Mountain?" Jonah asked.

"The what?" Inanna asked.

"That's not it's real name," he said. "That's just what we called it as kids. We thought it looked like a scary troll bent over, protecting treasure. And it's not really a mountain so much as a really big hill."

"Perhaps all this time it *has* been protecting something," Ava mused. "A thin spot between us and the Underworld…"

"I've heard crazier ideas," Jonah replied, then turned his attention back to the gods. "We used to go up there all the time."

"My question is why that spot?" Marduk added. "Why would they choose that place to release the shades? It's not exactly on our doorstep. Not quite the most strategic place to launch an attack."

"There's only a small number of locations from which they'd be able to release the shades," Hades explained. "This is likely the closest to us. I doubt the Fates have expected us to work it out. They might very well still anticipate having the element of surprise."

"Does the location have any advantages as far as the Fates are concerned?" Marduk queried.

"Well, in the vision, I was looking down into the valley. It's fairly narrow at the bottom, and the ground cracked open. That's where the shades escaped. Unless you were standing at the top of the hill looking down, you wouldn't see a thing until it was too late."

Satisfied with the answer, Marduk leaned back against the wall, arms folded across his chest.

"So, what do we do with this?" Vishnu asked. "We still don't know when the attack will occur."

"Marduk," Zeus said, "you're our most experienced in battle. How would you recommend we proceed?"

"I think we should relocate, and the hilltop will provide us with a vantage point when the shades erupt. We have some well-trained archers now. That could take a good number of them out before they have a chance to approach. And we'd have the downhill advantage. The visibility would be significantly greater there, as an attack here in this residential area increases the chances of us becoming trapped." His assessment was met with an overwhelming silence.

Jonah couldn't think clearly. He knew Marduk was right, but once they left the relative safety of the street and the Carter house, there was no looking back; the reality of that hit him like a sack of bricks. He looked up to see Tristan, ashen and fidgety, and felt some semblance of relief that he wasn't the only one overwhelmed by a sudden panic.

"I think we should do it," Zeus finally said. "The sooner the better." He turned to Vishnu. "How long do you think it will take to pack up what we need and organise everyone to move out?"

"At least a day. We could aim to head off the day after tomorrow."

Zeus nodded.

"Speaking of tomorrow," Ava added, "what time is it? I think my watch must be broken. It says it's nearly eight o'clock, but it's still light outside."

"Weird. That's what time mine says too." Tristan tapped the glass of his watch.

"I'll go check the clock in the loungeroom," Mallory stated as she left the room. Jonah studied the sunlight still streaming through the windows.

"Well, according to the clock, that's the correct time," Mallory declared when she returned.

"It's still daylight?" Jonah asked, turning to Zeus. "How is that possible?"

The god frowned and looked toward the others. "This isn't our doing."

"We don't know the full extent of the Fates' power beyond the fact that it exceeds ours," Inanna said. "It could be them, especially if they're drawing on their infinite army of shades."

"Why?" Ava asked. "How can endless daylight be a tactic?"

"Are they hoping we won't be able to sleep and will be too tired to fight?" Tristan asked with wide eyes and a weak smile, clearly only partially joking.

"I don't think that's the reason," Marduk said. "But I'm certain there is one. We just have to discover what that is before it's too late."

JONAH SAT UNDER what he now referred to as David and Bethany's tree. He could not find the same solace anywhere else. Resting his head back against the tree, he closed his eyes, trying to think of anything but what was coming.

"Do you mind if I join you?"

He opened one eye to find Ava hovering in front of him. He closed his eyes and shook his head, unconsciously holding his breath while he waited for her to sit down.

Well, you wanted a distraction, he told himself, reaching out to clasp her hand in his. Together they sat in silence, neither attempting to break it, but Jonah felt calm in the knowledge they were united.

HE STARTLED OUT of sleeping, which woke Ava beside him as well.

"Jonah? What's wrong?"

He looked at her blankly for a moment, disorientated after not having realised he'd dozed off. He struggled to hold onto the tail end of the dream he'd had, feeling it was important somehow. Turning from Ava, he glanced up at the sky to find the sun still unmoved in its position and intensity.

"Jonah?"

Tearing his eyes away from the heavens, he gave Ava a small smile. "I think I know why the Fates don't want the sun going down." Before she could say anything, he jumped to his feet, grasped her hand, and helped her up. Without another word, they headed toward Zeus, Enki, Marduk, and Vishnu aiding a group in loading the consecrated weapons into the makeshift carts.

The gods looked up as they approached. Zeus raised his eyebrows at the sight of Jonah's grin. "What's going on?"

"I think I know what the Fates are up to." Jonah clapped his immortal father on the shoulder. "But I need to check something with Hades first."

"He's in the house," Zeus replied.

Jonah headed in that direction, not needing to look back to know the gods and Ava followed.

They found Hades in the dining room with Mallory and Kali, standing over what looked to be some kind of plan for their departure. "What happened?" Mallory asked when she saw them.

"I'm not sure…" Zeus replied, glancing at Jonah.

"Hades," Jonah started, "in the Underworld, the shades are clearly visible, right?" Hades gave a slow nod, then looked to Zeus for clarification. "Is it the aether you told us about that makes them visible?" Jonah continued.

"Not quite," Hades slowly replied. "The vibrancy of the aether light is dependent upon the number of souls within at any given time. Why? What's going on?"

Jonah took a moment to compose himself, trying to contain his excitement in case he was wrong. "I think the Fates have made it permanently daytime to mask the shades."

"What do you mean?" Ava asked. "More light makes it easier to see something, not harder."

"No, I think he's onto something," Hades said, rising from the chair. "The glow of the aether and the faint illumination the shades provide are only visible in the Underworld, which means the only way we'd see them clearly enough to fight is in the dark."

"Do we know this with any certainty?" Marduk questioned.

"We don't know anything with certainty," Hades replied. "A shade has never returned to the mortal realm to test the theory. Yet it makes perfect sense, and the fact that the Fates appear to have bestowed us with eternal daylight would indicate they also think there's something to it."

"Great work, son," Zeus said with a proud smile.

"Hold on," Tristan said. "I don't mean to burst everyone's bubble, but how does this revelation help us?"

Jonah's smile faded. "It doesn't, really."

"No matter," Kali said. "I have a few tricks up my sleeve."

Vishnu glanced at her with wide eyes. "You mean…" Kali nodded.

"You haven't done that in centuries," Zeus said. "Are you certain you still can?"

"Are you questioning my strength?" Kali hissed.

"Yes, actually. I have to. It's been a long time since we ruled over this domain, and this is hardly a thing you can practise. A lot will ride on your ability, including mortal lives, and I'm not sure we'll have much of a plan B should you fail."

"I'll manage it."

"What of the repercussions?" Enki asked.

"The mortals will feel the initial effects. Mainly nausea, disorientation, and the odd bloody nose. But it will pass quickly enough and shouldn't inhibit their ability to fight."

"You're doing that annoying thing where you talk about us when we're standing right here," Jonah stated, scowling and folding his arms. "What the hell's going on?"

Zeus gave him a sheepish smile. "My apologies, Jonah. I'm not sure I dare say it aloud for fear the Fates catch wind of it, but I will try to show you." He held up a fist, then slowly moved the palm of his other hand in front of it.

"Oh!" exclaimed Ava. "You can do that?" She gazed at Kali, beaming with admiration.

"Do what?" Jonah asked, his scowl deepening with his frustration at being left out of the loop. Ava smiled up at him and, standing on her tiptoes, whispered the answer in his ear.

TRISTAN BUSIED HIMSELF helping with the preparations, doing the best he could to keep his mind on the task at hand.

"How are you, Tristan?"

He looked up to find Isis before him. For the first time since he'd met the goddess, he didn't feel the heat rush to his face at the sight of her. His heart felt too heavy with his burden to remind him of his attraction to her. Instead, he gave her a dismissive shrug and hurled another batch of weapons onto the back of the cart. He felt her gaze on him, bringing with it a nervous self-consciousness. The last thing he wanted was for her to witness his emotions taking hold.

"Do you know what you're going to do?" she asked gently before stopping him in his tracks with a single gentle touch on his arm.

Still, he couldn't bring himself to look at her. "I'm fighting. Of course I'm fighting. There's no way I'm letting my sister and my best mate face those evil bitches and their army alone." Isis didn't reply but left her hand where it was. Slowly, a warmth spread up Tristan's arm and into his chest, and he felt the heaviness of his decision melt away. "What are you doing?" he asked, finally feeling capable of meeting her stare.

"Whatever I can to ease your suffering, Tristan. Will you tell the others?"

"No. There's no point. I don't want them distracted by worrying about me. They'll know about it once it happens, and that will be soon enough." He paused for a moment, looking around as though someone might overhear him.

"What is it?" Isis prompted.

"It's just… I was wondering… you've seen it happen. Is it… Will it…" He broke off, his newfound acceptance faltering and his throat tightening at the thought.

"It will be quick. Regardless of where or how, it will be quick."

Tristan stared ahead at nothing in particular. After a little while, he flashed Isis a smile. "Well in that case, there's no need to be a bloody sook about it, then, is there?" His smile only slightly faltered as he loaded another bundle onto the cart.

CHAPTER THIRTY-TWO

A STILLNESS SURROUNDED THEM, heavy with anticipation. People sat in groups, though they barely spoke, knowing they needed rest before heading off in a few hours' time. Still, their minds and bodies resisted sleep while the sun remained so high in the sky.

In the Carter house, Zeus gathered everyone in the lounge-room one final time. Jonah felt too nervous to sit, instead opting to hover behind the armchairs in which Ava and Mallory had taken their seats. "I'll make this quick, as we all need to rest," Zeus began. "We're going to stagger our departures in half-hour blocks, each led by one of the gods. This will make it easier to defend ourselves should the Fates decide to pay us a visit along the way. I'll lead the first group. Ava, Jonah, Tristan, the three of you will come with me. Any questions?" The god scanned the room, and each of them shook their heads. "I have asked Mallory to stay behind. We still have a number of injured who can't travel or more importantly fight. Mrs. Carter has agreed to stay behind and care for them until we return."

Jonah looked down as Ava squeezed her mother's arm and rested her head on Mallory's shoulder. Mallory kissed her daughter's forehead, and Jonah placed a hand on Mallory's other shoulder. Without looking back at him, she covered his hand with her own.

"We'll be relocating the injured into the house," Zeus continued, "and since it's the Carters' home, they will be safest in here. The magical protections around the house will be reinforced a final time before we depart.

"Once we get to our destination, we have no certain expectation for when the shades will be released, so we will position sentries at viable viewpoints to give word at the first sign of them. Other than that, we'll be playing the waiting game, and it's up to all of us to keep everyone focused. Any questions?" Again, the room was silent. "Good. Now get some rest. First group departs in six hours."

Resting was the last thing Jonah felt like doing, and as Tristan and Ava joined him in moving the furniture about to clear space for the injured, he knew they felt the same way. Without a word, they went from room to room, moving and stacking furniture to make as much space as possible for the Carter house turned recovery ward.

Jonah tried not to focus on the nerves growing in the pit of his stomach, knowing they'd only build further with each passing hour. He ran over his training, as brief as it was, trying to recall everything Marduk had taught him. Jonah felt slightly more confident knowing he no longer had to aim so specifically in order to kill a shade, but he also knew one-on-one training was a far cry from fighting in battle. The knots in his stomach tightened when he remembered the Erinyes' attack—of how he'd failed to react. *What if the same thing happens? What kind of leader will I be then?* Mentally, he shook himself out of that negativity. There was no point working himself up about it; he'd find out soon enough if his courage would prevail.

AVA PAUSED IN making up the temporary beds in the loungeroom and let her eyes wander over the numerous family portraits hanging along the walls. Placing her hand across her stomach, she willed the ferocious butterflies to cease. Having spent the past few hours picking through her visions, she worried she'd missed some vital clue as to what was to come. The severe consequences of failing to have worked it out properly terrified her—like something happening to Tristan or Jonah which she could have prevented.

The first of the injured were carried into the room then, pulling Ava from her thoughts. She returned her focus to the distraction of making beds.

JONAH STOOD ATOP the driveway, watching the first group ready themselves to leave. Hearing footsteps behind him, he turned to find Mallory approaching, holding each of her grown children by the hand.

"Well, I guess the time has come," she said, giving their hands a squeeze.

"Oh, Mum." Ava threw her arms around her mother. "I don't want to leave you here."

"And I don't want to let you go. I'd be lying if I said I wasn't scared for the three of you. For all of us. But I have watched over you, witnessed first-hand the recent changes in you. It gives me some comfort knowing how powerful the three of you have become, even if you still don't quite grasp it yourselves. I believe we've gone through all of this together so you three will succeed. And I know Alex is watching over you." She kissed her daughter's cheek before holding her at arm's length. "Don't doubt your intuition, Ava. You've had an uncanny talent for it long before we knew anything of Oracles." She released her daughter, then wrapped her arms around Tristan's waist for a hug. "And you, Tristan, be fast, but stay focused. Look after your sister."

He kissed her on the head. "Come on, now, Mum. You know it's always Ava who looks after us." He turned to wink at his sister.

"And Jonah." Mallory held her arms out to him, and he stepped forward to take her hands in his. She pulled him closer for a hug. "I'm sure you already know this, but Alex and I have always considered you part of the family. Our son. I know you will do us all proud."

Jonah squeezed her tightly, his throat constricted with emotion.

"Time to go," Zeus called from the street, and Jonah stepped back. Ava and Tristan joined him. He looked up at the house one last time, wondering if they would see it again—if they would return.

"Off you go, now," Mallory gently instructed. "You know Zeus doesn't like to wait." Tristan stepped forward and pulled Mallory into a final tight embrace. His mother first looked confused by her son's uncommon display of affection, then grateful for it, and hugged him back.

"Now!" came Zeus' impatient bellow. Tristan released his mother, and without another look, turned and strode past Jonah and Ava toward the waiting group. They exchanged a brief glance before following him.

The first group made way for the trio as they moved to take their place behind the god. Zeus gave them a nod. "Keep together at all times," he instructed, then walked off to lead them toward battle.

They moved in sombre silence—no talking, only the sound of creaking carts and shoes scuffing along the road to accompany them. Jonah frowned when he thought he heard Zeus humming ahead of them, but he found himself enjoying the silence too much to say anything. He certainly wasn't in the mood to hum. But he did feel a certain surprising calmness, as though he stood in the eye of a great storm. As he looked around at what once used to be streets lined with houses and busy with traffic, he couldn't help but marvel at the surreal nature of it all. Despite his encounters with the Fates and everything he'd seen and heard, part of him still struggled to accept it as reality. Yet he also knew the world he'd once known—what he'd known of his own life—was gone. Even if they defeated the Fates and their army of shades, things would never be the same again.

With a sigh, he forced himself to rein his mind back into the present and turned his focus to the things they were fighting to protect. He thought of his parents, Alex, Mallory, and Tristan—and Ava. With each fleeting image, he felt his heart beat a little faster, and he swallowed thickly. Ava's hand slipped briefly into his, and he gave it a squeeze before releasing it, unable to look at her.

DESPITE THE DISTANCE, it felt as if they'd arrived at the hill in no time at all. The first group led by Zeus gathered at the base and gazed up.

"I thought it would look smaller than I remembered," Tristan murmured.

"Same," Jonah agreed.

"It's going to take everyone's efforts to get those carts up there, so get moving," Zeus instructed, making his way up the hill to get a look at the valley.

"I guess that means he's not helping," Tristan said dryly, then followed Jonah to the first cart.

It took a huge amount of combined force, but the group managed to half drag, half carry their carts to the top of the hill, where they stopped briefly to admire the view.

"It sure has changed a lot since we were up here last," Ava said quietly, staring down at what was left of the town in which they'd spent their childhood.

Jonah couldn't tear his eyes away. It was one thing to know the Fates were responsible for such widespread devastation; it was another thing completely to see it. Nearly everything had been so flattened, they could easily point out where the Carter house stood among the wreckage. "It's like this everywhere, isn't it?" he asked quietly.

"Yeah, man. I suppose it is." Tristan sighed and shoved his hands in his pocket.

"I get it now why it was so easy for people to find us. It's almost like a lighthouse, sitting on an island of despair..." Ava murmured.

"Bloody hell, sis," Tristan groaned. "Way to bring the mood down. I mean, I know things are dire, but that was a grim depiction..."

"You lot," Zeus called. "Over here." When they joined the god, he paused in his delegation of tasks for their group to speak to them. "We have an excellent vantage point up here. Visibility for miles. I've arranged for sentries to cover all views until we can determine exactly from where the shades will approach. The next group isn't far. I'm sending the rest of ours down to meet them, as they have more carts than we did. Jonah, Tristan, I want you to familiarise yourselves with the terrain. Memorise every rock, every tuft of grass. Ava, I'd like you to come with me." Zeus walked away. Ava looked quickly at Jonah and Tristan before hurrying after the god.

"He was joking about the grass thing, wasn't he?" Tristan asked.

"When have you ever known Zeus to joke about anything?" Jonah replied.

"Shit. Thought as much."

"HOW VIVID WAS your vision?" Zeus asked when Ava caught up to him.

"Fairly vivid. Why?"

"I'd like you to have a good look around. See if you can determine the exact location from your vision where the shades are released from the Underworld."

Ava nodded, not trusting herself to speak for fear she'd reveal her growing doubt.

She was all too aware that their survival rode on the accuracy of her vision, and nothing she did could undo the twisted knots of fear in her stomach. Closing her eyes, she forced herself to take a deep breath and focus. When she opened them again, she turned at the bustling noise around her and prayed for her mind to feel the pull in the right direction. She turned her head, vaguely aware of Zeus stepping closer, as though he knew she was on to something. Taking a few steps to the right, she paused, not certain of what she sensed. A vibration, as soft as a breeze, floated up over the hilltop. It came and went, as though the slightest change in the air disrupted its delicate path. Yet the closer she moved toward it, the more her confidence in her senses grew.

Reaching the edge of the hilltop, she opened her eyes and gazed down into the crevice at the bottom of the valley; it was only about a metre wide but ran along the earth past the hill. To one side was a pile of large rocks with an opening like a small cave. The vibrations were stronger here, and as she fought back a wave of nausea, Ava wondered if the Underworld could somehow sense her presence. It took barely a moment for her to recognise the gathering of stones as the very same from her vision.

"Is that it?" Zeus asked from beside her. Ava nodded slowly, frowning. "Are you not certain?"

Ava took a moment before replying, "Yes. I'm certain. That is the exact spot I saw in my vision. Still, doesn't it strike you as too easy? It's hardly inconspicuous."

"Why does it need to be? How many people are you aware of who currently search for entry into the Underworld? And if a mortal were to enter the cave, all they'd see is stone walls. The living can't just walk into the Underworld unguided."

"Then what now? How are we supposed to know when the shades are released? What if we can't see them in time, if we're not ready for them?"

Zeus placed his hand on Ava's shoulders. "We'll be ready." Without another word, he guided her back toward the group.

She looked over her shoulder, telling herself she only imagined the increasing vibration.

CHAPTER THIRTY-THREE

JONAH WATCHED THE hivelike activity on the hilltop. He lifted his arms behind his head to stretch out his aching shoulders and back. He was proud of the way everyone worked together. The others clearly felt the same—grateful for the distraction of an immediate task at hand, for having something to do other than wait for the inevitable. His nerves spiked once more in the pit of his stomach, and he lowered his arms with a focused exhale.

"Dude, will you check this place out?" Tristan exclaimed, coming to stand beside him. "We used to pretend we were fighting awesome battles on this hilltop. We'd never have thought one day it would be for real." Jonah chuckled at the memory, then fell silent, once again taking in the sight of it all. Tristan remained beside him, equally as pensive.

Jonah found himself alternating between bouts of nerves and sensations of detachment. A part of him still thought he'd wake up on the plane home from Greece to find this had all been a crazy dream. He glanced at Ava, who stood talking to Zeus, and another part of him wanted to reach out to her, to talk, to set them firmly back on the path they'd started the night they'd kissed. He didn't want to go into this battle without her knowing how he truly felt about her. Yet at the same time, he couldn't help but think it would jinx them, somehow.

Tempting fate... He smiled grimly at the irony.

JONAH NO LONGER had any concept of time; the sun still hung in the sky, unmoving. Most people settled in small groups or attempted to get what rest they could. Those unable to sit still, like Jonah, practised with their newly consecrated weapons. Instead of joining them, he found himself pacing, arms behind his back like some kind of general inspecting his troops, but on the inside, he felt nearly the complete opposite. He almost wished the battle would just start already, so they could be done with it, for better or worse. Deciding to bite the bullet and pull Ava aside for a chat, he tried to locate her in the crowd. The sight of Hades ducking through the throng toward Zeus distracted him instead. Despite how far away the gods stood from him, Jonah heard their conversation quite clearly.

"It has begun," Hades stated, grasping Zeus by the shoulder. Zeus returned the gesture, the two gods locked in a stare as an unspoken understanding passed between them.

Jonah hurried toward them and noted the other gods instinctually doing the same. "How long have we got?" he asked. Zeus looked to Hades for the answer.

"I can't say, exactly. Perhaps an hour? This is new to me. The Underworld has never been breached like this before, and I wasn't even aware that I'd know about it when it happened. All I can tell you is I feel the veil between the realms tearing and straining against the force behind it. I can say for certain it won't be able to hold for much longer. We need to be ready and in position."

Zeus nodded and looked to each of the gods in turn. "Gather your groups. You know what to do." He then turned to Jonah. "Come with me." The god led him to Ava and the Oracles, who sat in another circle but hurried to their feet at his approach. "We don't have long," Zeus stated. "Do you all know where you need to be?"

"Yes," Ava answered for them. "The Oracles will split into groups of two and three to make for more powerful shielding, spread evenly for as much coverage as possible. We don't know how strong the shields will be, but after the attack against the Erinyes, we're confident they'll at least be effective. Jonah and Tristan, I'll be with you."

"Ava, I—"

"Don't even try to stop me, Jonah."

"It's essential the Oracles hold their positions, no matter what," Zeus said. "They'll provide our only line of defence should we need to retreat."

"You can count on us," Ava affirmed, turning back to her Oracles in preparation.

Jonah followed the departing Zeus, hoping he'd have the chance to speak to Ava once this was all over. Without warning, the ground trembled beneath them, and Jonah braced himself against Zeus. "Was that…"

"I'd say so."

They walked to the edge of the hilltop and looked down upon the cave half-hidden in the crevice below.

"Is that it?" Jonah asked.

"It is."

"How is a whole army of shades supposed to come out of that?"

"I don't imagine it will remain that size for long," Zeus replied. As if on cue, the mouth of the cave opened, and the crevice widened.

"Yeah, now would be a good time to grab some weapons." Turning away from the edge, Jonah signalled for Tristan and Ava to join him.

"A call to arms?" Tristan asked, and Jonah nodded. Tristan looked over the contents of the crate inside one of their wagons and pulled out two short swords the length of his forearms. He swung them quickly through the air, testing how they felt. Satisfied, he held them at his sides, and Ava retrieved a dagger from the sheath hanging at her belt.

"Is that all you're taking?" Jonah asked, frowning in concern.

"Yes. Marduk carved it for me especially." She held it up for him to see the three of their initials engraved into the hilt. "And I can shield, remember? That should work, but if the shades do happen to break through it, I'll need something I can get to quickly."

Jonah's heart sank at the thought, and he distracted himself by grabbing a sword from the stack and holding it up to examine it. Part of him felt a little foolish, knowing it was made of wood despite its glistening black appearance. Yet he still felt the power of the Underworld's waters flowing down into his hand to travel along his arm. Lowering the weapon, he looked at his friends. "This is it."

"Group hug," Tristan declared and threw his arms around them, pulling them close.

"Watch out for the weapons," Ava shouted, then hugged Jonah and her brother in return.

They stood there, huddled together in silence. Jonah wanted to say something, anything, but he didn't trust himself to speak.

"Jonah!" Zeus' voice roared over the crowd, causing them to break their huddle.

Without another word, the trio ran toward the god, taking their positions just as the ground rumbled beneath them again. Jonah's heart thundered against his chest as he watched the earth crack open in the valley below.

The gods led each of their groups into position. Every human's face mirrored the expression on their neighbour's—fear, anxiety, and determination.

"Everyone is to hold their position until I say otherwise," Zeus declared, his voice like rolling thunder and reaching out to each and every one of them. Electric blue sparks danced across his body. The God of Thunder set his feet shoulder-width apart, short sword in one hand and his other palm ready to strike. "Kali, it's time!"

Jonah looked up to see the goddess standing in one of the now-empty carts. She closed her eyes and slowly lifted her hands to the sky, where she clasped her sword high above her head. Her skin took on an eerie, azure-blue hue as she chanted. Jonah's ears rang, and a vast shadow moved over them. Shielding his eyes with one hand, he tried to look up at the sky, but the sun was still too bright. Then he found himself clutching his forehead when a searing, white-hot pain pierced his brain.

"Hold your position!" Zeus bellowed. Every other mortal around them also struggled beneath Kali's power.

Her chanting voice rose in volume and speed, forcing the moon from its natural place until it hovered directly in front of the sun. The darkness felt as thick as ink after the prolonged light, and Jonah blinked rapidly to adjust his vision.

"Hold!" Zeus yelled.

When he looked down, Jonah found himself frozen in horror. The swarm of ghostlike shades spilled up from the Underworld, like thousands of ants fleeing a nest.

"Hold!"

Jonah wiped the blood trickling from his nose with the back of a hand, then returned it to his tight grip upon the water-christened sword.

"Shields!" Zeus commanded.

A rush of air pushed past Jonah when Ava projected her protective shield beside him, providing domes of white light around them like a beacon in the darkness. The act seemed to trigger an awareness in the shades, and they paused momentarily to glance up to the army waiting for them on the hill. Then what had at first been a random flood of shades now became a focused charge toward t1he living.

"Hold! Archer's, ready!"

Jonah's eyes locked on the approaching horde of shades, and it seemed he couldn't breathe.

"Fire!"

Arrows whistled from all around, flying up from the archers behind them in a wide arc before plummeting into the first wave of shades. When the weapons pierced the shades' luminescent blue exteriors, the rushing foes flashed a vibrant orange-red before releasing gut-wrenching moans and dissipating into nothingness. Awed, Jonah turned to Tristan beside him.

"This is going to be a piece of piss," Tristan declared, his short swords at the ready.

That flicker of his mate's confidence warmed Jonah with unexpected courage, and he prepared himself for the attack. The onslaught of arrows did nothing to slow or deter the shades as they hit the base of the hill and began their ascent.

"Archers, again!" Zeus commanded, and a second wave hurtled into the sky. As even more shades vanished before their eyes, Jonah's hope increased. Yet something about their anguished cries unnerved him; his chest tightened, leaving him slightly more nauseas with each vanquished enemy.

"Hold!" Zeus shouted again.

A single man had broken formation, now running from behind the protection of the Oracles' shields. "Helene! Helene, it's me. Are you okay?" the man shouted, oblivious to the shades closing in on him. A woman surged ahead of the masses, a ghostly apparition of her former self, and the man opened his arms. But she lunged for him and knocked him to the ground. The man's screams pierced the night as the body of shades drove on around them, swallowing both the man and his loved one beneath their numbers. A ripple of horror swept through the mortal army, but they could only watch and wait behind the shields. In mere seconds, the swarming horde moved past the man, leaving behind nothing but his desiccated remains there on the ground.

"Are you seeing this?" Tristan murmured. Beside him, Jonah couldn't answer, struck instead by the sudden, renewed brightness of the shades that had attacked that one man. "Shit..."

Despite that evidence, shouts and cries rose one by one from around them as those in the waiting army recognised their loved ones amongst the shades.

"That's my brother."

"Oh, God. Mum..."

"I can see my son!"

"They are not your loved ones anymore!" Zeus roared, sparks flying. "They are nothing but shades. Mere shells of the people you once knew. Do not be fooled. You must fight them, or you too will lose your life. We all will!"

Jonah glanced at Ava, who stood with arms outstretched told maintain her Oracle's shield, her eyes white orbs. He hoped that her trance had spared her from seeing the horror before them.

"Attack!" A massive clap of thunder came on the heels of Zeus' command. The god raised his arm and pulled it back, as though holding a spear, and when he hurled his arm forward, a bolt of lightning flew from his palm and into the shades, decimating those closest to its strike. For a moment, no one else seemed to move.

Jonah raised his sword high in the air and yelled as loud as he could. Hearing Tristan joining alongside him, quickly followed by other voices around him, he surged forward toward the shades, his best mate by his side.

AVA STRUGGLED TO control her breathing; each exhalation caught in her throat, threatening to break into a sob. She'd wanted to run after Jonah and Tristan as they'd charged toward the shades, yet she knew she couldn't. Having lost sight of them left her paralysed with fear.

Through her Oracle's vision, she still bore witness to the battle, though with a distorted perception, as if she viewed the scene through a crystal ball. Hearing a ferocious roar behind her, Ava turned her head as far as she dared to see an enormous lion thundering toward her. Inanna sat astride the beast, firing arrows into the sky. It seemed they would barrel straight into Ava, but in one mighty leap, the lion launched them both into the air and over Ava's head. Another mighty roar burst from the lion's open mouth when it landed, and it carried Inanna swiftly into the thick of battle.

Hades and Set ran past, wielding their swords and hollering their battle cries. The tattoo running up Set's back glowed from within. Isis and Enki flanked him from the right, commanding their short swords with such speed, Ava could barely track their movement. From the left came Vishnu and Kali, vibrant-blue and fierce. The awkwardness Vishnu carried in his mortal form had vanished; he now attacked the shades with ferocious swipes of all four arms. Kali appeared to dance alongside him as she glided and turned, sword in hand. A shade leapt danger-ously close, and Kali's arm shot effortlessly to grab the thing by the neck and pull it toward her.

A wave of despair gripped Ava when she recognised the shade as their neighbour. Kali sank her teeth into the shade's neck, all but severing it completely, and a thick ball of hot re-pulsion rose in Ava's throat. The goddess looked up and stared into Ava's eyes as she seemed to feed, her own eyes red and vacant. Unable to look away, Ava watched until the shade fi-nally vanished. Then Kali wiped a smear of luminescent liquid from her face, licked if off her finger, and continued after Vishnu.

A wall of fire shot out from beside Ava, startling her and followed by Marduk, his skin further encasing itself in dragon scales with each step he took. He casually aimed his bow into the enemy, releasing one arrow after the other, pausing every few steps to hurl fire into the swarm.

Screams of agony and despair rose up the hill from the mor-tal army, wiping away Ava's awe at the sight of the gods. She felt their anguish in waves as they tried to fight those they'd once called family and friends. "We need to push forward!" she instructed the other Oracles. "Take it slow and hold your shields. If you feel yourself slipping, stop and re-centre."

Mindful of every step, Ava scanned the fray for signs of Tristan or Jonah. Still, she knew them too well to think they'd remain on the edges of the battle; they'd be in the thick of it. "Please let them be okay…" she whispered and pushed forward.

TRISTAN PLOUGHED THROUGH the shades, not allowing himself the time for recognition. He avoided looking at their faces altogether, partly because he didn't think he could shove a blade into someone he'd once known and partly because he didn't want to see who would be the one to kill him. Yet with each slain enemy, his confidence grew, and he told himself that perhaps the prophecy had been wrong. "I make my own damn destiny!" he screamed, ramming each of his short swords into the two shades on either side of him.

JONAH WAS ONLY vaguely aware of the sky lighting up when Zeus' lightning bolts hit their marks or as Marduk belched fire into the mass of shades. It took all his focus to fight.

"I can't. I can't," cried a woman beside him, dropping her weapon as a shade lunged toward her and knocked her to the ground. Her scream before the shades devoured her was barely audible over the din of warfare.

Jonah acutely felt the pain and heartbreak in the cries of those around him. It grated on his nerves like sandpaper, fuelling him to cut through one shade after the other. He wanted it to end, to save them all from this suffering, but there was no time to think of anything beyond where next to strike.

Then he caught sight of Atropos amongst the shades. A cool, vicious smile spread across her mouth when she saw she had his attention. She stepped aside, the wall of shades parted, and Jonah froze. Running toward him were David and Bethany, their tiny faces distorted masks of maniacal rage.

"Oh, shit. Oh, no, no, no…" He wanted to run but could not. They charged at him, and he held his breath before raising his sword. With one mighty swing, he brought his weapon down again, felling them both in one powerful swoop. Jonah fell to his knees and howled up at the black sky, crushed by the weight of what he had just done, their faces dancing vividly before him. Gasping for air, he watched shades dissipate and mortals fall. Images of the bodies in the street after the Erinyes' attack flashed before his eyes, and he felt as useless now as he had then.

Only this time, he could do something about it. "Atropos, you bitch! I'm going to kill you!" he screamed. The Fate laughed, turning away to stroll back into the throng of shades and out of his view. Jonah swallowed. "We can't go on," he whispered.

AVA HEARD JONAH'S scream echoing over the fray and felt his anguish like a knife to her own heart. "Keep your shields up!" she instructed, then broke her trance and ran out into the battle. Shade after shade surged toward her, and she aimed her light at them with rapid hands, blasting them into nothingness in her determination to reach Jonah. Nothing else mattered.

The shades near Jonah closed in around him, and he still had not raised his sword. A mighty roar lifted over the violence, and Ava faltered only briefly when she saw Zeus, his face an angry blaze, barrelling through the shades and destroying them without even having to look, making his way toward his son.

Ava reached Jonah first, sliding to her knees beside him and casting her shield just before the shades struck.

Jonah looked up at her in surprise. "What are you doing? You're supposed to be with the others. Where it's safe." Ava only lifted a hand to wipe a tear from his cheek.

Zeus skidded to a halt beside them. "What happened?"

"Atropos," Jonah muttered, rising slowly to his feet. "She's here."

"Of course she is..." Zeus growled, turning to scan the crowd.

"There has to be another way," Jonah added. "We can't keep going on like this. Neither side is winning. We're killing more of them than they are of us, but at what cost? I don't know how much more anyone can take."

"Then do you propose something different?" Zeus asked.

HADES EYED THE expanse of the battle, mentally mapping the distance between him and each of the gods. He'd steadily worked his way to the edge of the fight, waiting for his opportunity. Zeus was preoccupied with Jonah, the other gods too caught up in the fray to pay any heed to the god of the Underworld. In a sweeping movement, he pulled his cloak out from under his shirt, draped it across his shoulders, and lifted the hood over his head. He waited for a moment to ensure no one had seen him, then hurried down the hill toward the cave. He had a score to settle.

"ATROPOS!" JONAH YELLED into the battle. "Atropos, let's make another deal."

"Jonah, we need to discuss this first," Zeus pleaded, half-distracted by the shades trying to pummel through Ava's barrier. Jonah ignored the attackers and left the safety of the Oracle's shield. He moved through the battle, his sword sweeping through shades as though he cut his way through a thick jungle. Ava and Zeus protected him as best they could, trying to follow closely.

"Atropos!" he called again, his determination growing with each step. For the first time in a long time, he knew what he had to do—how to be the leader they all needed. An eerie silence fell over the hill, the shades stopped in their tracks, and Jonah paused. Their enemies had frozen entirely, suspended in mid-motion, like someone had just flicked a switch to stop time itself. The mortals looked around in confusion and wary disbelief.

"Atropos!" Jonah called a third time. A wind stirred, sweeping up the hillside, and on the gust came Atropos and her sisters, weaving their way through the shades to meet him.

"You've finally come to your senses," Atropos said. Her sisters stopped slightly behind her. "Where is the Tablet, Jonah?"

"I don't know where the Tablet is." The Fate turned to walk away. "Wait," Jonah added. "I have a… a proposition for you."

"What makes you think we'd be interested in anything you have to offer?" Clotho asked, scowling.

Jonah ignored her, not taking his gaze from Atropos. "We end the battle, right here and now. We both know that neither of our armies will claim the victory. It's impossible. Instead, I propose something I think is of more value to you. Single combat."

"Jonah, no!" Ava cried.

Atropos narrowed her eyes at Jonah and merely said, "Continue."

"Me against your strongest shade."

"And what prize does the victor claim?"

Jonah took a deep breath. "If I win, you and your sisters piss off to wherever you came from and let us rebuild our lives. If you win, we'll give you the Tablet."

"You don't even know where the Tablet is," she spat.

"I don't. But I didn't say it hasn't been found." Jonah clenched his fists.

"Jonah…" Zeus growled.

Jonah looked up at his father. "You said you believe in me. In my ability to be a great leader. I need you to back that. I need your support in this." Zeus stared at him, any emotion tucked away behind his steady, immortal gaze. Then he nodded.

"What? Are you both out of your minds?" Ava shouted. "This is insane!" She grabbed Jonah's shoulders, forcing him to look at her.

"It's insane to continue a war no one can win," Jonah told her gently, "watching more and more of us die. I won't sacrifice anyone else. Not when I can do something about it."

Ava covered her mouth with her hand, unable to stifle a sob before she turned and stormed back up the hill. Jonah watched her brush past Tristan, who made his way toward Jonah now to see what had happened. When his mate stopped by his side, Jonah turned back to the Fates. "Do we have a deal?"

"On one condition. Once the battle begins, there is to be no assistance. No interference from any of your gods. If they breach this condition, you forfeit your life, and the Tablet is ours."

"Only if the three of you agree to the same," Jonah replied, meeting each of the Fates' glowers in turn. When he glared at Atropos again, she gave him a single, solid nod.

"Deal."

"Deal," Jonah declared, hoping they couldn't see the sweat on his brow or his trembling fingers wrapped tightly around the hilt of his wooden sword. He thought he was going to be sick.

"Then I know just the place for it," Atropos declared, smiling as she glanced at Zeus.

CHAPTER THIRTY-FOUR

HADES STRODE BACK through the tunnel in the Underworld until he came to the inner cavern. Below him, Charon sat in the Hades' throne and oversaw the boats delivering the newly deceased from the battle above. No longer needing to hide his presence, Hades lifted his arms and stepped off the ledge, effortlessly descending toward the watery depths below.

"What do *you* want?" Charon drawled.

"You can get out of my chair, for starters." Hades stalked across the water's surface, as only he could.

"And why would I do that? This realm is mine, now. You're a god with no domain."

"The Underworld can only be ruled by a god, and you are not one of us."

"No. I am merely an immortal destined to serve, to exist forever with no hope of rising above his station of eternal bondage."

"You are not a servant," Hades snapped.

"Oh, but I am. I deliver you souls, day in and day out. I am at your beck and call to cater to your whims. Tend to a realm of endless expanse without so much as a portion of it to call my own."

"That's what this is about? You betrayed me for freedom? Your own tiny realm? Had you come to me first, I could have given you both."

"You have the ability, yes. But I do not think you would have given me anything. You would have dismissed me as you have for eons. Mind you, I can't blame you for that. You made it easy to say yes when the Fates asked me to join them."

Hades silently looked Charon over from head to toe. "So they've taken the Underworld from me and given it to you. Look at you. You're still miserable. I know what you really desire."

"And what would that be, oh, powerful god?" Charon snarled.

"A consort. I've seen the way you watch the women ferried in here. If you relinquish your claim to my throne, I will allow you a consort and your own piece of the Underworld. On the condition that you also return to your position as ferryman."

Charon rose to his feet and slowly paced in front of the giant chair. "A consort of my own choosing," he demanded quietly.

"Of course," Hades complied. "As soon as you know—"

"Oh, I know. I want Ava Carter."

Hades opened and closed his mouth, faltering for a moment, "Ava? You've never met—why?"

"Because of what she means to them all," Charon spat. "She's become a symbol of hope and light to that disease you call the human race. I want to take it from them. Let them know my name. They can curse it if they must, but they will know who I am for generations."

Hades considered the repercussions of accepting such a proposal. The only sound now came from the soft trickling of boats gliding in and out of the cavern. "Very well. If I bring Ava down here to you, you take up your position of ferryman once more and relinquish your claim to my throne. Forever."

"Agreed." Charon flipped a gold coin in the god's direction.

Hades caught the trinket and took a final glance at Charon's malicious, black-toothed grin before he turned and made his way out of the cavern.

JONAH OPENED HIS eyes, trying to shake the disorienting cloud from his mind. He looked up at the circular stands towering before him in all directions, filled with those plucked from the battlefield on the hillside. Everyone looked as confused as he felt.

"Jonah!"

Hearing Tristan's voice, Jonah scanned the crowd for his friends. Only when Tristan and Ava waved their arms frantically in the air did he finally locate them. He took a step forward, then jumped when Atropos appeared beside him, followed closely by Zeus.

"Where are we?" he asked.

"Oh, I don't know what you mortals call it, but it reminds me of the Colosseum of old. Fitting, really." She clasped her hands together in anticipation. "What better location for your followers to bear witness to the fall of their great leader?"

As Jonah's clarity returned, he realised they stood in the middle of the Melbourne Cricket Ground—the M.C.G. It looked the worse for wear, the once magnificent green field now nothing but dry, dusty, overturned dirt. Two of the goalposts at one end of the field were snapped in half, and a large section of the stands was missing completely. Banners hung along the barriers had been half-ripped from their hangings, and shattered glass from broken spotlights covered the ground. Atropos swept her arm in a wide arc, and flaming torches appeared along the field's perimeter. "We want to make sure they can see you," she said, leering at him in the flickering light.

"The light will inhibit Jonah's ability to see the shade," Zeus growled.

"Oh, believe me, he'll have no trouble seeing his opponent." Atropos shot Zeus a smug smile.

"You don't have to do this," Zeus said quietly, clasping his son's shoulder.

"Yes, I do. It's the only way." Zeus only frowned, but he didn't try to deter Jonah any further.

"Any last words you'd like to exchange before we start?" Atropos asked with mock concern. She all but skipped around them in her enthusiasm to get started.

"I believe in you," Zeus said. "We all do. And these are not our last words." He nodded at his son before turning on his heel and re-joining the other gods in the stands. Jonah had no opportunity to respond.

"Remember, Zeus, no interfering from here on out," Atropos called out after him, but the god did not turn back to acknowledge her.

Watching his father walk away, Jonah found the enormity of what he was about to do kicking in. He looked back toward Tristan and Ava, hoping that seeing them would calm his nerves, if even just a little.

Clotho and Lachesis appeared on either side of their sister. Clotho approached him, carrying a shield, and she handed it to him without a word before returning to her sister's side. Lachesis brandished the consecrated wooden sword he'd left behind on the hill. As she held it out to him, she looked up and mouthed, 'Good luck.' Jonah could only stare at her in surprise, then she returned to her sisters.

"Are you ready to meet your opponent?" Atropos asked with a smirk. Her confident smugness only heightened Jonah's senses, and he did his best not to shuffle from one foot to the other. Taking his lack of response for consent, Atropos waived her arm to the right. The dry dirt swirled within an unfelt wind, and Jonah raised his shield against the flying debris. When the movement subsided, he lowered his shield to find an angry-looking hulk of a shade standing across the field.

"Okay..." he told himself. "He's big but not unbeatable. I've got this." But then the shade twitched and jerked, its spectral hue dimming then brightening, over and over. Jonah's mouth fell open; the shade's very mass increased before his eyes. Both mesmerised by the sight and paralysed with fear, he studied the monster Atropos had created, the outline of its figure bulging from within to reveal the faces of other shades fighting to free themselves from their new prison. A cry rose from the crowd as they too realised what was happening.

"Atropos!" Zeus bellowed from the stands. "This is cheating. If you proceed, you will forfeit the battle to Jonah."

"Actually, you are quite wrong." Her voice rang effortlessly across the stadium, as though she stood in front of a microphone. "The terms of Jonah's opponent were never discussed, only the terms of your involvement and ours."

Zeus lurched forward, but Enki and Inanna grabbed him by the shoulders and held him back, preventing his temper from getting the better of him. Yet even from where he stood, Jonah saw the angry red sparks flying off his father.

Turning his attention to the shade once more, he felt his mouth dry up, and he found it hard to breathe. The creature towered at least eight feet tall, its body pulsating with the swarm of shades piecing it together. Its own head was rotund and grotesque, with no nose or mouth—just two wide, gaping red eyes. It possessed no weapons. Jonah knew it didn't need them. It just had to get its hands on him, and he'd be finished. He forced himself to take a long, deep breath as the Fates turned and left the field. It was time.

TRISTAN LOOKED DOWN at Jonah and the monstrous shade, his jaw clenching in anger. Ava's hand trembled in his own, which only fortified his guilt. He'd been relieved that the battle was over, that the prophecy of his demise hadn't been fulfilled, but that didn't mean he wanted to see his best mate die. Tristan wasn't used to such conflicting emotions, and his anger and frustration built by the second.

"Those bitches," he muttered. "They can't keep trying to screw with us like this." From so far away, he couldn't see Jonah's expression, but he did see the slump in his mate's shoulders and realised Jonah had been defeated before he even started. "I don't bloody think so, you ugly shade bastard!" he yelled. Those around him turned and stared. Releasing his sister's hand, Tristan clapped once and stomped his foot hard on the concrete beneath him. The sound echoed around the silent stadium like a gunshot. He repeated it, and Jonah looked up at him. When he clapped and stomped a third time, Ava did the same, and one by one, those gathered in the crowd joined in this wordless show of support and defiance against the Fates. Soon, the whole stadium slapped their hands together and pounded the concrete in unison, the sound like rolling thunder.

THE GROUND BENEATH Jonah's feet vibrated with the strength of thousands. His heart pounded so fiercely, he thought it might burst from his chest. But it did not stem from fear; he felt empowered, as though he drew tangible strength from the support of those in the stands—those for whom he now fought. With renewed focus, he crouched into a ready position. The rhythm of the crowd's beat quickened, and Jonah knew he'd only have one shot to win. The massive shade lumbered toward him, and Jonah broke into a sprint.

A cheer ignited within the crowd, all but deafening him. Crossing the field with very little effort, Jonah covered the distance to his opponent. The closer he got, the easier it was to anticipate the creature's next move. The shade took a final stride toward him, and Jonah dodged to the left, skidding across the dirt between the creature's legs to come up behind it. The shade twisted its long torso to follow him, and Jonah leaped up onto the beast's outstretched leg, narrowly avoiding the thing's deadly grasp. Then he launched himself from the thing's leg and drove his sword into its hulking side. Another roar of encouragement echoed from the crowd; the shade's glow blackened around the embedded blade.

Then a searing heat radiated from Jonah's stomach, and he was thrown backward off his foe. He only briefly registered the shade's hand actually *inside* him before he hurtled through the air and landed on the dirt in a sprawling heap. The creature let out an almighty roar, yanking the sword from its body and hurling the weapon at Jonah. Jonah struggled to lift his head; the sword had landed somewhere in the dark, but it was too far out of reach.

He glanced back at the shade to see the blackening had spread, but still, the creature fought on. Jonah looked around helplessly for his shield, for anything with which to defend himself, but the smallest movement set the pain in his belly to screaming. And then the agony spread. He didn't need to look down to know it was bad. *No… it's not supposed to end like this…*

AVA STOOD FROZEN in place, paralysed by her fear for Jonah's life. Beside her, Tristan ran toward the barrier below them and tried to leap onto the field. But he was thrown viciously backward by an unseen barrier. "Let me out!" he yelled at the Fates. "He needs help!" His pleas unheard, Tristan lost his cool and kicked at the barrier over and over.

Now Ava watched her brother, and she was incapable of consoling or helping him, either.

Why didn't I see this? I could have stopped it! She cursed herself for not having tried hard enough.

"There is a way to save Jonah," someone whispered behind her. "But you have to come with me. Now."

Startled, Ava turned to find Hades close behind her. "How?"

"He doesn't have a lot of time. We need to hurry."

Without further question, she followed the god from the stands to the mouth of the tunnel leading to the changerooms below. Ava paused at the top of the tunnel and shot Hades a dubious glance.

"Trust me," he said, then walked ahead.

With no other choice, she followed him.

The smooth walls soon gave way to damp, dark stone, the fluorescent lighting replaced by burning torches. The temperature dropped, and she realised Hades now led her into the Underworld. Ava frowned, feeling as though she wanted to ask him something yet unable to grasp the exact words of the question she tried to form. The lack of clarity should have alarmed her, but she was too dazed to care. After a few more minutes, her muscles grew weak with fatigue, and all she wanted was to lie down and sleep. But the image of Jonah lying there in the dust entered her mind, forcing her to stay awake, and she held firmly to the vision. *Hold on, Jonah.*

JONAH RAISED HIS hands over his head, as if that would stop the monstrous shade looming over him. He waited for the end, but when the creature moved no farther, Jonah slowly lowered his arms. It stared down at him, so close he could see his own reflection in its glaring red eyes. But it did not move.

Pushing himself up on his elbows, he noticed even the contorted faces of the shades within the beast had fallen still in grotesque masks of horror. He moaned in pain, looking around to see the entire crowd had also been frozen in time.

What the hell?

He caught movement at the top of the stands opposite him, where a strangely isolated path of fog crept up over the top of the sails and spilled down into the stands. It swept over the crowd, snaking over the boundary that kept them all at bay and continuing onto the field. It drifted directly toward Jonah, then stopped a few metres away and rose sharply into the form of an old man. He was quite tall despite his stooping posture, as though he'd carried a heavy burden for a long time. He leaned on a walking stick of dark black wood, rough and unpolished. A braided silver cord was tied around the waist of his dark-grey robe, his long grey hair held back by a series of intricate plaits and decorated with feathers and stones. The man's beard flowed freely down to his waist.

A tiny rustle came from within his sleeve, and the head of a snake protruded, pausing to flick its forked tongue this way and that before it fully emerged from its hiding place. It slithered down the cane, then turned and twined back up and around until its head came to rest beneath the walking stick's handle. Jonah stared at the old man hobbling toward him, the only sound the repetitive tap and drag of the walking stick in the dirt.

"Jonah," the man began, his voice soft and gravelly, "it is an honour to finally meet you. I've waited a long time for this moment."

"Who are you?"

"Aesclepius. I'm an old friend of your father's. I've come to help."

"If the gods intervene, we forfeit to the Fates..." Jonah whispered, feeling weak and wondering if he was hallucinating.

"Fortunately for you, then, I'm not a god. My mother was mortal, the same as yours." Jonah frowned; the old man didn't even glance at the Fates' shade champion when he passed it, his gaze instead focused solely on the gaping wound in Jonah's belly. "And not a moment too soon, it seems." He leaned heavily on the staff and lowered slowly to his knees. The snake unwound itself from the cane, reached out, and moved gently over Jonah's body. Then it lowered its head into his wound.

"Wait!" Jonah protested. "What's that—" He howled in pain and collapsed back into the dirt.

"She won't hurt you," the old man said.

Jonah's entire body clenched to feel the snake writhing inside him. Flashes of white spots danced before his eyes, and just when he thought he was going to pass out, a strange warmth spread from his injury and wrapped around the rest of his body. He felt himself relax, somehow now with the strength to lift himself onto his elbows. It surprised him even more to find the pain had vanished. "Is it healing me?"

Aesclepius shook his head. "She's removing the toxin that was killing you. At least, it was killing you faster than the wound itself."

Then the snake emerged again, not giving him a second look as it left his body and wound itself back up the staff, glowing the same blue as the shades. It closed its eyes, and the blue faded until the snake was once again the same dark black of the staff, becoming one with the wood. Aesclepius reached into the folds of his robe and produced two vials of blood. These he held out for Jonah. "One of these will heal you. Give you life. The other is death."

"You're not going to tell me which is which?"

Aesclepius leaned on his staff and rose to his feet. "I'm afraid not. One's fate allows for only so much interference. I can provide you with the opportunity to live, but the final choice must be yours."

"How can it be a choice if I don't know which one will kill me?"

"That's why it's called fate, Jonah. Be well." Then the man turned and hobbled away. Jonah watched him leave, even as the wizened form evaporated into the fog and returned the way it had come.

Jonah sat up and inspected the vials for any clue as to how he was to choose the correct one, but as far as he could tell, they were identical. Taking a deep breath, he closed his eyes, put the first vial to his mouth, and yanked out the stopper with his teeth. He spat it out and downed the blood in a single gulp, grimacing at the metallic taste. Eyes shut tightly, he waited for something to happen.

A sudden, trembling roar made him open his eyes just in time to realize the world had started moving again and the shade's mighty arm once more made its rapid descent toward him. Clutching the second vial, Jonah rolled across the dirt and narrowly missed the creature's fist before it pummelled the ground.

Leaping to his feet, he bolted toward his discarded sword, sliding across the dirt like a runner into home plate and snatching the weapon with a firm grip. It took surprisingly little effort to stand again, and the renewed hope that brought him made Jonah grin. The cheers rising from the stands all but deafened him. "I'm alive, you ugly piece of shit!" he declared.

His massive foe merely stood upright again, the faces of the shades within it contorting in rage. The creature stalked toward him, and Jonah pulled the stopper from the remaining vile to pour its contents down the blade of his sword. Bracing himself, he let the monstrous thing come at him. His heart thundered, but whatever remained of his fear vanished completely when he launched himself toward the monstrous beast. With more strength than he knew he had, Jonah leaped into the air, his sword raised high. The creature pulled back its arm and prepared to strike, but it was too slow. Jonah let out a fierce roar and swung the sword down to plunge it deep into the beast's chest. He released his grip on the weapon and let himself fall to the dirt, rolling aside once more to escape the next blow.

The crowd erupted again. The massive shade stumbled forward, trying to pull the sword from its body. A blackness spread rapidly across its enormous form from where the blade pierced halfway through. It let out an enraged bellow, shaking the ground beneath them when it fell to its knees. Jonah stood, breathing heavily and eyeing the beast but certain it was no longer a threat.

But the ground didn't stop trembling, and a crack appeared in the dirt beneath the fallen shade. Jonah stepped back as the earth splintered in all directions. His enemy finally collapsed, its chest splitting open from the force of the trapped shades trying to escape their dying host. From within the cracked earth came a shocking hiss and a high-pitched scream, then the shades were drawn back down into the Underworld, clawing at themselves and each other until the very last of them had disappeared. The ground closed up with a loud crack, and with nothing left to sustain it, the once enormous shade was reduced to a blackened husk.

As if he watched the souls of the dead return to the Underworld every day, Jonah approached his defeated enemy and yanked the sword from its remains. The rest of the creature disintegrated into the earth.

An ear-shattering clamour of victory and praise erupted from the crowd, and Jonah raised his sword high in the air, unable to hold back his grin. He scanned the crowd and met Zeus' gaze first, his smile widening to see his father standing amongst the other gods and applauding. Then Jonah tried to find Ava and Tristan, bursting to share the explanation he knew they would want for his miraculous recovery. He found Tristan behind the barrier, but Ava no longer stood where he'd last seen her. With a brief frown, he found his concern was short-lived when Tristan hurtled over the field's barrier and sprinted toward him.

They clapped each other in a rough embrace, and Jonah's sword clattered to the ground. With Tristan's leap over the barrier now proof that it had indeed fallen, the crowd spilled onto the field from the stands, throwing cheers of relief and celebration.

"Dude, that was bloody awesome! I thought you were dead for sure. What the hell happened?"

"Long story," Jonah said, then released his mate. "Where's Ava?"

Tristan frowned and glanced back into the almost empty stands. "I don't know, mate. She was right there last I saw. Where would she even go?"

As if in reply, a deafening screech hurtled through the air above them. Everyone looked up to see Atropos plunging toward Zeus, her lips curled back in a sneer of hatred, palms open by her sides and her hair billowing around her face. To anyone else, this would have been an intimidating attack, but Zeus stood his ground.

"I will end you and your worthless progeny!" she screamed.

Zeus stepped forward, his hands in tight fists against his thighs—more in self-restraint than aggression. But the sparks still flew from his terrifying figure. "A deal is a deal, Atropos. Jonah won this battle according to our terms, upon which you cannot renege now."

"That's a lie," she hissed. "You clearly interfered. He was all but dead!"

"And yet he isn't. I'd like to claim the credit for such a mystery, but I was in the stands the whole time. As were you."

"It doesn't matter how you did it. You will pay for your deceit." Raising her arm, she slowly closed her hand into a fist with a malevolent smile. Zeus fell to his knees, clutching at his throat with one hand as he gestured with the other for the remaining gods to stand back.

"Zeus!" Jonah cried, forcing his way through the crowd.

"You are no better than the pathetic mortals who serve you. Or is it the other way around? You call yourself a god…"

Zeus glared up at the Fate, unable to speak, the red sparks shooting from his body with heightened intensity.

"I've waited a long time to end you, mighty Zeus." Atropos sneered and lifted her other hand over her head.

"Atropos!"

Jonah turned around, startled and confused by the voice calling out from behind him. There stood Lachesis, Jonah's forgotten sword in hand and pressed to her own throat. The crowd gave her a wide berth.

"What are you doing, you fool?" Atropos spat.

"We made a deal, sister, and we lost. If you end Zeus, I will take my own life. The Fates are nothing if there are only two. You will be powerless without me."

"You deceitful, idiotic…" Atropos turned her attention from Zeus and shot through the crowd toward her sister.

"This is not a threat," Lachesis muttered harshly, pushing the blade more firmly against her throat until small beads of blood bloomed against her ivory skin. Atropos stopped in her tracks, glaring, the air crackling around them like static with her rage. "This realm belongs to the mortals, for better or for worse. The deal is done. It's time for us to abandon the Tablet and leave these people to their original design."

The crowd waited, immobilised by tense anticipation. Then Clotho appeared before her sisters and placed a hand on each of their arms. A wind kicked up around the Fates, flinging dirt out into the crowd. Those closest raised their hands to shield wary eyes, and when all fell still again, the Fates were gone. The moon expediated its retreat from the sun, and the crowd blinked and lowered their heads against the sudden harshness of true daylight.

Jonah ran toward Zeus as Enki and Vishnu helped the god to his feet. "Are you okay?" he asked, placing a hand on his father's arm.

"I'm fine. Angry, but unharmed." He smiled down at his son, then pulled him into an embrace that would have crushed any man's bones but those of a demigod.

CHAPTER
THIRTY-FIVE

IT TOOK ALL of Ava's concentration to keep following Hades. She couldn't shake the dread that only seemed to increase with each shaky step. Occasionally, Hades stopped to wait for her or lend her a hand in navigating the rockier footholds of the Underworld.

"I'm tired," she said, pausing to lean against the cold stone wall. "I think I just need to lie down."

"No time for that, Ava." Hades draped her arm over his shoulders and lifted her back to her feet. "We need to move on. For Jonah."

The sound of his name gave Ava a small boost of alertness, and she forced herself to keep walking. With no concept of how long they'd been here, it surprised her when they reached one of the rivers. Hades left her to walk down to a large boulder on the riverbank. Its surface had split in a natural groove within which rested a wooden bowl. A flicker of recognition triggered in Ava's mind, but it was too dim, and she couldn't focus enough to recall it.

"Come." Hades gestured for her to approach, then lifted the bowl from its place. When Ava stood before him, the god placed the bowl in her hands. "Dip the bowl into the river and drink."

Ava glanced hazily from the bowl to the water and back to Hades. "This will help Jonah?" Hades nodded and stepped aside. Part of her thought this didn't make any sense, but she couldn't think clearly enough as to why. All she knew was Jonah was dying, and only she could save him; Hades had told her as much.

Crouching at the water's edge, she dipped the bowl into the river and slowly lifted it toward her face. Then she noticed the small, engraved symbols lighting up around the bowl's outer rim. She paused, trying to work out where she'd seen these before.

"You must hurry," Hades prompted.

Ava nodded, lifted the bowl to her lips, and drank deeply.

HADES REACHED DOWN and took the bowl from Ava's limp hands. Once he'd returned it to its sacred place within the stone, he bent to help Ava to her feet.

"Who are you?" she asked in a daze, blinking furiously. "Where am I?"

"I'm a friend," Hades stated, giving her hand a reassuring pat. "And I'm taking you home."

"Zeus," Enki said in a low voice, interrupting the god's embrace with his son. "Hades is gone."

"We don't know where Ava is, either," Jonah admitted.

Zeus' brow furrowed, and he exchanged a dark glance with Enki. "Stay here," he told Jonah and Tristan, then he took off through the crowd without an explanation.

"I'll let the others know," Enki said, as if that were a viable reason for him to head off in the opposite direction.

"Why is Zeus heading toward the changerooms?" Tristan asked.

"I have no idea…" Jonah said flatly, staring after his father.

"We're going to follow him, aren't we?"

"Absolutely."

WHEN THEY REACHED the mouth of the tunnel leading to the changerooms, they stopped to peer into the darkness. Only a faint glow of light came from within, but it seemed quite a distance away.

"Does that seem off to you?" Tristan asked.

"Yeah, mate. Pretty sure that no longer leads to the changerooms." With no verbal agreement necessary between them, they entered the tunnel at a jog. A flash of movement darted across their path up ahead. Their shoes barely made a sound when the concrete floor gave way to damp stone, followed shortly by the same change in the walls and ceiling.

"Holy shit…" Tristan whispered. "Is this the Underworld?"

"Sure looks like we're heading that way." Their descent only drew them deeper.

"Wait. Hades said mortals couldn't just enter the Underworld."

Jonah paused briefly, then shrugged. "We're obviously not having any trouble with it. I'm Zeus' son, so not entirely mortal... Maybe that means I can take you, too? Either way, I don't really care so long as we find Ava."

"Agreed." Tristan nodded, and they picked up the pace again.

They travelled down for what felt like ages. Then the silence of the tunnel shattered amidst Zeus' roar. "*Hades!*"

Tristan and Jonah exchanged a startled look, then took off running toward Zeus' voice. In seconds, they found themselves at a junction in the tunnel, the walls breaking off to the left and the right. The god's voice still reverberated through the stone walls, making it impossible to know where Zeus actually was.

"Which way?" Tristan asked.

Jonah closed his eyes, concentrating on the echoes of Zeus' warning shout as it bounced off the stone. "Right," he answered. "I think we should go right."

After only a few metres, they stumbled out of the tunnel and onto the loose shale of a riverbank. Using the river as a guide, they followed it in silence. Angry, muffled voices echoed toward them, as if travelling up the river itself, and they moved faster, trying to stay as quiet as possible.

"Have you lost your mind?" Zeus demanded.

"Of course not," Hades replied. "I'm simply doing what needs to be done to restore order."

"What the hell does Ava have to do with that?"

Without warning, Jonah and Tristan stepped into the enormous central cavern of the Underworld, Zeus and Hades standing atop the platform in the centre. Ava stood slightly behind Hades, staring wide-eyed and fearful at the angry sparks bursting from Zeus' form.

"Who's the sulky-looking bloke in the chair?" Jonah whispered.

"Pretty sure that's Charon. He's the creepy dude responsible for my hairdo."

Jonah gave a half nod in response, distracted by the way Ava clutched Hades' arm. "Something's not right…"

"No shit." Tristan took a step forward and slipped on the rocks, which sent him tumbling toward the river before he skidded to a stop.

"I told you two to stay put!" Zeus yelled across the water.

Jonah raised his hands in defence. "With all due respect, did you honestly think we'd sit back and wait if we thought Ava was in trouble?" Zeus only glared at them. Jonah grabbed hold of an empty boat floating past them. "Get in," he told Tristan. No one else said a word as the vessel took him and his mate toward the platform. Jonah thought Zeus' frown no longer carried anger but something else—some unexpected concern. Still, he tried to ignore the warning bells it set of within him, then he and Tristan left the boat and climbed up onto the platform.

"Ava, I'm glad you're okay," Tristan said, walking toward her.

His sister cowered behind Hades. "Who are you?"

Tristan jerked to a halt as if she'd slapped him, and Jonah swore aloud behind him. "Uh, I'm Tristan. Your brother."

Ava looked up at Hades, and the god turned halfway toward her to give a small nod. "Is he my brother too?" she asked, pointing at Jonah.

"No. You need not concern yourself with that one," Hades drawled.

"Asshole!" Jonah almost ran at the god. "What did you do to her?"

Zeus grabbed Jonah's arm to stop him from doing anything else, but he glared at the god of the Underworld. "You cannot do this. I will not permit it."

"Do what?" Tristan asked, looking frantically from one god to the other and back. "What's he doing?"

"It's the only way for me to reclaim my realm," Hades said. "Without the Underworld, I am nothing."

"And I want what was promised me," growled Charon, his silver eyes flashing.

Zeus turned toward the throne where Charon sat. "You…" he sneered, raising his arm and shooting an endless streak of lightning into the demigod, lifting him from the throne to hover uselessly in the air while the electricity coursed through him. "You dare address your sovereign in such a manner?" He directed Charon away from the throne and the platform and dangled him over the boats below. "You are the Ferryman. You will always be the Ferryman. The Fates are no longer here to defend you and your treacherous pursuit of a power that will never be yours. If you ever attempt such a thing again, I will toss you into the aether myself. Do you *understand* me?" His voice bounced around the cavern like claps of thunder; chunks of stone loosened and tumbled down around them. Then Zeus released Charon into an awaiting boat.

The Ferryman said nothing but slowly got to his feet and pulled the hood of his cloak up over his head. With a final flash of his silver eyes, he turned and thrust his staff into the river before gliding away.

"That was intense…" Tristan whispered.

"The Underworld is yours, Hades," Zeus growled. "But heed my warning. Do not presume to undermine me or my authority a second time." Hades offered a solemn nod. "Now release Ava to her family."

Hades eyed the ground at his feet. "I'm afraid it's not that simple."

"Wait, what? Why?" Jonah asked.

Hades sighed, failing in his apparent attempt to hide a sheepish smile. "She drank from the river Lethe…"

"Obviously," Zeus spat, the sparks flaring again. "Surely you have a contingency for such a foolish act."

Hades glanced back at Ava. "She must drink the blood of someone she loves. Only then will her memory be returned to her."

"Mine," Jonah announced without a second thought.

"Yeah, I totally would have offered," Tristan said, "but I think it'll be best coming from you." He patted his mate on the shoulder.

Hades withdrew a small, delicate blade from the pocket of his cloak and gestured for Jonah to approach. Jonah extended his arm, all too aware of how much fear he saw in Ava's eyes as Hades' knife slit his wrist. The quick flash of pain made Jonah wince, and he forced himself to watch the warm thickness of his blood flowing from the wound. Hades stepped aside and gently nudged Ava forward. She looked back at him, her eyes wide with panic. "It'll be okay," Jonah said. That seemed to be enough for her, because she grabbed Jonah's hand and placed her mouth firmly on his wrist. He grimaced at the sting and the unnerving sight of her taking long, slow pulls from his open veins until he started to feel lightheaded.

"Enough," Zeus commanded, placing a hand on Jonah's shoulder to steady him.

Hades grabbed Ava, who released Jonah's wrist, and everyone watched her in shared anticipation as she wiped the blood from her mouth with the back of a hand. She glanced blankly from one of them to the next. Jonah all but crossed his fingers, willing her to return to them.

Finally, her eyes widened in recognition, and her mouth dropped open. "Jonah!" She leaped forward and threw her arms around him. "I thought you were... I didn't know if you'd make it through the fight."

Jonah hugged her back fiercely, the relief blurring his vision just a little. "You're not getting rid of me that easily."

"Man, Mum would have killed me if that didn't work," Tristan muttered. Ava released Jonah and pulled her brother into another tight embrace.

Then she turned to Hades with a scowl and slapped him across the face, the sound echoing around the cavern like a stone whipped from a slingshot. Hades merely blinked at her, rubbed the side of his face, then turned. He walked casually to his throne and sat.

"Let's go home," Jonah said, a tired smile forming as the heaviness he'd carried around for weeks lifted just a little.

"There's one more thing..." Hades stated, leaning back against his throne. Then he lifted his hand toward Zeus, eyebrows raised as though he expected the god of thunder to know the answer. Zeus swore under his breath and turned away.

"What's going on?" Jonah asked, looking from one god to the other. Zeus paced the platform, and Hades propped his elbows on the throne's armrests and tapped his steepled fingers together.

"Do you want to tell them, or should I?" the god of the Underworld asked. A slight flicker of amusement tugged at the corner of his mouth. Zeus turned and glared at him.

"One of you better bloody well say something," Jonah hissed, the weight of dread returning full-force.

"One of you must remain," Hades said flatly.

"What?" Ava shouted.

"No mortal soul can enter the Underworld and freely walk out again."

Tristan swore, turning his back as he raised his hands behind his head and gazed up at the ceiling.

Jonah felt Ava's hand in his and squeezed it tightly. "Zeus?" he asked, half pleading his father for another option.

Zeus only raised his eyebrows. "I told you not to follow me."

Jonah swallowed thickly at the sight of something he'd never seen before in his father's eyes—defeat.

"You cannot deny your own devious, underhanded role in the way these events have unfolded, Hades," Zeus said in a low, threatening voice. "You've been bending the rules for millennia." Hades tapped his fingers to his lips, and Jonah couldn't tell if he was actually considering options or just toying with them. "Do not waste my time," Zeus added.

"Fine. I admit, without my part in this, there would have been no cause for the three of you to enter my realm. The will of the Underworld is unbreakable, and it does not allow entry without a price. Even with my making this concession, the fact remains as I just said. One of you must stay here, and the other two are free to go."

"I'll do it," Jonah announced. Ava buried her face in her hands with a strangled sob.

Zeus turned to him in surprise. "Jonah—"

"It's not a suggestion," Jonah interrupted. "You showed me I needed to believe in myself. To be a leader. That's what this is."

"No way, dude," Tristan said. "We should at least draw straws or flip a coin or something. I can't let you take this on by yourself. We're best mates, remember?"

"This is my destiny, mate. Has been from the start. I need to do this."

Tristan pulled Jonah into a fierce embrace. "You're my brother. You know that, right?" he said in Jonah's ear.

Jonah nodded. "Always. Take care of Ava." Unable to say anything else, Tristan released Jonah and gave him a pat on the shoulder. Then Jonah turned toward his father, and they clasped forearms before Zeus drew him in to clap his arms around his son. "Thank you. For everything," Jonah said.

"I wish there was something I could do," Zeus rumbled.

"I know." Finally, he stepped toward Ava, gently took her hand, and led her to the end of the platform away from the others. He turned her to face him, then lifted her chin so she had to look at him. Tears streamed down her face, and though she bit her bottom lip, her chin still quivered. "You know," he said, taking both her hands in his, "part of me wants to kick myself for not following my heart sooner. Especially when I think of all the time we could have had together." She closed her eyes and let out a little sob, but he squeezed her hands, and she opened her eyes to meet his gaze again. "But I've come to believe that everything happens for a reason. I've never felt that I had any control over my own life. That my choices had already been made for me long before I was even born. Except for one. My heart chose you the moment I met you, and I was a goner the first time you rolled your eyes at me." Ava giggled through her tears. "It didn't matter that we were only children. I knew. And I think you did too, even then." Ava nodded and squeezed his hands. "You're fearless, and you will lead an amazing life. For both of us. Ava Carter, I love you with all my heart. I always have, and I always will."

"I love you too." Ava reached up and pulled him closer. When their lips met, time seemed to stop, even in the

Underworld. Jonah drank in the fresh, soapy smell of her, the warmth of her hands in his hair, the curve of her lower back against his hand. He wanted this moment to be the last thing he remembered.

When he finally pulled away from her, Ava let out an involuntary whimper of hesitation, but her tears had stopped. He put a hand to her cheek, looked her in the eye, and nodded. Then he turned to face Zeus and Tristan one last time, steeling himself for what was to come. But Jonah didn't expect to see the unexplained glance shared between his father and his best mate, Zeus' eyes wide with some silent realization. Then Tristan turned to meet Jonah's gaze. He winked, turned around, and took off with inhuman speed toward the aether.

A terrified panic struck Jonah, and he lurched to run after his mate. "Tristan!" Ava screamed, but Zeus intercepted them with open arms, barricading them from the churning column of aether on the other side of the platform and Tristan's final moment.

TRISTAN HEARD THEIR cries, but he didn't falter. Jonah was wrong—this destiny was Tristan's. They'd grieve over losing him, he knew, but they would have each other. Jonah and Ava had finally admitted what everyone else had known for a long time; their bond was a rare thing, especially now. In the second before he launched himself from the platform and into the aether, he felt the remnants of Isis' touch on his arm. Then he embraced the brilliant flash of white light waiting to greet him.

CHAPTER
THIRTY-SIX

JONAH DIDN'T KNOW how long they sat there, slumped on the platform, clinging to each other in their sudden and overwhelming grief. When the tears finally dried, they left behind an aching hole in his chest.

Jonah looked up to see Zeus standing before the aether, his hands clasped behind his back. The throne, however, was empty. "Where's Hades?" Jonah asked. Ava lifted her head off his shoulder to also settle her gaze on Zeus.

Zeus turned. "Oh, he skulked off once his debt was collected. I imagine he's around here somewhere." Jonah gritted his teeth, silently cursing Hades for the coward he was. Zeus glanced around the cavern, then stepped toward Ava and his son. "It's time for you to leave."

Jonah stood, then helped Ava to her feet. "We're ready." When Zeus merely gazed at them with a concerned frown, Jonah added, "You *do* know the way out, right?"

"I do," Zeus said. "But I'm afraid I can't lead you through it."

"What is that supposed to mean?" Ava asked, her eyes wide.

"You've heard of the curse of Orpheus?" Zeus replied. Jonah groaned.

Ava put a trembling hand on his arm. "Jonah, what do we have to do to get out of here?" The words came out in a terrified whisper.

"All you have to do is follow me, Ava," he said, amazed that he'd thought there would be an easy end to this. "But if I turn back one time, even if it's just to make sure you're behind me, you'll be returned to the Underworld. And you'll never leave." Ava just stared at him, her eyes wide.

"We can do this," he assured her, reaching out for her hand. "Trust me. And Tristan didn't… do what he did so we can spend the rest of our lives stuck down here."

Zeus brought a hand down on his son's shoulder. "The Underworld will ensure this won't be easy for you, Jonah. It will find ways to torment you. Drive you mad, if you let it. But if you love Ava and Tristan, you'll keep your head forward and persevere."

Jonah nodded and pulled Ava into his arms. "Are you coming with us?" he asked his father.

Zeus shook his head. "No. But I'll be waiting for you on the other side." He lowered his hand, then met Ava's gaze. "You cannot help him on the journey out of here. If he falls, he has to pick himself up. If he calls out to you, you must not answer. If he stops walking for any reason, do not approach him. It will be a long and fretful wait for him to resume the task, and the outcome is entirely in his hands. But have faith in him."

"I do," Ava said without hesitation.

"Good. Jonah, you can leave the way you came in. Once you leave this cavern, Ava must be behind you. And—"

"I know," Jonah finished. "Don't look back."

Zeus nodded. "I will warn you, the return journey will feel a lot longer than the path into the Underworld. Don't let it stop you."

Jonah nodded, then took one final glance at the aether. Grief once more clutched his heart like a vice. *Thank you.* Then he had to tear himself away before clearing his throat and leading Ava back to the river. When they reached the edge of the cavern, he turned back a final time and raised a hand in farewell. Zeus returned the gesture, his solemn frown doing little to ease Jonah's nerves.

"Let's go." Ava released his hand and reached up to give him a kiss. "We can do this."

Jonah wrapped her in an embrace, savouring the moment as he tried to fight back the self-doubt already trying to undermine him. With a deep breath, he released her, then led the way back up the river. He listened intently for the sounds of her pursuit— the crunch of her shoes on the loose shale lining the riverbank; the odd sound she made when she momentarily lost her footing. Reassured even by that, he found himself fuelled by the knowledge that they did this together.

AT THE TUNNEL'S entrance beside the river, Jonah wondered if Zeus had been wrong. So far, the trek had been easy; what if the Underworld was releasing them without a fight? As if in reply, a low chuckle echoed around them, and Jonah berated himself for daring to hope any of that were true.

"You call yourself a leader, Jonah?" The voice rose from the tunnel, low and menacing. "What kind of leader lets a friend sacrifice himself?"

Jonah clenched his jaw so fiercely, he felt it pop, but he kept going.

"Have you thought about how you'll tell Mallory that your selfishness killed her son? Think of the pain in her eyes. The disappointment every time she looks at you. The flash of recognition that she trusted you when she shouldn't have."

"Shut up!" Jonah yelled and picked up the pace.

"The Carters took you in as one of their own, and you repay them by killing their son. Do you honestly believe you can ever set foot in that house again?"

Jonah fought back the hot tears threatening to overwhelm him, the voices blaring at him from every direction. When a harsh cackle sounded too close to his right, he reeled away and tripped, driving his knee into the hard stone. Pain radiated through his leg, and he squeezed his eyes shut, refusing to give in to the voices. Yet when he tried to stand again, he felt so tired. Every movement became a tremendous burden, heavier than the last. *They're right,* he thought, kneeling in the tunnel. *It should have been me. I should have found a way to stop him.*

"Jonah." A soft, stern voice cut through all the others. "Get up."

He lifted his head to find an old man before him, dressed in a white robe. "You're Abgal..." he whispered.

The old man nodded. "You must get up. The longer you take, the harder this will be."

Jonah pushed himself up off the ground, groaning with the effort; it felt as if someone had strapped weights to his back and forgotten to tell him about it. When he looked back up to ask how far he'd walked, the old man was gone.

Steadying himself, Jonah forced one foot in front of the other. He conjured a memory of Ava smiling, hoping it would give him the strength he needed to move on; instead, all it did was stir an intense longing to turn around and see her face—to make sure she was okay.

"How could she still love you, after everything you've done to her family? Her father and brother are dead because of you. They would have been better off if you'd never come into their lives at all."

"I didn't have a choice!" Jonah screamed.

"Of course you did," the voices hissed. "You could have left with your aunt when she moved away. That would have been best for the Carters. But you're selfish, Jonah. You stayed because *you* wanted them to be your family. Now look where you are. You destroyed them."

A sob burst out of Jonah's chest, leaving behind a throbbing ache as if it had ripped a hole on the way out. Yet he pushed himself forward; he had to lead Ava to safety, even if she wanted nothing to do with him when they left this place.

"That's right. You know she's just using you to get out of here. But once she's free, she'll be done with you forever."

Jonah swung his fist out at the invisible voice, connecting with the stone wall instead. With a shout of rage and pain, he cradled his injured hand and jumped when another Abgal appeared before him.

"That was a foolish thing to do," the old man said. "You need to keep moving. There's not much time."

"Is Ava still behind me?" Jonah whispered.

"You know we cannot answer that. Move."

Jonah closed his eyes and willed himself to be stronger. Just as before, when he opened his eyes, the Abgal was gone. He managed a few more steps in welcome, relieving silence, but then the voices returned, louder and more persistent than ever.

"To think your parents died for you. How ashamed they must be now, to have wasted their lives for nothing…" A cloying sweetness overwhelmed his senses, and another sob broke from Jonah's steely resolve. He tripped again, broken by the wafting scent of his mother's perfume, and fell to the ground. "That's right… and you can barely remember what she looked like, can you?"

Jonah rested his cheek on the stone floor of the tunnel, unable to stop the tears. For the first time, he realised he'd never really cried over his parents' deaths. Now, it felt as if he'd lie here forever, mourning them for eternity. The voices cackled and hissed, taunting him. Then two pairs of bare feet appeared before him, and Jonah lifted his aching head to see two more of the Abgal.

"Focus. You need to focus. The past has gone. Look to the future. If not for yourself, do it for Ava. She's counting on you."

With trembling legs, Jonah pushed himself onto his feet and roughly wiped the tears from his cheeks. "I'm not ashamed, and I'm not afraid," he yelled, then broke into a jog. "I hope you can hear me, Ava," he called out, careful not to turn around. "Let's get the hell out of here."

THE HARASSING VOICES neither abated nor lessened as Jonah pushed forward, but now, Jonah felt their intended barbs bounce right off him. He didn't know if this resistance came from the long-overdue emotional release concerning his parents or the help of the Abgal, but he felt stronger, both mentally and physically.

Up ahead, an Abgal stood to one side of the tunnel, his hands clasped in front of him. The old man nodded as Jonah passed him, which only nurtured Jonah's confidence. Still, he reminded himself to maintain a steady pace, not wanting to move too quickly and risk losing Ava. That seemed unlikely even now; she'd run circles around him in their realm. A small smile flickered across his face, and he wanted nothing more than to look into her eyes and hold her when they got out of here.

"You know she's already gone, don't you? She hasn't been behind you for hours, now. Pity. She had such a bright future…"

Jonah's footing faltered at the words, the possibility of it being true making his heart skip a beat or two. The urge to turn around was unbearable, and while his brain told him no, every part of him longed to glance back and see her there behind him, safe.

"Remain steadfast," said the sixth Abgal, stepping from the shadows of the tunnel. "Focus."

By now, Jonah didn't think he had the strength left to see this to the end. His heart pounded against his chest, crazed with the terror of losing her. It didn't matter what else the voices said; he focused solely on Ava, telling himself over and over that she wouldn't leave him—that he hadn't failed her too. When the end of the tunnel came into view, Jonah blinked against the sudden light. Then he saw the final Abgal waiting for him and jogged up the last steep incline.

"Is this it?" Jonah asked.

The Abgal nodded. "At the end of the tunnel. You can never re-enter the Underworld."

"Fine with me." Jonah placed a hand on the old man's shoulder. "Thank you. All of you." The seventh Abgal bowed his head deeply, then Jonah lifted his hand. Taking a deep breath, he faced the end of the tunnel and sprinted the last few metres.

The light was so drastically blinding after the Underworld's darkness, his hands went instantly to his eyes, shielding them until they adjusted. Against the eye-watering glare, he found a dark figure standing where the tunnel ended below the stands. When he could finally focus again, Jonah saw it was Zeus standing there with his arms folded and a massive, proud grin spreading across his face.

"Welcome back."

Jonah's breath hitched. "Is Ava…"

Zeus nodded. "It's safe to turn around."

Jonah spun on his heels, expecting to see Ava behind him, but instead, he found the entrance to the Underworld had disappeared, replaced by the changeroom tunnel. He took a step forward, a knot of fear twisting his insides. He thought he might vomit. *No, Ava. I can't lose you too.* Before he could take another step, a shimmering haze spread across the entrance, and Jonah squinted, unsure of what he was seeing. As Ava stepped out toward him, the frown fell from his face. He closed the gap between them with a desperate leap and wrapped his arms around her.

"I'm here," she whispered, as though reassuring herself as much as him.

Jonah kissed the top of her head, feeling both unable to speak and overwhelmed by his gratitude that she was okay. Finally, he pulled back and looked down at her. "What happened? I thought I'd lost you."

"You almost had. The Underworld put up some kind of force field, trying to keep me there long enough for the exit to seal. But the Abgal were there. They helped me through."

Jonah embraced her again, not wanting to let her go while his mind turned to Tristan and what he'd sacrificed to get them out of there.

"Is everyone okay?" Ava asked, gazing around at the now empty stadium. Jonah looked around them in surprise.

"Everyone is fine," Zeus replied. "The other gods returned with them to the town. The two of you have been gone for days." Zeus advised.

"We're here though," Caitlyn announced as she stepped out from behind Zeus, "We were never going to leave without you." The girl ran toward Ava and hugged her and Jonah both. When Jonah looked up, he saw the other Oracles rising from where they'd been sitting together in the stands, waiting for them to return.

"You didn't have to do that, but thank you," Ava said, smiling at them all. That smile faltered when she kept searching the group.

Caitlyn followed her gaze. "I'm afraid we lost Winnie, Kai, Otto, and Zia." Ava covered her mouth with her hands, and tears filled her eyes.

"I'm sorry," Jonah whispered. He placed a protective arm around her shoulders, and Ava took a deep, shaky breath. Then she smiled quickly again at the Oracles, but this time, it was in share mourning.

"Is it really over?" Caitlyn asked. Ava glanced at Jonah, who could only nod. Then Caitlyn took a deep, determined breath. "So what now?"

"I could use some help from you and the other Oracles," Jonah said. "I think it's time to tell the world what happened."

"Consider it done."

"ARE YOU READY?" Ava asked, squeezing Jonah's hand.

He took a quick look around the circle of Oracles surrounding them, now just a little smaller than before. "I am." Then he nodded and signalled for them to begin. Breathing deeply, he listened to their hushed chanting, trying not to focus on the gaping hole of Tristan's absence beside him. The chanting rose in volume, and when Ava stiffened beside him, he knew it was time.

"Survivors! Here and around the world… The battle is over. The Fates have been defeated." As soon as he said the words aloud, he felt as though a huge weight had lifted. The stress and anxiety fell away, as though they'd been sucked back into the darkness of the Underworld beneath them. "We've been through hell and back to get here. Yet you stood together, even when a victory seemed impossible. When some of you had to face those you loved. When every one of you did whatever it took to survive. None of us have come out of this without losing someone close to us. I know the pain is unbearable." He paused and caught his breath, his emotions threatening to spill over into his voice.

"Among the horrific number of lives lost, four of our Oracles also fell. Winnie, Kai, Otto, and Zia. They gave their lives to protect you. Also"—Jonah forced himself to continue, now completely unable to hide the trembling in his voice—"we lost my best friend and brother, Tristan Carter. He sacrificed his own life so Ava and I could be free of the Underworld. This is a loss I know I will never recover from. But now, we *can* say these deaths were not in vain. Now, we can rebuild our world, free from the threat of the Fates, and carry on a new life—a better life—for all of us. And for this Earth and the generations to come.

"The Tablet of Destinies is safe, but should there ever come a time when that changes, we can't give the Fates another reason to re-envision their crusade. We have to be better in this new world, for our children, and our children's children. To keep them safe, too. No matter who you are, or where in the world you live, we are in this together, and I am honoured to be a part of it." He released Ava's hand, ending the transmission while he still thought that was the best place to end it.

Jonah felt unable to move, the reality that it was in fact over finally sinking in. Tears swam in his vision, but he made no move to wipe them away. Instead, he looked up at the sky with its brilliant blue hue and wisps of clouds. He heard the light wind weaving through the stands, playful in the silence. His jaw quivered as he smiled with a newfound appreciation.

SIX WEEKS LATER...

Jonah stood behind Ava in the Carters' driveway, his arms wrapped around her waist as they looked out at the night. It amazed him how quickly their rebuilding efforts had taken shape, the houses around them now looking more like homes than the remnants of destruction. There had been no talk of money or of who was entitled to what; the only currency now was a willingness to pitch in together. It helped that the gods hadn't left them yet. Their strength, both physically and emotionally, had been invaluable to them all.

A few of their neighbours walked past, raising their hands in greeting before they turned in for the night. Jonah and Ava returned the gesture, smiling. "You're quiet," Jonah told her.

"Just thinking." Ava leaned back into him.

"What about?"

"That it's weird to feel both happy and sad at the same time."

"I know." Jonah sighed. Not a single day had gone by that he didn't miss Alex and Tristan, but having Ava by his side had also made him happier than he'd ever thought possible.

"Thought you two might like a cup of tea," Mallory announced as she walked down the driveway, steaming cups in hand.

"Thanks, Mum," Ava said. "How's it going in there?"

"Good. Most of the injured have recovered, but they seem to enjoy hanging out together. It seems my house has become a bit of a community centre. But I don't mind. It's nice to be surrounded by their conversation and laughter."

"Good evening." Zeus strode up the driveway toward them and stood beside his son. The god took a moment to gaze out over the newly rising neighbourhood, rocking back and forth on his heels.

"Everything okay?" Jonah asked.

Zeus nodded. "Yes. Everything's fine. Just enjoying the quiet of the evening, as you seem to be."

"Okay..." Jonah exchanged a bemused smile with Mallory. Raising his cup to his lips, he took a swig of tea, then lowered his cup when he noticed a strange orb of white light, no larger than a golf ball, hovering in the middle of the street. "Can you guys see that?"

"See what?" Ava peered in the direction Jonah pointed. Zeus cleared his throat and stopped rocking to stand perfectly still.

"It's... growing." Despite his better judgement, Jonah walked cautiously toward the light.

"Jonah, be careful," Ava whispered, but she too followed a few steps behind him.

"It's okay," he said. "I don't... I don't think it's dangerous." He couldn't say how he knew this, but he also had never felt this safe before.

The light expanded into a brilliant golden orb, spinning and turning in the air right in front of them. Before Jonah could get too close, the orb let out a bright flash. He flinched back and stopped, rubbing his eyes and waiting for his vision to clear. When it did, time seemed to stop, and his mouth dropped open on its own.

"Tristan?" Jonah had to try twice before he could swallow, and he blinked a few times, thinking this had to be either a hallucination or some kind of vision. "Is this real?" Smirking, Tristan stepped forward and embraced his best mate. "Holy shit!" Jonah cried and hugged him back, unable to grasp that Tristan was there before him, flesh and blood.

Ava let out a little squeak, her hands flying to her mouth, and only when Mallory threw herself at her son did Ava move to do the same.

Tristan opened his arms for the rest of his family as well. "Don't cry, Mum," he said softly, then kissed the top of her head.

"How— Are you— What happened?" Jonah finally blurted.

Tristan only grinned. Mallory stepped back and held him at arm's length, looking him over from top to bottom. "You're... different," she said.

"I'm a god."

Jonah burst out laughing. "Bullshit."

"Dude, seriously. They made me a god!"

Jonah turned to Zeus, who had stepped up behind them and looked particularly pleased with himself. "The apotheosis of a hero," Zeus said. "A loophole, if you will. Tristan's selfless act made him a candidate."

"Why didn't you tell us?" Jonah asked, glaring at his father.

"It wasn't his news to share," Tristan said. "I wanted to surprise you all, and I had to wait until I was strong enough to join you in this realm."

"Hold on," Jonah said, shaking his head. "This is still... You're an actual, legitimate god?" His disbelieving grin finally broke free, matched by Tristan's own.

"Sure am. I mean, I have a lot of work to do and a hell of a lot to learn—"

"But he'll have all the assistance he needs to transition," Isis said, walking toward them to slip her arm through Tristan's and gaze up at him.

"Does that mean you get to stay here with us?" Mallory asked.

"Not exactly. I can come and go whenever I want, once I get better at it. But I can't stay. I'm a god now, Mum. I'll have important things to do." He laughed, and Mallory wrapped her arms around her son's waist, squeezing him tight.

"I'm just so glad you're okay."

"I know, Mum. I'll come around as often as I can, but even when I'm not here physically, I'm with you."

"Wow," Ava said. "If anyone thought your ego was huge *before* this..." That brought a rise of laughter all around. "I can always count on my family to keep me grounded and humble."

"In all seriousness, mate," Jonah said, putting a firm hand on Tristan's shoulder and still unable to believe what he felt there was real. "What you did for us... I was furious at you, man. And devastated. But... you saved our lives." He put his arm around Ava's shoulder. "Thank you."

"What are mates for?" Tristan reached out, and they clasped forearms.

JONAH STROLLED THROUGH the cemetery, his hands shoved in his pockets. He'd taken to visiting his parents more often, especially on the nights he couldn't sleep. He nodded in greeting to each of the Abgal he passed, who busied themselves as always with maintaining the sacred site.

Taking his usual seat at the foot of his parents' graves, he shook his head and smiled. "You wouldn't believe it," he started, then relayed the story of Tristan's return. His eyes welled with pride and relief, and it seemed everything had just now started to sink in. When he finished, he leaned forward and placed his hands over the earth covering their graves. Closing his eyes, he pictured them both, standing side by side in eternal youth, the Tablet of Destinies nestled softly between them.

"Keep it safe for me, Mum and Dad."

ZEUS STOOD ATOP the hill, looking down at the new houses the neighbourhood had painstakingly rebuilt in the last few weeks. The Carter home no longer stood out among the others as a beacon, yet it was still easy enough to spot. An unseen aura filled the space around it, not quite glowing but sending out a warm, welcoming invitation to anyone who passed by.

A wind swept up, whipping the long grass against his legs. "Atropos," he said sternly, never taking his eyes from the Carter house.

"Zeus." The Fate stepped up beside him, and together, they stood in silence, looking out at the changed world before them. "It's hard to believe it's so peaceful now, after all that's happened," she said.

"Would you say it was worth it?"

Atropos shrugged. "I'd say it's too early to tell. What would your son think if he knew you and I had instigated this from the start?"

Zeus sighed. "He'd never forgive me. Jonah's been through too much. It would also be too much to ask for his forgiveness now. He must never know."

"It will remain our secret," Atropos replied. "My sisters would be equally as unforgiving should they ever discover what happened between us. I still maintain it was a necessary evil." She paused, then finally turned to look up at the god. "Do you think they'll do better this time?"

Zeus looked down at her and frowned. "They have to."

ABOUT THE AUTHOR

Liz Butcher resides in Brisbane, Australia, with her husband, daughter, and two cats, Pandora and Zeus. While writing is her passion, her numerous interests include history, astronomy, the paranormal, mythology, reading, art, knitting and music—all of which fuel her imagination. She also loves being out in nature, especially amongst the trees or near the water.

Liz's previous works include numerous short stories published in various anthologies and her own short story collection, *After Dark*.

Facebook: https://www.facebook.com/lizbutcherauthor/
Website: http://lizbutcherauthor.wixsite.com/lizbutcher
Twitter: @lunaloveliz